Peter and Paul

Nigel Timms

Visit us online at www.authorsonline.co.uk

A Bright Pen Book

Copyright © Nigel Timms 2010

Cover design by the author ©

All rights reserved. No part of this publication may be reproduced, stored in a retrieval system, or transmitted in any form or by any means, electronic, mechanical, photocopy, recording or otherwise, without prior written permission of the copyright owner. Nor can it be circulated in any form of binding or cover other than that in which it is published and without similar condition including this condition being imposed on a subsequent purchaser.

ISBN 978 0 7552 1288 0

Authors OnLine Ltd
19 The Cinques
Gamlingay, Sandy
Bedfordshire SG19 3NU
England

I

1

Mervyn looked with love on Lucy.
"What?" she said.
"Nothing. Just looking."
"Hm."
"Hm to you."
"What do you mean, Hm to me?"
"Nothing."
"Nothing will come of nothing."
"Come to bed."
"Merv…"
"You know you want to."
"Hm…"
"*Ein schöner, gemütlicher Nachmittagsfick…*"
"Oh, that's not fair… you know what German does to me…"
"*Ja, ich weiss…* come here."
"But we must set the alarm."
"Because if we fell asleep and missed evensong…"
"The Reverend Peter would be upset…"
"There'd be no one to play the organ."
"Because I'd been playing on your organ…"
"You only married me for my organ skills…"
"You only married me for my top C…"
"And your pert little B flats, Topsy…"

Knock knock knock.

"Damn."

"Hello? Anybody in?"

"Another five minutes and I would have been..."

"Merv! Behave. Hello, Pru, come on in."

"I'm not interrupting anything, am I?"

"Alas, no. Want a coffee?"

"Thanks, Mervyn, don't mind if I do."

"Take a pew. Sorry we haven't cleared the lunch things away yet."

"Don't worry about that. If you can't relax a bit on a Sunday afternoon..."

"Exactly. In fact I was just suggesting to Lucy before you came in that we ought to..."

"Milk, Pru?"

"Just a splash, Lucy, thanks. I've just seen Alan going into the vicarage."

"Would that be Alan the connoisseur of counterpoint?"

"He spoke to me again after mass this morning, Mervyn. He was very upset."

"Poor chap. I hope you assuaged his grief with C of E coffee and stale biscuits."

"And now I suspect he's gone to share his views with the Vicar."

"Alan is very generous with his opinions."

"Did you hear what he said about Jack Green's installation?"

"Let me guess. An imaginative and finely crafted re-thinking of the *corona spinea* symbol, a poignant reminder of the Passion of Christ..."

"No, Lucy. He said it looked like someone had left their hedge trimmings in the church."

"Can this be the same aesthete who made our Easter joy complete by saying that Messiaen's *Joie et Clarté des Corps Glorieux* made him think of electro-convulsive shock therapy?"

"Lucy... I've told you before not to speak French to me when we have visitors..."

"Shut up, Merv..."

"Anyway. He says that before you came to the church everyone in the congregation could join in. Now it's like a concert, he says. He says he doesn't feel he's taking part in the worship at all. He says he just has to sit there for ages while you lot- that's us in the choir, by the way, Lucy- show off how clever we are. You need to remember that what was suitable for your college chapel at Cambridge isn't appropriate for a parish church in the Cotswolds, he says."

"Is that all?"

"And you play the hymns too fast."

Mervyn smiles a tight little smile, slowly turning his souvenir of Cambridge coffee cup round and round, as if inspecting it for flaws. Then he sighs, puts it down and folds his arms on the table.

"Well, well, well," he says. "Good old Church of England, eh?"

Balance. Compromise? The Middle Way. But what on earth was he going to say? Peter, pen poised, pondered the parish retreat. Pah. Such a nuisance, he fumed, that his curate Tim was once more in need of a cure himself. He had had to take the ruddy retreat on for him, of course he had, obviously he couldn't cancel. What had Alexandra said? *Quis curabit curatores* was it? Quite funny, but she's too quick to show off her little learning, she is. She will mature. Pity about Oxford. Swansea, indeed. Sasha, one has to remember to call her now, of course, the name chosen by one's parents being inadequate to convey one's preening self image to the adoring world. Wilderness of this world. Arrogance of the teenager. He peered out of the wisteria-framed window of his comfortably book-lined, after many years of study, study. The garden, no wilderness now. A lovely garden, I hope you thank the Lord for it every day, Deirdre had said that time, when she was painting her picture of the church. Oh I do, he had replied, but you should have seen it when he had it all to himself! Not original, but it made her smile. He could see little Alice, his younger daughter, dear little girl, lying on a sunbed in the centre of the sunny Sunday afternoon lawn. Wonder what she's reading. Good that she reads. So many children don't, lack the concentration, motivation indeed, when the easy stimulation of the screen is available at the touch of a. Hm. Button. But...

On. He bent his head and wrote about sin. Let not sin therefore reign in your mortal body, he wrote, so as to obey the lusts thereof. Romans. Six? Check that. Yes, here it is. Verse twelve. And the wages thereof, that is, death. Poor Father Michael. Got his wages. Good funeral, though, moving. Miss him. Where is that from? Here. Verse twenty three. Unsatisfactory, though, all this. Done it so many times before. Paul beginning to pall, ha ha. Don't seem to be making any... *progress*.

Jack, Jack, Jack. Jane stopped scrubbing, watched the suds slip off a saucepan and into the sink. *Think.* What am I going to do? Why compromise? He is a way out. But... She lifts her head, stares blankly out of the ivy-framed window of the steamy kitchen. There's little Alice on her sun lounger reading. Enjoying her lovely long summer holiday, looking forward to going to the cottage tomorrow, she'd said, but so disappointed that Daddy can't come. Daddy's got to take the Parish Retreat, Jane had explained, because Tim who was going to do it for him is Not Very Well again. And Jack, who just happened to have been passing and so had just dropped in for a coffee by a remarkable coincidence just happened to be free next week and would just love to have a few days in Wales she'd been a bit too quick to suggest it and he'd been far too quick to accept it and Peter obviously thought it was all a bit bloody odd but said, well, Jack has become a sort of friend of the family, hasn't he? Too bloody right he has...

Jane bent her head and attacked another saucepan.

Progress. *Pilgrim's Progress.* Yes. Peter peered at the bookshelves, somewhere here, surely: ah. Yes. As I walked through the wilderness of this world... I dreamed; and behold, I saw a man with his face from his own house... a book in his hand, and a great burden upon his back. ..."O my dear wife," said he, "and you the children of my bowels, I, your dear friend, am in myself undone, by reason of a burden that lies hard upon me." Yes. A burden, it is. Can't go on like this. Something has to give. Some movement out there on the lawn. Made him look up again. Oh *God*. It's him. Ignore. Got to get on. Death came into the world through Man's disobedience. Man was tempted by the woman, and he yielded to that temptation. Better to marry than to burn... Paul again. O my dear wife. A great thing is a good wife, above silver and gold, she is. Jane. Hm. When did we last..? Can't remember. Husbands, love your wives, and be not bitter towards them. Colossians three nineteen? Yes, well remembered. A good wife, Jane. Does the washing up. Well of course she does, I'm too busy...

"Peter! Peter, can you go out..."

"I'm a bit busy..."

"Peter! In the garden! That bloody man again..."

... lifted her eyes from the cards and saw there, at last, in the golden candlelight, the tall manly figure she had dreamed of so many, many times before. A thrill ran through her whole body, and she would have cried out to him, but he moved quickly towards her, his dark, handsome face gleaming, his finger on his full lips. Say nothing, he whispered, carry on with the Reading of the Tarot. His smell was in her nostrils now, male, earthy and good, maddening. With a trembling hand, she turned over the next card

"Alice!" Oh *God*. "Hello there. Lovely day, isn't it?" The Toad, advancing over the sunny lawn as if he owned it. "Look at you. A real little lady of leisure. You'll get sunburned, fair skin like yours. Camomile lotion, that's what you'll need. Cooling. What are you reading?"

Little Alice shrank into the sunbed, drew her thin legs up tight, hugged them defensively. How dare he come into their garden like this when she was. Only wearing a. She pulled the sunhat right down over her face, suffered him to snatch the paperback.

"*Cartomancer*. Ooh. A tale of the occult, is it? Naughty girl."

Arms folded tightly across her bare chest, she watched him with narrowed eyes from under her broad brimmed straw, the big bald ugly reptile, as his fat fingers flicked through the novel, his pink tongue playing with his froggy lips. Revolting. Mummy said mustn't say he's fat. Rude. Corpulent, Mummy said.

"Cartoman*trix* it should be, if she's female. You know, like executor, executrix, victor, victrix? Silly stuff anyway, by the looks of it." He chucked it down. Just *chucked* it down on the grass. And *stared* at her, at *her*, yes, her *body*. Filthy Toad, go away.

"How old are you now Alice? Nine? Ten?"

"Did you want to see Daddy? Because I think he's inside."

"Yes. But there's no hurry. Such a lovely day." He paused, still staring. Actually *staring* at her... "Lovely..." he said again, nodding, with a horrid sneery smile, all twisted and- ugh. "Camomile lotion. Smooth it into the skin. Very cooling. Mm..."

Ugh. Go *away*...

"Is that you, Alan?" Thank God. Daddy.

"Alice and I have been having a little talk."

"That's nice."

Alice said nothing, picked up the novel, curled herself up again tightly, turning her back on him. He'd lost her place for her, hadn't he. *Bugger*, total Toad bugger. Silence. One of those awkward ones, by the sound of it, but that was Daddy's problem now. She flicked through the pages, found the place. Then the Toad was suddenly off on one.

"About the service this morning, Vicar. That mass setting. Unsuitable. Completely unsuitable. I've had to listen to a number of complaints. It's a parish church, not King's College Cambridge…"

"Alan, for goodness' sake…"

"Some members of the congregation were very upset. They couldn't join in, could they?"

"I don't think they were supposed to, Alan. Byrd's four part mass isn't really a congregational setting…"

"Precisely my point. So what was Mervyn doing? Sometimes I think that man deliberately sets out to sabotage the worship…"

"Come inside and have a cup of tea."

"I don't want tea, I want something done about that man. He seems to think he knows the lot about church music, but…"

"A cup of tea, yes. He did his postgraduate thesis on Dufay, you know."

"I don't see what that's got to do with it."

"Reconstructed the Requiem from fragments he found in Holland somewhere…"

"We're a parish church…"

"I know that, Alan…"

Alice listened to the voices fading away as the two of them moved towards the house. She sighed, frowned, heard the back door slam shut. Horrid Toad. Sasha said he was a pee-doh, but she wouldn't say what that meant because she was Too Young and in any case she'd learn all about it next year in impersonal socialist elf lessons. With a trembling hand, she turned over the next card, and the shocking face of Death leaped at her, its skull-like features twisting malevolently. Derryn took the card, glanced at it briefly, held it up in front of her face. There, he said, his voice low but quivering with passion- see what the powers predict! Elise shuddered. Death? she gasped, whose death? That, my dear Elise, breathed Derryn hoarsely, his eyes burning hotly, is what you and I must find out! Together! End of chapter.

Alice folded the paperback around her souvenir of Penzance bookmark, and stood up. Ouch. The disgusting Toad was right though- too much sun. She ran to the back door, paused with her hand on the knob, peering through the glass. He was there. After a moment, she went in anyway.

"Completely unsuitable for what is supposed to be a *Parish Communion,* Vicar, a service for all of us *together*, not a concert for a few smart-alecks to show off their post-graduate whatever it was…"

"I'm sure we can sort this little problem out easily enough. I'll put the kettle on." Peter flicked the switch, passed a hand over his beard: Lord save me from the congregation of naughty men…

"Well I don't think it's a little problem. Not something you can just brush away."

Flakes of dandruff, Peter saw, had snowed onto his clerical black shirt. Crossly, he brushed them away. "For goodness sake. Do sit down, Alan."

"Thank you, yes, yes, but do you see the point I'm making?" The chair creaked as Alan fatly or corpulently sat. "Good afternoon, Jane."

"Good after. Noon, Alan."

Jane scrubbed. Viciously. A roasting tray. Suds splashed out of the sink onto the window through which she had watched him lingering lecherously round her daughter. Toad, the girls called him, and bloody right too, perv that he was. Still be there now if she hadn't sent Peter out to get him away from her. Where was she now, though?

"Mum?" Oh. Hovering by the door, glancing at *him,* doesn't want to come in while he's.

"Ah. The sunbathing beauty. A little pink, she is I think! There, did you hear that, Alice? I'm a poet, but you didn't know it. Did you?" Horrible man.

"Mum?" For Christ' sake. Tea towel, where?

"Come on then, what is it?"

What it is is into the downstairs bathroom for the aftersun: but being too much in the sun's not the half of it. There's change on the way. Perhaps. Does she sense something?

"Mummy, why isn't Daddy coming on holiday with us?"

Jane glanced back towards the kitchen, pushed the door to with her foot. "Well, Darling…You see…" She gathered Alice's long fair hair in both hands, bunched it on top of her head. "Here, hold it out of the way while I do your shoulders."

"Why isn't he?"

"I've told you why. He's very busy."

"He's always very busy. I want him to come too."

"Well… it's difficult for him, you see. With Tim being not very well. And anyway, as I said, he'll be driving down to join us at the end of the week. There." Jane patted Alice's little flat bum and opened the door to shoo her out. "Now go and get a T-shirt on."

Alice let go of her hair, went up on tip toes for a kiss. Mwah.

"Why don't you have long hair, Mummy? You've got boy hair."

"Silly. Run along."

"Hi Mum, Ali. What's up?"

"Oh, Sasha, I *told* you not to smoke in the house…"

"What's that bloody Toad doing in the kitchen?"

"….and not to swear."

"Bloody's not swearing though, is it, Sash? My English teacher says bloody."

"I'm not surprised, the way you write."

Alice sticks her tongue out at big Sis, who blows smoke at her before hipswaying away.

"So how come *Jack's* coming?" Alice wants to know.

Good question.

"Well, *I* don't see why we have to have a choir at all, quite honestly. Many churches these days- more, ah, shall I say *modern* in outlook, are moving towards the idea of a *music group* to lead the singing of, of how shall I put it, more *contemporary* music."

"Alan, look…" Peter shuts his eyes tight, rubs them, pushing his glasses up onto his forehead. "Mervyn's put in an enormous amount of work to train the choir and…"

"Mervyn, Mervyn. It always comes back to *Mervyn.*"

"Mervyn's cool," pronounces Sasha, still hipswaying, centrestaging the kitchen. "I quite fancy him, actually. Pity he's married."

"Sasha, really…"

"Onlyjoking… ah," taking a can of lager out of the fridge, "This is the stuff to give the troops."

"You drink too much, young lady," Alan is headshakingly sure of this, "Binge drinking is one of the main causes of…"

"If I might remind *you*," says Sasha, ringpulling, frothslurping, "our Lord Jesus Christ himself no less once turned twelve stone jars of water into wine in Cana of Galilee. Now if that wasn't a binge…"

"Sasha, please, Alan and I are having a talk…"

"A biblical binge…"

"Sasha!"

"What?"

"Would you leave us, please?"

"But I thought we were discussing the main causes of something or other. Don't you want the Young Person's point of view? All right, all right, I'm going. If you want me later, I'll be sprawled on my bedroom floor choking in a pool of my own vomit…"

Jane, having sent her younger daughter on her way duly anointed and not much the wiser regarding *Jack,* suddenly stopped dead in the hallway. She could hear Alan's implacable complaints and Peter's plaintive protests in the kitchen. She knew she ought to go in and be a good clergywife but suddenly realised she just couldn't any more. Just… couldn't. All that was over. She turned her back on the pros and cons of worship songs, shaking her head in disbelief; how had she ever been able to care about such things? She found herself outside the bathroom again, went back in and locked the door, resting her forehead against the cool woodwork. No more. It's all too much. It's been so long, so long since…

Once upon a time, in that fairytale undergraduate never never land, it actually used to be exciting, to be part of Peter's world. But that was all such a long time ago now…

Peter's world of make-believe. There's no getting away from it. It *is* all a make-believe, isn't it, like a child's game that wouldn't stop, should've stopped for adulthood, but wouldn't, couldn't stop, not once you're locked into it by family and friends and the expectations of the world you live in. And by marriage. Such a marriage…

Help. Help… Let me out! She went to the washbasin, leaned on it with both hands. Down the plug hole. My life. Gone down the. But perhaps not. She raised her head, and her reflection came to meet her in the cracked mirror. Perhaps not, if *Jack…*

Jane tried to see herself as Jack must have seen her that day when she suddenly decided to drive to his workshop, when she realised…

He must have liked the way I look, she thought, turning her head this way and that. Must have liked my Boy Hair. Funny Alice! I used to like it long, but not now. Mine not as fair as hers, though, more auburn. Might get some tints. Not too old for that. Mirror mirror on the wall. Who is the. Sasha's colour comes from Peter, of course. Very black hair he used to have, sharp stubble too, had to shave twice a day till he grew his beard out. She gets her looks from him all right, not me, lucky girl, handsome bastard he was in those days. Her straight nose, high cheekbones. Not like me and Alice.

Alice looks more like... like me. Little tilty uppy noses we've got, though actually my jaw line's still quite good... bit jowly these days. Lay off the booze. Not unusual for sisters to look different. Alice is just getting to look more like me. Not him. That's all...

Sasha's got my eyes, though. So proud of her, at Speech Day, so tall, confident, with her new bobbed hairdo, fabulous figure she's got now, shaking hands with all the bigwigs like a real grownup she was.

A real grownup. Not a pretend one like me. Getting old. Was that it, then? Was that my life? Is that all that there's going to be? Just that? Jane saw her reflection splinter and dissolve as she began to cry.

Elise began to cry. Derryn's huge black mare snorted impatiently, stamping her big hooves on the cobbled street, eager to be gone. In a single swift movement, he mounted her, took control of her.

"Farewell, my dear. Don't cry. We shall meet again... very soon!"

"Oh, Derryn, don't leave me- I'm frightened!"

He leaned down from the saddle and took her small hand in his, lifting it with his cool leathern glove, and pressing it to his hot lips. Oh! How she yearned to go with him!

"Fear not, Elise!" he said, his eyes gleaming, "Fear not! Remember you have the power of the Cards! I shall return." The mare whinnied as he tugged on the reins, turning her head away, and then suddenly her iron-shod hooves shattered the silence of the night, striking fire from the cobbles as he urged her into a swift clattering canter. Elise stood like a statue, her hand still raised as it had been when he kissed it. At last she turned her palm, and would have waved after him, but already he was out of sight: suddenly she felt cold, alone, and more frightened than she'd ever been before. She

"Mum?"

Jane had wandered into the sitting room.

"Are you all right, Mum?"

"Sure. How's the sunburn?"

"You've been crying!"

"Oh God. Is it that obvious?" Jane wiped her eyes, said, "I'd better go and wash my face."

"Oh, Mummy..."

So it's back into the bathroom for more heart to heart, there's always more, it seems. Not that you can share everything with a ten year old. Or with a precocious eighteen year old, no she couldn't talk to Sasha about... she hadn't told either of the girls quite how far it had gone with Jack, hadn't even admitted it to herself, really. Was she in love with him?

What was it *like* to be in love? She'd been in love with Peter once, she supposed. But that hadn't been like this thing with Jack. With Peter it had just gone on from one thing to another until it had seemed obvious to everybody in the Intercollegiate Christian Union that yes, there was something a bit special between Peter and Jane and somehow it just seemed inevitable that after Oxford he'd be ordained and they'd marry and she'd be so lucky, what with him having attained a condition of almost complete sinlessness... yes some twat actually said that, can you imagine... and it was clear that the Lord was surely with them and she'd just gone along with it because it just seemed just, just...

"So you will speak to him then, Vicar."
"Yes, Alan, I'll speak to him after evensong."
"Because as I say, some people might feel that they were no longer able to take part in services which so clearly are designed to exclude them."
"Yes."
"Exclusive, that's what it is. Inclusive, it should be. Get more young people involved."
"You'd like that, Alan, I know." Shouldn't have said that.
"I would."
"Goodbye, Alan. See you at evensong." Or that, because...
"I don't come to evensong, Peter, you know that."
"Goodbye, Alan." Being vindictive. Why? Oh God.
"Yes, well, goodbye and- well, you make sure you remember to speak to, to..."
"To Mervyn, yes, goodbye." Go *away*.
"Right."

Shut the door on him at last. This won't do. Please Father God, bless Alan, please help me not to to to. Hate him. No, it's hopeless. Oh look on us thy servants with compassion, forgive us our weakness, in our weakness we know not what we do. Lord, what would *you* do? Jesus? ...Jesus? ...Lord? Nothing.

What was I doing before...? Writing. Notes for the retreat. Oh no! He isn't coming to that too, is he? Have a look at Tim's list. Oh Lord, he is: I'll have him banging on to me every day next week as well.

Damn the bloody man.

Sweet Jesus, forgive us our infirmities, help us to love our neighbours as ourselves, help us get more young people involved; oh yes, well: he'd better stay away from Alice, damn him.

Damn.

…because it had just seemed right. Right to abandon hope of a career for herself, right to take up her cross and follow Peter to that bloody little hole of a house in Oxford, right to lie on her back staring at the cracks in the ceiling, street lamp right outside the window there was, funny what you remember, flat on her back while he pumped the X chromosomes into her to make Sasha, God how the old bed squealed and complained, she never squealed or complained though, no, the two of them just lay there under him and took it, took it, took it

Like he wanted, yes, that was how he wanted it…

Because she'd promised…

"What are you thinking about, Mummy?"

To love…

Jane found herself half asleep on the sofa, one arm round Alice. She sat up, rubbing her eyes, and then looked down into her daughter's open, smiling little face, feeling as if it were a mirror showing her her own younger self, back in the time when she still had hope, before she'd ever got involved with Peter and his literal-minded friends.

…honour…

Had that been it? Was she just feeling alone in the world? Out of the context of home and school, had she been that desperate for identity? And after Dad's funeral it had seemed natural to spend more time in church… and Mum had changed so much, so quickly…Suddenly she felt anger start to boil in her, and quickly looked away lest it taint the precious image of her innocence which she saw in Alice.

"Mummy?"

"It's nothing, dear. Come on, it's time for supper. And then we finish our packing, and then early to bed. Long drive tomorrow. Early start."

…and obey.

2

lay on her back staring at the cracked ceiling while the mooncast shadows of branches shifted and shifted endlessly across it. At last she could bear it no longer, and casting off the coverlet went barefoot to the window, pulling her silken nightgown tightly round her body against the chill midnight air. Her breath misted the cold glass, and she cleared it with a corner of her gown. The dark trees were swaying menacingly in the wind, clouds brightened and faded as they raced across the face of the full moon. Suddenly she caught her breath: a chill ran down her spine. *She was not alone in the room!* But that was impossible, she'd locked the door- surely! Behind her, the faintest susurrus as of cloth brushing on cloth: her eyes strained in their sockets but she could not bear to turn around. It could not be! *It could not be!*

"Elise..." The voice was soft, sibilant, seductive. "Do not be afraid."

Infinitely slowly, she turned towards the bed. In the bright moonlight, she could see the dark form of the vampire stretched out, his head upon her pillow. His eyes sparkled like wicked jewels, and his fangs gleamed, white, bright, enticing. As if drawn by an irresistible force, Elise found herself moving, step by trembling step, closer to the bed.

"No," she gasped, "No- you can't force me to do this. I will not." But still she drew nearer and nearer.

"Do not be afraid," he repeated gently. "For you are most highly favoured. And highly flavoured too, I daresay. Well- we'll find that out soon enough." And smiling, he raised his arm, took her hand in his, and gently drew her to him...

"Where are the girls?" Peter prowled around the kitchen, as if he expected to find them hiding in a corner somewhere.

"Alice is in bed. Sasha's watching the telly." Jane sat down, crossed her legs, flicked a crumb off the table. "We need to talk."

"That Alan. I'm afraid I was quite rude to him this afternoon."

"Now."

"Though I don't think he noticed. Too thick skinned. Or just too thick, ha ha. What shall I do about him? Do you want coffee?"

"Tell him to fuck off. We need to talk."

"Jane. Really. No need for..." What's got into her? "Well, what? We're talking, aren't we? It's good to talk! That's what we used to say. *It's good to talk!*" This last in a silly voice which Jane did yes dimly remember used to be a thing they'd shared once. From an advert, was it? Who cares. So tired. Peter, listen.

"Peter..."

"Was that yes to coffee?" Spoon in one hand, jar of fair-trade decaff in the other. The grain in the table top swirled and swirled. Jane put both hands flat on it to steady it. She shook her head slowly.

"No to coffee, then," he went on, God how he went on these days, "It's decaff, won't keep you awake. Do you know how many people there were at evensong? Four. Not counting the choir. More in the choir than in the… You know, I think Alan may have a point. I mean, it *was* more like a concert than. You know, it was like on radio three on a Wednesday afternoon. The music's much more important to the choir than the worship. That can't be right."

"Peter, I can't go on like this any more."

"What? Like what?"

"Pretending."

"Pretending?"

"I have to pretend to believe in a supernatural God, in you as a priest, in myself as a mother, in what we're doing to the girls as parents, it's all just make-believe, none of it's real, Peter, can't you see?"

Peter, peering, pours boiling water into a Souvenir of Canterbury mug. He can't see. The steam rising from the mug has misted his spectacles. He puts down the kettle, pulls a handkerchief from his trouser pocket, removes his spectacles and polishes them. Then he replaces them, after which so doing he thrusts the handkerchief back into his trouser pocket and

"Peter!"

settles with both hands his spectacles more securely on his nose and having carefully added semiskimmed picks up the mug of coffee brings it to the table

"I'm serious."

and pulls up a chair and sits down opposite her. Coughs. Runs his finger round his neck, hooks out the plastic dog collar, drops it on the table. Undoes the top button of his black clerical shirt.

"It's rather late. Darling, couldn't we…"

"Discuss this in the morning? No. Because in the morning you'll be *too busy* getting ready for the parish retreat and in any case Jack and I are taking the girls down to the cottage, or had you forgotten that?"

Jack and I. The words hang in the air, still resonating strangely.

"No, I…" Peter takes the mug, raises it, sips, puts it back. "Hadn't forgotten." Silence. "Interesting young man, Jack."

"Haven't you got anything to say?"

"What do you want me to say?"

"I've just told you I can't go on like this! React! Or am I expected to deal with this all on my own?"

"Jane, are you trying to tell me that you... that you've *lost your faith*?"

"Ah no, you're not going to catch me like that. Losing your faith's all part of the same game, isn't it? 'Heard about Jane? She's lost her faith, poor thing, better send Dominic round to have a word, help her through this difficult time in her life.' Oh no. I'm not a Christian Union groupie any more, following you holy boys around like, like... That was years and years ago. All that's gone. Gone for good. You can forget it."

"Jane, keep your voice down- the girls..."

"Will know about it soon enough."

"But have you? Lost your faith? After all that we..."

"Listen, Peter. This is how it seems to me. It seems to me to be obvious that because of circumstances beyond our control, we are born. After a little while, we become aware of various things going on. Eventually, we cease to be aware of them. And that's it really, isn't it?"

"You can be very depressing sometimes," Peter muttered, lowering a sugar lump into his coffee so that the brown stain rose up its flanks until it made his fingers wet and he let it go. "This sort of talk..."

"I am very *depressed* sometimes. This sort of talk as you call it is common currency out there in the real world, Peter. You must have noticed."

Suddenly he's angry. "Why are you behaving like this all of a sudden...?"

"It's not all of a sudden. All these years... Come on, it's obvious. I've changed. I took a bloody science degree, or had you forgotten that? I've come to realise..."

"Now look here, Jane..." really getting very cross...

"And no, it's got nothing to do with *Dorwin* and *Darkins* as you have so *amusingly* said so many many *many* times please *please* don't say it again. I am no longer the stupid little innocent who used to leave her brains outside with her umbrella when she used to go into college chapel with you to play vicars and tarts or whatever the hell we thought we were doing in those days: I'm not *her* any more, Peter, I'm *me* I'm different- look at me! Will you look at me! Peter!"

But Peter had shut his eyes, saying nothing, waiting for her to stop, and for his own anger to go. She'd seen him do this so often, admired him for it, even. He thought he was praying to God to keep him from falling into wrath, well, he *was* praying to God et cetera. Playing the game. The same old game. Waiting for her to... Jane couldn't keep it up any longer. She groaned aloud and sagged in her chair.

"Peter, isn't it *obvious* what's wrong?"

One of those awkward silences, Alice would think. Peter opened his eyes again, picked up a spoon, noted briefly the distorted self portrait it offered him, and immersed it, probing for the crumbling cube at the bottom of the cup. "No, it isn't obvious to *me*..." he said, frowning. He put the spoon down, sipped the coffee, grimaced. "I don't know why I did that. I don't take sugar. Hey." Smiling thinly, he looked at her. Hey, he said again, and leaning forward reached across the table, trying to tilt her chin up the way he did when she was feeling down. It was one of their things, one of their couple things. She moved her face away from him.

"Don't do that."

"What's the matter?"

"What? I've just told you. How many more times? You *know* what the bloody matter is." This also just, possibly, too loud, Sasha still watching telly is she? Peter glanced around looking for...

"Ah, well, yes. I suppose I do," he said, quietly, trying now for the soothing tone. "I'm really very sorry." He blinked, sipped his coffee.

"Well? What is it?"

"What?"

"What the matter is with me. I want to hear it from you in your own words. I want to know that you understand. Show me you know how much all this hurts me!"

"Well, you seem to have lost... lost your..." He gesticulated aimlessly.

She turned away sharply, biting her lip: would have cried out. She stood up, went to the window, but at this time of night there was nothing to see but her own angry reflection. What's the point, she thought.

"Well, I..." Peter was on his feet too, hands still waving feebly, sketching some sort of gesture, a farewell, a blessing?

"...Jane?" But she was gone. Gone.

Elise, he breathed. His left arm was round her shoulders, holding her trembling body in a masterful embrace. He smelt of the thrilling night, of the harsh wind howling among the pines, all the wild, hidden life of the dark world outside. Slowly, gently, his right hand caressed her cheek, then slipped down beneath the smooth silk of her nightgown, and cupped the opulent roundness of her breast; his fingers found the firm nipple, circled it, stroked it: carried away on an irresistible wave of pleasure she felt her back beginning to arch, her head falling back on the soft pillow, offering her naked neck to his deadly kiss

the opulent roundness. Opulent. Where's the...

Opulent. a. Rich, wealthy; abounding, abundant, well stored. f. Latin *opulentus*.

cupped the opulent roundness of her breast. Roundness of. Her breast. His fingers found the firm nipple, circled it, stroked it: carried away on an irresistible wave of pleasure she felt her back beginning to arch, her head falling back on the soft pillow, offering her naked neck to his deadly kiss.

Then all at once the vampire drew back from her and froze, listening intently it seemed. From the depths of her abandon she could hardly speak, but faintly whispered, "What is it?"

"Hush! Listen!" He half rose from the bed, turning his head to catch some faint sound. Then she heard it too, though the wind in the pines half hid it: the unmistakeable rhythmic pounding of hoofbeats. With a terrible oath he leapt to the window, flung open the casement. For a moment he stared wildly into the night, then turned back to her, his face a twisted mask of rage.

"I shall return!" he yelled, "I shall have you yet, though I have to pursue you through all the worlds to the end of time! You shall be mine, Elise!"

With a loud scrunch of ironshod hooves on gravel the horse drew up in the yard below. She heard the rider dismount, stride to the door and hammer urgently upon it.

"Elise! Elise!" It was impossible to mistake Derryn's voice- he was back! "Open the door! Elise!"

The vampire howled with rage. She saw him flail his arms wildly, a mad black silhouette against the moonlight: then all at once he changed, shrinking into his bat form. For a fraction of a second she saw the leathern wings beating in the window space, and then he was gone into the night. A terrible crash came from below as Derryn broke in the door, and then his booted feet were pounding up the stairs: he plunged into the room.

"Elise! Are you here? Please God he hasn't taken you!"

"Derryn!" Her voice was weak, but it was enough to guide him. As his eyes became accustomed to the moonlight, he snatched off his rough leathern riding gloves, and smoothing her tousled hair away from her face, took her head gently in his hands, turning it from side to side to see if… but there was no wound, not a scratch. He exhaled a great sigh of relief.

"Elise…" he gasped, "Oh, Elise. I thought I had come too late…"

"Oh, Derryn."

then feet were pounding up the stairs. A terrible crash as Jane slammed her bedroom door.

"Mum?" Alice half rose from the bed, turning her head to catch any sound. Was Mum crying again? Nothing to be heard. At last she could bear it no longer, and folding *Cartomancer* around her souvenir of Penzance bookmark she put it on the bedside table and casting off the coverlet went barefoot to her door, pulling her silken nightie tightly round her body against the chill midnight air. Nothing to be heard on the landing either. For a moment she watched her Mum's door, then went and leaned over the banisters. Down below, faint noises from the television. She crept downstairs. At the end of the hall, she could just see into the kitchen. Daddy was sitting hunched over a mug at the table, very still. He didn't see her. Should she? He might be angry. She snuck back to the sitting room. Through the half open door she could hear the telly. She went in. All the lights were out. On the screen, a lady was taking off her dressing gown and getting into bed to the accompaniment of creepy music. She didn't look very happy. There was a candle by the bed. She blew it out, and the room flooded with blue moonlight. In the glare Alice looked round and saw her sister sprawled on the sofa. Sasha waved a can at her.

"Hello, little Sis, what are you doing down here?"

Alice jumped onto the sofa and cuddled up. "I heard Mummy coming upstairs and I thought she might be crying again."

"Was she?"

"She banged her bedroom door."

"Ah."

The music swelled louder, and a dark shadow fell over the lady's face. Her eyes flicked open, and she looked all sort of scared and surprised but actually quite excited too. Then it changed and you could see this really cool bloke was there by her on the bed with like dark curly hair and a white shirt half unbuttoned so you could see his

"He's got a really hairy chest."

"Sh. He's the vampire."

"That's like in my book."

Then he pulled at some strings on the front of her nightie so that it sort of fell away and you could see her
"Hey…"
"Quiet."
tits or breasts rather and the nipples, firm nipples.
"Firm nipples."
"*What* did you say?" Sasha choking with laughter, spilling lager everywhere…
The lady in the bed sighed loudly and arched her back and the vampire man leaned over her to kiss her and then it changed and there was a closeup of his mouth about to kiss her but suddenly it stretched horribly and his eyes went all mad like and then there were these huge huge fangs and Alice screamed!
"Alice, what the fuck…"
And all the lights went on and then there was their father standing in front of the telly ranting at them wanting to know what Alice was doing up so late and didn't they know they should get a good night's sleep before their early start in the morning and how many of those cans have you drunk today and all the time he was banging on they could see behind him on the telly naked writhings and he couldn't see what was so funny and then the lady's going oh oh oh so loud he turned round to look and saw her opulent et cetera and then it was all outrage and switch this filth off but no one could find the remote and in the end he just went and yanked the plug out of the wall. Then he really started in so Sasha sez OK OK I'm off to bed but that wasn't good enough and it was look here Sasha this, and are you listening young lady that, all the way up the bloody stairs and Alice felt the tears coming and said Daddy, but he turned his face to her a twisted mask of rage it was like in her book and You can shut up as well, he yells at her so she couldn't help it carried away on an irresistible wave of misery like in her and then she felt her eyes beginning to well up and then she was howling following them up the stairs and then Mummy was somehow there as well and everyone was on the landing yelling at once and and and

Sasha locked herself in the bathroom, dropped her jeans and sat on the loo peeing, trying not to listen to the alarums and excursions outside. After about a minute it suddenly went quiet. Mum would be sobbingly putting sobbing Ali to bed, Dad would be downstairs storming round extinguishing lights and securely locking doors. So now is the time to make a break for it. There is a tide in the affairs of nen, which taken at the flood, leads over the landing and into her room before he comes back up.

There, made it. Parents. God. Feel quite shaken up after all that yelling. Temper on him when he gets going.

Parents. Aye, there's the rub, she thought, as she stretched out on her bed and lit a fag, that big imaginary parent in the sky. The trouble that idea's caused. Fact is, what you see is what you get. Try telling that to Dad. Fantasist.

Sasha watched the neat white cylinder's elegant adagio curl of smoke, rising, vanishing. Every one a little suicide, they say. And yet a cigarette is the type of a perfect pleasure, according to Oscar Wilde: it is exquisite, but it leaves us unsatisfied. Wanting more. Ring Jess? In a minute.

Try telling anything to Dad these days. Never mind metaphysics, what about how pissed off with him Mum is all the time. He must have noticed. How she looks at her *friend* Jack. Who just happens by an amazing coincidence to have a week free to take us off to the cottage, Dad being Too Busy again...

Jack. Bloody hell. Not much to look at, is he. Half starved, hungry looking. Lean. Such men are dangerous. Artist. Is he? Of sorts. Real scruffy, anyway, looks the part. Tatty jumpers with holes in, ripped jeans, big hands... Cassius, that's it. Let me have men about me that are... corpulent. Not if they're like bloody Toad.

Jack, though. Who'd have thought it. Mum's bit of rough.

Go and tell Dad now. Wake up, will you? Friend of the family indeed. What if he makes a pass at Mum? What if she goes for him? Dangerous. End of happy family. Of unhappy family. End of something, anyway. Of the world as we know it. Perhaps Dad would like that. Bit of eschatological excitement.

Or, what if he just doesn't care? It's over already, isn't it? They don't sleep together. Separate rooms. P'raps he's turning a blind eye. P'raps he hopes she will get off with Jack. Or are they shagging already?

Depressing, somehow...

What if it's really serious, and she goes to live with him? Takes Ali with her, leaves me out of it, I'll be at Uni, and poor deserted Dad has to live all on his own, playing his supernatural mind games... but is that what he wants? To be left alone? But imagine. Jack. Stepfather? Him? Oh God. She can't be serious. How old is he anyway? Younger than she is. A toyboy. Would I go or stay here? Stupid stupid... don't need all this just before...

But yes I'll be out of it anyway next term. *Ich geh'. Ich wandre in die Berge.* Play *Das Lied* now? No. Too tired for Mahler. Sash closed her eyes, visualising the Beacons, seeing herself wandering there, or on the hilltop in Gower where she'd sat with Jess, gazing and gazing at the swerve of shore and bend of bay…

Sasha leans over, stubs the fag out in her souvenir of Dublin ash tray. Which threatens to dissolve in tears but no, it's just the smoke getting in her eyes, isn't it- Sasha doesn't cry… will not…

Parents. God.

Phone. Jess? These jeans too tight. Must change that bloody ringtone. Got it. Thumb. Yes. It's Jess.

"Jess… Awful. No, really. Talk to me, Jess, be the voice of sanity…"

3

She's up for it and she's lovely, thinks Jack, isn't that all I need to know? I like the way she flashes her eyes at me, the way they crinkle up when she's giggling, or how she'll just look at me sidelong, that long hot look that seems to say oh come on, come to bed… come to bed *now*. She must be *amazing* in bed. Jack closes his eyes, imagines undressing her. His cock stirs. But then he says to himself, you're kidding yourself, my son. One: look at it long term, where's it going, eh? How old is she, anyway? Two: the other thing. Always. The baggage. It's the baggage they come with. The girls for a start. Look before you leap, will you? Jack finds he's half asleep. Opens his eyes. Sits up. Holds his hands out to the fire. These cottages never seem to get warm, even in the summer. Damp too. Bloody weather. Changeable. Poke those logs. Get a good blaze going. There.

He crouched on the rug, stared at the little fire he'd made, his head empty, waiting for the pictures to come, let them show themselves… but there's nothing to see. Not yet. After a while he stood up yawning and stretching, rubbed the small of his back, fair old drive that'd been, went into the little kitchen. Cuppa tea. Further than he'd thought, too. Rain belting down most of the way. Funny how close it is to Bryn's place. Like driving back into the past. Strange journey altogether. They hadn't said much to one another, really, nothing about *them*: couldn't, could they, with the two girls in the back with the rest of the baggage. And why were they so moody? Little Alice, usually so polite, silent, just reading her book. Sasha only grunted when he spoke to her. Caught a glimpse of her now and then in the mirror, listening to music on headphones, staring sullenly out of the window. She's a looker, all right, though. Had he upset her somehow? Time of the month or something. Lot on her mind. Uni next term. Jane was quiet though, was she embarrassed? At how far it had gone, might go? Now they were together for a week without Peter, it was suddenly... real. Jack, searching in the bags they'd brought, found Fairtrade teabags, and semiskimmed. Any bics? Ah, *dark* chocolate digestives: someone knows what's good for them. Munching, he pulls open a cupboard. Mug. *Atomkraft? Nein danke* sez a smiley face. What the fuck?

Glad they've gone out, anyway. Soon as they'd unpacked they were into cags and boots. Walk those blues away. Did I want to join them? Took one look at surly Sasha and No, bit tired after the drive, I'll get the house sorted, have some supper ready when you get back, how's that? That's fine, though actually Jane if it was just you and me and not the girlies too... *Then* actually... straight into bed, hey? He takes his tea back into the sitting room, wincing at the wallpaper and the ghastly oil of their church it was supposed to be, done by a friend, she'd said. Daubed by a dickhead, he'd thought. *Actually* though... if it was just her, he could. See himself. Getting really involved. Where would *that* lead though? What am I getting into here, thinks Jack...

"Mummy, are vampires real?"

The steep and rugged pathway wound up the hill behind the cottage through darkly dripping woodland: Alice, cagged and booted against the threat of more rain, splashed doggedly along behind Jane.

"Vampire bats are real. They drink blood."

"Same as Christians, you know." Sash races past them and jumps up onto a fallen tree.

"Oh, really Sasha..."

"*Hic est calyx novum testamentum in sanguine meo,*" she proclaims, uplifting an invisible chalice to the fan vaulting of the trees...

"Sasha..."

"*... qui pro vobis fundetur.*" And she slurpingly mimes guzzling the lot.

"I'm giving up Latin next year."

Sasha licks her supposedly ensanguinated lips, leaps down and grabs little Alice under the arms, swinging her off the ground and round and round until she squeals...

"That's because you're too silly, go on, admit it, you're too silly..."

"Ow... I'm too silly..."

... then wrestles her to the ground, and kneels over her, cagoule spread out like vampire wings, baring her teeth.

"Aha! A tasty little morsel! I cannot wait to sink my teeth into her sweet, juicy, tender little neck..."

"Ow, Sash, gerroff me..."

Jane turned and plodded on up the rocky path, soon leaving the shrieks and howls behind. Sasha seemed to have perked up a bit. She doesn't like Jack. Neither of the girls knows what to make of this... situation. Neither do I. What am I doing? Trying to get my life back. Back from Peter. And bloody Paul.

Sasha's got no time for religion. Hasn't been to church for... ages. She has a choice. Not like the Vicar's wife. Clever girl. Proud of her. So proud. Where did she learn all that stuff though? They didn't do the mass in Latin classes. Or perhaps they did. That weird Classics man. What was his name, Ablative? Something like that. Sash said she fancied him, but then she says that about everyone, just to be provoking. Tell them anything to get them interested, he would. That filthy story of the old man who couldn't poke it in and out any more so he got a slave to do pressups under his bed to jerk him up and down while his girl bounced away on top. How angry Peter was when she came out with that during Sunday lunch, in front of Graham too. And when he said it's lascivious and she said no, it's Petronius I had to laugh. Sasha. I wonder if she's. Ever. Must've by now. All the girls do now. Not like us in Oxford then. All us little Christian virgins trimming our bloody lamps to keep the flame bright for the bridegroom, which in my case turned out to be Peter... But is she on the pill? Most mothers would know, but I... Can't really talk about. With her. But she'll be fine, she's too clever to get herself in trouble. I hope. All that Latin. Oh yes, the mass. The *marse*, as the Anglo Catholic mafia or marfia in Oxford used to call it, poncing around in their frilly cotters. How we used to laugh at them. What a bloody fool I was, why did I waste my life on. On all that *crap*. Because of Dad. Because of my upbringing. Because there was no choice. Despite doing a science degree, getting a first, could have done anything in those days. If things had been different. But then there wouldn't've been Sasha. Or Alice. Everything's predetermined, isn't it. It's obvious. Though not to Peter. What am I going to do? Oh, no not the bloody waterworks again. Lachrymose. I feel so. Labile, there's a good word for it. For me. Here's the stile, old wood beginning to rot, seen better days it has, feels a bit wobbly. Yes. Well, mustn't go seeing images of our own decay everywhere we look, must we.

She climbed over- whoops! careful- and set off across the open hillside, out of the woods at last. Perhaps.

Jack squatted on the edge of an armchair by the fire, sipping his tea, a little nervous to be honest, yes, bloody hell what am I getting into here? Look before you. At his open air show in Burford, that was the first time. What a cheery smiley face as she asked him about his exhibits. Bright eyed. And the sound of her voice and way she moved as she walked around. What was it? Something about her, right there in the first couple of minutes, something *special*... She'd liked his twisted spiky *corona spinea* and bloody Peter had talked a lot- God he does always talk a lot- all about the symbolism of Our Lord's suffering or some bollocks like that and he hadn't really listened until he said, So what about making one for our church? Hey- a commission. No problem, Vicar, name and address please. And it had gone on from there, hadn't it? Saw quite a bit of her during the installation, found himself thinking about her all the time, making excuses to drop into the vicarage. "For a coffee…" But he'd never have made the move. It was her. One day last month out of a clear blue sky- bingo! There she was in his workshop. Out of the blue. It was funny how she didn't say anything. He was beavering away on an interestingly shaped log he'd found, stripping the bark, waiting to see what it had to say to him, when he got this spooky feeling like he wasn't alone. He'd had the door propped open- maybe it was the light altering as she stepped through. Gave him a hell of a turn so the chisel slipped and ouch! And oh God sorry Jack did I startle and she runs up to him and takes his hand and there's the bright red running and just for a second she was going to, yes just for a second it seemed as though she was going to kiss it better her lips were open so close so close. He looked at his bleeding finger, looked into her eyes, kept looking deep, deeper what is happening here oh my God oh my God he thought while he gently took his hand away from hers, put his finger into his own mouth, tasted blood. Sucked it. That was nearly you doing that, wasn't it, his eyes kept on saying and yes, hers answered, yes, it so nearly was.

"Ouch."
"Do you need a plaster?"
"Nope."
"Does it hurt much?"

"Nope nope."
"Who's there?"
"I won."
"I won who?"
"I won who give you a kiss."
And he did and her heart was pounding he could actually feel it as he held her and kissed her again and again and …

…and she tasted the faintest flavour of his blood as he kissed her and, and in the end she had had to break away and sit down and oh I'm sorry, she had said, I'm so sorry. In sudden sunlight, Jane sat down on the outcrop at the top of the hill, got her breath back, watched the shadows of the clouds shifting slowly across the valley floor. The weather changes so fast here. How fast her heart had pounded as she realised what she'd done. Even now, here on the top of the hill, she shook her head in disbelief. But he had raised something in her that there was no saying no to. She had been drawn to him, and there she'd found herself, there in his workshop on a rickety old chair, almost in tears she was with the strangeness of it all, but knowing that now, if she wanted, she could make love to him, he'd let her, more than let her, he *wanted to*, she'd actually felt his, his… *cock* pressing hard against her as they kissed and she *did want to* so much, but… I'm sorry, she'd said again. Sorry? he'd replied, leaning back against the bench, take it easy, Jane. You don't need to be sorry. Sorry for what? Jane? The grasses before her on the hillside flared flat in great waves that hissed as the wind swept them, buffeted her as she sat there. But she wasn't saying sorry to *him*, was she, not to him, no. She'd sat there, in the cluttered workshop, buffeted then too by what? By the gale force of what she'd done: she turned her head away from him, as if from an abyss so confused she was now, she'd stunned herself, didn't recognise herself anymore she was all so *out of context* she was lost she was about to run away back to the familiar, back to a self she could recognise; but then she found he was standing right in front of her, so close, he took her head and pressed her face against his… oh he smelled earthy, good, maddening no I can't. Even think. Mustn't. Sounds so silly. Pressed her face against his… bulging jeans. There. That's what he did. I have admitted to myself at last that yes that is what he did and I loved it. *Loved it.*
"Mum!"
"Mummee!"

Their tiny figures are out of the trees and waving and it's going to be a race to the top now, is it? She waved back. Here they come. I've got about another minute to myself. I need more time. I need more time, I said to him, standing up, please understand... I looked up into his eyes, noticed their colour again, yes, a startling green. I need more time. I laid my hand on his stubbly cheek, stroked it, searching his face for... what? Reassurance? He smiled: kindly? Understandingly? And I reached round, felt the short curly hairs on the back of his neck, drew his head down to me and I kissed him again, *tongued* him, up on my tip toes oh I kissed him so *hard*. So good. And then I said something stupid like I've got to go now, but I must see you again. Very soon. Stupid, silly nothing words, but how do you dismantle a situation like that? There aren't any rules. You just have to make it up as you go along. Sure, he said, kindly, I think it was, yes he's kind somehow in a way that Peter never was, is, no was. Too late now, Peter. I do understand, he said. And added, I think about you all the time, you know. And he squeezed my little hands with his big craftsman's hands and...Yes, I said, all the time, I think about you too...

"Yoo-hoo...!"

And somehow I was back in the car and the next thing I knew I was turning into the drive and Peter was there and the girls too just like nothing had happened

"I'm winning!"

just like nothing had happened but because of what had happened it was all different to me. I saw them all with new eyes, nothing would ever be the same again...

"I won! I won!"

I won I won I won who give you a kiss

Something clicks for Jack. He suddenly thrusts the poker into the heart of the fire, goes quickly out to the wood stack. Running his hands over the piled logs he waits for them to tell him: ah, this one. A flattish piece, no bark, a rough rectangle. Back into the cottage. Taking the glowing poker from the fire, he carefully burns the runes Hoegl, Odil, and Beorc into the wood. Causation, homestead, regeneration, he thinks urgently, then blots out the words and tries to let the concepts become feelings become patterns, sharp, bright, in focus. Bind, bind. The baggage they come with. That was the problem with all of them. Why should Jane be any different? He holds the smoking rectangle in both hands, whispers the names of the runes, and bind, bind, he thinks, seeing the patterning of them, willing them to work for him. Better than before! Then loudly he makes the spell whole and good: *ka!* He carefully places the charged talisman on the mantelpiece and goes out again. Always before there'd been something about the women he'd known, something to keep him away from them or them away from him. In his car is his stone knife, a razor sharp flint bound into a polished wooden handle: a parting gift from Bryn. His only real teacher. For a moment he looks at it, remembering, wondering what Bryn's doing now. Not far away. Then turns to the little stone cottage, hers, with a faint smoke from the chimney, and the woods climbing above it. She's up there somewhere. Her little cottage. Hers and Peter's, that is. Look at it. Great place, location, location... helluva location, get away from it all here, all right. Used to belong to his parents, she'd told him, till they finally snuffed it thank God, she'd said. Didn't get on with them then? he'd asked. Bloody hated them, she said, you've no idea. Quite savage. Surprised him, not like her. She'd said clergy don't live in their own homes so need to have somewhere to go when they retire, in the meantime it's a nice little earner with the holiday lets, helps with the school fees. She's up there, on the hill. She's lovely. Does he love her, though? How many times he'd thought himself in love! And it had always turned out... bad. Emma from school with her horses and her bloody family, more concerned with pleasing them than giving him anything of herself... well, he just didn't fit in their world, did he. And yet she was so surprised when he broke it off. Because he'd met Millie. He hefts the knife in his hand and goes out of the yard, running a little way up the slope into the wood behind the cottage. It starts to drizzle again. Millie, oh yes, she'd been so beautiful he couldn't believe it, but.... well, she didn't fit into *his* world. Her shopping, her clothes, her makeup, her complete lack of any recognisable values beyond what the media threw at her. How long did that last? A couple of weeks? Yes, just a couple of weeks that summer before he went to art college: his nude drawings of her made quite an impression when he showed them to his teachers. Turned her into art. An expression of what she'd never be herself. Timeless beauty expressed in pictures of a frivolous flippant little... Goodbye, she'd said, as he got onto the train, see you. And that was that. Wonder where she is now. He finds a birch sapling with long pliant shoots, greets it by its name, *Beorc*, reverences it, asks its help, eases thin strands away with the flint. As always, the action reminds him of Bryn, how gently he'd worked the wood, always going with what it had to say, never forcing it, letting the form and the purpose of it emerge naturally, allowing the magic to run through every piece he did. Letting it become itself. How lucky he'd been to meet him, to be able to stay with him, learn from him. Million to one chance. What a teacher. Not like that crowd of pseuds and money grubbers at college. Bryn taught him craft. Including the craft of the runes, though that was later. Ah, but it had been during those first months with Bryn that he'd met Cathy: she was a teacher too, or at least that was her job description but Jesus what a bore she turned out to be in the end, pretty face though she was: on and on about school school Melin Fach Primary was it? Little mill, that meant, she'd said. Ground her down all right. Depressed, demoralised. Coffee and too many biscuits at break, she said, worried about getting fat. Marking every night. Crying over the too many exercise books. Red ink and red bloodshot eyes. Cathy bloody Pritchard in her clicky clacky high heels and her tight little business suit ready for a parents' evening, tense and all ready to burst into tears, hair stretched up in a bun? Bloody school, she was always tired out, couldn't cope, and he couldn't handle it either. Why had he got involved with her? Because she was beautiful, of course. To look at. But Bryn was against it right from the start. Leave her alone, he'd said, she's no good for you, boyo. Too fragile for you, inexperienced in the ways of the world she is, like you. He ignored the advice, he'd learned nothing, still as green as. Oh he'd loved something in Cathy but in the end there was too much baggage, too much to carry. How she'd wept when he... And there by the stream of course there is, there's an Alder, hail *Iss*, he whispers, and gently removes a small sprig, foundation, guardian of the project, yes. Alder and... and Elder, of course, plenty of that faery tree to ward off harm. *Feoh!* How she'd wept when he said it was over. So he moved his things out one morning when she was at school and never went back. God, how he drove that day! Bryn was outside his workshop when he finally pulled up in the old banger, everything he owned on the back seat: he was leaning on the gate smoking a pipe, it was as if he'd been waiting for him. Where have you been all this time, he'd said- those were his first words, and then, you'd better come on in, looks like we've still got a lot to do. After that he didn't leave until one day Bryn said, well, I suppose that's it, off you go and go well, Jack. And gave him the lovely little knife as a keepsake. On the way back to the cottage, he is already weaving the birch strands together, the strands of all our lives, making a circular wreath. At the front door he binds it to the handle of the knocker so that it hangs flat against the woodwork.

He fetches the talisman, notches it at the corners so that the Alder and Elder can grip it tightly, and threads it into the centre of the wreath. Then he twists and winds and pushes and tugs hard at it, until it is one solid ring, with the magical runes showing clear and bold in the midst. He steps back to look at it whole and complete. It's raining steadily by now, but he just wipes it from his eyes and keeps on staring, willing, wanting her Jane, Jane, oh, so much. Third time is the charm. *Jane.* Work for me this time, please… then, *Ka!* he calls again, and goes inside to make the supper.

"I won!"
"I let you win, little Sis."
"No you didn't, you can't run as fast as me, you smoke too much."
"Cheeky little…"
"Ow, stop it…"
"Look, girls: a rainbow."
I shall set my bow in the clouds, and it shall be a sign of the covenant that is betwixt me and the earth which I have made, thought Jane. The beauty of it, the beauty of it all. Alice sat by her Mum, cuddled up. I'm cold, she said. What, even after all that running around? I wanna go back to the cottage. Jack said he was making us dinner, didn't he. Yes, he did. Is he a good cook, then? I don't know, replied Jane, and tasted again the still strange bittersweet flavour of her hopes and fears of Jack. How little she really did know about him, his family, his past. Past loves. Was there someone else, somewhere in his life? She wanted to know what secrets were hidden away behind that, that *attractive* face. Jane shut her eyes, visualised him. Kindly, understanding. But who *was* he?

"Who *is* Jack, anyway?" Sasha, standing aloof, trying to light a fag, sheltering the flame in a fold of her cag. Jane opened her eyes, looked from the rainbow's inhuman splendour to the lovely face of her daughter. How she loved her. So proud. Even if she did smoke too much. And drink…
"Well?" Sasha wasn't going to let it go.
"What do you mean?"
"You know what I mean. He's come from nowhere just in the last few weeks, and now he's taking us away on holiday. What's going on?"
"Are you and Jack having an *affair*?"
"Ha! That's right, little Ali, no point beating about the bush, is there? Jesus."

Jane looked back at the rainbow, the covenant betwixt. Fading now. The mystical union that is betwixt Christ and his Church. Those whom God hath joined together... Fading. Gone soon.

"Jack's become a very good *friend*," she said at last.

"Right." Jane caught the mocking tone along with a carping note of cigarette smoke on the wind.

"We're *not* having an affair."

"But you and Dad are like on the rocks, yeah? That was one hell of a row last night."

"I... we just..."

"Are you and Daddy going to get *divorced*?"

"Ali, you really have got a knack for getting straight to the point, haven't you? Cut-the-crap Ali, we'll have to call you."

"I'm not crap. *You* are."

"I didn't say you were..."

"I want Daddy."

"Daddy's coming on Friday."

"I want Daddy *now*."

"Oh, grow up, Sis, you sound like a baby."

And she's up and off running blindly down the hill, stumbling and weaving a little way until she tumbles and lies still. There is a faint cry, then nothing.

"Shit," sez Sash.

"The fact is, Sasha," said Jane, as the rainbow finally faded away, "Jack..." It would be dark soon, she noticed. That was the last of the sun for today. Look at those misty rainclouds beginning to drift back into the valley. "Jack..." But she didn't know what she was trying to say.

She shook her head, sighed. Sasha takes a last drag, chucks the fag away, goes and put her arms round her mum, leaning her head on her shoulder.

"Oh, Mum."

"I don't know *what* I want right now. But perhaps you're old enough- no I mean I'm *sure* you're old enough- to understand. The fact is, I *told* your father, told him *very* clearly, though I don't think he really understood, that I felt I was *living* a *lie*. I don't see things the way I used to. Religious things, I mean, of course. Something's matured in me or developed or... No, I'm not expressing myself very well, am I? I felt I had to tell him that in all honesty I can't support him any longer as a priest because it's become obvious to me that the church is all bollocks..."

Sasha's sudden explosion of laughter made her jump: then she realised what she'd said, how absurd it all was, and Bollocks, she repeated giggling, and then she stood up and yelled to the whole world: "Bollocks! great big round pendulous hairy bollocks!"

Sasha, convulsed, rolled off onto the grass and lay on her back bicycling her legs, going bollocks, ballocks, bollocks...

"It's all bollocks," Jane was screaming now, "All of it. Boll-ocks!" She ran to Sasha, fell on her, hugged her, still bollocking away: "Blasted benighted bollocks!" she bellowed.

"Beautiful blissful bouncing bollocks!"

"Beatified bollocks! By the beatified bollocks of St Benedict!"

The two women had to stop in the end, their sides were aching, tears streaming, laughter this time, though, thought Jane, how long is it since I wept for joy. Gasping, panting, they lay still at last, flat on their backs, staring up at the impassive grey of the evening sky. Then they found they were not alone. Absurdly upside down as it seemed from where they were lying, Alice crept into their field of vision, her face crumpled, miserable, muddy. Shit, she's back, thought Sasha. Poor Alice, she's still upset, thought Jane. But it was *only pretend*.

"Opulent bollocks!" laughed Alice, and jumped on them both.

4

Perfect timing, thought Jack, when he heard them exclaiming and laughing outside. They'd found the talisman, then. And cheered up a bit by the sound of it. Good. All ready? He glanced around the room. Starters on the table- oops, the wine. He went to the fridge for the bottle of white, opened it, and by the time he got back they were inside, kicking off boots, all talking at once.

"Did you make that funny thing on the door while we were out? We did woodcraft at school last year. I made a fish."

"Have I got time to change before dinner? And Alice- we must get some of that mud off you. Into the bathroom with you."

"Oh, Mummy..."

"I'm parched. Mm. New Zealand. Always reliable."

Jack finds himself on his own with Sasha, who pours herself a glassful, swirls it, tilts it, sniffs it. That glossy black bob of hair. Quite a girl.

"Mm. I'm getting pears and mangos and elderflower and… drunk too, later on, I hope." She flashes him a stagey grin and takes a mouthful. Slurp, swallow, ah. "Good stuff, Jack. What's it mean?"

"Pardon?"

"The runic. I guess it's not just there for decoration."

"Oh." He pauses, leans one hand on the mantelpiece, runs the other through his curly hair, rubs the back of his neck. "Well, it's a spell," he says, to no response. He feels he ought to say something else. "It has to do with making things happen that are going to happen anyway, but somehow making them happen more deliberately, more positively."

Sasha, nose in glass, has been looking at him speculatively, saying nothing, but now she slowly lifts one eyebrow. Then she quickly necks the rest of the wine and grabs the bottle.

"Sorry, Professor Bumblebore," she sez, refilling, "you've lost me there."

Jack laughs. "It doesn't matter. Just think of it as a little good luck charm."

"All right, I will. If you say so, Prof. Thank you very much. And what exactly *are* you hoping will happen this week, deliberately, positively or otherwise?"

"…"

"Ah, the bathroom's free."

"Oh, Jack, you *have* worked hard. This looks delicious. What's the matter?"

"Nothing. Sit down, do."

"Mummy, I'm sitting by you."

"All right, Dear. Where's Sasha?"

"She just went out to the, er…"

"Oh. P'raps we ought to wait. Oh, yes, thank you, Jack."

"Can I have wine too, Mummy?"

"Alice, I… oh well, why not. Just a splash, Jack, not too much…"

"Is that all right?"

"Lovely."

"Well, cheers."

"Cheers, Jack, and thank you again."

"Cheers, Mummy, Cheers, Jack."

"Chee... oh dear." Sasha is framed in the doorway. "My glass appears to be empty. Again. Fortunately, I see that there remains a modicum in the bottle..."

"Oh, Sasha..."

"Mummy, are you going to say grace?"

Silence. Jane doesn't know what to say. Every mealtime, for years and years, their family has said grace. But now... She glances at Jack.

"It's difficult," she begins. "You see..." But Jack seems to understand.

"Look," he says kindly, "I don't see any harm in remembering the Good Earth which produces our food. That's a kind of grace, isn't it? So I'll say, Thank you, Earth, for feeding us. I'll say that for all of us. There, how's that?"

Jack smiled around the table, picked up his knife and fork.

"Do *you* think vampires are real, Jack?"

"Vampires?"

"Don't take any notice of my little sister, Jack. She's quite batty. Ha ha. *Joke.* And *don't* stick your tongue out while you're eating, Alice. It makes what is already quite an unpleasant sight utterly obscene."

Jane stared at her plate. This was what it was like, then. To have lost your. No. It can't be right to see everything in terms of loss.

"You all right?"

"Yes, fine, Jack, sorry." And she started to pick at what was, she realised belatedly, really rather good smoked salmon. Really rather good smoked... she hated herself for that. Her bloody *vocabulary* even was still... Her inner voice still spoke with the accent of the vicarage dinner party: really rather good smoked salmon, don't you think, Peter? Very good, Bishop, really wonderful. Jane's done us proud again... haven't you, Dear? Do you think I might just have another drop of the... Oh, when I was a clergywife I thought as a clergywife but now I am become a woman I have put away clerical things...

"You like it, Jane?"

"It's really rather."

"Well?"

"Good. Oh dear."

"What?"

"Never mind."

"Jack?"

"Alice?"

"I was thinking, whether you think vampires are real or not?"

"You mean human vampires, like in horror stories?"
"Yes."
"No."
"Oh."
"Do you like horror stories?"
"I don't think *Cartomancer* is a horror story exactly. My English teacher says it's written in a mixed-up john-ray."

Sasha snorts, puts a hand to her mouth, reaches for her glass. "Sorry."

"It's about this girl, Elise. One day she finds this old pack of cards in the attic and she starts playing with them and has a vision of this handsome man Derryn his name is and she tells her granny who says she's got the gift but it's very dangerous and she mustn't tell anybody and she's got to be really careful because she might be meddling with the powers of darkness, so…"

Alice prongs another piece of really rather good, chews briefly, swallows.

"So anyway, she starts having these funny dreams about Derryn and vampires too and then one night she's all on her own in the house and she starts playing with the cards and suddenly there in the room with her is Derryn himself and…"

"Your English teacher would hold his head in his hands and say in a very sad voice that you are merely retelling the story, instead of Identifying the Novel's Significant Themes."

"Oh… yes he would, too. How do *you* know that?"

"Because he used to teach *me*, silly."

Jack is still wondering where he's heard *Cartomancer* before… sounds familiar. But why is Jane so quiet? Staring at her empty plate. He nearly speaks to her, but says instead, "So, Sasha: what are *you* reading at the moment?"

"Me? I'm not reading anything, of course. I've done my exams, and so obviously shan't open a book again until I get to uni."

"Uni?"

"Versity, yes. *Abertawe.*"

"Where?"

"Swansea."

"Ah. And what are you going to do there?"

"What everyone does. Read a bit, write a bit, get drunk, meet the love of my life, lose my virginity. Though not necessarily in that order."

"I see… and why Swansea?"

"Ah…" pouring herself the last of the bottle, "well you see, there's the matter of Welsh boys to be decided."

"What's so special about Welsh boys?"

"For goodness' sake, Jack, if I knew that I wouldn't need to go, would I?"

"I still think you should have applied to Oxford," says Jane. "Jesus College was stiff with Welsh boys when your father and I were there."

"The college may have been stiff, but do you have any evidence that the boys were? Oh, sorry, Jack, for all I know you might be a Jesus man yourself. Are you?"

"Not in any sense of the word, I assure you."

"Thank Christ for that. Well it looks as if I shall have to do the necessary research myself. It's a dirty job, but someone has to do it. At least, I *hope* it's a dirty job."

"Sash, what're you talking about?"

"Oh you'll find out in your personal socialist elf lessons. I suggest we let the topic drop now. It is after all rather *hard*."

You could never tell with Sasha, thought Jane. Always teasing. But was she just trying to hide something with all her talk? Perhaps she really was. Still a virgin. Perhaps she's a bit afraid of. There had been boys around, all right. On the pill was she? She'd never said, they'd never talked like that. Why not? Most mums were able to. Sasha just didn't want to. Boyfriends? When Neil was there at Christmas, she'd got her on her own in the kitchen and tried to. Are you and Neil… *going out*? Sasha had looked her in the eye and said, No, we're *going* to stay *in* and watch a DVD, OK? She glanced at Sasha now, so proud, smiled at Jack, pushed her plate away. Nice boy, Neil. Pity about the guitar playing…

"Did you enjoy that, Jane?"

"Yes, thank you *so* much." Ouch.

"All done? Great. Give me your plates, I'll get the main course."

"Let me help you."

"Jane- you just sit still and let the magic happen."

"Magic?"

"Yes, little Sis, didn't you realise? Jack can't *cook*. He just draws runes on the *hob*, and then… *ka!* A little goblin comes and makes his dinner for him."

"That's just silly."

"Yes. I think it probably is."

"Are you sure I can't help?"

"Quite sure."

Hob? In the kitchen, Jack carves chicken: but his mind is racing. Hoegl, Odil, Beorc: hob. She can't read runes, can she? And *ka* she'd said, the word of completion, of binding. Coincidence. No, couldn't be. There's something knowing about her. Christ, how old is she anyway? Eighteen? Wise for her years. What on earth is going on? He put the knife down, pulled the lace curtain back from the little window. Almost dark now, the trees looming shadows. He feels… just a little bit scared. If he's honest with himself. Just a bit. What was going to happen? What did he *hope* would happen? He had a sudden vision of himself, standing here in a strange kitchen, in a strange country, cooking for strangers. All is strange. He felt a moment of panic. Deliberately, he released the dingy lace and rubbed his eyes. Identity. He wasn't sure who he was for a moment. We rely on our environment for our identity. Who'd said that? Out of context, we are no one. He realised he was missing his own little home, his workshop. Ridiculous. A howl of laughter from the other room. He couldn't hear what they were saying. He started putting slices of chicken on plates. Talking about him? Why not? They did, he presumed. But what did they say? What think? Now more laughter, and Sasha pretending to be an electric guitar. What was that? Neil, did she say? He concentrated on plating up. Make it look good. May it be good. May it work for me this time, *please*.

"How's it going?" Sasha, pulling open the fridge. She squats, looking for the other bottle, hauls it out, slams the door and holds it up to him like a trophy- tra la- but not before his sculptor's eye has shown him. Those haunches. Those tightly bejeaned… This is ridiculous. Her daughter, for Christ's sake

"You all right? Want a hand?"

Well, she's a lot more friendly now. Drunk, of course. "No, thanks, really, I'm just plating up now."

"Great. Ah, there's the opener. I prefer screwtops, don't you? Quicker." She winks, and she's gone. This is ridiculous, one glance at her daughter's tight little butt and I'm trembling like a leaf. Incestuous. Shit. *Shit*! In the cupboard there's a bottle of Scotch. No. No point in just getting drunk! Need to learn to deal with it in the future, if… *if*. He concentrates again on plating up. I suppose people just get used to it. No, it's because she's bloody fascinating! How did she *know*? Bit of garnish. Green salad leaves. There. Presentation is everything. Like on the telly. All done? Right. Here goes!

"*Voila! Coq au vin!*"
"Thanks."
"This looks lovely, Jack."
They pick up knives and forks, begin.
"Mummy."
"What, dear?"
"Whisper."
"All right, Darling, now what is it?"
"He said… cock."

5

Slowly, gently, his right hand caressed slipped beneath smooth silk nightgown opulent roundness fingers found firm nipple circled stroked it: carried away on an irresistible she felt her back beginning her head falling soft pillow her naked neck his deadly kiss

Sleepily, Alice turned the pages. Here.

"Elise…" he gasped, "Oh, Elise. I thought I had come too late…"
"Oh, Derryn."
"You must use the Cards again. It is the only way to learn his terrible purpose."
"I'm frightened." She turned her head away, her lip trembling. "So, so frightened."
"You must." He gently turned her face to him. In the moonlight he looked so confident, so strong, so handsome. From outside, she heard his mare neigh and stamp.
"Oh, Derryn," she gasped, "Derryn."
He moved closer to her, so close she could feel his warm, urgent breath on her cheeks.
"Elise," he whispered, and then all at once they were kissing, long, passionate deep kisses that seemed long seemed

Alice yawned.

passionate deep kisses that seemed to bear away all her fears and grief on a great flood of emotion. Oh the manly taste of him! Oh the bliss! Oh Derryn! Oh that this would never end!

"Elise! Are you all right? What's going on?"

Derryn drew back from her, leapt from the bed and strode to the door just as Elise's ancient grandmother came tottering in, her creased face painted yellow by the flickering candle in her hand.

"And who might you be," she demanded in her creaky old voice, "breaking into my house in the middle of the night and finding your way to my granddaughter's bedroom?"

"Oh, Grandmother, this is Derryn. It's all right..."

"It is not all right. I demand to know..."

"Madam, there is no time." Derryn's deep voice was commanding, authoritative. "Elise must use the Cards of Power at once. A great evil is abroad this night."

"Cards? What do you know about the Cards?

Alice slept.

"Cards?"

"Tarot cards. I've got a pack in the car. Shall I fetch them?"

Jane watched the froth on her coffee going round and round, put her spoon in to stop it. Made her feel dizzy. Or was it all that wine. Funny how Sasha could drink all night without showing any sign of... "If you like."

Jack smiled at her and stood up. He put a hand on Jane's shoulder, squeezed it.

"Are you too tired?" His voice was low, kindly. The hand moved to the back of her neck, stroking up under the back of her silly boy hair... Her lips parted, she almost gasped with the sensuousness of the contact, felt herself starting to blush, and glanced at Sasha: but she seemed to be lost in admiration of Deirdre's painting of St Jude's.

"No, I'm fine." She put the frothy coffee spoon in her mouth, sucked it, tilting her head round to look into Jack's green eyes, narrowing her own. What the hell. What she'd shared with this man already! And how much more there might be... now she really was blushing. She dropped the spoon with a clatter, smiled, laughed outright at herself. She clasped his wrist briefly."Do get them, please."

"I love the way your eyes crinkle when you laugh." He pecked her on the cheek, and went out. Sasha pushed her chair back, got up stretching and then went to inspect the painting more closely. She sighed loudly. "Patron saint of desperate cases and lost causes, wasn't he?"

"Who?"

"Saint Jude." She quickly sat by Jane, leaned in close to her face so that their hair touched and the wings of her bob made a little black private tent. "Mum, Mum-*ee*, listen, if I were you and you were me, you'd say to me that he doesn't seem quite *suitable*."

"When have I ever had the chance to comment on *your* choice of, of male company."

"Male company indeed. Come on, Mum, get real. This is all a bit *strange*, isn't it? We hardly know him and yet… You should see the way you look at one another."

"You don't know what…"

"What?" But he was back.

"Here we are. I'll just move these plates."

When he'd cleared the table, Jack sat opposite them, shuffling the pack. Jane watched his big craftsman's hands, thought she could see the scar where he'd cut himself that day, started remembering how she'd felt when he kissed her. He put the pack down, and she met his gaze. I want you, she thought, but I want you to be… not to be…

"So what happens now?" Sash takes out her fags.

…that is the question.

"Up to you. I can do what I call a general reading for your present situation, or you can focus on any one issue that's concerning you…"

Jane puts her elbows on the table, props her chin up with her fists. Her lips are pursed. The word "bollocks" echoes in her memory. But. She so wants him to be…

"You can use the cards for something called Pathworking, too, but that's not really something I'd, er…"

"Use to wear away this long age of three hours, between our after supper and bedtime," sez Sash, who knows her Shakespeare.

"Ah, right," agrees Jack, who doesn't.

"Can you tell me the future?" Jane, wistful, really wants to know, but knows he can't, nobody can, cards or no bloody cards. "Oh, Sasha, you're not going to smoke in *here* are you?"

"What will happen, will happen," says Jack, shrugging. "But…"

"But you can make it happen more deliberately or er positively or whatever, yeah I think I remember. All right, all right, I'll go outside for a *shmoke*. You can *do* Mum while I'm gone, Jack." She pauses at the door, though, like they do in every movie exit you've ever seen. "Do her with the *cards*, I mean."

"Sasha, *really*."

"And then when I'm back, you can *do me too*." And with a wiggle of her eyebrows, she's gone. Jane sighs, shakes her head.

"Sorry about her, Jack."

"Stop saying you're sorry."

"Sorry. Oh. damn." He kisses his fingertips, places them on her lips. She takes his hand, kisses it hard, lets it go.

"I really want to do this reading, Jane. I want you to know about me. What I could do for you…" He sat back grinning at her.

That's who he is, Jane thought suddenly, grinning back, *out*-grinning him surely… With his curly brown hair and his bright green eyes, he's not just any old Jack, he's Jack o' th' Green…

he's a woodland faun, (O oui, let me spend my après-midi with you my dear…)

he's an aging Puck (but not aging *too* much! Younger than me… how much?)

he's everything I want and I want him *so much*. I think.

"…Well?"

She takes a deep breath, holds it a couple of seconds, staring at the pack: then she exhales suddenly and says:

"Deal the cards, Jack."

6

No signal? For fuck's sake. Dark out here in the yard too. Just the light from the primly curtained window behind which my mother is being *done*. Ha, that's fu-nny. Actually, not funny, not really. Get this fag lit at last. Not funny. Parents fighting, splitting. Why? Why can't they bloody grow up? Because they missed the chance to, long long ago, of course. Sounds like they, how shall I put this to you, ladies and gentlemen of the jury, let me put it to you that as soon as they found any security, any meaning in their lives, anything which would give them approval and status, value, no matter how small or peculiar the pond in which these two queer fish swim swam swum to find it, they clung on to it, white knuckled, against all common sense and reason. Not that fish have knuckles, mixed metaphor, ha ha. They stopped growing. Hardened. Ossified. Twats. But I do love 'em…

Sash doesn't cry. Ever. Sash leans against the drystone wall of the yard, takes another drag of her fag, wipes the back of her other hand across her eyes, but she doesn't…

That was quite a brainstorm actually, should write it down. Or tell Jess. Yes, Jess, yes… Jess. Bloody phone. *Why* isn't there a fucking signal? Calm, calm. It'll be because of the hill up there, the bloody Welsh remoteness of the place. Climb up the top, then, ring her from there. In the dark? Get lost, wander around for ages, still might not work after all that. Ah fuck it. Wonder what she's doing? Neil's gig tonight. Pity to miss that. Wonder if she went. Jason wanted to take her. *Jason*, God. Every time he gets back from a walk he has to bandage his knuckles where they've been dragging along the pavement. I wouldn't have minded going, though. Hear Neil play again, he's good. Good looking, too. But no, oh no, Neil, no. Not getting into my knickers, are you, Neil. Not really my type… when I played you Mahler and you said it didn't have much of a beat… But when you got up close… when I kissed you on the sofa when we were supposed to be watching the DVD at Christmas and you got *aroused* I could tell and yes Neil I was curious to see but no it was late and of course Dad didn't mind driving you home. But you minded, didn't you. Sorry about that. One thing to be grateful to Mum and Dad for. Boys were never even on the agenda, were they, not after prep school. Gave me a fighting chance. Chance to grow up a bit before. Not like those poor bloody slags you see hanging around the town at night. Drunk, shrieking, puking. Pushing their tits out at everyone. Pushing prams all too soon, serves 'em bloody right too, though single mumhood's a lifestyle choice now, it seems, seems to be what they want. Or what the impersonal urge of the species to reproduce wants. 'Course at a nice posh girls' weekly boarding school fine tradition of academic excellence outstanding Ofsted reports like wot I went to you never even see a boy except at the weekends in church, and I was far too grand to talk to them, thank God or Dad actually who practically *was* God in those days.

Sash thinks about Neil. When he got up close. What it was like lying by him on the sofa and kissing him. Where he put his hands. What he wanted her to do. But Sash didn't…

I shall miss school. Not just Jess and the others but the whole thing. By the time you're in the upper sixth you really appreciate it. And being Head Girl was- just *so* cool. Fabulous teaching, well, most of it. Mr Empson, wow. Eng lit on a stick. And Ablative Absalom- that story about the old man who couldn't poke it in and out any more... so he got his slave to, do pressups! Under his. He was funny. Absolutely. One or two right wankers, as always- eternally grateful to the RE department autoeroticists in particular for inoculating me against God, sorry Dad but it's all for the best. But Swansea- sorry, *Bach,* I mean *Abertawe*- will be a right fucking hole compared to a girls' weekly boarding school with a fine tradition of. Have I done the right thing? (and why did that thought make me glance up at the sky? Old habits...) You should apply to Oxford, said nodding Dad, glasses gleaming with enthusiasm, I could have a word for you at Jesus... Dad, no, I said, it doesn't work like that any more. As if I'd want to go there anyway as Your Daughter. It's not that, Sasha, it's the whole thing, he said, practically on his knees, the Oxford Experience. Being at Oxford. No, Dad, I said, I want to experience being, not being at Oxford. I need the sea, anyway. If you'd swum in the sea like I have, caught the waves, if you'd clung to the sharp rocks and felt the rollers pounding the cliffs, cracking back out of the cavemouths, if you'd known the sunny serenity of those little secret bays don't be stupid, he'd said, sneering. Secret little bays indeed full of plebs with their picnics and radios and the racket from the jetskis of the Birmingham Navy all day long, you're out of your mind. I shalln't be spending bank holiday weekends there, Dad. And have you, Sasha, have you *seen* the Swansea campus? Have you? Yes of course I have. Oh my Lord, Sasha. Patched and peeling. When I think of the opportunities you've had...

Sash could have applied to Oxford. But Sash wouldn't...

Because she'd got it all sorted. There wasn't really anything she wanted to study at uni but *ideas* and given her background and consequent inclinations there weren't any ideas she wanted to study more than ideas about *being*. She'd only just realised that it was possible to experience being, what it meant to be *conscious* of being... ah. Headspin. She'd worked all that out during the last summer hols, that best of all summer hols, the one between lower and upper sixth when you've read enough by now to be able to really read properly for the first time, start to get the references, make the connections, run alongside the big boys and girls of literature, find out what for yourself why the really good teachers were always so enthusiastic, yes, it was because their subjects actually were *fucking awesome* and she couldn't wait to get back in September and tell them so... there was so much to find out! And the long beaches and gentle hills of Gower were going to be her research laboratory, no matter what Dad said, not the screaming tyres of Grotford. *Because* what was meant to be just a surfing holiday at Rhossili that magical summer had turned out to be a surfing and neuroscience and life the universe and *everything* supercamp with Jess and her Amazing Mum. Well, and her dad and her couple of funny little *bothers* too. The twin bothers! Someone's spelling mistake ages ago, immemorial family joke now, funny how they still find it funny... They were off doing Boy Things most of the time, thank goodness. That hol had been a life-changer. Such a *surprise* to discover so *much*. That you *could* discover so much, and just in a few days. Jess's mum Julia... wow, what a brain. Scientist, like my own dear Mama. Actually not like her *at all*... Julia the professional. Julia the lecturer. Books on it. Idle chat about waves had started her off that morning, paddle out into the sea, catch a wave, ride it, what is a wave, waves in general, mathematical expression of a wave, then brainwaves, yes electrical waves in your brain creating illusion of continuity and therefore individual consciousness emerges as a phenomenon *wha*? *you're losing me* no it's easy listen self awareness emerges in response to environmental stimulation *hold on you'll just need to...* refresh rate varying between 25-40 hertz in waking mode which is pretty crap not even as good as a computer monitor but it's all you've got my dears one day the sensation will cease to arise and that will be that... ...*run that past me again. I think my refresh rate is a little on the low side.* This ought to help, then, Julia said, pulling me another can of lager from the coolbox before asking me what I thought language was. And off she went again. That holiday had been the start of something, all right. Came just at the right time. I was ready. Pointed me in the right direction. A ten day crash course in how absolutely fucking fascinating it would be just to try and get hold of what it really means to *be*. Oh, Hamlet, eat your heart out, that was for *real*. Something new and amazing every day from Jess's Mum. And something new and amazing every night from Jess...

Sasha lights another cig...

Because the point is if you're right Julia then where does that leave Dad, I'd asked. And Mum, and…

The sun was blazing down that afternoon. We'd been in the sea all morning. Gavin had taken the bothers off somewhere in the car and there were just the three of us lazing in the long grass near the tents, afterlunch sleepy, a little bit drunk. I've only met your dad a couple of times, replied Julia, smoothing suncream into her arms. He seems very nice. You're not answering the question, says I, and then, sorry, that wasn't very polite. It's all right, Sasha, she laughed, I should be the one apologising. It's an important question for you, and a difficult one, right? I don't want to criticise your dad. But sometimes… you see it's difficult to talk about the way the world works with religious people because you feel somehow you shouldn't blow their house of cards down: sorry that sounds terribly patronising… I don't want you to think I don't value spirituality, Sasha, it's more a matter of being perfectly clear *what it is*… what you think you're doing when you practise it. I suppose in the end it's all about whether you think religions are human inventions or not. It's obvious to me that they are, along with the whole supernatural thing. Your dad presumably thinks they're not, and I wouldn't want him to get the impression that I thought he was deluded. Why ever not, Sash wants to know. If he's built his life up to now on an illusion, shouldn't someone tell him, before he wastes the rest of it as well? It's not that easy, says Julia. Take my parents, for example… I couldn't bring myself to tell them what I really think. I let them imagine I'm temporarily lapsed, or something. Couldn't bear to… *break their spell*. That's it, really, I think. Couldn't bear to see them spiritually *bereft*. And to know it was my fault. Human kind cannot bear very much reality, right? Perhaps with a professional Christian I wouldn't pussyfoot around, though. Tell him- or her- what I really think, maybe. I'm not sure. I'm not sure what I'd say to your father. But Julia, what do you really think? I need to know. Well Sasha I suppose I think a clergyman is someone who is committed to promoting a view of our existence which I guess I would say is, well, anecdotal at best. Where do they imagine the natural sciences fit in? What do they think the supernatural could possibly *be*? How do they deal with humanist ethics? Your poor father- he must find it very difficult to hold on to his beliefs sometimes. Yeah, it's a real white knuckle ride in the church today, sez Jess yawning, rolling onto her tummy and unhooking her bikini top. Do my back would you, Sash?

Sasha had a last drag, dropped the butt and stepped on it. *Breaking their spell.* That was what she'd been trying to bring to mind ever since Jack told her about his runes. Cold out here now. And they've had long enough gawping at one another across the table. She approached the door where Jack's green spell lurked in the darkness. As she let herself in she ran her fingers over the black runes, smiled. Hob, indeed.

7

"Hi."
Ah. One of those *awkward* silences. Well, excuse *me*.
Sash goes upstairs.

"The Hierophant, the Fool. The Emperor, the Empress. The Star. The Green Man. The correspondence is… breathtaking."
"What do you mean, Jack?" Jane sounds a little impatient here, is getting, to be perfectly honest, rather tired. Of all this nonsense. What is she getting herself into with this man? It's not too late, she thinks. You've only got to keep your hands off him and you can go back to Peter, no harm done. But there is no going back to Peter, not now… And I *do want him…*
"In this pack, the Hierophant is a girl, pre-pubescent or only just entering young womanhood. Like Alice. That sort of girl's potentiality, her intellectual curiosity and yes I have to say it her... *budding sexuality…*"
"For goodness' sake, Jack."
"… do attract a certain kind of Fool. You told me, didn't you? Alan, his name is, right?"
"Don't drag *him* into it. For heaven's sake…"
"The Emperor is Peter. Authoritative, in command."
"That figures."
"A wielder of power. But see- the card is inverted. Here, he represents the negative, the, you know, not positive but oppressive, er… *insensitive* male power that's kept women under, women like you, in subjection, for centuries. Love, honour and *obey*, I expect you said, when you married him, didn't you?"
Kept me under, all right, she thought, shrugged. "Sure."
"Did you mean it?
"What?"

"Did you obey him?"

"...Yes."

"So. Is your marriage an equal partnership? No."

"I don't think it was ever meant to be. In that kind of religion..."

"Is it a marriage at all? I mean now, after all these years of you growing apart?"

"Of course it is."

"Are you sure? Tell me about when you were first married."

"What do you mean?"

"What was the sex like?"

"Jack!"

"Did you get what you expected from him? Did you get what you wanted?"

"Jack, really..."

"Have you *ever* had what you wanted from him?"

"I... I suppose the Empress is me."

Jack waits. Answer the question, he thinks, but says, "Exactly."

"So who's the pole dancer? Don't say it's Sasha."

Jack laughs, picks up the Star card, which shows a beautiful naked girl dancing in a swirl of galaxies and constellations. He expects to make an amusing comment, or tease Jane with the image: but suddenly his laughter is gone. The freezing blackness of the interstellar spaces... it makes him dizzy- and is the girl reaching out to him? He feels a chill on his spine, but a possibility of warmth too... rightness... he cannot speak. This card has spoken to him, but its message has nothing to do with Jane. *Feel my reality*, it says: every card would speak as strongly as I, were it not that you are a complete charlatan and...

"Jack?"

"Sorry?"

"I was wondering, if you thought *she* was supposed to be Sasha? The pole dancer."

"Oh, right." Jack runs his hand through his hair, pulls himself together. Bit of a shock that. Now what? Make something up. "Sasha? It's the Pole Star she's dancing with, then. The card represents spiritual insight, connects our ordinary world of the sun with the highest spiritual plane, pure undifferentiated joy in being. Sasha? Sure, why not?"

Well obviously because... but Jane remembers that what is obvious to her these days isn't obvious to other people, necessarily. So she picks up the last card of the spread, holds it up by Jack's face, as if comparing them.

"So, Green Man," she says. "What have you got to say about yourself?"

In the soft glow of the reading lamp, Alice lies sound asleep, one hand still resting on her open book. Gently, Sasha removes it, automatically glancing at the text.

"Elise must use the Cards of Power at once. A great evil is abroad this night."
"Cards? What do you know about the Cards?"

Bloody cards everywhere tonight, thinks Sasha, sitting softly on the edge of the bed.

"There is no time to explain," says Derryn urgently. "Quickly, Elise."
Without a word, Elise goes to her chest of drawers and takes the pack from its secret hiding place. Placing it carefully on the top of the chest, she pulls the frayed ends of the silken bow, so that the black wrapping cloths fall away, and takes the fateful pack to the little table, shuffling the cards as she goes.
"This is not good," complains her grandmother

Damn right, old lady, thinks Sash, not very good at all. But she keeps reading.

"Evil may come of it..."
"Be still, old woman! A greater evil will certainly come if we desist," Derryn rebukes her. "Give me the candle. Now, Elise, a spread of six. Cruciform. *Now*!"
Derryn tilts the candle so that a pool of hot wax runs onto the table, and plants in it firmly the luminous length. By its sinister flickering light Elise finishes shuffling the cards, as he draws up a rickety chair. She sits and looks up at him, her large eyes fearful. He puts a hand on her shoulder, squeezes it. "Do not be afraid. You have the gift." His voice was lower now, even kindly. His hand moved to the back of her neck, stroking slowly up under the back of her long, flowing hair... Her lips parted, she almost gasped with the sensuousness of the contact, felt herself starting to blush, and glanced at her grandmother: but the old

woman's eyes were closed, her lips moving silently as if praying. Elise took a deep breath, held it a moment, and then sighed out suddenly and quickly began placing the cards, face down: one in the centre, then one above it, two below it, one on each side of the first- the cross was made!

"Elise," Derryn's voice was no more than a whisper, "Reveal the first card!"

Sasha folded the book around Alice's souvenir of Penzance bookmark, and put it down on the bedside table. She took her shoulderbag from the other bed, and stood for a moment looking at her little sister. What was she going to dream of tonight? Cards of Power and a great evil abroad in the night? At least she was reading something. Ought to see in her an image of my own childhood, sigh for lost innocence, kiss her lovingly on the forehead, so that she stirs in her sleep and mutters something cute and vaguely relevant to our present situation before snuggling down et cetera et cetera. Some people would too: funny how I'm set up not to. So, switch out the light carefully so that it won't click and wake her, and go back downstairs. Fourth one creaks? Yes. On the bottom step I wait: faint voices from the dining room. Go in? By going in, I change everything for them. The power! No, leave them to it. Go the other way, into the grotty little room we call the study. Not that it's seen much study lately. Dark. Dark, the interstellar space... ouch! Bloody coffee table or something, careful, break my fucking neck. Here's the pole of the standard lamp. Click. Fiat lux. I decided not to disturb them. That would be scanned. Everything in my past experience, all my conditioning led me to turn in here instead of. No decision really possible. It just happens the way it was always going to happen. I am responsible, but as agent only: it's not my fault. What happens as a consequence of. Those bottles still there? In this cupboard they used to be. Ah. Brandy. Brilliant.

So there was never any possibility that Sasha would not lie on the sofa, feet up, taking a good swig from the bottle. Or that after a moment's reflection she would not pull a paperback from her bag, and begin to read. Where now? Who now? When now? Unquestioning. I, say I. Unbelieving. Questions, hypotheses, call them that. Keep going, going on, call that going, call that on...

Jack came in from the kitchen with more coffee. Jane had gone to sit in one of the armchairs by the fire, was leaning forward, poking a little life into the embers. He handed her a mug, sat in the chair opposite her, stretching his legs out.

"So," he said, sipping. "That's me. What about you?"

Me? What about me. I'm nothing...

"Come on. You've had my life story. Your turn."

Jane sighs. Life story indeed. Some bloody big gaps in it then. He's told her about Emma, Millie, others. Art college, A dozen odd jobs, here there and everywhere, turn his hand to anything it seemed. So different, so alien he is. And he's only... he's... he's at least, it must be ten years younger than... I had to hear all about how he had his stroke of luck- bit of money from some sales, found the workshop to rent so cheap- couple of decent exhibitions, few more sales, commissions... Peter's crown of thorns. Steady money at last. It's just that he's lonely, unfulfilled, he says. Yeah, aren't we all. And then I met you, Jane, he says... me. Right. Actually, I haven't done too badly. The girls. So proud. Why run myself down. What's this man like? He's brought up no children, his life has been a self-indulgent mess, he's a great tangled forest, dangerous, dark and full of unknown hidden ways, frightening. I can't find the man in all that, can't see him, couldn't possibly see how to get close to him. Wouldn't want to, now I know so much... But I *was* close... And I *do* want...

"Jack," she said, "there's not much to tell. About me. I met Peter in my first year at Oxford and I've stayed with him ever since. I did think about a job in industry- but in the end I felt I was called to be with Peter. We had the girls. That's it." Some bloody big gaps, but that's it. She looked into the dying embers, sipped her coffee, put it down. "Oh, Jack."

Jane slipped off her chair, crouched by the fire. She took the poker again, but it was just about out. Nothing to be done. At last she leaned back groaning, rested her head on his thigh.

"Jack, what am I going to do?"

Jack leaned down to her, kissed the back of her head, breathing her scent, stroking her hair. "Sit on my lap," he said, "Come on, Jane."

Awkwardly, she did as she was told.

"Kiss me," he said. She did that too, but was tight-lipped, unhappy, soon broke off, turned her head away from him. She stood up, leaned on the mantelpiece with both hands, and stayed there, head bowed.

"Do men always expect to be able to tell women what to do?"

Jack got up quickly and fetched the Scotch from the kitchen, and a couple of tumblers. She hadn't moved.

"Want a Scotch?"

Nothing. Jack snatched the cap off the bottle upended it till the bright gold splashed in anyhow swirled it smelled its harsh reek swallowed half the spirit caught his breath clack the glass went back on the table he saw her wanted her went to her where she was leaning with her bum stuck out stood close took her hips in his hands pulled her back into his pushing pulsing crotch working it round and round and moaned his cock stiffened against her between her squirming buttocks she must have felt his erection yes she groaned harshly and pushed her arms straight on the fireplace her arse back harder shifting her weight from one side to the other and he slid his hands off her jeans and up under her jumper onto the soft warm sides round onto the quivering smooth belly sliding them forward now and upwards feeling for her full breasts as they hung there swaying in their cradling bra and then his left hand slipping down between her legs

She twisted away.

"Oh, Jack, not yet." Jane went to the table where the tarot still lay scattered: she snatched up the Green Man, glared at it.

"Not *yet*? What are we waiting for?"

"For me!" She dropped the card, grabbed her hair with both hands, staring wildly at him. "I'm frightened, Jack! I'm afraid of what I'm doing to Peter, the girls, you! Can't you understand?"

Jack watched her face working, saw the terrible conflict in her. Felt some of her fear. He could almost smell it. He couldn't speak.

"Good night," she said suddenly, "I'm s..." She stopped herself, shook her head furiously and was gone.

8

Jack lay on his side staring at the darkness. His cock throbbed in his hand, he couldn't sleep... He twisted away from the duvet, sat up on the edge of the bed. The window was a faintly glowing rectangle. He got up and dragged the curtain back. A bright moon rode scattered cloud above the wooded hill. He found the catch and opened it wide, gratefully felt the cool draught flow over his naked body. This was ridiculous. More of that Scotch would dull his senses, knock him out. Who cares. He went to the door, opened it a crack. Total black, total silence. He took his bathrobe from the back of the door, swathed himself in it, switched on the bedside lamp- it would give him enough light to find his way down. Outside the room he listened again. No sound from either of the other two bedrooms. He went downstairs stealthily: a loud creak from one step. Into the dining room, light on. The table, cards, bottle. He snatched it up, no top on it, hefted it, drank deep.

"Impressive."

He convulsed: it slipped away from him, crashed onto the table, rolled, spewing liquor: Sash caught it just before it fell, raised it to him in a mocking toast, said Cheers old boy, and put the spout in her mouth. He watched her throat working as she swallowed, eyes closed, swallowed... and cracked it back onto the table. She remained there, head down, shuddering, one hand clasping the base of the bottle, the other fisted on the tabletop to steady herself, for she was, Jack could see, very drunk already and what with the shock to her system of all that Scotch too...

"Are you all right, Sasha?"

She raised her head, regarded him unsteadily from between the the black bobbed wings.

"I'm pissed," she said, "so I guess I'm all right." She lurched closer to him, put her hands on his shoulders, looked him in the eye or thereabouts. "Have you," she asked reasonably, "fucked my mummy yet?"

She swayed, held on to him tighter, tight, very, I must be very tight, she went on mumbling, very, staggering but forcing him back against the table then holding him there very tight with one hand while the other slid down quickly seeking his cock. Sasha get off he muttered he tried to catch her hand, push her away but Ah no you don't she said Be reasonable I am her daughter I have a right to know and shoved him so bloody hard in the chest he fell back on the table and his robe fell apart and there it was for fucksake look at it and lo it was hard and upstanding A fine big one and with opulent ballocks too, she said, Not that I've got anything much to compare it with, anyway, it looks nicely tumescent and as it were ah pre-ejaculatory from which I conclude that you have not in fact recently shoved it into my yummy mummy. Right, lover boy?

But by now Jack was off the table clutching his swinging cock and balls and scrambling up the stairs bouncing dizzily off the walls as the Scotch hit him hell's bells that bloody girl and he made it to his room at last, shut the door, fumbled with the light, got it switched off somehow and flung himself onto the bed, hauled the duvet up to his chin and lay on his back staring at the reeling cracked ceiling while the room went round and round and the mooncast shadows of branches shifted and shifted endlessly. Couldn't sleep, though. Couldn't stop thinking about her. That bloody girl. Bloody beautiful she is. At last he could bear it no longer, and casting off the coverlet went staggering barefoot to the window, pulling his nightgown tightly round his body against the chill midnight air. The dark trees were swaying menacingly in the wind, clouds brightened and faded as they raced across the face of the full moon. Suddenly he caught his breath: a chill ran down his spine. A tiny click from the door behind him: *He was not alone in the room!* But that was impossible- surely! And then, almost inaudible, a susurrus as of cloth brushing on cloth: his eyes strained in their sockets but he could not bear to turn around. It could not be! *It could not be!*

"Jack…" The faintest whisper right on the edge of hearing: soft, seductive. It came again: "Jack."

Infinitely slowly, he turned towards the bed. There in the shadows, he could just see the pale naked form stretched out, her head upon his pillow. As if drawn by an irresistible force, Jack found himself moving, step by trembling step, closer to the bed.

"No," he breathed, "No- you can't force me to do this. I will not." But still he drew nearer and nearer, till he stood right over the darkly shadowed bed. He felt a hand brush his thigh, caress it slowly, lingeringly, before it slipped higher beneath the rough towelling of his bathrobe, and cupped the opulent roundness of his balls: then the fingers found the firm base of the stiffening cock, encircled it, stroked it: stroked it again and again. Carried away on an irresistible wave of pleasure he felt himself about to come, and "Oh", he gasped aloud, "Oh, Sasha…"

Then all at once she drew back from him and froze, listening intently it seemed. From the depths of his abandon he could hardly speak, but faintly whispered, "What is it?"

She howled with rage, and leapt from the bed. In the faint moonlight he saw her flail her arms wildly like the ghost of a mad white bat as she tried to gather her pale silken nightgown about her; then she flung herself at the door. For a fraction of a second she fumbled sobbing for the clattering latch, found it, threw the door back and was gone: her feet pounded away along the landing, and a somewhere a door slammed with a terrible crash.

Little Alice woke to bright sunlight streaming through a gap in the curtains. She sat up and saw Sasha sprawled snoring on the other bed, and wondered not for the first time why her big sister so often went to bed with all her clothes on. Breakfast, thought Alice, and went downstairs. Nobody about. Why do grownups sleep so much, she wondered. About to go into the kitchen, she noticed the table. What was all this? As she got closer, her nose wrinkled at a strange powerful smell, unpleasant but somehow familiar. Something had been spilt all over… but what were these? Cards! Oh My God thought Alice Oh My God it's like in my book but they're real! Wide eyed, she looked in gasping astonishment from card to card… It's all true after all: it's not just made up, there *are* such things! These must be real Cards of Power! But whose are they? Mummy's? Sasha's? Jack's? Who is the Cartomancer? What terrible secrets grownups have! Who would ever have guessed it? Six cards lay in the foul-smelling pools on the table. Near them was… the rest of the pack! Did she dare? She lifted her eyes from the cards and looked up at the cracked ceiling, listening, listening. Not a sound. Did she dare? She crept round the table so she could reach the pack, her heart beating wildly. The Cartomancer grownup, whoever it was, would be so angry if they knew. Then she thought, oh no, if there are real Cards, there must be real Vampires too, and her stomach heaved. Her back went all cold, and she felt her hair pricking at the back of her neck. Her neck… what if… With a trembling hand, she turned over the next card, and the shocking face of Death leaped at her, its skull-like features twisting malevolently.

Little Alice opened her mouth as wide as it would go and screamed and screamed and screamed…

II

1

"Death?" rasped Peter. Clutching the lectern, he peered inquisitorially through his spectacles at the half circle of ageing parishioners as if expecting that some of them would accept the offer immediately and slump to the parquet floor. But one way or another they clung on. Mrs Mountjoy clutched the arms of her chair, white knuckled with *timor mortis*; the Major glared angrily out of the window over his *pince-nez* as if expecting to surprise Death lurking in the shadows of the shrubbery. Eric was fidgeting, bored or wondering what was for lunch, or wanting the toilet. Evelyn's eyes were on the baroque plasterwork of the ceiling as she polished briskly her spectacles, the better perhaps to search for some imagined heaven beyond it; Glenda blew her nose neatly, shifting her bottom on a hard chair; Mrs Travers wiggled her little finger vigorously in her ear before inspecting myopically the waxy result. Alan, arms fatly folded across his corpulence, had been admiring the gleaming chromework and brassy cymbals of the drum kit, no renaissance polywhatsits here, and the glossy black mass, ha ha, of the splendid grand piano, though Bechstein too Jewish for Christian worship surely he thought, ha ha ha: he had admired also the slender girl with the flaxen hair sitting up straightbacked motionless on the stool next to it, her hands in her lap, her eyes closed, her face expressionless. Hm. His chair creaked as he plumply uncrossed and recrossed his legs, moistening with reptilian tongue his wide lips. Peter let go of the lectern, put his palm to his mouth and coughed. Agitated his beard. Couldn't seem to clear his throat. How he used to enjoy these parish retreats: but look at us now, he thought, God look at us now. Death, be not proud. Life, you've got nothing to shout about either.

"Death?" Peter said unto them a second time, "Death came into the world through Man's disobedience." Disobedience, yes, he nodded around his audience: an inaudience they are really, he thought, frustrated, and found his eyes drawn, not for the first time this disappointing morning, to the girl on the pianostool. Comely. White polo shirt, shortsleeved. Pale, freckled arms. The inevitable blue jeans, rather frayed. Bare feet. How beautiful are the feet. Of them that preach. He found he had lost his train of thought.

"Man was tempted by the woman, and he yielded to that temptation," he gasped at last.

Eric, he saw, was now frankly yawning. This was hopeless.

"But since by man came death, by man came also the resurrection of the dead." He couldn't get any purchase on the familiar words: they slipped away from him, meaningless. My God my God why hast thou forsaken. A disappointing morning. Forsaken me. He had not done well, good and faithful servant though he thought he. Finish the quotation, then shut up. Thought he was. "For as Saint Paul says, As in Adam all die, even so in Christ shall all be made alive, and now we're going to have a *song*," he all but shouted. What is the matter with me, Peter thought despairingly. He looked over at the girl again. Still motionless. But she'd said she'd... Come on, I said it's time for the *song*! Weren't you going to...? He frowned, frustrated, cleared his throat. Not asleep, was she? From the parishioners there grew now the muttering quietly coughing noseblowing muttering footscraping muttering cacophony of inattention that seemed to be their default condition, certainly when music was imminent, let alone immanent. "At least, I *hope* we are going to have a song..." Suddenly her eyes flicked open, straight at him. Hit him. An otherworldly cornflower blue. But a slow smile softened their intensity.

"Of course we are. I was just thanking Jesus for your beautiful words."

She laughs me to scorn. But no: she was sincere, and as Peter realised that, he saw the extent of his loss made plain: *he used to be able to talk to Jesus like that too*. He felt his eyes well up. No, you cannot make me... so he sniffed and watched her, my God my God why, watched her with a melancholy envy as she picked up a guitar from the floor at her feet and stood with an easy grace, hoisting the sling over her shoulder. The action lifted her top so that he caught a glimpse of naked belly: then for a moment as she settled the instrument there was a tightening of the fabric over her tiny breasts, showing him how pert her nipples were and he looked away, reminded of Jane when they'd been at Oxford together and how in those days *he'd spoken to Jesus like a friend*. The girl with the guitar now eagerly dancingly hipswayed across the room to the tall French windows, her long flaxen hair swinging, twanging the steel strings into tune as she went. Like she's going to meet her lover, he thought, and then, *Ah- she is*. For a moment she paused on tiptoe, the instrument silent now, her back to them all as she stared hard into the sundrenched garden: and it did seem as if she was looking for something or someone out there. She waited: and somehow stilled with her waiting stillness the mutterers, the natterly chatterly prattley fidgeting suddenly ceased. And out of her stillness, as if from a great distance, her music began: broken chords for a broken world, fingerpicking out for Peter all the pain of the row with Jane, his sorrow for Sasha, how she'd become so difficult and… and poor little Alice, how little time he'd had with her and what kind of a world were his children growing up into and who was Jack anyway and what had he been thinking to suggest they should go away together without him: *Jane!* He felt so low, all thy waves and storms are gone over me. When did it start to go wrong?

But by now she had turned from the window and, sarabanding swaying towards them to the guitar's humming and strumming, she sang in a clear sweet voice Jesus my love, come down from above take me away to be with you for ever Jesus oh oh I love you so when will you come for me I shed a tear in exile here but you will comfort me when you appear you will return till then I burn with love for you my king when you appear all of my fear will disappear I know on that great day the world will end but Jesus, Jesus my sweet friend I know that you will

Take me and enter me
Fill me with ecstasy
Then I shall come:
Yes, yes I'll come,
With you to…
Heaven

2

Lunch.

Briskly, Robert installs himself opposite Peter. Places his bowl of soup just so, draws towards him the jug of water, salad bowl, lettuce, prays: Bless this food to our use and ourselves to your service, amen, says he, then breaks crusty bread, immediately beginning to mop up with it fragrant yellow gobs of nourishing homemade vegetable soup. A hungry man.

"It's good," he says chewing, "to have you at Windwood again, Peter. It's been a long time." Long time, he nods, yes. "You should come down more often. And bring the family with you next time," he adds, admonishing with another chunk of wholemeal Peter for being on his own before scooping, mouthing, chewing some more. "You should. Is Jane all right? And the girls? Alex was it, and the little one was…?"

"Alice. And Alexandra insists on being called Sasha now."

"Does she. Why?"

"I don't know."

"Is it because…?"

"I don't know why it is."

"You don't? I see." He pours water. "Well, are they?"

"Well enough." But I am so laden with this burden, that I cannot take that pleasure in them as formerly: methinks I am as if I had none. Peter toys unhappily with his bowl of soup, a pilgrim making no progress, aware of munching Robert watching him, waiting for him to say more. Terrible row last night. When the morning was come, they would know how he did: he told them, "Worse and worse." He also set to talking to them again; but they began to be hardened. No, Robert, my tongue cleaveth to my gums.

Around them on benches at the long refectory tables parishioners mingle with residents. No rule of silence here: fellowship rules, and that rules out self indulgent introspection let alone the monkish practice of listening to Holy Writ read out. Not that his lot would be silent for long anyway. Alan, he notes grimly, has somehow levered his bulk in by the guitarist girl, and is holding forth at length, while she nods and smiles dwarfed at his side. Giving his opinion of Byrd's polyphony no doubt. Bit old for him, I'd have thought: she must be all of eighteen. Damn: uncharitable nonsense. Pray for him later I must…

Peter looks back at Robert and smiles weakly: can't help envying the easy authority in the handsome head with its short white hair and beard neatly trimmed, no nonsense there. He picks up a paper napkin, wipes at his own overgrown moustache. The nightly growth that fringed his lips, Sasha called it: this was amusing, apparently. "Yes, they're well," he adds at last, not very convincingly he feels, but. There you are.

Robert reaches for the Cheddar cheese and a change of subject.

"How did it go this morning, then? Good session?"

"I didn't feel I did very well at all, I'm afraid..." Peter picked up a piece of bread, crumbled it onto his plate without eating. "The best thing was the song. That girl over there. Didn't catch her name. She offered to sing for us and was really quite remarkably good."

"Fran? Remarkable girl altogether, is our Fran, said Robert, buttering bread, paring cheese. "You don't know about her, of course: she joined us since your last visit."

"Remarkable?"

"Quite a story. Fran's not her real name. But it's what she wants us to call her."

"Why do girls..? Sasha..."

"Some story. Let me tell you. You should try this cheese."

"No thanks."

"Mm. Really is very good. Well, *Fran* as she wants to be known first came down here with a parish group." He munched. "A few months ago. From Oxford. Student. Gave it all up."

"Ah. The rat race of modern life. More fulfilling working here."

"M... wait." Mouth full again, chew, swallow it down. Appetite of the man. "You haven't heard the half of it. When I say she gave it all up, I mean *all*. She sold all the stuff from her flat, the car her doting parents had given her, the lot. Went into an Oxfam shop with a couple of bags of odds and ends and a cheque for several thousand pounds. Before the old dears in the shop had managed to pick their jaws off the floor she'd started taking her clothes off too."

"What?"

"Apparently there was quite a scene. I got all this from her parents when they came down here after her. That was quite a scene too, I can tell you." Robert grins mirthlessly at the memory, finishing his sandwich. He shakes his head, shrugging. "To cut a long story short, the Oxfam ladies took pity on her and gave her some old jeans and a sweater and a pair of trainers from stock and off she went. Thumbed lifts to get down here."

"That's incredible."

"That's what happened. I found her on the doorstep one morning with nothing except the clothes she stood up in and a big smile. Told me Jesus had shown her Mark chapter ten, the rich young man, the one who wanted to know how to inherit eternal life, right?"

"She said that?"

"He'd kept the law from his youth. But one thing was lacking."

"He couldn't bring himself to sell all his possessions and give the money to the poor... but she actually did?"

"She actually did."

"And the parents came after her, you say?"

"They were furious. With me. Thought I'd brainwashed her, like they do in these *cults*, you know? Well, we talked, prayed. They're a Christian family, but thought she was taking things a little *too far*. Very Anglican! In the end, though..."

"She got her own way."

"There speaks the father of a teenage girl."

"Sasha doesn't... yes, she does." Bloody Swansea, for heaven's sake. "Women... do tend to get their own way." And he wondered bleakly about Jane.

Robert took an apple, smelled it, crushed with strong white teeth a large bite out of it.

"Then there was the boyfriend," he crunched.

"Pretty unhappy too, I guess."

"Harry, I think she said his name was. Poor lad. Having your girl go off with someone else is never very pleasant. But when you've been jilted for Jesus..."

"Rather damaging to the self esteem. Or not, I suppose. Strange. Well. What a story." Peter looks at her with new interest. She's doing all the talking now: Alan has met his match, apparently.

"So here she stays. Works hard, cleaning, cooking, anything. Makes music for us. Won't accept any money for what she does, of course. You're not eating."

No, I'm... really not very..."

"Got to keep your strength up."

"She seems to've made quite an impression on Alan."

Robert swivels round to have a look, turns back grinning. "She makes quite an impression on everyone. Me included. The only thing is, though, she's..."

"What?"

"No, talk to her yourself. I wouldn't want to, well… you'll see." For a moment Robert is silent, looking at the apple core as he twirls it by its stem. Then he looks Peter in the eyes and says, "I was sorry to hear about Father Michael, by the way."

"Oh. Yes. A great shock. Heart attack…" Death, again. Wages of. The dead praise not thee, O God, neither all they that go down into silence. Poor Michael. Dead. Wages of sin indeed. Ridiculous. Never known a better man. Adam's sin really. And Eve's. The woman tempted the man and…

"Hm." Robert drops the apple core on his plate, puts his elbows on the table, steeples his fingers, purses his lips, eyes downcast. "May he rest in peace. He used to love coming here." He looks up at Peter's troubled face. "Is any one else… giving you support?"

"Support?"

"He was your spiritual director, wasn't he?"

"Yes. No. No one. Not like that."

"Perhaps a little chat. After supper. Say about eight o'clock?"

Lord, thou hast found me out. Peter looks at Robert sharply, then drops his eyes to his plate and kneads his brow and wonders why he's become so ready to hear implied criticism everywhere. For a moment his eyes prick, it's like when the girl said she'd been thanking Jesus… He looks at her again, still talking animatedly to Alan, who looks strangely quiet.

"A little chat? What do you mean?"

Robert reaches across the table, places a large hand on Peter's arm, squeezes it affectionately, kindly.

"Don't misunderstand," he smiles. "I'm not criticising. You're not yourself, though, are you? I can see it in your eyes. Come and talk. This evening. So. What are you doing this afternoon? The prayer walk?"

Through the wilderness of this world, solitarily in the fields, sometimes reading and sometimes praying… and also to condole his own misery.

"Yes."

"Good. I'll see you later."

3

Then said Evangelist, pointing with his finger over a very wide field, "Do you see yonder wicket gate?" And Pilgrim, peering through his spectacles said no at first but then actually yes I think I do after all. Off you go then, said Evangelist, across the lawn and through the gate. God bless. But Pilgrim answering said unto him, alas, I cannot go so fast as I would, by reason of some of these folk being a bit doddery on their feet, not to mention this burden that is on my back. No matter, I'll look after them, replied Evangelist, you go off on your own. Have a bit of time to yourself with the Lord. So he thanked him right heartily and went on with haste, neither spake he to any man else by the way; nor, if any asked him, would he vouchsafe them an answer. So, in process of time, he got up to the gate. Now, on the gate there was written, "Please shut the gate." So after he had passed through he latched it carefully after him lest he break the country code or in any other wise offend.

Now there was in that place a forking of the path, and Pilgrim, having been forewarned by Christian, followed not the broad and easy way to the left hand which would have led him down unto the beach but trod rejoicingly rather upon the steep and rugged pathway up through the woods on the right hand; though in truth he rejoiced not so greatly after some couple of hundred yards as it was indeed pretty blooming steep like stairs it was and the weather being humid and the burden on his back weighing heavier it seemed good to him to stand awhile and with a fair white cloth of linen having his initial P embroidered in one corner to wipe his streaming brow withal. Steep like stairs it is, he thought and turned looking down the way he'd come and he was minded then of little Alice following after him up the stairs in his house and how she had said unto him, with tears and heartfelt supplication, Daddy, and he had turned on her in his wrath, looking down at her looking up at him and saying, And you can shut up as well, don't you think I've got enough to deal with, with her I don't know who she thinks she is, and your mother up here too going on and on, without you whingeing and whining go to bed you silly little girl, that she wept the more bitterly. And at that remembrance a great sorrow filled him that he groaned aloud and sighed and beat his breast, for he knew right well the saying of the Apostle Paul in his great epistle to the Colossians namely Fathers, provoke not your children to indignation, lest they be discouraged

And I have sinned, forgive me, forgive me, Jesus, he prayed. But answer came there none, save only the the distant mockery of the gulls and the sighing of the wind in the trees for it was actually quite breezy up here and rather less humid which was a relief. And espying in that place a conveniently fallen tree, he stepped aside from the path and sat upon it right gladly.

And calling to mind that this was after all a prayer walk and not just a jaunt in the woods he prayed again, saying our Father, which art. And he had a sudden vision of himself, himself a father though not in heaven, sitting there wretched in the windy wood. All was strange: the shifting patterns of sunlight on the undergrowth, the heady stench of wild garlic. He felt a moment of panic. Deliberately, he removed his spectacles and rubbed his eyes. Identity. He wasn't sure who he was for a moment. We rely on our environment for our identity. Who'd said that? Out of context, we are no one. Ridiculous. I am that I am. Another condemnatory chorus of shrieking gulls. He wondered what they were saying. He knew what they were saying. Oh, Alice, he prayed, forgive me. Lovely little girl with her long fair hair and her trusting look and her silly book about vampires, was it? Sweet little tilty uppy nose and her big eyes oh how she reminded him sometimes of Jane. How she was before. And in the photo album too those funny pictures of how they used to be before. Before all this, this. He pictured her like she was in her school photo so proud of her new uniform and said to her I'm so sorry, little Alice, how can you ever forgive me Alice, my little daughter this is ridiculous I love you so much please forgive me. Ridiculous. And there came upon him then a terrible realisation of what he was doing so that he recoiled from the thought that he was praying to his little daughter for forgiveness, only God can forgive sins, but he couldn't remember if that was the scribes and Pharisees who said that or if it mattered or who he was just squatting here on a log like an idiot after all, his specs dangling from his fingers.

Then was Pilgrim ware of voices as it were of a great multitude of murmurers complaining up the path behind him and recognising them to be the voices of those very souls whose cure he had he rose up in haste lest they should catch him up and confound him with their jabbering fellowship and setting his spectacles firmly on his face more or less legged it the rest of the way up the path and out of the woods at the top and on a sudden lo! the great and wide sea also. There go the ships, he saw. And there is that Leviathan, presumably, though not currently visible, whom thou hast made to take his pastime therein:

could we but stand where Moses stood and view the landscape o'er, not Jordan's stream nor death's cold flood could fright us from the shore, he thought. And so he stood awhile, uffish, manksome, buffeted by the wind, the glossy coarse grasses flicking or flaring flat before his feet, falling away in shallow terraces to the cliff edge. Dangerous. Like her.

Now Pilgrim was not sure, for his geography had ever been but hazy but he had an idea that the low hills he could see over the sea there on that other shore, in the blue hazy distance beyond the shining sea, were the hills of Wales, and was it not in fact Swansea and Gower directly opposite, and that put him in mind of his dangerous older daughter Alexandra that is ycleped by herself Sasha, that she might be herself more onely, and defy him the more greatly, and on every occasion possible, not in drinking strong liquor and smoking fags alone, but how she further went against his rightful paternal wishes not to mention Saint Paul's (for did not that Apostle write to the Colossians three twenty Children obey your parents in all things: for this is well pleasing to the Lord) by making application to Swansea and not Oxenford for all his earnest entreaties that she should bethink her of the manifold advantages and benefits of the Turl, the High, the Bod, the Broad, I don't know who she thinks she is.

Dangerous. We pray thee too for wanderers from thy fold, oh bring them back, back to the faith of old. Oh God, behold Alexasha in thy mercy help her find her way back to faith and hope and, and the other thing, charity, yes. Charity shop, for heaven's sake, Oxfam, see Sasha doing that. What an amazing. Fran, was it? Why? For Francis or Frances I suppose for him of Assisi he gave it all up what if I did? Give it all up. Wonder what her real name is. What her parents called her. But is that her real name or is your real name something you have to find out? Oh God help Sasha if that's what I must call her she's known to you Lord by whatever name is just as. Sweet Jesus help her through that wicket gate whirled round this wicked world so dangerous what will become of her?

And Pilgrim prayed most earnestly for his eldest, his dear child, oh it was that school that did it with that smart English teacher Alec Empson was his name was it with his cunning ambiguities corrupting the once so blindingly obvious *certainties*. All up with that now, all is relative, language flowing over the surfaces of this our wintry world. Everything a metaphor. Thy radiance bright awakes new joy, transforming clay. What am I thinking?

What? Think what? Who? Think now who is thinking? I. Say I. Oh God. What does that mean? Prayer walk this is, yes, well, pray then. I was glad when they said unto me, we will go into the house of the Lord. Then were the disciples glad when they saw the Lord. And so was Jane. At my ordination. Glad. So what has happened to us? Look at the sea down there, the miles and miles of gleaming sea. If I take the wings of the morning, and remain in the uttermost parts of the sea, even there also shall thy hand lead me. Words, words. But what else have I got?

Sasha. Forgive me.

Praying to my. Wrong. Hold her before God. Hold all of us. In his hand. He's got the whole world. Mervyn would cringe at that. See him now. Cringing politely, refraining from giving us the Byrd. And Alan frankly smirking. Words, words, hopeless.

Now Pilgrim remained long in that high place and would fain have remained longer, for 'twas good Lord to be there, even building perhaps a tabernacle or three but there came to his ear once again that murmuring of fellowship drawing near so that he rose up in haste and cast about him for the path which would lead him down to the next prayer point, for he had been well briefed by Evangelist. Keeping well away from the cliff edge which was now he saw it yes actually pretty jolly lethal to the unwary he came at last upon the stile over a fence and saw beyond it the way down even as Evangelist and Christian had helpfully described it. Pilgrim therefore mounted the the stile, old wood beginning to perish in the harsh sea air, seen better days it has, feels a bit wobbly. Yes. Well, mustn't go seeing images of our own decay and failure everywhere we look, must we. He climbed over- whoops! careful- and set off with a will, coming down from the mount of revelation, not that much had been revealed, more concealed, ran a little way, easy, jog jog jog, down we go, faster, faster, down so steep here oh half hurls earth for him off under his feet, yes, Jesuitical they were but he had enjoyed them, poems Gerard Manly hop skip and a jump down here running along now Sasha gave him for his birthday not one for poetry really but he was pleased she'd thoughtfully got him something he could relate to at any rate there's hope yet yes and perhaps faith too and the other thing charity.

And it was even as Christian and Evangelist had foretold, for there was not much farther on a low cairn of stones, a mere child's sketch of an altar it was, though, disappointing, and a rough wooden cross too: someone had been to a DIY and bought a couple of planks and some nails and banged it together any old how. Shoved it in the ground. Prayer point three. Jane.

It seems obvious to me that because of circumstances beyond our control, we are born. After a little while, we become aware of various things going on. Eventually, we cease to be aware of them. And that's it really, isn't it? Isn't it *obvious* what's wrong?

It isn't obvious to me, Jane. Walking around the cross, he found a stone lying in the long grass. He dug his fingers in under it, plucked it out of the earth. Heavy. What would Dominic say? During the pilgrimage of this our life, there are times when the cares of this world grow up around the struggling plant of faith, choke it. Come unto me, all ye that are heavy laden, and I will give you rest. Laden, he bore the heavy stone to the cairn, placed it. Felt the release of not carrying it. There is more joy in heaven over one sinner that repenteth, than in ninety and nine that have no need of. No. No, Dominic. She's not an OICU groupie any more, following us holy boys around like, like… All that's gone. Gone for good.

He would pray for Jane. Picture her. How she was, before… When did he first see her? This morning, when. Guitar. God, her. When a tightening of white fabric on. On those pert little nipples. *Jane*! Ah, remember, how she was when. Before we. Can't see her now. How she is… with him. Who is Jack anyway? Pretending, she said. I have to pretend to believe in God, in you, in myself, in what we're doing to the girls, it's all just make-believe, none of it's real, Peter, can't you see? Peter crawls onto the little cairn and claws his way in, clutches the stone, it's real to me, would bury himself in it this altar of the Lord this home. Holy. It must be. Oh how amiable are thy dwellings.

Jane. I pray thee too for her, her and Sasha, wanderers from thy fold, oh bring them back, back to the faith of old. Oh God, behold Sashajane in thy mercy help them find their way back to faith and hope and, and...

Jane. We used to pray together. God, remember how we used to. Before. Before we let our bodies off the leash.

Peter thrusts his body into the loose pile of stones, would tunnel inside, he is a miner a mole a caver clawing his way into a choke of fallen stone he is fallen man he has sinned he has suddenly become aware of voices near at hand murmuring complaining louder now he twists around in the rockpile and looks about him wildly crazed they pursue him his parishioners would not understand: this kind of grovelling prayer is not on their servicesheets: he must escape and slithers down and finds his feet in the grass and frankly flees them, runs headlong down the broad path panting now oh now how sure he jogging is he jogs along must reach the shore before they find him oh how beautiful upon the mountain are the feet of them that preach the gospel of them that reach the peace of the beach.

   Flat sand, and suddenly silent. Even the nagging commentary of the gulls is gone. Stand still a minute, listen: they'll never find me down here. On either side, cliffs rear up: look at them, huge, and how crazily tilted they are. Those layers of rock. Strata, that's the word. Before me across the wet sand the sea and sky. And Wales where they. Jane and. Listen: ah, not quite silent after all; the faintest music, a plashing of the eternal waves. Eternal. Eternal Father strong to save. Her. Jane. No good, can't see her. Not with Jack. Some prayer walk this, hopeless. Forget it. Words slip away, can't get a grip. Which way now? Along here to the left, the shadowy side, sun going down that way behind, west that must be then, get out of the sun, too hot here. The tide must have only just gone out, very fast here, goes a long way too, huge tidal reach Robert called it biggest in the world except for somewhere in Newfoundland. Strange, that. Why? And the bore or boar is it? Not this far down. Get that further up the estuary. Spectacular to watch. Dangerous if you're in a little boat I suppose. How's that work then? Something to do with the river water meeting the sea. All the rivers of our lives flow into the one eternal sea of life oh yes use that in a sermon, good. Feet sinking into the soft sand still wet, footprints in the sands of time I'm leaving. These trainers really mucked up now, doesn't matter. Story about Jesus walking by your side, parallel footprints, then only one set, why so, why did you leave me Lord no that was when I carried you. Can't remember it now. My God my God why hast thou forsaken me, and art so far from me. Psalm twenty two. Dark in here under the cliff, but cool after the sun up there on the hill. Wet rocks black, dank, rank with seaweed smell and barnacles sharp to the touch. Cool pools in the sand here under the overhang. Wonder if there's a crab? There's a rock pool. Sea anemones, waving their arms about, poke your finger in they'll grip it. Sting you? Not here. Tropical ones perhaps might. Get myself in here, into this shadowy corner, sit down for a bit, take the weight off. Off my feet, off my back. Into the valley of the shadow of.

   Death.

   Death be not proud. Where's that from? Sasha said it. Some poem. Holy sonnets, that was it. Who wrote that, I asked her. Dunno, she said, now I've taken my exams I'm done with poets, ha ha… see her laughing, mocking? Oh dear.

Oh but it's peaceful here. Lean back on the cool rock, and close my eyes for a moment. Dangerous. Might go to sleep, get cut off by the tide coming back in, no escape except climb up the cliff. Couldn't make it, fall off. Drown in the sea. All thy waves and storms are gone over me. Drowsy.

Whang!

What? Blasted football, who…?

"Sowwy, Mister."

"Callum, leave the jenna manna lone."

"It's quite all right, please don't worry. Here's your ball, Callum," unhandily chucking it at the boy, who grunts something like cheers, chests it, knees it, keepy-uppies it once, twice, misses the third, picks it up, hoofs it goalie fashion into the distance.

"Callum, gerear now!"

"Am cummin!" And he's gone, thank goodness, no sorry, oh pray for Callum and his mother or aunt or big sister or could be anyone really got to pray for someone but how, how come it's all so different these days. Used to be able to talk to Jesus once. Several people on the shoreline now, walking in the waves, some of them. Not on them, ha ha, though it does look as if. Optical illusion. But just suppose by some miracle all suddenly so blessed, like Saint Peter till he lost his. Like she lost her. Jane. Look at that dog. Dogs love the water, not like cats. Why is that? No reason really why cats couldn't swim as well as dogs. He's coming this way. Patter of paws on wet sand, hello, boy! Girl? Girl. Hello! Patting dog on head actually not as good as on belly cats prefer head stroking not going to pat this one too wet with going in the sea and smelly nothing worse than wet dog, like when the dishwasher went wrong and all the glasses stank. Sniffing at me. How she wags her tail! Throw something for her. No, then she'll want to play for ever, follow me home. Bitch.

"Sheba! Sheba!"

Funny how often dogs called after Sheba, arrival of the queen of. At weddings Mervyn plays it Handel is it when she visited Solomon in all his glory he was not arrayed like they did not show me the half of it she said. Solomon son of David shagger of bathing beauty Bath Sheba wife of Uriah the Hittite

"Sheba!"

There she goes now off like a shot off a shovel to her owner. What sort? Labrador, is she? Labrador, where is that? Near Newfoundland is it where the tide is even bigger than here, never really took the time to study the world map which is strange since all this world is God's creation one ought to at least have the decency to take an intelligent interest in what He's been up to with his let there be this and let there be that and seeing that it was all very good. What is the matter with me! Stupid thinking like that. Irreverent. God. *God*? I used to be able to talk to…

Getting a bit cold in here now actually. Move along the cliff towards the sea, catch the last of the sun. Tread carefully here, twist your ankle if you're not. Ah! The sound of the sea getting louder. The dog walkers are gone, there's no one else here now. Here where the water slaps right up against the rocks, climb round into the sun over the sharply barnacled shattered boulders into the next little bay, the warm sun's rays almost horizontal now as it sinks in the west the colours rich and vivid and ah! Who's that in the water?

It's *her*.

Shrink back, don't let her see me. Watching her.

What is truth? I come to bear witness. By bend of bay and swerve of shore she dances for her lover on the ribbed sand in the shallow rippling sea, ever at play in His presence, surfeet splashing sparkling in the low rays of the setting sun, dances for Him who will come, dances to welcome him, come, Lord Jesus. Pilgrim leans on a rock watching. He has come to the brink, shrinks on the shore, will not venture o'er, will not join her dance. Look at her leaping at the water's edge, flaxen hair flying in the air, the white polo shirt and the blue jeans, limbs rising and falling with the spray in arabesques of invocation. How I envy your excellent motion, your patterned devotion, rhythmical motion of praise, praise of him, but for me too, me: watching you I praise too. Oh, and the colours, unreal from the low angle of the setting sun. She glows, a gold and white and blue jewel. A living stone in the wall of the heavenly Jerusalem. Oh that he could take her and place her on the cairn of his heart, burrow in with her into the edifice of faith and be forever free from sorrow, free from sin. And as he watches her something blooms in him, ah, she is so lovely so lovely ah no Onan I could there's no one around just me and her I could I could

4

Ulysses
Death in Venice
Uncommon Prayer
So long, God, it's been divine
A Woman's Glory: St Paul and the Eternal Feminine
Stand Up, Stand Up for Jesus: Studies in Christian Tantra

By a man's book shelf shall ye know him.

Abraham and his Seed. Lurid cover. Have a look.

"We've got to get rid of the b-bastards, see? They are an affront to to to…"
"To God, I know."
"To God. And we will never achieve the g-greatness, which He promised to to to…"
"To our forefather Abraham, yes."
"To our forefather Abraham until we g-get, get, get…"
"Rid of the bastards. I see. If you whet that blade any more there'll be nothing left."
"Bastards. There'll be nothing left of them by the time I've f-f-f-"
"Finished with them?"
"Fucking slit their bastard throats, man."
Jesus took the knife and the whetstone out of Levi's hands and laid them gently on the table. Then he sat down on the bench next to him and put his arms round him.
"Levi," he said softly, and all at once the big fellow was sobbing like a baby. I'd never seen anything like it.
"So bloody angry," he wept. "They make me so, so…"
"Bloody angry," said Jesus, "I know." And he went on holding him till it was over.
I went to the window; pulled the shutters open. Let there be light, I thought. Outside, the street was empty. It had been raining, I saw. On the just and the unjust alike. At any rate, the Roman patrol had gone.

"By their bookshelves shall ye know them! I'm so sorry to've kept you waiting, Peter. Bathtime and bedtime stories seem to take much longer nowadays than I remember from when our Emma was a little girl herself. Sara's just making us some coffee now. But you've been able to entertain yourself. That's good. Sorry about the mess in here…" Robert picked a couple of magazines and a newspaper off a chair, added them to the pile on his desk as a gesture in the direction of tidying up.

"Yes. No, I do understand. It used to take ages getting Alex- I should say Sasha- off to bed when she was little. Great long stories, and then prayers…"

"I'm not a believer," stated Robert, as he fitted himself into an armchair, accidentally bewildering Peter before continuing, "in bedtime prayers. They'll come to the Lord in their own way eventually, in a way which is uniquely appropriate to their psychology and to their social and linguistic environment. That's what I told their mother, anyway. Ha! Bit mischievous actually, shouldn't tease. Emma's not very interested in *theory*, as she calls it. And as for her husband… Do sit down, Peter."

Peter put *Abraham and his Seed* back on the shelf, sat down obediently.

"And who is the lucky son-in-law?"

"Now *you're* teasing. Well, I deserve it. Adrian? He's a lovely, straightforward boy. Bit *too* straightforward in some ways. Not a reader. Well, that sounds critical, doesn't it. He's a good boy. Teaches, you know. Science. In what he calls 'a large rural comprehensive.' Don't think he's enjoying it very much. Anyway, it's been good for him and Emma to get away without the children for once. They're having a week in France, you know."

"What's it like being a grandparent? Do you enjoy it?"

"At the moment? No. Roll on, Saturday! But when they've gone, I expect Sara and I will be saying how sweet the little things are and going over all the funny things they did. You know how it is. Absence makes the heart grow fonder, and all that." Peter found himself wondering how true this was in his own case. "Are you missing your family?"

"My family?" Ah. This was Robert finding a way in to their little chat. But at that moment he was rescued by the grand entrance of the coffee.

"Here you are then." Big friendly Sara sailed into the room and hove to by the coffee table. "Hello, Peter," she said, docking the tray on the low table between the two men and beginning to unload it. "Didn't see you at supper. Have you had something to eat?"

"It was a bit late by the time I got back from the, from my walk. I wasn't really hungry."

"Some of your dear old parishioners were asking where you'd got to. I told them you'd been taken up to heaven in a fiery chariot."

"You didn't!"

"True. Have a biscuit."

"Peter is o' th' chameleon's dish. He eats the air, promise crammed."

"You'll have to excuse my ageing husband. He talks complete nonsense sometimes, don't you Grandpa?"

"The Dane, woman, the Dane!"

"See what I mean? There's nothing to be done, I'm afraid. Do tuck in to the biscuits, before he gobbles them all up himself."

"Begone, wife," says Robert, urging down the piston of the cafetière with one hand while patting with the other her considerable arse. "The game is afoot."

"We know all about your games," she said, smacking his hand away and smirking sidelong at Peter. "Don't let him keep you up all night with his nonsense. If you need rescuing, just scream." She kissed Robert on the top of his head. "Mwah. See you later." And she was gone, leaving Peter to wonder how the two of them managed to talk like that while he and Jane could barely stand one another's company. Robert concentrated on pouring coffee, the thin trickle sounding surprisingly loud in the suddenly still room.

"I envy you. You and Sara. So easy together, it seems. So easy." He shook his head sadly. "Not like…" Robert glanced up at him, started pouring a second cup.

"Not like, I think you may have been going to say, you and Jane…"

"We. No. Jane and I. We seem to have grown apart."

"Milk?"

"What? Oh, yes, please."

Peter got up, went to the window sighing. The day was far spent, the night was at hand. The shades lengthened, and very soon the dark trees would be swaying menacingly in the wind, clouds brightening and fading as they raced across the face of the full moon. Nightmare. Let there be light, he thought. He pulled the lace curtain aside. Outside, the garden was empty. It had not been raining, he saw. On the just or the unjust. No Roman patrols either. Abraham and his seed indeed. So bloody angry... He realised he had clenched his fists, relaxed them, dropping the lace. He took his glasses off, rubbed his eyes.

"Grown apart, you were saying."

Peter turned around. For a moment he hardly recognised Robert: had forgotten where he was. Identity. Out of context. That was the problem. Who was Robert, anyway? He hardly knew him. But perhaps that was the point. Easier to talk freely. Perhaps. Confused, he put his glasses back on, adjusted them.

"Sorry, I was...yes. Grown apart, you could say that."

"It was you that said it." Robert thrust out his legs, made an airy gesture with one hand. "The floor is yours. Do you want to talk about that?"

"Yes."

"Come and drink your coffee."

Peter perched on the edge of a chair, took up his coffee cup, sipped, made a face, put it down."

"Is that all right for you? Not too strong?"

"It's fine."

"Sara likes it strong. When she makes coffee, she makes coffee. And when she makes water..."

A silence began to lengthen. Peter, still edgy, stood up again, put his hands in his pockets. Where to start? At the beginning. But where was that? He noticed a poster on the wall, took a couple of paces towards it. An aerial view of a line of climbers making their way across a snowy ridge, dwarfed by their surroundings. In the Himalayas or somewhere, by the look of it. *It's not where you've come from, it's where you're going to*, advised the caption.

"She says she can't go on pretending any more."

"Pretending what?"

"That she believes." Another poster showed a bronzed athletic youth on a rock face in brilliant sunshine, empty blue sky behind and below him as he clung on to an overhang by his fingertips and one toe. *If it's going to be, it's got to be me.* "Apparently she's been pretending for some time now to believe in God, in me, in the way we're bringing up the children," he told the young climber. "The whole of our life together, in fact. It seems that the strain of keeping up this pretence has now become too great for her. She says she can't go on." He turned to Robert. "That's it. That's what my problem is. Now you know." He went back to the chair, sat down, took his coffee and a biscuit. Your turn, Robert.

"So. She's lost her faith, you might say."

"That's what I did say to her. But she won't accept that that's a meaningful thing to say. I think what she's getting at is that you can only really say that someone's *lost* their faith in a context where *having* faith is a real possibility. Which for her it no longer is. I suppose that she just feels that how she feels now is, well, normal."

"Normal." Robert made it sound like a swear word. "Who was it who said the other day that they thought religion was part of the problem, not part of the solution? One of our, er, *politicians*." Robert stirred angrily, but waved the anger away. He smiled at Peter. "They've got a point, of course, our secularist brethren. Though I'm not sure how many of them fully understand it, let alone live up to it. There was always this great paradox at the heart of the old supernaturalist faith, wasn't there: if you only behave morally because you know you'll be punished with hell fire if you don't, then you're not really behaving morally at all, are you?"

Peter started to say, "Old supernaturalist..?" But Robert pushed on.

"You have to actually *want* to live well because you can see for yourself that it's the right thing to do. Even in the depths of nihilistic despair. My God my God why hast thou forsaken me, yes, even on the cross. There's been so much written about this, you know, the idea of human autonomy, but people don't read, do they? It's obvious. You have to get rid of the idea of an all-seeing sin-punishing God first or authentic moral behaviour is impossible."

"It isn't obvious to me," said Peter, realising as he said it that he'd been saying things weren't obvious to him quite a lot recently. But this was… "I don't understand. Get rid of God?"

"Of an obsolete idea of God. Which is probably what Jane finds she can no longer pretend to believe in. Whereas you- perhaps- have not got to that point yet."

"What point? The point where I lose my faith too?"

"Come on, Peter, you know faith isn't a thing like that, some odd thing to be lost like a chap might lose his hat or his umbrella or something: it's a living process, a relationship with the world, a way of seeing… it changes."

"This is our faith," affirmed Peter the Vicar. "We believe in one God, Father, Son, and Holy Spirit…"

"Yes yes yes. But meaning what?"

"You know what it means!"

"I know what it meant when I was twenty. But I'm not the same person now. I've changed."

"That's what Jane said. That she'd changed, since we were at college together. I don't understand. No, I do, I mean, of course I understand how people change as they get older, have kids, get on in the world. But the certainties of faith, how can these ever change? Did Jesus die for our sins, or did he not? Jane used to be so sure of that. I remember her saying, when some atheist in college asked her why she was a Christian, it's because Jesus died for my sins. She quite simply knew Jesus died for her sins. How can that change?"

Robert opened his mouth as if to answer the question, but changed his mind. Leaning forward, he poured more coffee. A thirsty man. "One of the greatest problems I find in organising collective worship here is that everyone is at a different stage in their spiritual growth. Of course, having a strong unchanging dramatic ritual such as the old mass used to provide a common focus which people could relate to in their own ways, but that's mostly gone from the church now. Not the mass, I mean, obviously, but the possibility of accommodating wildly different spiritualities in the same service. It's a language problem. These days liturgy all seems to be aimed at people with a mental age of about ten. Which is fine for ten year olds of all ages. The rest of us have to pretend, see? And it can be a strain keeping up that pretence. But there," he laughed, "if Sara were here she'd tell me to stop riding my ruddy hobby-horse around the room. This is supposed to be about you. And Jane. Tell me some more about Jane."

"What about her?"

"How did you meet?"

"We were at the same college. And she was in the Christian Union. We saw a lot of one another."

"What attracted you to her?"

"I don't know."

"Oh, come on. Long legs, nice tits?"

"Robert, really…"

"Well?"

"It wasn't like that. I admired her. The way she used to praise the Lord in church, dancing sometimes, with a tambourine! I got to know a lot about praise music through her. Not just worship songs, either. She sang in choirs too. Renaissance polyphony, like my organist Mervyn likes to have sometimes. Causes problems for me. People like Alan.

But that's another story. No, it was her faith, and her good nature, really. Her kindness."

"She was kind to you, was she?"

"She did a lot of good works."

"So. How did the relationship develop?"

"Well, as time went on we just seemed to be spending more and more time in one another's company. Worshipping together. Going to concerts. People said there was something a bit special between us. I was due to be ordained after I'd done my year's training, and she being a year below me, well, we'd both finish with Oxford at the same time and it made sense to get married then, just before I started in my first parish."

"Why did you get married?"

"Like I said. There was this special thing between us. Everyone remarked on it. We obviously got on really well. It made sense."

"Nothing else?"

"Well, she wanted to make her mind up about what to do after Oxford. She'd got this really good degree, in science of some sort, and so of course there were a number of opportunities for her in industry, should she decide to go down that route. But she didn't."

"Science of some sort? What sort?"

"I'm sorry?"

"Biochemistry, engineering, theoretical physics?"

"Oh, I see. I'm not sure. She used to spend a lot of time in the labs down Parks Road, I remember. Tried to tell me about it, but it was all Greek to me. Actually worse than that, I was quite good at Greek. Well, New Testament Greek. Fairly good. Forgotten a lot of it now, of course."

"No conflict between her scientific studies and her religious beliefs, then?"

"Conflict? No. I've never been able to see why people think that might be a problem. God made a beautiful, complex world, and understanding how it works is part of understanding His creative purposes, isn't it?"

"I see. But she had a chance to make a good career for herself, with those qualifications."

"Oh yes. She went for interviews, Rolls Royce, BP, I can't remember now. I think she was quite successful, could have had a job with any number of big firms."

"But she decided to become a curate's wife instead."

"She decided that in the end she wanted to support me in my ministry. For which I have been very grateful ever since."

"Right." There was a long pause during which Robert watched Peter with growing astonishment. "Anything else?"

"What do you mean?"

"Let's try another approach. What does she look like?"

"Jane? Well- she's. She..." Peter shrugged, grinned, spread his hands. "She's about so tall, quite good looking..."

"What colour are her eyes?"

"Her eyes? They're... sort of. I don't know really. Why?"

"Hair?"

"Shortish. Used to have it longer."

"Any other distinguishing features?"

"You make it sound like a missing person inquiry."

"It is, isn't it?"

Peter thought about this. Yes, she's gone missing all right. When had he last seen her? Really seen her as she was? He let his mind wander back over the years, tried to visualise the pictures in the photo albums. What did she look like in those days? As a young mother, holding baby Alex? As an undergraduate?

"I find it quite hard to find the words. I'm not very good at describing..."

"Peter, forgive me, but I want to ask you again. Why did you marry Jane?"

Peter just stared at Robert, shaking his head slowly. "I don't see why you keep on asking me that. I've told you."

"You've told me all sorts of things," said Robert. "Given all sorts of reasons. But not the one I would have expected." He leaned forward expectantly, but Peter was silent. "The obvious one," he urged.

"Obvious?" Nothing seems obvious to me, he thought sadly.

"Didn't you *love* her?"

"Love her? Of course I loved her."

"But it wasn't at the top of your list, was it? In fact you didn't mention love at all." Robert fell back in his chair, arms spread, point made. "Did you?"

"Well, I suppose I took it for granted that you'd realise I loved her."

"Did Jane have to take it for granted as well?"

"I'm sorry, Robert, I don't see where this is going. I'm confused. That was all years ago, anyway. I want to know what I'm going to do now.

I'm supposed to be going over to the cottage on Saturday to join her and the girls and."

"And..?"

"There's this man. Jack. He's become a sort of friend of the family, I suppose you'd say. He's an artist. Made an installation for the church. Really quite good. But."

Robert got up decisively and went to the metal filing cabinet, pulling out the bottom drawer which made a suggestive clink...

"He's gone with them, you see. Drove them over there so I could have the car to come here. Seemed like a good idea, solved a problem: he fancied a bit of time in the hills..."

... produced a bottle, glasses...

"Trouble is, I think he fancies Jane a bit too."

...and placed them on the table...

"And the way she looks at him..."

...and unscrewed the cap, sloshing in a couple of decent shots. He knew his stuff, all right, it was a goodish midrange single malt. What the doctor ordered.

"So. There's another dimension to it. As you can see, the doctor has prescribed a dose of the medicine on the table before you. Alas, its effects are palliative only; but a full and perfect cure may not be immediately available."

"I'm not saying there's anything going on, Robert. But I'm not saying there isn't." He felt all the pent up jealousy, the hot resentment, the frustration, ready to burst out. "I don't normally drink. Much. But." He snatched up the glass, tilted it and swallowed shuddering the neat spirit. "Ugh. Well, as you say, it's medicine of a sort."

"More?"

"Go on, then."

"You say he's taken all three of them to this cottage of yours? Well, it's not as if he's got her on his own. Jane's well chaperoned, isn't she?"

"I suppose... Oh dear. Shouldn't drink any more of this," Peter remarked, drinking some more, "I suppose she is."

"Do you still love her?"

"Yes! No. I don't know..."

Ah, what does it mean to love? English is inadequate, suggested Peter, who had done enough Greek to know the difference between eros and agapë and was always glad of an opportunity to explain it to anyone prepared to listen, which Robert was not, really: being not only fully apprised through his wide reading of the difference already but beginning to realise also that Peter was a little too ready to deploy conversational smokescreens whenever they got close to what seemed to him to be the root of the problem facing him.

Agapëistic love, Peter was saying, the love of God with all our heart and with all our mind and with all our, our, the other thing, strength yes, thank you, and of our neighbour like ourself enjoined upon us by our Lord himself

Yes yes yes, agreed Robert agreeably, but we're talking about your love for Jane, and…

Erotic love, love as of a husband and wife, Peter would not be deflected here, is of course quite a different matter. And he went on to include in the scope of their discussion the love communicated by the little verb phileïn, is it, my Greek's a bit rusty, he admitted. Love as liking only, as in I like ice cream or I like playing chess or…

Well now Peter you obviously liked being with Jane in that sense, interrupted Robert with just a little asperity, we can admit you must have been a Jane-o-phile, he said laughing a little dryly at his not really very funny sorry Peter let me top you up attempt to lighten the tone and tried furthermore to assure Peter that from his description of college life it was clear too that he had loved Jane and everybody else in the place with an agapëistic fervour which he had to admit seemed to have been wholly admirable but that, *that*, he pressed on, waving Peter's attempted commentary aside, isn't really the point is it? Because, he urged, when I asked you just now if you still loved her I obviously meant in the sense of a man and wife- erotic love. Come on, Peter, this is the confessional: when did you last make love to her?

A silence began to lengthen. Peter, still silenced by this question, swallowed the rest of his scotch, stood up, put his hands in his pockets. He took a couple of unsteady paces towards the posters on the wall. The line of climbers still made their way across the snowy ridge, dwarfed by their surroundings. *It's not when you came last, it's whether you're ever going to again.*

"I can't remember exactly. Some time ago."

"A long time ago?"

"Quite a long time." The bronzed athletic youth on the rock face still clung onto his overhang by his fingertips and one toe, in brilliant sunshine, empty blue sky behind and below him as he clung on hard. Hard on. *If it's not going to be, just use it to pee.*

But suddenly Sara was in their midst with I'm so sorry Peter oh Robby I've just remembered I promised Emma I'd email and it's getting a bit late so I wondered if you'd mind if I just used the computer and Peter was saying oh no no not at all we were just finishing which he could see was expected of him they'd arranged this hadn't they if we're not out by half nine for God's sake come in and say you've got to send an e-mail or something or I'll be here all bloody night with the man.

So, said Robert as Sara cleared a scatter of papers from the keyboard and unhandily began the laboriously peering and prodding process of Logging On, it's been good talking to you, and Yes, it's good to talk, replied Peter automatically with a twinge of something like nostalgia for a lost world of ease and almost happiness. Here, have you got a good book to read, asks Robert, waving a hand at the shelves, did you see anything you'd like to borrow while you're with us? People don't read enough. Robbie, says Sara, I've just been reading a message here from someone who says that he can enlarge your penis for you. Do you think I ought to take him up on his offer? And they're both convulsed in laughter, this is obviously one of their couple things, how Peter envies them their ease, their simple sensuality oh Jane Jane Jane. What a mess. What am I going to do? He goes to the bookshelf, takes down *Abraham and his Seed*, and shoves it into his jacket pocket. Says thanks, Robert, night Sara, see you tomorrow: and he leaves them to it, what ever it is, goes outside. The night air hits him. Scented, heady. Walk for a bit.

5

So Peter found himself in the garden, walking- unsteadily - in the cool of the day. I walk in the cool of the day, hm. After briefly inspecting this thought for possible blasphemy, he blessed it on its way. No Eden this, though pleasant enough out here on the lawn with the darkling wood over there and the scented shrubs here and oh look out there the sea itself, silvered by an early moon. More like twilight, anyway- it is nearly dark. Must be what, half nine o'clock on a midsummer night. Like that play. Saw Alexasha in that. At her school. Queen of the fairies. No fairies here though. Wait. There's one.

Skipping across the lawn towards him. White shirt gleaming in the dusk. It's her.

"Hello. Peter, isn't it?"

"Yes. "

"It's a beautiful evening. I've been thanking Jesus for it."

"Right." Peter sat down suddenly, legs giving way. Ooh, that drink. His head sank onto his chest, was he was going to be sick? No. Well, that's something.

"Are you all right?"

"Yes, I'm fine. Sorry- bit under the weather."

"You've got a burden to bear, haven't you? It was obvious this morning. Do you want to share it? We could lay it before the Lord." She sat down on the grass by him, put an arm round his shoulders. He raised his head, found her face was very close to his, ducked down again. "Hey," she said, and he was appalled to find her fingers reaching under his beardy chin, raising his face to hers. She was very close, and he could feel the heat from her, smell her sweat, not unpleasant though, and not really surprising either after all that dancing around. But so close. Suddenly she wrinkled her nose. "Hey, you've been on the booze." She flicked her flaxen hair, whispered in his ear, "Come on, Pete, don't hide it from the Lord. He's here to help."

Helpless, he turned into her embrace, one hand on the grass to steady himself, the other somehow on her thigh. The sheer attraction of her. He saw her brilliant eyes, her small pretty nose, parted lips…

"Oh Jesus," he said.

"Oh that's so good, Pete," she gasped. "Oh Jesus, listen to Pete. Hear his prayer."

Her right arm was round his shoulders, holding his trembling body in a masterful embrace. She smelt of the coming night, of the gentle breeze starting to whisper among the pines, all the wild, hidden life of the hours of darkness. Slowly, gently, her left hand caressed his cheek, then slipped down across his raggedy beard all untrimmed as it was not like Robert's and slid under his jacket and then down over the smooth cotton of his shirt and finally cupped the opulent roundness of his tummy. Carried away on an irresistible wave of pleasure he felt his back beginning to arch, his head falling back, saw the first stars peeking out…

"Hey, Pete, don't go to sleep on me!"

"Sorry. I am, yes, rather tired, I must confess." Peter let himself down, lay all the way back, stretched out fully, his head falling back on the soft lawn, offering his naked neck to her loving kiss as she nuzzled up, her head on his chest so that her hair was in his nostrils ah so lovely and there was no doubt about it now he had an erection all right, oh yes, on no this wouldn't do at all. He'd resisted her temptation once today already. Becoming a habit. He got himself up awkwardly on one elbow, smiled down crookedly at her.

"I shore you on the saw, saw you on the, at the beach today," he said, nodding, he was yes, he had to admit it, fairly drunk. "Dancing in the waves."

She lay on her back, looking up into his face. "I was dancing for the Lord," she said, "hoping he would come for me. I'm so looking forward to his coming. Did you like watching me?"

"What do you mean?"

"Men do. Like that poor man who came down here with you, Alan. He has a terrible demon of lust in him. But I think I managed to help him deal with it."

"How?"

"I just prayed with him about his sexual preferences."

"Good God."

"Amen. But you still haven't shared your burden. Come unto me, all ye who are heavy laden, and I will give you rest."

"My wife doesn't understand me."

"That's what Alan said."

"It's getting cold."

"Yes. We could cuddle up a bit."

"All right then. How's that?"

"Mm. Better."

"She's lost her faith."

"Your wife has?"

"Myes. Mm. That's nice."

"You could tickle me just here if you like."

"Here?"

"Mm. Saint Paul says in one Corinthians seven that if any man has a wife who is not a believer he should not divorce her, for the unbelieving wife has been sanctified through her husband. Ouch. Just gently."

"Sorry."

"He also says that those who marry will have many troubles in this life."

"He does?"

"Verse twenty eight. And then he goes on to say verse twenty nine that those who have wives should live as if they had none, for the present world is passing away. Will you kiss me?"

"Fran…"

"I'm sorry, Peter, I shouldn't have. Asked that. It's just that it gets a bit lonely sometimes, you know? Waiting."

"Waiting for what?"

"Waiting for Jesus to come and take us away to be with him in heaven. St Paul says verse twenty nine the time is short, but…"

"But it's been two thousand years and there's no sign of him yet? Sorry, that was…"

"Pete… do you think I did the right thing?"

For a little while they lie huddled together under the sky, silent, waiting.

"Was that a spot of rain?"

"Yes." She sits up, looking at the sky which is now quite overcast. It's almost completely dark now. "It's been lovely talking to you, Pete. And thanks for the cuddle."

She stands, holding a hand out to Peter. He takes it, and she heaves him groaning to his feet. The rain is suddenly upon them.

"God bless," he says. "Sleep well."

She replies surprisingly with a snatch of song.

"…*es kommt an zu regen. Ade, ich gehe nach Haus.*"

"What's that?"

"It just came to me. From my life before. I used to love Schubert. Among other things." Her voice seems to crack somehow. Her face is wet. The rain- or is she… *crying*? "Good night," she says quickly, and sprints away from him across the lawn to the house, leaving Peter alone to trudge through the cold rain after her towards the distant light over the front door.

6

Back in his rooms, Peter steps dripping out of a cold shower, goes towelling himself back into something like sobriety, back into the little bedroom. Why did he marry Jane? Stupid question. He found himself quite resenting Robert and his let's be honest stupid questions. Because he loved her, of course. Of course he loved her. It was because he loved her that he had to marry her. Because it was better to marry than to burn. And he did burn. But it was better to stay unmarried, as St Paul was. Better. Says so in Holy Writ. Perfectly clear.

Naked, Peter sits on the edge of the bed. There's *Abraham and his.* Abraham. Something to wear and something to eat. Ha ha. *And his Seed.* And here's his watch: nearly midnight, late. Must get some sleep. And a bible. Look it up. One Corinthians seven. She knew it well, Fran did, he thought, as he read it through. All those verses. Better to marry than. Better to stay unmarried, though. Here it is. Do not deprive one another, except by mutual consent and for a time, that you may devote yourselves to prayer. Then come together again, so that Satan will not tempt you through your lack of self control. Listen. Quite silent. Wonder where she sleeps. If she's asleep now. Wonder how old she is. Not much older than Sasha. And I could have. She wanted me to. And me so old for her, well. Such a slender little thing. So fragile she felt in my arms. But God her body, what would it have been like to. My seed. Into her. Well I didn't. Satan will not tempt me through my lack of. He put the bible back, wrapped himself in his bathrobe, got into bed, switched off the light.

Lack of self control.

He had not lacked self control.

While their secular friends at college slept around and got into all kinds of trouble, making their lives miserable and neglecting their work with late nights, furious whisperings in corners, angry recriminations, shamefaced visits to the doctor, he and Jane had been such a happy couple simply because they had had no sex at all. He remembered that time at the Christian Union when they'd been discussing extra-marital sex and someone asked Jane giggling how it felt being in love with a great Christian boy like Peter and not having being able to have sex with him until they were married and he'd been so proud of her when she said I don't mind at all not having sex with him (glancing at Peter and blushing just a little) until we are married because if we keep ourselves pure Jesus will reward us in heaven and it will just be so worth it.

And then they'd got married in the college chapel of course and after the reception off they went in his old banger of a car to the little honeymoon hotel in the Cotswolds and when they checked in as the Reverend and Mrs it all seemed suddenly real no going back now and scary too and she cried a bit when they got upstairs, he remembered her sitting on the bed weeping while he got the cases unpacked, but she soon cheered up after he had asked Jesus to look on them and bless their marriage now they were married, yes, that was the thing. They were married. Therefore…

Downstairs they had lingered in the dining room over coffee and, expensively indulgent but, hey, you only get married once, liqueurs. But it was getting late. They were the only ones left in there. They couldn't put it off any longer.

In the bedroom.

In the bedroom she'd shyly taken herself off into the en suite with her nightie and he'd tried to pray his usual before sleeping prayers but the only before sleeping thing he could think of was what was going to happen when she came out and then it was too late because there she was getting into bed and smiling at him with her crinkly eyed smile that he'd seen so often but now it was all so different and he had a moment of panic

He had a moment of panic, sat up in bed, switched on the light. Had he really snarled at her with something like contempt, aren't you going to say your prayers? Had he really left her open mouthed, rushed into the en suite, stripped and stood quivering under a cold shower? Had he really gone back into the bedroom naked, his erection standing up like a weapon? Had he… the shame. He fell back onto his pillow, twisted his face into it, sobbing, tried to hide from the memory of it.

She had gasped when she saw him like that, said, Well, my prayers have been answered! But he saw nothing funny in any of this, pulled off the covers and straddled her, saying God, God, I burn, forgive me! And he ripped her nightie off her, tearing it, so that she squealed at him something like Hey, steady on, take your time, but he was all God, God, God, forgive me and he clamped his hands on her breasts kneading them like dough forgive me God I burn and poked with his big cock all over her thighs her belly anywhere but the right place and then he suddenly roared, shuddering, seed squirting on her face, in her hair, and he collapsed onto her knocking all the air out of her rolled onto his back and lay panting, groaning, God, God, forgive me, lay not this sin to her charge it is the way of women thou knowest Lord, Lord how they tempt us with their bodies oh forgive her, God forgive me for I did burn.

At last Peter could bear his memories no longer, and casting off the coverlet went barefoot to the window, pulling his towelling nightgown tightly round his body against the chill midnight air. His breath misted the cold glass, and he cleared it with a corner of his robe. The dark trees were swaying menacingly in the wind, clouds brightened and faded as they raced across the face of the full moon, which gleamed brightly now on the wet lawn where he had lain with her who had given up everything for the Lord, who was for ever dancing for the Lord, who looked eagerly for his coming, and hoped she hadn't made an awful mistake... And he thought Oh God, for how many years has Jane thought that she made... an awful mistake... And he remembered something she'd muttered one night long ago, as he lay gaspingly convalescent in the bed beside her, something he hadn't understood at the time, but it had stayed with him because it was so strange... only now did he realise what she'd meant and wept again. At least I'm not just a doormat, she had told the cracked ceiling: I suppose being a prayer mat is slightly better...

7

"I'm sorry I screamed, Mummy. I was frightened because it was like in my book."

"I know." Jane put her mug down deliberately on the table and managed to remain- she thought she could perhaps manage another two minutes- sitting calmly opposite pyjamad Alice, sweetly innocent of all this *shit* watching her shovelling down the cornflakes, apparently quite recovered. Resilience of children. See me bounce back from this one. Never. Or is it just the inauthenticity of their imaginative worlds. Inauthenticity. There's a word. How long does it take to get over being frightened by a stupid nonsense of a vampire story with its pathetic apology for characters who all run round spouting clichés and oh God but who was she to criticise after being frightened by a stupid nonsense of a, of a man like Peter and the spouting clichés of him and the, and the pathetic apology for a life she'd been led into with him? Make-believe. All of it? The children were real enough. Peter, though. And church. Spouting clichés. And *Jack*. Bloody *Jack*. What were they going to *do*? She pulled her dressing gown tighter around her nakedness. Chilly in here this morning. Have to get dressed in a minute. But don't want to go upstairs yet. Don't want to see him. Or Sasha... But oh God we're here for a week: what are we going to do? She dug her fingernails into the palm of one hand so that the pain brought her back to the present moment and said: "We're all a bit... you know, Alice. Not quite ourselves."

"It's confusing. Aren't you going to have any breakfast, Mummy?"

"I don't know." Jane decided to take a sip of coffee, and did so, putting the mug down afterwards without spilling a drop, indeed, without hurling it at the wall at all. Poor little Alice, what have I done to you? "Maybe in a little while I'll have some. What do you mean, Dear, what's confusing?"

"Why do you say the like, you know supernatural things like vampires and all that is not real, if Jack has Cards of Power?"

Jane glanced at the sideboard where she'd chucked the bloody things. "Look. They're not 'cards of power' Darling, they're just playing cards with silly pictures on them. For playing games. There's no such thing as magic. Jack just likes… playing games." With, for example, Sasha.

And after I finally…

The bastard.

…decided…

Bastard, bastard.

…that after all these years of frustration and self denial I would finally give myself…

"Uh, Morning. God, my head."

"Sasha," Alice points out, "was wearing those clothes yesterday. Why did you go to bed with your clothes on, Sasha?"

"Because I was too pissed to take them off, I guess. Is that coffee?"

…and all the time he was only interested in your tight curves, you… and here I sit all flabby and old…

"In the kitchen."

"Right. Bloody hell."

Alice watched Sasha stumbling away in search of coffee, whispered "Mummy, did Sasha get very drunk?"

"I think she must have done."

"Are you cross?"

Cross? *Cross*? Poor Alice. She wants me to draw a line for her, thought Jane, taking a deep breath, no, *really* deep, as if about to submerge herself but for how long? How much longer could she stand this? No, get real. Look at Alice's big innocent eyes. Have to help her, keep going for her. She wants to know if Sasha's behaviour is acceptable (no it fucking isn't what *did* they do to get to the point where he just assumed that it was her) but how will we ever know when our behaviour crosses from acceptable to unacceptable if there's no one to mark out the boundaries, to point out landmarks along the way (how about being eased away from your lover by your own daughter, pretty damn unmistakeable landmark that) as we journey from

"Mummy?"

childhood to adult life? Oh for God's sake. Here it comes again, the waterworks, but no not yet not yet. How will we know, for that matter, even when we've *got* boundaries: especially if they've been marked out by a first century paranoid obsessive who's convinced himself that the world's going to end within his own lifetime and that his own peculiar little personality is going to persist beyond the death of his lustful but strenuously celibate body? Bloody Peter and his bloody Paul.

"Mummy?"

"What?"

"Aren't you?"

"What?"

"Cross?"

"No."

"I'd be."

"A little girl once had a teddy bear," said Jane, her voice cracking alarmingly, "which suffered from being cross-eyed. So she called it Gladly." Alice just stared at her. "Gladly my cross I'd bear."

"I don't get it."

"No, neither do I any more." Jane smacked her hand down hard on the table so that all the breakfast things jumped. So did Alice.

"Mummy..!

Sasha came back from the kitchen slurping frowningly at a mug of coffee. "Where's our Jack, then? Still in bed?"

"How should *I* know?" snapped Jane.

One of those awkward pauses, Alice recognised, Sasha frozen in mid-slurp, Jane glaring at the table, so she contributed helpfully, "Sasha, I was frightened when I saw Jack's cards on the table."

"Yeah. So was I," said Sasha with the ghost of a smile, but caught Jane's eye, read in it with a sobering shock suspicion, then furious accusation, then an awful despair, and added, "Or was that just a dream." Oh. Digging myself a hole here, she thought, said quickly, "Going out for a fag," and was gone.

Outside, Sasha found herself swaying on her feet in the fresh air, almost deafened by birdsong. It had rained in the night, she saw, picking her way across the sunlit gravel to the wall. And it always smells so good after rain. Seems I'm still a bit pissed. Becoming the default position, have to watch this. Whatever had she drunk? A lot. Brandy, reading Beckett very late, keeping going on going on. Ought to get more sleep. No signal still. Oh, Jess. And then whisky too, and yes what *had* all that funny stuff been about with Jack? She stopped dead. His cock out. That actually happened. One frame at a time, last night replayed itself to her now, image after image. Jesus. Had she really said..? And seen..? And..? She balanced the mug on the wall, climbed up, her slept-in clothes rasping on her skin. Another slurp of this coffee. Must've just gone up and collapsed on the bed. After… Ugh. Feel all dirty. Mouth like the bottom of a parrot's cage, ha ha. Have to have a bath in a minute. She put the mug on a stone, took out her fags. Packet a bit crushed, only three left as well, fuck. And lit up, thought about Jack. And his big. Bloody embarrassing. Having to face him. After that. Worse than embarrassing actually: and then the mug toppled off the wall and shattered with a bang and oh shit the booze cleared and the full enormity of what she'd done finally hit her. Mum! God, when she looked up and glared at me like that *does she know*? Sasha felt her stomach heave, and not just with the booze, no, this was … And it's not just if she knows it's *what it means…* She must know. She was a little girl again, being told off very *very* severely for being so *so* wicked, but this was much more serious, Jesus this was fucking awful, worse than anything she'd ever done before when she'd had to sit crying on the naughty step. Sitting on the wall, staring into the empty yard, she felt flushed, her heart beating, very close to tears, he must've *told* her, they must both be absolutely fucking *furious* with her…

The empty yard? Sasha slipped off the wall, looked round the side of the cottage, down the lane. Where's his bloody car, then? She stood wretchedly in the dry patch on the gravel where it had been, sucked hard on the cigarette stub, chucked it away, folded her arms tight under her breasts and bit her lip. Don't want to go in. Can't face Mum. Oh fuck, he's even taken the bloody silly wreath off the door what if he's just fucked off and left us here what if Mum really loved him and now he's gone and she'll never see him again and it's *all my fault*!

She went in anyway. Better face it. Couldn't stand outside all bloody day. Alice was still at the table, busy with toast and marmalade.

"Where's Mum?"

"Gone up to get dressed."

Sasha got herself some more coffee, sat in an armchair by the fireplace. Better face the music, she thought. Feel so grotty. Oh God, here she comes. This is it.

But Jane said nothing. Sat herself at the table, staring at her empty plate. Sasha watched her mother with some fear. It was obvious she knew. How was she was going to deal with it? Pretend nothing had happened? No way. Or perhaps she really doesn't know, in which case why is she so bloody upset? O God let's get it over with.

"Where's Jack?"

Jane pursed her lips, moved a knife a couple of millimetres. "You seem very interested in the whereabouts of Jack," she said, with a awful calm.

"I just wondered if you knew…"

"He'll be down soon, I'm sure." *Doesn't she know he's gone*? thought Sasha. Jane went on, her voice icy. "I seem to remember him saying that he liked to get his eight hours. By which time I will have… will have…" But she had, she found, forgotten what, if anything, she had been going to say. And it was getting harder not to sob. Alice, though, was being helpful again.

"By which time you will have made us all a lovely picnic and then Jack will take us off for some Vigorous Exercise in the Hills. That's what you said yesterday, isn't it Mummy?"

"Yes, Alice," said Jane, "That's what I said yesterday. Now go upstairs and get dressed. Please."

Something in Jane's tone surprised and hurt Alice a little bit. Crestfallen, she got down from the table, went towards the stairs. "OK, Mummy."

Sasha waited until she'd gone and then said, "So…"

"Yes, Alexandra?"

Sasha felt utterly crushed.

"You want Jack, do you, Alexandra? Why don't you go and wake him up? Take him a cup of tea in bed! I expect he'd like that!"

Sasha didn't know what to make of this.

"What did he tell you, Mum?"

"He didn't *tell* me anything. He didn't *need* to!"

Or this. He didn't need to tell her anything- she's obviously furious with her- no, don't get it. Careful. Tread carefully.

"I was just so upset, Mum," Sasha began cautiously, leaning forward elbows on knees, hands fisted on her cheeks, staring into the cold grate. "I had a real go at him, I'm afraid." No reaction. Try some more. "You see I just hated the way he seemed to be forcing you into a relationship far too quickly. You didn't seem *ready* for it." Glance at her: she hasn't moved. "Oh God that sounds terrible, patronising, it's nothing to do with me is it but it's just because I love you so and and let's be honest Mum *I* wasn't ready for it either. God, that sounds so selfish. But I was frightened for Dad too. He doesn't have a clue how much you love Jack, has he? Look I know you *do* love Jack and I'm so glad for you but what *about* Dad? And Alice. She's so confused. She couldn't understand why Dad wasn't coming till the end of the week. Just didn't see where Jack fitted in. As it were." Bugger. No time for jokes. "Gosh, sorry, look I'm *trying* to be serious. I *know* you're in love with him, and like I say I'm *so* happy for you. I know things have been bad with you and Dad, and Jack did look like a chance for you to be really happy, like Jess and me. But… I was so stupid last night. Oh, I just lost my temper, and I was drunk, I suppose. I was so angry with him. I'm ever so ever so sorry. But it's too late now. I'm afraid I might have ruined everything for you. I just wanted you to be happy. You have to believe that."

A long silence developed into a very long silence. Sasha massaged her brow, closed her eyes. Oh, she'd thought she was so bloody smart and grown up: but she should never have interfered. Selfish, stupid. Too drunk, too stupid.

"Like Jess and you?"

Sasha opened her eyes. She hadn't realised that Jane had come to sit in the chair opposite her. She was leaning forward, her head tilted quizzically, her expression not unkind.

"Oh. Yes. Jess and I have been lovers for about a year, now." Putting it into words made it a reality in a way Sasha had not experienced before. Strange.

Jane almost smiled, said, "Well. I… I did wonder why an attractive girl like you… I mean why you and Neil, for example, never… And all that stuff about Welsh boys last night. Oh, Sasha, you are funny. I suppose this is what they mean when they talk about 'coming out,' is it?"

Sasha smiled at her crookedly.

"I guess."

This was big. Jane wanted to say so much, feel so much, but her own misery kept getting in the way.

"Then… what *is* this with you and Jack? She *had* to ask.

So she doesn't know! And he's gone. But she doesn't seem to know he's gone.

"He really said nothing about me last night?"

"No, I haven't spoken to him... not actually spoken to him, since I went up to bed. Leaving him down here. With you."

"So you thought that Jack and I... no way! Oh, Mum, how *could* you?"

"Because..."

"Because what?"

What can I say, Jane thought. I can't tell her... she couldn't meet Sasha's eye. Looking away, she said, "I went to his room. Very late."

"But you said you didn't speak to him."

"I didn't."

"Oh." Sasha felt she was getting well out of her depth here. She really didn't want to think of her mother mutely shagging this man...

"He thought I was you."

"*Mum*!"

"Why would he think that, Sasha?"

Because I'd made a grab for his cock, because I'd seen his bloody great cards on the table. Because he must've thought I was hot for him. Bloody hell. But since he's not here any more, there's a way out.

Sasha looked her mother in the eye, said: "I don't know."

Jane stared back. "You said you had a go at him. You mean you argued with him, yes?"

"I was really pissed and stupid, but, basically, yes. I did."

"You didn't give him any reason... to think... to explain why he would have thought..."

"*No*." That was true enough; true enough for Sasha to keep up the eye contact anyway, thought it was becoming painful by now. Jane finally looked away. Sasha's signal to move. She flew at her mother and flung her arms around her, got in close, under her guard, trying for the refuge of intimacy. "I told you, Mummee, last night. I don't think he's quite *suitable*."

Jane let herself be held, hugged, comforted? Maybe. By this young, energetic person she had somehow brought about. How assured Sasha was in her body! (Jess, for heaven's sake...) How uneasy Jane felt by comparison, as if she wasn't at home in her body, as if her flesh was somehow alien, unclean... bloody Paul again. At last she roused herself, looked Sasha in the face, moved one wing of her glossy black hair back, kissed her cheek, smiled weakly.

"All right, Darling," she said, "That's it, then. I'm going up now to tell him it's over. He'll have to drive us home and then it can just be over. A mistake."

"Mummee, I don't think you can."

"What?"

"Tell him."

"Why not?"

"Why do you think I kept trying to ask you if you knew where he was? I mean, if Jack's in bed getting his eight hours, why's his car gone?"

Derryn closed the ancient wooden door quietly, and smudged out with his leathern riding glove the mystical pentacle chalked on its rough planking. Its protection was not needed now. His handsome brow furrowed, he turned away from that fateful house and faced the dark night. Over the swaying pines, storm wracked clouds brightened and faded as they raced across the face of the full moon. Somewhere an owl hooted its strange unearthly call. Although his mind was a turmoil of conflicting emotions, he took care to tread softly, for he did not want to wake Elise or the old woman: he made his way across the mysteriously shadowed garden to where his mare stood patiently waiting. He stroked her strongly arched neck, grateful for her strength and loyalty, before unhitching her reins from the fence. Head bowed, he led her a long way along the rough track before mounting, and even then walked her until they were a good mile from the house. Then at last the rage burst in him, and with a cry of mixed fury and anguish he urged her into a gallop, faster and faster, away into the night

Someone came up the stairs at a run, pounded along the passage. A door rattled, and then Alice heard her mother's voice: a cry of mixed fury and anguish, thought Alice, yes. Just like in my book. And then, oh dear, what's gone wrong now? Grown ups' stuff, she thought, and helping herself to another dark chocolate digestive from the packet she'd liberated from the kitchen, read on.

fast and faster, away into the night he rode: his tireless mare's iron-shod hooves drumming past forest and moorland, splashing through fords, clattering through sleeping hamlets, on and on, ever further away from that house of horror. And always as he rode he thought of Elise, of her beauty and vulnerability: but mostly he went over and over in his mind the terrible revelation of the cards, that awful secret, and the terrible fate which he had so narrowly escaped.

So it was that as the first faint glimmers of the coming dawn began to lighten the leaden sky in the west, he finally came to the overgrown track which he knew led down into the hidden valley where dwelt Eldan his master; he who had shown him The Way, an age ago it seemed: and now it was his only refuge.

Down that steep and stony track he turned his mare, walking her now, for in that early hour it was still gloomy down there where the rough stony track wound under the trees, and ever and again he had to duck his head under the overhanging branches and he feared also lest she should stumble. But at last he reached the valley floor, and, hearing the endless trickling of the stream like an old friend's welcome, would have felt some ease in his heart, for he knew he would be safe here, at least for a while: but he was denied that comfort, for like a dull pain there came back to him the promise he had so reluctantly made, and which he now knew would have to be broken.

Another twist in the track took him clear of the trees, and at last he could see his master's humble dwelling. He dismounted, and led his exhausted mare through the first flutings of the dawn chorus up to the tree by the barn. He tethered her, and approached the cottage. All was shut up, wrapped in early morning stillness: doubtless Eldan was still asleep. Loath to wake him, Derryn wrapped his riding cloak about his tired limbs, and settled down to wait with his back against one of the great trees which sheltered the little house.

Derryn would fain have watched, that he might go to his master as soon as there was any sign of movement within: but the great exertions of the past night weighed heavy upon him. After only a few moments his chin sank onto his chest, his eyes closed, and he slept.

III

1

Bryn Bryn Bryn!
Who's a lucky boy, then?
Bright early morning summer sunshine on gentle green slopes, sheep-flecked, rising and falling like waves of deep emerald, sloping down to the water where music passes by him so softly as he sits fishing, rod in hand, so clarinet cool it is in the lakeside's Sabbath rest, with softest shuffle of brush on snaredrum, gentlest adagio beat of bass where bobbing in lapping sparkling water his float nods to him at the end of his line: *Good morning, Bryn, you Fisher King! What are you after now?*

Bryn became aware of himself wondering what he was after now, knew he was only just awake: he eased himself back into the dream before it faded and... and....

And a kite soared high
In the azure sky
And a jewelled dragonfly
Fluttered bright in sunlight and perched glinting on the end of the pliant rod he held in his hands and spake unto him, saying:
Bryn Bryn Bryn!
Catch it catch it catch it catch
Catch that salmon! Rod, his own rod in his own hand. Salmon of wisdom. Mair, sez a sheep close by, oh, that's magnificent, keep going, *Magnificat* and see with what big letters I am writing to you in my own

hand and and and his seed for ever see- see it all now as we set out upon the Medinarrational Sea once more, *Sŵn y Môr* stormy though, Malta tempestuoso- Luke hear and see the bright float's sudden plunge under the shining surface: Ah, strike! line tightens on the throbbing rod and Oh! the joy of it! wind him in, wind him wind, wind, oh so stiff to turn appaullingly stiff and hard the apostold it differently
Can't... can't...
Unlucky boy, Bryn! Unlucky...
Dream on! Stay with it!
Catch it! Can't!
You Fisher King, you fucking can...
Stay with it! Look, look into the deep dreamy water. There. You never know what's coming. Who's coming? Paul. Paul? He strained his eyes wanting to see, see through the swirling water the shadowy form he's hooked, winding the stiff reel on the throbbing twitching rod, wind him in, here he comes the poor little preacher the salmon of wisdom's just under there see its shining silvery length just under the surface- there! There!
Bryn Bryn wind him in
Can't stop for you, can't stop for you
He can't stop turning the reel, can't quite see, wakes up in bed
Cock-a, cock-a, 'course he can
Bryn Bryn
Paul!
Bryn finally woke to birdsong and fine bright sunshine piercing the flimsy curtain: a fine day after all this rain! Ah! He stretched himself out in the bed, warm, content, found he'd got a hardon, took the thick throbbing rod in his hands. Pretty good at his age! He turned his old grey head on the pillow, saw with delight the thick mane of blonde hair next to him, gloriously backlit gold by the piercing sensuous sunbeams.
Bryn Bryn Bryn!
Who's a lucky boy, then?
Who's a cock-a doodle?
Dwy, dwy, do!
Lifting the cover off her, he marvelled as he always did at the sumptuous contours of her naked back, her slim waist, the opulent swell of her
Swell, swell,
'Course she is, 'course she is

swell of her buttocks. He turned into her, easing the twitching rod between her thighs, his mouth on her neck: her smell swamped him; his senses swam in the warm lake of her sleepy acceptance of him as she went over yawningly sighing onto her tummy, opening her legs and lifting her hips so that he could enter her from behind. Ah! Strike! He was in, and Oh! the joy of it! Throbbing rod, he thought, and ah! Again and again he thrust into her winding her in, round and round windingly until she twisted around on him and *Aroswch*, she breathed, still half asleep, *Aroswch: 'Dwy* ...He knew what she wanted, pulled out of her, rolled onto his back so she could mount him, and she straddled him and

Yes lucky Yes lucky

Cock-a doodle doo

she took his cock-a doodle doo *Dwy*... in her hand and put it into herself, and rode him, dreamily rode him faster and faster as she came closer and closer and closer and then she was there and so was he and the world was drifting into a dreamy bliss beyond words beyond being...

Where is the salmon of wisdom, Bryn?

Still in the lake boy. Wind him in! In! Inspiration... wind blows where it listeth...

Can't can't cant

Can Bryn, can Bryn

And *Mair*, sez a sheep, *Mair,* by Saint *Mary, Mair*...

Gabriel to Mary came and entered in her

Where is the salmon of Solomon's wisdom? Entered in her, eh? Bra. Ham. Seed for ever, 's all over now, Saul of er Tarsus least of the apostolic suck session goes on going on. No, he can stop whenever he wants to it's all one, man and wife is one flesh fresh salmon caught out there with his rod in his hand who is it who is it

Wind him in, Bryn,

Wind him in, Bryn

Bright summer sunshine on gentle green slopes, sheep-flecked, sloping down to the water, loud with birdsong, calm of hills above where wind blows where it listeth clarinet cool

Bryn Bryn Bryn!

Who's a lucky boy, then?

Bryn reawoke to brighter sunshine piercing the flimsy curtain: a fine day after all this rain! Ah! He stretched himself out under her sleepy weight, warm, content, flaccid, flowing on drifting downstream through gentle meads in pastures green she leadeth me the quiet waters, quietly gently

Pretty good at your age!
Pretty good at your age!

gently easing the sumptuous nakedness of her off him, he got up on one elbow and contemplated with delight as she settled again the thick mane of blonde hair spread about her lovely face with its finely shaped jaw, the full lips parted slightly, the flared nostrils, the almond eyes now lidded, serene in after orgasm languor; the delicate but strong tendons of the neck, the graceful lines of the collarbones, the lovely parting of the breasts on either side of the sternum. Very gently he gathered the luscious flesh of her right breast till he cupped it and put his lips to the nipple: it was firm but yielding as he ran the tip of his tongue around its aureole so that she shuddered deliciously, muttering *Paidwch, Bryn, paid...* He kissed her brow, murmured *Ah, Cariad... Diolch, Cariad...* rolled away across the bed and landed his feet on the floor. A fine day! He put his hands on his knees and levered himself up. Pretty good at his age! Fishing. A good day for fishing... Why fishing? Why not? He dragged his old ragged trousers on, armed himself into a tattered jumper, worked his toes into his flipflops and staggered happily off into another new day. Life was good!

Having pissed and crapped, showered and shaved, cheerful Bryn flung open the front door and advanced grinning into the sunny garden, loud with birdsong. And saw the car...

He saw the car, crouched like an ugly metal beast in the yard by the workshop. Someone in it. Who? Stride up to it. Asleep? Rap smartly on window. Stirrings. Creakily groaningly down comes the glass. Oh for God's sake.

"Hello, Bryn."
"What the fuck are you doing here?"
"Ran away again. Sorry."
"Pooh! You stink of booze! Are you pissed?"
"Oh, er... well."
"At this time of day?"
"What time is it?"
"I don't know! Early!"
"I ran away."
"So you say! Who have you run away from this time?"
"A woman."

"A woman! Oh, fucking great. No bloody change there then. Oh fuck."

Bryn flaps his arms, frustrated, walks briskly, agitated, from the car to the wall which he makes to punch but thinks better of it, he's not worth grazed knuckles, is he, and back he goes again flapping frustrated frigging fuck, he says, "Well damn it all," he says. "This is…"

"What's the matter?"

"Awkward."

"God, Bryn. I couldn't think what to do. I'm so tired. Wait till I tell you. I just came here because…"

"Because it's what you always do when you've made things too hot for yourself somewhere. When are you going to grow up. Ach! Bloody hell."

A silence. Jack reaches for the ignition key.

"Sorry, I'll go."

"No you bloody won't. Not in the state you're in. You'll bloody kill yourself or some other poor bastard. You'd better come in. But it's awkward, see? Awkward. Well, never mind, we'll just have to deal with it. And I thought it was going to be such a fine day. Come on."

So Jack follows Bryn into the old familiar kitchen, and it feels like coming home. Nothing much has changed. Bryn throws himself into the old armchair by the range, takes his smoking kit from the little niche in the wall, and stuffs his pipe, critically considering Jack as he stands there for a moment dithering in his half drunk state, but perhaps showing a little sympathy too? Bryn may curse a lot, but he's got a heart of gold. Hasn't he. And a soft spot for our Jack. Jack the lad, eh? For fuck's sake.

"For fuck's sake don't just stand there dithering. You know where the kettle is. Make yourself useful at least. We'll have a brew."

"So what's the problem?" asks Jack, frowningly filling the kettle. "Why is it so awkward all of a sudden?"

"You'll see soon enough," says Bryn, through a cloud of smoke. He shakes the match out, chucks it in the grate. "And I really thought it was going to be such a fine day. Ah well. Like I said. We'll just have to deal with it."

Jack found a couple of mugs, tea.

"So how's business? Making much?"

"Enough. You'd be amazed how much demand there is. People appreciate fine craftsmanship. And I've been writing more. Quite a lot in fact. Had another one published since you were here last. Hasn't exactly flown from the shelves, but... Anyway, I'm not too badly off. How about you?"

"I get along."

"Hm. So what have you been up to, then, you randy bastard, that you have to come flying back to old Bryn in the middle of the night, with your tail between your legs, half pissed and useless as ever?"

Jack makes the tea, hands him a mug, takes his own to the other chair. There's a pair of very skimpy panties on it. He holds them up between finger and thumb.

"Are these part of the problem?"

"Never you mind them, boyo."

Jack drops them on the rug, sits down.

"I got involved with the wife of a customer. Thought I was in love."

"For fuck's sake."

"She was lovely, Bryn. Give me a break."

"So what went wrong?"

"It's a long story."

"We've got all day, apparently."

"There was a misunderstanding."

"Ah."

They both sipped their tea. Misunderstandings were well understood by both of them.

"What kind of misunderstanding was it this time?"

"I thought she was her daughter."

"Explain."

"It was dark. I was being wanked off. I thought it was the daughter doing it. It wasn't."

"That is some misunderstanding."

They sipped their tea again. Misunderstandings like that were remarkable even by their standards. Then Jack realised they were not alone. On a pair of long, naked, *sexy* legs, wearing nothing but one of Bryn's old shirts that left her decent by an inch, towelling her hair, she came in. And stopped, dropped the towel, her mouth open in disbelief.

"Jack?"

"So, Bryn. I see what you mean by awkward." He leant down, picked up the panties. "looking for these, Cathy?"

2

"I did not think I should ever see you again," she gasped. "Oh Derryn, hold me, hold me tight. I have been so frightened. Why…?" Amanda clung to him desperately, rejoicing in the hard feel of him, his familiar manly smell. "Why have you come back, Derryn?"

Alice reached for the dark chocolate digestives. Only two left. Save them for bedtime.

"Amanda, my love, I must speak with Eldan. Is he within?"
"He is still asleep. But he will be so angry with you. When you left…"
"I know. I know you are his now. And I did make a promise to him. But alas, I must break that promise now. I must see him. Only he can help."
"Derryn!" She broke away, leaned on the tree with one one hand, digging her fingernails into its rough bark, while with the other she covered her face, and he saw her shoulders heaving with silent sobs.
He looked towards the little cottage, started to move, but suddenly she was in front of him again, her upturned face a tragic mask.
"Please, Derryn…"
"I have to face him. I need his help."
"Take me away with you."
"What? Impossible. All that was between us is over. It could not be."
"You don't know what it's like… with him." Her voice was a mere whisper. Her eyes searched his face, and he saw something in them he recognised, something more than fear… something he had seen in Elise: a deep dread, a horror.
"Amanda, what are you saying? What has been going on here?"
"He does things. At night. Terrible, terrible things. He makes me…"
"What?"
She swallowed hard, her face crumpled, an she looked away.
"He makes me do things with him…"
"He makes you…? What things? Amanda!" He took her by the shoulders, almost shook her. "Tell me!"
But she was silent, listening, it seemed. Then she caught her breath, and her eyes found his again: they were wide with fear.
"He is awake! He knows you are here!"

"How can you tell?"

"Can't you *feel* it?"

And indeed Derryn could feel something strange: the early morning sunlight in the garden had altered somehow; a tension was in the air, and no birds sang. For a moment all was still; an unearthly stillness, as if the world held its breath. Then Derryn saw the cottage door opening, and Eldan's tall figure appeared on the threshold, his long white hair and beard strikingly bright in the strange distorted sunlight.

"So. Derryn," he called, his voice harsh and grating. "You have returned after all. Amanda, won't you bring our guest inside?"

"Alice! Are you up there?"

"I'm in my room, Mummy."

"Sasha and I are going to walk to the village. Do you want to come too?"

"I thought we were going for some Vigorous Exercise in the Hills."

"Jack's had to go away, unexpectedly. Do you want to come to the village?"

"Can I stay in and read my book?"

"If you like. Are you sure you'll be OK?"

"Yes Mummy."

"We won't be long. Back in time for lunch, anyway."

"OK Mummy."

"Mind the vampires don't get you, little Sis."

Sticking your tongue out isn't a very effective rebuke when you're in your bedroom and your big sister is downstairs, but it satisfied Alice; and there's No Returns either. She snuggled down again, and turned over the page.

"So what are you going to *do*, Mummee?" Sasha tucked her arm into Jane's and skipped into step with her.

"I'm going to *think*."

"About Jack?"

"Jack was a *mistake*."

"What if he comes back?"

"He can go away again."

"Oh, Mummee." Sasha hugged her mother's arm tight, said, "So here we are stuck in a cottage in darkest Wales with no car and nothing to do but introspect. We'll go mad, mad, mad."

"We can play Scrabble."

"That would help us go mad more quickly, yes."
"We can walk up on the hill."
"Did that yesterday. Boring."
"We can walk into the village."
"Good idea. Oh, wait- we *are* walking into the village. Boring."
"You can tell me about Jess."
"Not boring. But mm. Well, bit *personal*. Let's talk about you and Dad."
"That's personal too."
"Yes, but he's my Dad as well as your... Is it too soon to call him your ex?"
"Oh Sasha! That's a terrible thought."
"But one that needs thinking, right?"
"I suppose."

They reached the end of the shady lane and turned onto the open road which led to the village. Here the sun was hot; and they walked on without speaking for a while, letting themselves listen to what their minds came up with. I *told* him, told him *very* clearly, Jane heard the familiar phrases reeled out again- how many times she'd gone over those hopeless arguments, she was sure he never really understood- that I felt I was *living* a *lie.* I don't see things the way I used to. When did I finally realise? Years ago, really. But now, something's matured in me or developed or... I had to tell him that in all honesty I couldn't support him any longer as a priest. I can't live with him either. When did it become obvious to me that the church is all ballocks? Ballocks or bollocks, it was all the same to her. How funny up on the hill laughing with Sasha. When did it become obvious... It was years ago. How many? Before Sasha was born? Yes It was over between us almost as soon as it started. If I'm honest. Was there *ever* anything there? I'm getting mixed up. Which way round was it? Did his behaviour in bed- justified to him by churchy friends as being Christian purity- put me off the church, or did the church's demands for Christian purity- communicated to me by preachy him- put me off him? Or is that just two ways of saying the same thing? Or am I going mad already?

It came to Sasha to wonder what must it be like to feel your relationship is at an end after so many years, for Mum, for Dad? In Sasha's world of schoolgirl gossip, relationships had come and gone, changing like the weather, it seemed: it hadn't been unusual to hear girls at school talk of mums and dads breaking up, of step dads, of mum's boy friends, of dad's new woman. And of course some of the girls changed boy friends every weekend, it seemed. She thought of Jess with a warm glow and a little tingle of excitement: they'd been steady for nearly a year. But she found herself wondering what it would be like if she and Jess split up- unimaginable, but these things happened. She felt an awful emptiness inside, she missed her so much already after only a couple of days- was that a foretaste of what it would be like? A horrible empty aching void? Being all alone in the world with no one to turn to and say, hey- look at this, did you hear about that? But Jess wasn't just someone, she was herself, her special self, her lovely lovely irreplaceable self. Sasha clung tighter to her Mum, so that Jane smiled at her wryly and said, you OK? Sasha nodded smiling back tight lipped and began to wonder if she'd be able to steer her into the pub after they'd done their shopping. And whether she'd be able to get a signal in the village. Ring Jess. Yes. Then they came to the little non-conformist chapel standing back from the road just outside the village.

"Bethel."

"What's that, Dear?"

"Up there over the door. Beth-El. House of God."

They stopped to look. Gabled, end-on to the road, the slate roofed house of God was a trim rectangular building, painted white, with a short flight of worn steps up to the arched doorway. Plain glass windows, also arched, on either side of the door, gave the façade the appearance of a faintly surprised or possibly slightly snooty face.

"Want to see if he's in?"

"Sasha, really."

"We could leave a card to say we called and how sorry we were that he was out."

They were grinning at this when the door opened and a very old bespectacled gentleman with long white hair and beard emerged, saw them smiling up at him, and waved.

"Mum, it's him!" hissed Sasha to giggling Jane, and waved back, yelling, *"Bore da, Arglwydd: shw mae?"*

"Hello! Sorry, I'm from Wolverhampton myself. Lovely day."

3

Let us get up early to the vineyards, let us see if the vines flourish. If the flowers be ready to bring forth fruits, if the pomegranates flourish, there will I give thee my breasts.
(The Song of Songs Chapter 7, verse 12)

"I want him dead. I want him dead!"

"Don't cry, Mother. It upsets me to see you unhappy."

"How can I be happy while crowds gather outside the palace every day to hear him howling in his prison…"

"They can't hear him in the street, Mother."

"Howling that my marriage is a sin…"

"It *is* a sin, Mother."

"Howling, howling…"

"Have some more wine, Mother."

Herodias grudgingly took the golden goblet, gulped. Wine was her only comfort now that her husband seemed to have lost interest in her. When did they last have sex?

I am sorry, that must seem shocking: but I am trying to portray the thoughts of a wicked and sensual woman here. You, gentle reader, do not have such thoughts, and neither do I; or at least, God help me, not very often. It is terrible, sometimes, what one has to imagine in order to justify the ways of God to the seed of Abraham.

Let us picture then, for alas we must, this rapidly ageing but still very attractive, alluringly clad woman. Herodias is the wife- queen indeed- of King Herod, called the Great, but great in fact only in the magnitude of his insecurity and the murderousness of his efforts to maintain himself in what power he has, though he has that only by courtesy of the hated Romans. Reluctantly, then, for I almost fear defilement as if touching pitch, I invite you to join me in imagining her swaying on her feet as she drains the dregs of the wine, wiping her wet lips: letting her perhaps unsteady gaze come to rest speculatively and not without envy upon the precociously developed young breasts and long lithe limbs of her reclining daughter, (I know, I know- courage!) who was now yawningly inspecting her long painted fingernails. Nubile, yes, ready for it was she, already? She'd started her periods: if they're old enough to bleed, they're old enough to butcher. Yes. Why not. Use her.

"It's your Father's birthday tomorrow, as you know…"

"My Father is dead."
"Oh Salome, please…"
"But since man and wife are one flesh…"
"Will you listen to me!"
"Two men and a wife in this case..."
"Salome!"
"That's an awful lot of flesh. Especially when you consider how fat- sorry, corpulent- my new uncle-father actually is…"
It was a resounding smack which echoed off the lasciviously frescoed walls. Immediately Herodias regretted it, not because she cared a damn for Salome: but the bruise might show tomorrow and…

"Hello, Peter. I wondered if I'd find you in here."
Oh *God*. Thought I'd be safe in here. Better put it down and be sociable.
"Robert. Hello there."
"*Abraham and his seed*, eh? Enjoying it?"
"Oh, well, I've just been dipping into it really…"
Robert snatched the paperback, flicked through the pages, sniffed, chucked it back at Peter, who caught it clumsily.
"Good, that's good. Staying in this afternoon?"
"Yes, I just fancied having a quiet read actually," mumbled Peter, miffed, trying to find his place again. He chucked it at me. Just *chucked* it…
"And what are the parishioners getting up to while you laze around in the library?"
While I? "Fran's teaching them some gospel songs." Laze indeed. "Alan was very keen."
"He does seem to have become very keen. On Fran."
"He won't get anywhere with her, though, will he? She's spoken for."
"I suppose in a sense she is. She loves the Lord in a very… real way." Robert picked up a copy of the *Church Times*, read the headline, tutted, chucked it down. "She tells me, by the way, that she had an interesting conversation with you."
"Really?"
"Late last night. After you left."
"Ah. Thank you for that, it was… helpful talking to you."
"She says her conversation with you was… helpful, also."
"Oh, good."

"Yes, it is good. Very good. Quite an evening, in fact, for helpful conversations."

"Apparently."

"She tells me that you were a sympathetic listener. That's good."

"I try to be."

"And that you talked about faith."

"Faith? I suppose we did a bit. I can't honestly remember much about it. Your scotch whisky, Robert- strong stuff."

"Strong stuff indeed. Your talk this morning showed signs of being rather less forcible... how shall I say, a little morning afterish?"

"I beg your pardon, Robert, I may have been feeling a little tired but I thought I managed to give a reasonable session..."

"I don't think any of them had actually read *Pilgrim's Progress*."

"So?"

"They found some of the references a little obscure. Didn't really see what you were getting at. And to be honest, neither did I. Your comments on Saint Paul... on faith... Peter, are you sure you're all right?"

"What do you mean?"

"I'm sorry, Peter. I don't want to be critical. But I do have a responsibility to the people who come here. And to the residents. I have a responsibility to Fran, for example."

"What are you trying to say?"

"Fran is on a very individual and highly personal journey. It would be a shame if she were deflected by any assault on her faith. At the moment it's all she's got. Don't prick her bubble, Peter. Don't knock away the only prop that's holding her up."

"As I remember it she voiced some doubt. But we all have doubts, don't we?"

"Do we?"

"Don't you?"

"Do try and get to dinner tonight, by the way, and have a chat to some of the parishioners: they're not seeing much of you, are they? And I get the feeling they're becoming a little confused."

"Robert..."

"I'll catch you later. Things to do. Good bye, Peter."

Peter's turn to wonder if Robert was a little too ready to deploy conversational smokescreens whenever they got close to what seemed to him to be the root of the problem facing them all. He sighed, and looked out of the window at the lovely gardens basking Edenic in the sun. For a moment it seemed such a perfect world. As it was in the beginning... Then he found himself wondering what Jane was doing. With Jack. He caught a vision of her, quirky, quizzical, *attractive*. He wanted to... hold her. And more. He saw her lying on her back, indecently naked, one arm across her eyes, ready for him to, to... or for Jack to... he thrust the thought away, get thee behind me, Satan. Indecent. What evils: sin, and, of course, its awful consequence, death.

...and she needed her to look her best.

"Listen, daughter. This is what you will do. No, shut up and listen or I'll hit you again." She gripped the furiously pouting little girl's trembling wrists, holding her close, and hissed into her ear. "Salome! Listen! So. This is what you will do- you will dance! Yes, dance! It is the King your Father's birthday feast tomorrow night. When he is drunk or should I say drunker than usual, and he is bored with the fire-eaters, the acrobats and the Egyptian magicians I will tell him that it is time for you to make your own special contribution to the festivities: that you will dance for him. It will be a... sensual dance, gradually revealing more and more of that young flesh which you and I both know he lusts after, the lecherous pig."

"No."

"I say yes."

"No. You pile one sin upon another. You add to incest the incitement to paedophilia."

"To what? What nonsense is this?"

"A Greek word meaning the illicit love of children. Markos told me."

"*Markos told me*." Herodias couldn't sneer the words enough. "And since when has the illicit love of children been part of your lessons with that old goat? I hope he didn't give you a practical demonstration."

"Mother!"

"He will have to go."

"His lessons are the only interesting part of my life."

"You are becoming too clever for your own good. Listen. You will dance, dance the Egyptian dance I taught you, veiled with seven veils. After each of the seven parts of the dance, you will shed one veil. It is your Father's custom to give a reward to entertainers who please him. If he asks you what you would like, come to me, and I will tell you what to ask for. If all goes well, I will reward you too. Handsomely. You will be glad you co-operated."

"What will I wear under the veils?"

"Daughter, please don't ask any more questions. Do it- do it for my sake."

For my sake. For God's sake. For the sake of our Lord Jesus Christ. Sake. Funny word, sake. Use it all the time, never really thought. Where's the…

sake[1] n. 1 (for the sake of something) for the purpose of or in the interest of blah blah. 2 (for the sake of someone) out of consideration for or in order to help someone 3 (for God's or goodness etc sake) expressing impatience, annoyance, urgency or desperation

Impatience… annoyance. Urgency. Desperation.

expressing impatience, annoyance, urgency or desperation fr OE sacu contention, crime sake[2] Japanese alcoholic saker large falcon saki tropical American monkey Sakti variant spelling of Shakti: hm?

Shakti (also Sakti) n. *Hinduism* the female principle of divine energy. fr Sanskrit śakti power, divine energy.

Female principle of divine energy...

Sakti, sal, North Indian tree *Shorea robusta* fr Hindi sāl, salaam, n. a gesture of greeting or respect in Arabic speaking and Moslem countries v. make a salaam fr Arabic (al-)salām ('alaikum) peace (be upon you)

Peace. My peace I give to you, not as the world giveth, give I unto you…

Peace…

Salable adj. variant spelling of saleable well who'd've thought it. Salacious.

Salacious adj. having or conveying undue or indecent interest in sexual matters derivatives salaciously adv. salaciousness n. fr Latin salax fr salire to leap + ious. To leap. Upon her. Upon her undue interest or indecent was it yes interest in sexual matters. Salacious like lascivious that horrible story Sasha told when Graham was there so embarrassing she is she has no shame Jane neither giggling lasciviously just what you might expect

Urgent interest in female energy. Then peace. For a while.

I know little of what old Markos would probably have referred to as the Terpsichorean muse: but can say with certainty that the drunken hopping and swaying which passed for dance at village weddings in my childhood would have had little in common with the kind of indecent spectacle one imagines might be offered for the entertainment of kings like Herod. So I must steel myself once again and so must you for more wickedness: for in truth it came to pass that little Salome danced a sensual dance for her unclean unclefather- a dance suggestive of delights she could not have fully understood at her age: we could seek to forgive her, she knew not what she did, though her mother knew all right, indeed had trained her gestures to a peak of erotic perfection. Yes, oh yes: there on the glassy sea of polished marble gleaming in the bright lamplight she danced for him till he wanted to come, oh yes, he has come to the brink, to the shore of the sea of abandonment. Look how he drinks her in like heady wine as her lithe limbs fly over the shining surface, driven by drumming, dark hair in the perfumed air, the veils waving and falling with the singing of the pipes in arabesques of invocation. Oh, how he loves her excellent motion, her patterned devotion to him, to him, it was all for him, rhythmical motion of limbs so soft yet strong, supple. The colours, unreal in the lamplight. She glows, a gold and white and blue jewel. A living stone in the wall of the heavenly Jerusalem. Oh that he could take her and place her on the altar of his heart, burrow into her, the edifice of faith and be forever free from sorrow, free from sin. And as he watches her hungrily, eats and drinks her with his eyes, gorges himself with the sight of her, something blooms in him, ah, she is so lovely so lovely ah no oh no Onan I could they're all watching but I don't care I could I could…

I could. I could have too. This is too, too much like, like. Enough of this too urgent interest in female energy. Hunger. Gorged. Get some tea. See the blasted parishioners.

4

In the crowded refectory, Alan waves across the heads of the many, beckoning. Peter, standing unhappily with his doubtless fairtrade cup of tea and plate of home-baked carrot cake, feels he has to go to him.

"Fascinating, Vicar. That girl has such a way with music. You should have heard us- we were really singing well. To the Lord. Really spiritual, it was. Surely you can see how good it would be if we were able to sing spiritually like that on a Sunday morning?"

"Alan…"

"Music with a bit of a beat, that's what we need, not like Mervyn's boring bird music…"

"There are plenty of beats in Byrd, Alan; about eighty per minute on average I should think, but yes yes yes I know that's not what you mean... Yes, yes it might attract the young people, of course you are always so interested in attracting the young people aren't you... well the choir is quite young actually if you think about it, younger than the protesters in the congregation, anyway, younger than you, certainly... yes of course I was young myself once, yes I used to bang a tambourine with the rest of them, don't you think *growing up* comes into it somewhere? Immature? Yes, I do frankly. I think it's a matter of spiritual maturity rather than calendar years. Well I suppose in a way I am saying that, yes. I think you are, in many ways. Wallowing in your own ignorance. I'm sorry, I don't care. It's about time someone did. Well do that, then, what do you think we have different denominations for?"

God, that went badly. Peter finds his cup is rattling on its saucer, so violently is he trembling. He puts it down on a table, clattering, tea slopping everywhere. He takes a deep breath, turns for the door: but the way is barred. Robert.

"I couldn't help overhearing. Do you mind if we have a word?"

Peter finds that he is still holding his plate of carrot cake, absurdly, as if offering it to Robert. Should he? As propitiation? He places it by the edge of the small pool of tea on the table, and looks round the, he suddenly realises, unnaturally silent refectory. The many headed mutely watch them both leave. Neither speaks until they reach Robert's little study. Sara is frowning at the computer monitor.

"Oh, hello, boys. I hope you don't want any more whisky, Peter, I don't think there's any left."

"I'm sorry if you think I drank too much last night, Sara."

"Now, I didn't say that, did I, Peter."

"No, but you meant it. Why can't people say what they think?"

"You've been doing a bit too much of that this afternoon." Robert is harsh, even angry, Peter realises.

"So?" I can be abrupt too.

"Sara, love, I'm sorry- would you mind if I had a word with Peter in private?"

"Oh. Yes, I suppose I don't mind. Goodness. Bit upset, are we? I'll just log off..."

"Leave it! Just leave it and..."

Sara, chastened, is nevertheless too much of a creature of habit not to pause at the door to ask if they'd like some coffee bringing in. Robert informs her ominously that they've just had tea, and she is gone.

"Do sit down, Peter."

If it's going to be, it's got to be me. I don't think I know quite who I am any more, Robert. And as for what's going to be..." Peter touched the glossy rock wall, wondered what it would be like to be as sure footed and energetic as the shining youth clinging to it.

"Please..." Robert was indicating the chair where Peter had sat last night. Suddenly feeling very tired, Peter fumbled his way to it, while Robert fitted himself into the one opposite.

"I just... can't see..."

"Peter, I blame myself. After what you told me last night, it was inexcusable that I let you try to carry on this morning. The burden must be... too great. An outburst like that just now was... inevitable. The natural restraints, the little white lies that oil the wheels of... well they just go, don't they? When you're feeling..."

"Saint Paul's wrong, isn't he?"

"I'm sorry?"

"About Jesus coming back soon."

The change of gear was a little sudden for Robert, who had been motoring nicely. He scratched his head, said: "He was a man of his time."

"But we have been reading him as if what he has to say applies to us now."

"Much of it does."

"Pick your own verses. Do it yourself doctrine."

"I think everyone has their own approach to scripture, don't they?"

"I made a terrible mistake. I must've been blind. I think this business with Fran- I mean Jane: well, no, actually Jane *and* Fran... yes... I'm beginning to see."

"I'm afraid I don't..."

"A terrible mistake. All those years ago. And now I'm having to deal with the consequences. But who am I? Who would I be, out of context?"

And then the phone rang. Robert hesitated, wondering if it would be best to ignore... no. You never know.

"Hello. Oh. Oh, right. Better put her on, then. It's for you."

"Me?" Accident, illness, I'm ringing to say that it's over, I'm taking the children away... "Hello?"

"Hi, Dad, it's little old me. How's life at the funny farm?"

"Sasha?"

"Got it in one. How's it going? Thought I'd give you a ring... Dad? You there?"

"Yes. Sorry... this is... unexpected."

"From now on, the unexpected is to be expected. Or so I'm told. How are you, anyway?"

"Well, to be honest, I'm a little bit..." Peter glanced at Robert, who was indicating tactful inaudience by riffling through papers on his desk. "Look, Sasha, I'm a bit busy... did you want anything in particular, or..."

"I'm going to put that on your gravestone, Dad: 'I was a bit busy.' Just about sums it up. I rang because I cared about how you're feeling, if that means anything to you at all. We didn't exactly part friends, did we? Or have you forgotten about that row on Sunday night?"

"Oh..." Peter thought his heart would burst. "Oh, Sasha. I love you."

"Love you too, Dadee. I'm sorry we had a fight."

"Me too. I... How's Alice? And Mum?"

"Alice is still ploughing her way through her badly written and in my opinion unsuitable for an impressionable young girl book of horny vampires and Mum is just getting back from the bar with another round of refreshing lager beers. Say hello to Dad, Mum."

"Hello to Dad, Mum."

"Jane? Is that you?"

"It was the last time I looked."

"Jane, are you... where are you?"

"We're in the pub. In the village. We've been here since. Oh, I don't know, all afternoon. And yes I am a bit pissed if that's what you wanted to know. It's called having a good time. Are you having a good time?"

"Yes. I thought you were going to walk in the hills, not spend all your time in a pub."

"Ah. Yes. There's been a hitch. In the hillwalking department. No transport, see."

"But I thought Jack was going to..."

"Yes. Yes, I thought Jack was going to as well. But he didn't. He's... gone away."

"Gone away? Why?"

"Er... He suddenly realised he had to be somewhere else."

"You mean he's just left you there?"

"Looks like it."

"But... look, listen." Peter glanced at Robert, who was still pretending to read: a bad actor, he was all ears. "Listen, Jane. Things are a bit difficult here, actually, and I'm just wondering if. If it might best for the best if I came over."

"What, now?"

"Yes."

"But what about the retreat?"

"I don't care. I want to be with you." A long silence. "Jane?"

"Sorry, I just had to take a drink. You're going to leave your parishioners all on their ownsomes so as you can be with your family?"

"They'll be better off without me. It's not going well." Robert, Peter saw, had given up acting and was now staring frankly. "I can be with you this evening. Then tomorrow we'll go walking. How's that?"

"It's, er... different."

"Don't you want me to come?"

"Well..."

"Say you want me to come! Or say you don't! Just say!"

Robert wants to say something, but Peter impatiently motions him to silence, turns his back. "Jane..."

"Well, you'd better come, then. Alice will be pleased."

"Right." Though why just Alice? Doesn't matter. "I'll get my things together and be off at once. I... I love you, Jane."

"See you later then." Click. End.

"What will you say to your parish group?"

"I shan't say anything. Goodbye, Robert."

"Peter! You can't just leave them..."

"Yes I can."

"What shall I tell them?"

"Tell them it's a family matter. Which it is."

"I think I ought to ring Graham."

"You can't frighten me with purple, Robert. I'll speak to him myself in due course."

"I'm not trying to frighten you, man- think! What if they get to him first? What sort of a tale do you think the likes of Alan will tell?"

"He'd better not say anything. Or I'll tell the police how he looks at my little daughter. You can tell him that from me. Goodbye Robert."

Robert had plenty more to say but Peter found himself ignoring all that and flung the door open and nearly knocked Fran over.

"Peter! There you are! I heard you having a row with Alan and wanted to see if there was anything…"

"I'm afraid I'm going to have to go away. My family. On their own, in the cottage…

"Go away?"

"Yes, I'm sorry. I… need to see them really… sorry."

"Fran, I'm afraid Peter's feeling…"

"Don't go away now…"

"Going to go and find out who I am. Out of context. Sorry, I'm not making much sense. Got to get out of here, anyway."

"We could go to the chapel and…"

"No, I've really got to go."

"Now?"

"Now."

"But I wanted to…"

"What?"

Fran's face suddenly crumpled, and she ran. Ran awkwardly knock-kneed along the corridor to the firedoor, bashed the bar and was gone into the bright sunlit garden.

"I seem to be upsetting everyone today, Robert. If I've upset you, I'm sincerely sorry. I'll just get my stuff from my room. Goodbye."

Peter held out his hand. Robert took it, nodding slowly.

"All right. So be it. I'll… get them all together before supper and have a word."

"Thank you. Thank you very much. Goodbye."

In the dazzling dusty carpark, Peter fought with an overwhelming awareness of everything he was seeing, hearing, causing to happen. The clunk of the central locking unlocking, the creak of the door opening. His senses were running wild: he smelled the hot plastic interior of the car, a whiff of wisteria from the terrace behind him, felt the weight of his bag as he slung it onto the back seat, almost jumped at the apparently mocking cackling of a passing gull. I can't handle all this, he thought, nauseous. But forced himself in behind the wheel, shut himself in, in the stifling heat. Seatbelt on, start the engine, down with the windows. And then out again because it was so bloody hot he didn't want his jacket on, did he, so there he stood by the chuntering motor peeling his sticky jacket off, balling it, chucking it anyhow into the back who cares let's go, go… then he realised there was a little group on the terrace watching him: Alan, of course, Eric, a couple of others,

Robert. He got back in quickly, pulled the door shut bang clutch first handbrake and gas... faster and faster over the scrunching dry gravel, a cloud of dust in the rear view mirror hiding his past as he raced down the drive...

He still had half an eye on the mirror when someone leapt out of the bushes in front of him. His body had the car slithering to a stop before his mind had caught up with the fact that he'd nearly knocked Fran over. The passenger door opened and shut and there she was next to him, gasping with exertion and fear.

"Drive!"

"You want to come with me?"

"Please!"

"But Fran..."

"You've no idea what it's like back there. *Please!*"

Peter watched himself set the car in motion and accelerate it furiously into the future.

5

"Bethel."

"What's that, Dear?"

"Up there over the door. Remember? Beth-El. House of God."

Again, they stopped to look. Faintly surprised, or possibly slightly snooty, the little chapel's face looked back at them. There was no sign of the white haired ancient.

"I'm going to have to face up to it," said Jane, holding on to Sasha with one hand and her shopping with the other. "This is not going to be easy. Having your Dad here, I mean. I mean, after all that nearly happened. With Jack, I mean. But that's not the worst of it. Come on, we'd better get home. Alice's been on her own for hours." And they set off again, unsteadily, in the direction of what for the moment they thought of as home.

"What is the worst of it, then?"

"The worst of it? The worst of it, is that."

"That?"

"Yes, that, all *that*," tossing her head back towards the chapel. "God, et cetera. I just can't go on pretending. I've *told* him. You know that. I've told you I've told him. But he can't understand."

"Or won't."

"Can't, won't, it's all the same."

"No it's not. If he really can't understand, then he can keep his own beliefs. But he knows that if he made the effort to understand truly what you're getting at, he would indeed understand, and would therefore lose his beliefs."

"Sorry, you've lost me. I knew I shouldn't have had that last pint. Need a pee as well."

"The radical view always undermines the conservative view. If the conservative understands the radical, it ceases to be conservative. That's how it works. So they don't listen. They can't. If they do, it all falls apart around them."

"What does?"

"Well in this case, theological realism. Are you all right?"

"Just going into bushes. Hold the shopping for me."

So Sasha stood and waited, watching the cars go by and thinking about when she'd been able to call Jess at last: the relief of hearing her lovely voice, of being told she was loved, of telling her she loved her too, oh that was all there was to say and they both knew it was so but how important to hear it said again and again. She was happy! They were both happy! How could it ever end? Yet love affairs did end. You heard about it all the time. Why?

At first Derryn could see little. After the bright morning sunlight, the interior of Eldan's cottage seemed impenetrably dark.

"Come in, Derryn. Come in and sit down. And explain what brings you here, contrary to your promise."

There was a menace in the words. Derryn had expected him to be angry, but there was something more than anger here- some darker threat. As his eyes became accustomed to the gloom, he made out the shape of his old master sitting at one end of a long table which was littered with the tools of his Craft: rolls of manuscript, leather bound books, crystals and scrying glasses, wands, pattens, cups, swords, and strange instruments at whose functions he could only guess. Amanda stood behind his carven seat, her eyes downcast. Derryn hesitated a moment, then sat down at the other end of the table.

"I know I said I would not come again," he said urgently. "But I had to. Only you can help us, Master. A great evil has arisen in the land. Surely you must know what I am talking about?"

"A great evil? Really. How... terrible for you." Eldan reached behind him, took Amanda's hand, raised it to his thin lips, kissed it. Derryn thought he saw her shudder. "Amanda, my dear, be absent. Leave us. This matter is not for your sweet ears."

Amanda threw a desperate glance at Derryn, full of pleading-warning, even? She sobbed, and fled into the shadows. Somewhere a door banged shut.

"So." Eldan's voice was a reptilian hiss. "So what is it, this... great evil of which you speak?"

A door banged shut. They're back at last.

"You said you'd be back in time for lunch."
"I'm sorry, Darling, I did, didn't I? Oh dear."
"It's my fault, little Sis, I led our mother astray by giving her to drink strong drink. Mea culpa, mea maxima culpa."
"I'm starving. And I'm definitely giving up Latin next term."
"That's because you're too silly to study it any longer. Where's the booze?"
"Couldn't you have got yourself a sandwich, Alice? Oh Sasha. Haven't you had enough lager?"
"What's the Latin for sandwich, then, if you're so clever?"
"Arena uter, God *I* don't know, the Romans didn't have bloody sandwiches, they just used to tickle irritating little girls to death like this..."
"Ow! Mum, gerreroff me..."
"Here's a thing," says Sash, dumping Alice on the floor and sitting on her, "which, little sandwich, you don't know. Our dear Papa is going to be with us this very night! There! What say you?"
"Tonight? I thought he was coming..."
"On Saturday, yes. But owing to a *strange* disturbance in the *time-space continuum*, he will in fact be here... Oh God, I can't be bothered." Sasha got off Alice and cracked open a can. "You explain, Mum, while I drink this strong lager and cause irreparable damage to my liver and lights."
"What's she on about, Mum?"
"She? I'm your sister, Ugly, not a mere pronoun. Mm. This is good stuff."
"Daddy's coming tonight. Change of plan, that's all."
"When's Jack coming back?"
"Jack isn't coming back."
"Why not?"

"He's... been called away on business."

"He's Jacked off. Ha ha."

Jane glared at Sasha. Not funny. Though no way was she going to say why.

"Sorry, Mummee, joke. Jokes? You know, like Alice's face?

"You're horrid. And I want my tea. When are we having tea? I'm starving."

6

Peter stopped at the toll booth and chucked a handful of coins clattering into the metal basket. In the bowels of the machine, little Welsh gnomes weighed them, found them not wanting, lit their green lantern and let the barrier be raised. *Croeso, Sais.* As he drove off again, Fran woke up, yawning.

"Where are we?"

"We are in Wales."

"Wales? I must've been asleep for ages."

"You seemed to fall asleep as soon as we left Windwood."

"No, that was when I woke up."

"Eh?"

"From a horrible dream."

Fran didn't seem inclined to say anything else, and he drove on in silence. But in his head the insistent echo of Robert's authoritative voice, weighty with warning, wouldn't leave him alone: Fran is on a very individual and highly personal journey, he had said. Don't prick her bubble, Peter. Don't knock away the only prop that's holding her up. He began to feel the stirring of what might have been panic: what was he taking on here? Not for the first time since leaving Windwood, he wondered what Jane was going to say when he came in and dropped Fran on the mat.

Then he realised she was crying.

"Oh, Fran..."

The sound of his voice triggered something in her, and she gasped, bit her hand, twisted her legs.

"Look, I think we'd better..." There was heavy traffic, he couldn't look at her properly. But the resourceful gnomes of Cymru had fashioned a sign: *Gwasanaethau*, it announced, adding reluctantly for the benefit of the *Sais*, services. Glyphs of knives and forks make its message clear to those with no skill in either language, thought Peter wildly, applying the brakes. The rearview mirror suddenly blazed with headlights, horns blared, and hot with fear and shame Peter somehow got them up the ramp, round the roundabout back over the fistshaking cursing motorway and into the sudden limbo of the service area. He ran the car swiftly over to the far side where the many parked not, nosing up against a fair grassy bank, switched off, breathed a sigh. The relief.

But no, for she was out, off and up the bank in a moment: she flung herself face down on the grass. Peter followed slowly, rehearsing words of... comfort? Counsel? What? Her shoulders heaved: she made a strange rhythmical keening noise, over and over, an endless lament, it seemed. He sat by her, waiting. At last he could bear it no longer and touched her shoulder.

"Fran..."

She rolled onto her back, lay with one arm across her face, silent now, but still trembling. Just like Jane when she was waiting for him to... he saw the peaks of her little breasts, the delicate skin of her exposed belly; felt a moment of terribly powerful desire, dragged his gaze away from her, turned his back on her, cursed her, cursed Jane, cursed bloody Saint Paul. Who had ruined all their lives, he saw. And when that thought arose in him, he really did think he was going mad.

Then he realised that she was laughing. He twisted round in surprise, and there she was, peeking up at him from beneath her arm, still shaking, but this time as if in the grip of some incredibly funny joke.

"I've..." she could barely speak, "I've been such a bloody fool, haven't I?"

Peter could only stare. Abruptly she stopped laughing and sat up, rubbed her eyes, worked her hair back behind her ears.

"I must look such a mess. Have you got any money?"

"Money?"

"Yes, money. You know, cash, the folding stuff, beer vouchers? Don't you still use it out here in the real world?"

"Oh. Yes. Yes of course." Fran followed him back to the car, watched while he found his crumpled jacket, took out his wallet. Licking her lips, she leaned in close to inspect its contents.

"I haven't got much," he said ruefully. But I can get some more at the cash machine, I suppose. Would a tenner do for now?"

"It would." And she snatched it playfully from his fingers. "Chee-ars, Peter. Give to the poor," she said with a cheeky grin, "and you will have treasure in heaven. That's Matthew nineteen, verse twenty one, in case you had forgotten. So, *you* ought to be all right then, come the glorious day- they don't come any poorer than me."

And she was off. What on earth was he going to do with her? Take her back to her parents. Obvious thing. Get Jane to clean her up a bit, she could have some of Sasha's clothes, they're about the same size- no, Sasha's taller. Not much, though. Oxford, was it she came from? Drive her down there tomorrow. Ring them up first of course. Wonder if they'll be glad. To get their prodigal daughter back. Actually that's not right, she didn't waste her substance on riotous living did she? On the contrary. I wouldn't give much for the fatted calf's chances, anyhow. Always assuming she wants to go back to them. She was pretty quick with that tenner. Where's she gone? Swallowed up into the crowd. He climbed back up the bank, sat down, wondered what he'd do for money if he gave up... Oh it was too difficult. The cottage helped with the school fees, but there would be university to pay for too. *This is insane*, he thought. What am I doing? What thinking? Why am I sitting here in this ghastly place when I ought to be... I'm supposed to be running a parish retreat. Not retreating myself, running...

Ring, ring. Ring. Peter realised that his phone was ringing, ringing. Numbly he took it out, let his finger touch its button, let it rise up to his ear. Peter, peter... peter? Dimly he heard himself saying hello? Peter it's Robert. I'm worried, where are you? Worried? Why worry? What? ...with you? What? I said have you got Fran with you? We can't find her anywhere and someone said they'd seen her getting into your car. Peter? We've gone away. Away where? Where are you now?

It's hard to say. People are doing the usual things.

What?

You know. Arriving, getting out of cars. Eating, drinking, wandering around in circles.

No, I... where *are* you, Peter? Have you got Fran with you?

Fran? No, she's here somewhere. Can't see her just now.

Peter, you're not making sense. Where are you?

I'm here.

There are so many of them. Lost sheep, every one. Look at that one with his baggy England shirt hanging over his paunch and his baseball cap on back to front with his burger in one hand, phone in the other

Peter...

And his woman in her sunglasses trailing behind with their little boy with his spiky hair and his can of Coke and his poor little brows in a tight frown

Listen, man...

Their faces are masks of resignation, hopeless, yes, it's the hopelessness that hurts, and I'd wanted to reach out to them all my life tell them about Jesus yes that was the point wasn't it to bring new life to the weary take my yoke upon you and lean on the gospel light risen with Christ we are even that family shutting themselves into their car saved sheep they are too all saved from sin their sin that put them in here goats from sheep when saw we you hungry Lord or in prison and goats visited you not insomuch as goats you did it not goats goats for the least of these demonic cacklers the lost the damned the ghosts

"There you are."

"Yes, here I am."

"Been on the phone?"

Peter realised that he still had it in his hand: he looked at it with surprise, put it to his ear. Dead now.

"Robert. He wanted to know if I'd got you with me."

"What did you tell him?"

"I... can't remember. I think I said you were here. Sorry, I'm finding all this a bit of a strain. What are we going to do?"

Fran sat down by him crosslegged, tearing the cellophane off a packet of fags. He watched, astonished, as she lit up.

"Oh... that is brilliant. I think I've missed having a smoke more than anything. Well, that's not quite true," she giggled. "Actually, I've missed having sex more than anything."

Peter looked away from her. That awful desire again. Curse it.

"This is hopeless," he said. "What are we going to do with you?"

"What would you like to do with me?"

Peter became aware of his heart pounding, his cock beginning to stir at the awful possibility. He said nothing, but realised he was looking at the Travelodge next to the carpark. She glanced at him, followed his gaze, understood, looked back at him speculatively.

"Ah," she said, and exhaled twin jets of smoke through her nostrils. "Who was it who said, anything not forbidden is compulsory?"

He looked at her. How lovely...

"You wouldn't want to..."

"I might." She took another drag, flicked off the ash, watched him through the drifting smoke with narrowed eyes.

"How can you have changed so quickly? Yesterday you were dancing in the sea, begging Jesus to come and take you to heaven. Only this morning you were singing him happy clappy songs with the likes of bloody Alan. And now you're saying you might want to spend the night in a motel with a man you hardly know…"

"Pretty cool way of getting to know him."

"Fran! Please…"

"Have a fag."

"I don't smoke."

"Please yourself."

"I ought to take you straight on to the cottage, before it gets too late. You could get cleaned up a bit, borrow some clothes from Sasha. My daughter. She's about your age, size, bit taller maybe. My wife Jane would make you a nice meal, you could have a good night's sleep and then in the morning I could run you over to your parents' house. Where do they live?"

She stretched out her legs and lay back on one elbow, stubbing the fag into the grass.

"That's one possibility," she said, smiling.

IV

1

"Learning, Jack. It's all about learning."

Bright summer sunshine smiled on gentle green hillsides, sheep-flecked, rising and falling like waves of deep emerald, sloping down to where the peaceful water lapped, sparkling round the float bobbing at the end of the line: and a jewelled dragonfly perched glittering on the end of Bryn's rod.

"I just can't get my head around it, Bryn"

"You can get used to anything in time, boy."

"Yes, but…"

High above their heads in the clear azure a red kite soaring keen-eyed spread its wings to catch the updraft. Sheep, distant, cried for *Mair*.

"It's a bit strange, Bryn."

"It is, yes. But…"

Bryn stuffs and lights his pipe.

"But what?"

"…it's when the strange things happen that you really start learning."

"So what have you learned from the strange thing that's happened here?"

"Cathy coming to stay, you mean? Ooh. All sorts. You'd be amazed."

Jack leaned back onto the grassy bank, shut his eyes. Visualised Cathy in Bryn's shirt. The shock. I'll bet he's learned a thing or two all right. And me? I'd learned so much from Bryn, thought Jack, or so it had seemed. But what was it worth in the real world, the world Jane lived in? The cards, the runes, the woodcraft. It hadn't got him very far. Nearly bankrupt, if the truth be told... Disconsolate, he dozed, on the brink of a dream, found himself weaving through a tangled woodland, in and out around the black boles of ancient oak and ash he ran, slipping on drifts of dry leaves, ducking under low looming branches, crashing through curtains of hanging foliage, leaping mossy fallen trunks, but she was always ahead of him, a slender pale figure, twisting and turning, half seen, half sensed, never any closer...

She? Who?

Jack opened his eyes suddenly. Bryn was still puffing away contentedly, watching his float. Him and Cathy. Incredible.

"So, Bryn, let's get this right, she just turned up one day, did she, and decided that she wanted to stay here with you. Yes?"

"You heard her yourself. She told you how it was."

"I can see how she couldn't stand her bloody teaching job any more, and who can blame her for that, but what amazes me is why she came here."

"She told you why, didn't she? I was the only person she could think of who'd understand. All her friends thought she was mad to pack it all in. And she was hardly going to come to you after you ran out on her, was she?"

"Her parents?"

"Oh, come on, Jack. Oop! Here we go." Bryn was scrambling to his feet, winding the suddenly screaming reel, his rod a quivering arc: there was a violent thrashing in the water. "Pass me the net- hurry up!" Bryn held the rod in one hand and with the other eased the net under the struggling fish. He scooped it up and landed it.

"The salmon of wisdom, eh, Bryn?"

"Brown trout. Get another couple and that's supper tonight. Where's my priest?"

"Priest?"

"Little club. To dispatch our fishy friend humanely. Here it is. So!" Bryn removed the hook from the dead fish's lip, set about re-baiting it. "Shove him in the bag, will you?"

Dispatched. Dead. Sent on its way by a priest. Its body bagged up, supper.

"What is learning?"

"Eh? Learning?" Bryn was busy casting, winding; then he settled the rod on its rest and sat down again. "You know what learning is. You can see it in people. The way they change. Become able to do new things. Take Cathy now. She's learned. She's changed. Not the same woman you knew, is she?"

"That's true. And how about you?"

"What about me?"

"You said you've learned. From having her here."

"Mm."

"So? How have you changed?"

"Difficult to say. Having her around sort of... well it's helped me get my ideas together, see? I've written more and done it better since... Nah. I'm not putting this very well, am I? That sounds really naff, makes her sound like a *muse*: huh. It's been more like sharing a process of becoming, becoming more alive... And it's great to have the sex. Ooh, sorry, that's a bit tactless, ha! Well fuck, man, you did ask. No, to be honest, I don't know. I feel a change is coming for me, though. A big one. Can't see it yet. Don't suppose I will see it till it's here. I'm... working on it. With her."

"How exactly?"

"Ah." Bryn knocked his pipe out in the palm of his hand, started to re-stuff it. He glanced sideways at Jack. "That's maybe where you come in. Oh yes, I don't believe you're here by chance. Maybe..." He went silent, frowning at his float.

"Maybe what?"

"You still working with the *hud*?"

"The heed, the old magic. Yes, I try to."

"What have you done, in the last week, say?"

Jack felt a reluctance to speak. The failure of the runes, the disaster with the cards... the cards! He'd left them...

"Your silence tells me something is not right."

"You're right, Bryn. I haven't done well."

"Hm. Trying to push things along too fast again, eh?"

"Maybe."

"That was ever your weakness. Learn patience. Take up fishing."

"Are you serious?"

"No. Not that it would do any harm. But listen... oh damn, we're in again!"

Again the bent rod, the taut line, the reeling in, the threshing of the struggling fish, the net, the deadly priest, the bag.

"I am working," said Bryn, when the line was cast once more and his pipe was going nicely, "with Cathy, on a rather difficult but very rewarding form of magic which I have not previously had the opportunity to, ah, explore."

Strangely pompous for you, thought Jack. "Go on."

"I'm beginning to wonder how wise it is to involve you, to be frank. You're such a fucking teararse you see, I'm afraid you might bugger it all up."

"Oh, thanks."

"You're welcome. No, it's just that, as I think I said a minute ago, I don't believe you're here by chance. So maybe…"

"You want to involve me? In the magic?"

"Maybe."

"If I don't bugger it up."

"I'll have to think about it. Hello!" The float dipped, nodded, was still again. "Ah. Just a nibble. Come on, fishes. We've one for Bryn, one for Jack. One for Cathy now!"

"When I knew her she was all tense, all the time. She wouldn't wander round the house in nothing but a shirt in those days. Not her. Cried a lot. Hated her job, hated herself, it seemed to me. I just couldn't take it. What happened?"

"You've heard what happened. She told you."

"I want to hear it from you. Seriously now. How can a person change so much?"

"All right, seriously. People do change, Jack. In the right circumstances. I was able to help her in the first place just by giving her space, I think. Not judging her. Not putting a value on her behaviour, you know? I was surprised to see her, God knows. But I thought, ah well, these things don't happen by chance, it's part of some pattern I can't see the whole of right now. So she stayed. Yes, that was it: I was able to give her space, time. No pressure."

"But Bryn, man, you're not just giving her space and time, you're bloody shagging her. How did that get going, eh?"

"Now then, Jack, now then. Well, like I say, there was no pressure. I think that, during that time I was able to give her, she came to realise that her… sexuality you might say wasn't like, you know, like some special project she had to get right, something she had to deal with or else. Are you with me? Seems to me, once she was away from her impossible job and her frantically fucking friends with their bloody tarty clothes and makeup and chasing boys she realised sex wasn't something out there you had to try and grab a piece of, no, it was just part of her being herself. Being here with me being myself, she could be herself, see? Do say if I'm boring you."

"Go on."

"The way I see it, what changed her was being able to feel that she didn't have to force things along, didn't have to try to live up to somebody else's idea of what she should be like. She could just get on with being how she is. Not worrying about what she looks like or what people will think about her. Letting herself be."

"What did you do? I mean, once she was here? Just carried on with your life, did you?"

"More or less. Got on with things in the workshop, wrote a bit, walked in the hills, went fishing. Sometimes she'd come with me, sometimes not. She slept a lot at first. Some days she just sat by the fire: it was still winter when she came, bloody cold it was. Then she took to watching me in the workshop. We started talking more, spending more time together, still not worrying about a thing. Spring came, summer. Gradually she opened up. Opened up like a beautiful flower, boyo."

"Are you in love with her?"

"*Cwestiwn dda...*"

"What's that mean?"

"It means, good question. How the hell are you ever going to do the *Hud* right if you won't learn the fucking language?"

"Haven't got the patience. Or the memory. Or the concentration, or..."

"We're in again! Hand me the net... Ah, *uffern tan,* it's just a fuckin' perch. Come here boy, while I unhook you. It's back in the lake you go. Too bony aren't you? And taste like shit. Here, pass us another worm, will you Jack? Thanks. 'But as for me I am a worm and no man: a scorn of men, and an outcast of the people'. Outcast. Cast out. Further out, away from the muddy bank where Mr. Perch likes to go, eh?"

Jack watched glumly as Bryn stood up and flicked the rod hard, so that the float and the weighted hooklength flew far out into the glimmering lake. A splash, a pause, and then up popped the little coloured float.

"Well?"

"Well what?"

"Are you in love with her?"

"The relationship between any two people is unique to them. You say they're 'in love' and you think you've described their relationship. But you haven't. All you've done is labelled it. Given them something to live up to. Or to be trapped by. Jesus, Jack, what is the matter with you today? Ah. That's a stupid question."

"So how did this unique relationship go from opening flowers to opening legs?"

"All right, Jack. Your eyes are naturally green, but their colour is much more intense than usual today."

"I'm not jealous."

"So what are you angry about?"

"Angry? I just wanted to know…"

"Look, there was no sexual pressure on her- how the hell could there be? I'm an old man, after all- I wasn't expecting her to want me physically as well. But we just came closer and closer together. I was being natural- being myself like I always am- try to be- so she became herself, like she'd never been before. She was quite surprised to find out what she was like, I think."

"So one day she just crept into your wanking pit and… oh God, sorry."

"Yeah. Well. It's all right, Jack. As soon as I saw you in your car this morning I knew this was going to be a bloody difficult day. But like I said, you can get used to anything in time. Learning, remember? It's all about learning. Especially the strange difficult bits. The painful bits."

"She's happy, then."

"Seems to be."

"That's nice for her. I had hoped it would be like that for me, with Jane."

"Jane? Oh, the wanking woman with the daughter."

"Yes, that's the one. God, what a fool I was."

"Fool, yes, that's your card all right, if you thought you could give one another the kind of space I've been talking about. A married woman for Christ's sake, with children…"

"She came out to my workshop. She wanted me. It was obvious how much she wanted me, Bryn."

"But the pressure on her, Jack- from her family. It was never going to work."

"She wanted to leave her husband. At least, I thought she did. It was just her and the two kids, in a cottage, away from it all…"

"But you weren't away from it all, were you? You took it all with you. All that baggage. And it sounds as if you had half an eye on the daughter too, eh?"

"That was a misunderstanding."
"So you said. Come on, fish, one more."
"She was very drunk. Had real go at me."
"Who? The daughter?"
"The daughter. She's too clever by half. Read the runes."
"Runes? What runes?"
"I made a talisman. Put it on the front door. Hoegl, Odil, and Beorc."
"Causation, homestead, regeneration. A long time ago it was I taught you runelore. Don't use it much myself. Not these days."
"But she read it, Bryn."
"Hm. Well, anyone can learn the names of the runes. Spell out Hob. Doesn't mean she's learned to use them properly, any more than you have, by the sound of it. Hung it on the front door, did you? Bloody hell."
"What's wrong with that? You taught me…"
"Always trying to push it along, aren't you? You're supposed to let them speak in their own time, not stick 'em up where all can see like a notice saying 'Hey, everyone, I'm a bit weird, but come on in and you'll find I'm up for a fuck.' You'll be telling me next you did a Tarot reading for her. Eh? Oh God, you did."
"It was breathtaking… the correspondences…"
"…Were unbelievable. Course they were, since you were using the cards as a tool of, I don't know, sexual courtship let's call it, rather than one of spiritual growth."
"No, but Bryn, one of the cards really hit me… the Star…"
"I daresay it did. But you can't just dip into these magical practices when you please, man. I tell you, out of the context of proper study- hard bloody work I mean, not just pissing about- they mean nothing. It's like these people who only go to church at Christmas. You can't just turn up once a year and expect it to work all by itself."
"What do you know about the church?"
"More than most of the clergy you'll meet round here. They seem to think it's some kind of social club."
"Jane's husband's a priest."
"Ha ha! You don't say. Well, Jack, you do pick 'em, don't you." Bryn lifted up his little club, weighed it in his hand. "Jesus was called the fish. Iesus Christos Theou Huios Soter."
"Don't get it."
"Jesus Christ, of God the son, saviour. Acronym: Ichthus, a fish. And he was dispatched by a priest. A high priest. Annas."

"I thought it was Pontius Pilate."

"Pilate would never have heard of him if the priests hadn't wanted him dead. Or so the stories go. You must read the Bible sometime. It's interesting. Ha! At last! Landing net, please!"

2

First shalt thou build thy temple not made with hands. And this shall be the form of it: before thee an arch with a fair garden beyond, with sweet birdsong and morning dew on scented flowers of springtime that do sway in gentle breezes, and in the midst thereof Raphael standing with sword raised high. On thy right hand an arch likewise, beyond it a garden in full heat of summer noontide sun, loud with insects as swarming bees and the like and in the midst thereof Michael in shining armour standing with his lance and beneath his feet a serpent crushed. Behind thee an arch also, beyond it a darkling garden of eventide, in gentle rain, with falling leaves brown and yellow and a stream flowing with a sound like faery music through the midst. There stands Gabriel, and in his hand is a cup of marvellous fine silver richly worked. Beyond the fourth arch on thy left hand all seems dark, for deep midnight is there and silence of midwinter too: only faint stars in a black sky show thee Uriel [*the manuscript becomes indecipherable at this point- Ed*]

Cathy closed the book and put it back on the pile on the table. She unfastened her belt, dropping the baggy trousers she'd pulled on when she'd seen Jack, and stepped out of them, unbuttoning Bryn's old shirt. This she shrugged off as she went through the back door, stepping naked onto the little sunlit patch of grass behind the cottage. Halted, she faced east, and raised her arms, breathing in deeply, held the pose for a moment, then exhaled slowly, at the same time lowering her arms to her sides and closing her eyes. There she stood in the midst of the garden, limbs gleaming in the brilliant light, like a statue but for the breeze playing gently with her long fair hair, open to the four elements of the world as the eastern arch arose in her imagination; and beyond it, with sweet birdsong and morning dew on scented flowers of springtime, the stern piercing eyes of Raphael.

"Who are you that would build this temple not made with hands?"

English. Somehow she'd assumed... no matter. Bryn said to accept, to allow, to judge not lest she be judged...

"My name is Cathy Pritchard."

"I asked for your name."

"That is my name. I am Cathy Pritchard."

"Cathy Pritchard. Teacher. At Melin Fach Primary School. Depressed, demoralised. Coffee and too many biscuits at break, worried about getting fat. Marking. Crying over the too many exercise books. Girl friend of the impatient importuning Jack Green. Jack... Green. A hard name to say. It sticks in the back of your throat. Cathy Pritchard in her clicky clacky high heels and her tight little business suit, tense and ready to burst into tears, hair stretched up in a bun? No. She is not here. I can only see you, standing easy, naked as the day you were born. New born you shall be, perhaps. I ask again: who are you?"

"I am not... the same. But I am..."

"Changed. Into whom?"

"I am... I have no name, Raphael. I am free of her: I have no name now. Raphael- name me! You can tell me who I am!"

"Hardd."

"What? Hearth...? ...Hard?"

"The hard shell of clicky clacky Cathy is gone: ...athy. ...athy. Hardd."

"Hardd means beautiful..."

"That is how you seem to me, Hardd."

"And what of Cathy? Is she dead?"

"No. But see, with my sword of discrimination I part you from her. You are new born from her. You have outgrown her. You shed her as a growing crab sheds its old shell. Be beautiful, be Hardd..."

"Must I be called Hardd in the world?"

"It is your inner name, your secret name. Tell it to no one, for it will give them power over you to know it."

"Not even Bryn?"

"That is something for you and for him to discover together. Are you close enough to exchange your true names? As for the rest of the world, let them call you Cathy and marvel at who you are now, how you have grown, relaxed into bliss..."

And it seemed to beautiful Cathy-hardd as though Raphael leaned forward and placed his left hand on her head, blessing her with all the scented urgent new growth of spring, while pointing with his sword at the arch of summer.

"Go now, Hardd, seek Michael of fiery summer sun…"

As she turned to the south, Hardd became briefly aware of the grass beneath the soles of her feet, between her toes, of herself in the real world. How Cathy would have screamed and squirmed at the thought of standing naked outside- even here where there was no one to see. She felt tired, wanted to rest, but Raphael urged her on. And Bryn had said it would be hard work. *Gwaith hardd-* beautiful work.

"Beautiful hard work, yes, Hardd, but are you hard enough? Come through the arch into the heat of my high summer garden and see how long you can stand it."

The voice of Michael was loud, brassy, his face imperious. Mocking? Yes, that too. Bryn had said there would be tests along the way, traps. He had also said that it was not right to pass through the arches- not yet. Hardd could smell the rich summer scents, honey, roses, a thousand flowers growing in profusion: and the heat was intense; it was like standing in front of a furnace. Drifting for a moment back to her everyday awareness, she knew the sun was truly scorching today, felt the old Cathy's fear of sunburn- heard a voice from somewhere saying, camomile lotion. Smooth it into the skin. Very cooling. Mm- but she forced that down and raised her face to outstare Michael's blazing eyes.

"It is not right that I should enter your realm just now. I am new born, not yet strong enough for what you offer. The time will come. For now, please bless me Michael of Fire, as Raphael of Air did, and as you have been strong in treading down the serpent of the easy lie, help me to be true to truth, to…"

She ran out of words, let herself simply be with the massive presence of the archangel, stern but, it seemed, kind. She bathed in his benevolent warmth, his heat. Heat. And yet became aware of another voice, soft, suggestive.

"Silly, stupid. Sunshine's so so strong on your soft sensitive skin," hissed the serpent, crushed beneath Michael's feet, but not yet quite defeated. "How long do you think you can stay in this paradise garden? How long before the allure of the forbidden fruit overcomes your fine faith in Bryn's magical presence? Jack. Yes, stupid, silly, think about Jack. He's young. You used to yearn for his big long cock so slick in you it was oh yes you certainly certainly could have young Jack jacking in you, jack, jack, jacking in you again come on, come, you know… ooh yes… yes…"

So tired. She felt herself swaying, fought for balance: not just in the lust for Jack- that sudden shock left her reeling all right- but trying to

remember to keep going, not give up, this was the hard work Bryn had warned her about, so difficult to concentrate though...
"Michael, Michael- please help me..."
"Who did you say you were, now? Do I know you?"
"Ca... Ca... no, Ha..."
"If you can't stand the heat..."
"Hardd... I am beautiful..."
"Heat..."
"Hardd..."

3

Jack and Bryn came chattering into the garden, stopped dead when they saw her.
"Jesus Christ."
"Here, boy," said Bryn, dropping the fishing tackle on the ground. "Take the bag. Get those trout gutted and... there's some taties and onions in the- oh, you'll find them. Go on. Leave her to me. I think I know what..."
He made his way carefully across the patch of dry grass, stood hesitating a few feet away from where she was, naked, otherworldly.
"Is she..."
"Go on. It's all right."
Jack didn't move. Couldn't. There was a magnetism in her incongruous figure, an extraordinary potency. As he watched her, the light in the little garden seemed to intensify, deepen: all at once there was a gust of wind that set the trees rustling and then, absurdly, too theatrically it seemed to him, a distant rumbling of thunder. The sun went in, and all at once Jack sensed a danger and an overwhelming unease. Bryn stood in front of her, peering into her wrapt face. Then he glanced at Jack, and tossed his head towards the cottage- go in, he mouthed. Reluctantly, Jack picked up the bag and went into the kitchen.
There was her shirt on the floor. Instinctively he gathered it up and pressed it to his face, inhaling deeply. Her smell- yes, must be- but nothing he could remember. How long ago had it been? He dropped it, dumped the bag on the drainer, and took out the fish.
He had finished working on them and was chopping onions when he became aware of Bryn leading Cathy, very slowly, by the hand. They

passed by him like ghosts, through the kitchen to the staircase. Thunder sounded again- closer this time, and rain pattered on the window. Jack ducked his head. He looked at the three fish lying on the chopping board. I know just how you feel, he thought. Gutted.

Bryn led her into their bedroom, and there she stood, her lips moving soundlessly, her almond eyes half open, but looking at nothing he could see. He felt her forehead- hot. How long had she been out there? Cool in here now, but still- all right to leave her for a moment? Yes. Into the bathroom- camomile lotion? Here. Smooth it in. Very cooling. He took it back to the bedroom- she hadn't moved- and lifted the thick mane of blonde hair spread about her lovely shoulders so that he could anoint them, very gently, tenderly, and her back too; then her face with its finely shaped jaw, the full lips parted slightly, the flared nostrils, the eyes still fixed on vacancy; the delicate but strong tendons of the neck, the graceful lines of the collarbones, the lovely parting of the breasts on either side of the sternum. He gathered the luscious flesh, easing the ointment onto her, and as he worked, she began to stir, moaned, shivered, licked her lips. He kissed her brow, murmured *Ah, Cariad... Cariad...* And then she said, very clearly, Thank you, Gabriel.

It was as if she had slapped him. *How could she know?* He was still gaping at her in astonishment when she caught her breath, and her eyes flicked open.

"Oh, Bryn!" And then she was laughing and crying all at once, joyous- she flung her arms around him, hugged him. "Oh, it was hard work, all right- just like you said it would be. But, Oh, Bryn, the beauty of it, the..."

She stopped suddenly, turned away from him. Beauty. She sat on the edge of the bed.

"What is it, Cathy? What are you remembering?" He was still in shock from her use of his true name.

"Oh. Bryn. I..." She searched his face urgently. What to say? "I want to tell you everything, but..."

Bryn sat by her, kissed her cheek. "You don't have to say anything. Especially if it's difficult. Give yourself time. You can write the experience down. Meditate on it."

"No. I want to. Raphael told me..."

"Raphael?"

"...told me my true name."

"Ah... That's... truly wonderful! I am so pleased for you, Cariad. Did you also speak with the other angels?"

"Not all four. I couldn't keep it up any longer. Michael exhausted me, and the... the horrible..."

"Did the serpent speak?"

"Yes."

"I see."

A silence, during which they both became aware of rain beating on the window.

"It's pouring. It was raining in the garden through the arch in the west. It was such a relief to be able to move on to Gabriel. He blessed me, but then I had to just thank him and... come back."

Bryn took her hand. So it was a coincidence. Or a vital connection. Time would tell. "I'm sorry. I felt I had to bring you back. Perhaps I shouldn't have meddled. It would have been good for you to build the whole temple today."

"No, Bryn, I'm glad you came for me. I was utterly spent. It was enough for one day. I should have brought myself back after meeting Raphael. But I was so thrilled- I just thought I could go on for ever. But Michael, ah, that was so difficult. And then- well somehow Gabriel was really kind, and gentle. He reminded me of you."

"Why?"

"I don't know. A feeling about him. Very male, but not threatening. So wise." She kissed him on the lips. "Shall I tell you my true name?"

"As long as you have to ask that, the answer's no. But perhaps, soon, we will tell one another our names."

4

"Bryn! How is she?"

"Fine. She's fine. Having a shower. Down soon. Well, have you managed to ruin our supper yet?"

"Les pom-dur-ter so-tayed avec les onions are dans les oven keeping warm. Les sauce fromagois is congealing dans this saucepan here. Les trwar pwassons are dans the grill pan awaiting immolation when you're ready. OK?"

"OK. Christ, look at the rain. Bit of a sudden change, eh? Imagine if this had come on while we were at the lake. What have we got to drink? Water water everywhere but not a drop- ah. This'll do. Given me by a satisfied customer, it was. Get it open, will you, while I light my pipe. What a day. What a day."

Bryn sat in his favourite chair and got his pipe going, watching Jack ransack the kitchen looking for the opener.

"I prefer screwtops, don't you?" he said, through clouds of smoke. "Quicker." Jack froze. "What's the matter?"

Jack looked at Bryn, trying to remember where... ah, right. "Nothing. You just reminded me of something, someone... Oh for God's sake, where is it?"

"Try the drawer by the sink."

"Hoo-ray."

"Now pour us a couple of large ones and come and sit down. Thank you very much. Ah. Not bad. So. What are we going to do with you, young Jack o' th' Green?"

"What would you like to do with me?"

"I'm not sure. Finish your education, perhaps."

Jack took a big swig of wine, rolled it round his mouth, swallowed. The tannins gripped his gums, made him grimace.

"Of course, if you just want to bugger off back to your wanking clergywife, that's fine with me. It's just that- well, you know, something tells me you're here for a reason."

"So you keep saying. Look, Bryn, I think I must have been a bit mad getting involved with her. What you said earlier was right. It was never going to work out."

"But there was a need in you. And that need's still there."

"I think it's over. With Jane. I think it is."

For a while they sat in silence in the darkening room, listening to the rain pounding outside. Then Jack said, "Perhaps I could at least stay here tonight. It's not a great night for travelling."

"Of course, of course. Good God, man, I couldn't turn you out into the storm."

"In fact, to be honest, I'm not too sure what to do anyway. I'm not making much money."

"Welcome to the club."

"I was thinking, before this thing with Jane came up, I might just have to take some ordinary job. You know, anything. Anything where I get paid and don't have to think. Stacking shelves."

"I can offer you something much better than that."

"Is it to do with magic?"

Bryn nodded, exhaled smoke, seemed to withdraw into himself. Jack took another swallow of the wine, and then Cathy was there. Bryn was on his feet at once, went to her.

"*Cariad! Sut wyt ti? Wyt ti eisau bwyd?*"

She nodded. Wanting to eat, yes, Jack could follow that much. And wearing some proper clothes for the first time today as well, thank God. Jeans and a shapeless sweater, but you know what's underneath that, don't you, son, hissed a voice in his head, sumptuous sensual...

"*Dewch at y bwrdd*. Jack, you can get those bloody fish under the grill now. Come on, Cathy, sit down here at the table and try a glass of this bloody red ink."

Bryn's English sounded laboured, as if it were for Jack's benefit only. He'd rather talk to her in Welsh, Jack thought, their own private language, shutting him out.

"No need to be polite. Sharad oosh Cumraig os gweloosh whatever it is, if you like. I might as well get used to it if I'm going to stay."

"Jack's going to stay?"

"That's one possibility."

"I don't know how I'd feel about that... I might as well be honest."

"You'd be unhappy if he stayed? You said this morning, let bygones be bygones."

"I didn't know he was going to stay then, did I?"

"Look," Jack called unhappily from the cooker, trying to turn the fish without breaking them, "if it's going to be difficult, I'll be off first thing in the morning. I've had enough grief the last couple of days- I don't want any more."

"It's got nothing to do with what you and I had going before, Jack. It's what Bryn and I have now... I don't want to lose any of that, and..."

"Why should you?" Jack came up to the table, swallowed some wine, made a face. "I'm not going to interfere. Like you said, let bygones be bygones. It's all over between us. Has been for months. Nearly a year, isn't it?"

She stared at the table in front of her. It was all over between Jack and Cathy Pritchard. But a hissing voice in her head made her wonder how he'd get on with Hardd... Hardd and he... it might be different this time, no, for the first time...

She became aware that Bryn had taken her hand, was squeezing it. She looked into his face, read no jealousy there but no unawareness either, he knew, understood what she was thinking, surely. She leaned into him, relished his male strength, very male he was, but not threatening. So wise. She kissed him on the lips.

"Jesus, the bloody trout are on fire!" Jack leapt across the room in time to save the fish. Himself, he was beyond saving, he thought, as he found some plates. What was going to happen? What did he *hope* would happen? He had a sudden vision of himself, Christ, was it really only last night? *Déjà vu.* Standing in a strange kitchen, in a strange country, cooking for strangers. All is strange. Again. He felt a moment of panic. But Bryn was not a stranger. He rubbed his eyes. Identity. Cathy no stranger, but changed. A changer. And who was he himself? He wasn't sure who he was for a moment. We rely on our environment for our identity. Who'd said that? Out of context, we are no one. He realised he was missing his own little home, his workshop. Ridiculous. A howl of laughter from the table. He couldn't make out what they were saying- they'd gone back into Welsh. He started putting fish on the plates. Talking about him were they? Why not? They did, he presumed. But what did they say? What think? He concentrated on plating up. Make it look good. May it be good. May it work for me this time, *please*.

"How's it going?" Cathy, pulling open the fridge. She squats, looking for another bottle, hauls it out, slams the door and holds it up to him like Sasha... This is ridiculous. That was... It's Cathy, for Christ's sake.

"You all right? Want a hand?"

Expressive form of her. "No, really, I'm just plating up now."

"Great." She winks, and she's gone. This is ridiculous, I'm trembling like a leaf. Shit. *Shit!* On the sideboard there's a bottle of Sŵn y Môr. No. No point in just getting drunk! Not after last night! Need to learn to deal with it in the future, if... *if.* He concentrates again on plating up. I suppose people just get used to it. You can get used to anything in time, boy. Bit of garnish? Green salad leaves. There. Presentation is everything. Like on the telly. Would we give this to our customers? Well, it's all we've got to offer. All done? Right. Here we go again!

"*Voila!* pwassons grillay!"

"Thank you, Jack, and diolch, Byd."

"Amen."

"Thank you, Earth, for feeding us?

"It is meet and right so to do."

They ate in silence. Cathy felt Bryn's presence more than ever, his sheer benevolence of being. Was this love? She glanced at Jack. I certainly, certainly could have young Jack, jacking in me again, come on, come, you know… no. There was no comparison. The reptilian voice was just that, a voice, an expression of something felt all right, but to be accepted, worked with gently, integrated, its dangerous energy turned to the good.

"That was good." Bryn pushed his plate away, got up from the table. "Learning, Jack. It's all about learning."

"Have you decided what to do with me yet?"

"Give it time, boy, give it time. Gently now." Bryn came back with the Sŵn y Môr, poured a slug into Jack's glass, sat down again.

"Cheers…"

"Iechyd da. Cathy?"

"Dim diolch."

"It's a bit strange, being back here with you after all this time, Bryn. And you, Cathy. You've changed…" Jack realised that he didn't know quite what he was trying to say, took another mouthful of Welsh whisky.

Bryn stuffs and lights his pipe.

"…it's when the strange things happen that you really start learning. Remember what I said to you earlier on, when we were fishing?"

Jack leaned back in his chair, shut his eyes. Strange things. He visualised Cathy naked in the garden. The shock. I'll bet he's learned a thing or two from her all right. And me? What have I learned from him? I thought I'd learned so much from Bryn, how gently he'd worked the wood, always going with what it had to say, never forcing it, letting the form and the purpose of it emerge naturally, allowing the magic to run through every piece he did. Letting it become itself. Ah. That was it. The craft's a metaphor. It's yourself you're working on.

And your relationships with others.

At this, Jack opened his eyes suddenly. Bryn was still puffing away contentedly, watching Cathy. She was watching him. Just being with him. Him and Cathy. Incredible. How gently he must've worked with her, always going with what she had to say, never forcing her, letting the form and the purpose of her emerge naturally, allowing the magic to run through everything they did together. Letting her become herself. Ah.

What are we waiting for, he'd said impetuously to Jane last night, after he'd grasped and groped and thrust at her half yielding but not yet ready was she, but did he care? He saw her standing there gripping her hair in both hands, staring wildly at him, and telling him, We're waiting for me, for me, she'd cried, and then I'm frightened, Jack! I'm afraid of what I'm doing to Peter, the girls, you! Can't you understand?

He couldn't, not then. Now, looking at Bryn and Cathy in their serenity, he shuddered with self disgust. No comparison. How could he have been so stupid?

"Bryn?"

"Jack?"

"You're right, as always. I need to finish my education. When can we start?"

Bryn smiled, and poured them both some more… Sŵn y Môr.

"We already have," he said.

V

1

"Mummy! Daddy's back!"

"Let me confirm that for you, Mother- the random remarks of my little sister frequently relate little if at all to reality. Ah. That does indeed seem to be the family car crunching onto the gravel, our paternal parent your husband hunched over the wheel. But wait- what fresh madness is this? He is not alone…"

"Mummy! Daddy's brought a lady back with him."

A lady? Jane made her way through from the kitchen, wiping her hands on a tea towel. It seemed a very long way, and uphill too. What ever now? She joined the girls at the window, so that as Peter and Fran got out of the car they were met with the three of them staring out like a framed family portrait. Fran grimaced and opened and closed her hand in a nervous half wave: Peter sketched a sort of apologetic shrug as he ushered her towards the door.

"Ooh, she's beautiful- like Elise in my book."

"She's cute, all right. What do you make of this, Mummee?"

"Looks like he's found himself a girlfriend." Jane couldn't believe she'd said that: her stomach turned over. Must be all that lager.

"What, like you've got Jack?"

"Alice, for God's sake…"

"Don't you *dare* mention Jack…"

And then the door opened and there they were. Nobody seemed to be able to remember the next line. Peter had a go at introducing…

"Er… Fran. This is."

"Hi."

"Jane, Sasha, Alice."

"It's nice to meet you all."

"Nice to meet you too," said Jane, lifting an eyebrow at Peter, but he was still trying to remember what came next.

"Pete's been really kind," Fran improvised into the silence, grinning round at them all. "Rescued me."

Pete? Nobody called Peter Pete, thought Jane. What the hell's going on here? "Rescued you?" she asked, "Where from?"

"Bloody Windwood. My own fault really. It's a long story."

Wide eyed, Alice turned to Jane. *She said B...*

"Good," sez Sash, suddenly businesslike, enough of this pratting about, "we like long stories, don't we, little Sis?"

"Mm?"

"Her eloquence is breathtaking, *nicht wahr?* You look as if you could use a drink."

"Ah, yes! Drinks!" That was it- Peter had found his place in the script. "Let's all have a drink and then we can sit down and... and..."

"...you can tell us all what the hell's going on," smiled Jane sweetly. But then her stomach heaved again as she remembered what she might have to tell him...

"Yes, well." Peter sat heavily in an armchair by the fireplace. Suddenly exhausted. "Sasha, I'm sure you wouldn't mind sorting out... I don't know what we've got..."

"I do. And I don't. Mind, that is. In fact, try stopping me." She stepped closer to Fran. Cute, yes. "And what, exactly, would you like," she purred, "to *have*?"

Fran was up for this. "What, exactly, are you *offering*?"

"So what's going on, Peter?" Jane felt she was choking. Now that he was actually here, where she and Jack had...

"I had to get away."

"What am I offering? Why don't you come and see..."

"I should be delighted. Lead on, Macduff."

"Get away? Why?"

"Why did Jack go off, anyway?"

"It's lay on. Not lead on. A common mistake..."

"I beg your pardon."

"Granted..."

"Never mind Jack," muttered Jane. She felt him glance sharply at her. She'd been too ready with that. Careful! Quickly she hit the ball back. "What's happened?"

"Look, Jane, I've got so much to tell you...

"...Though why anybody should want to lay on Macduff, when Lady Macduff was available and presumably much more comfortable to lie on, I really don't know."

"He couldn't lie on her. He'd had her murdered earlier in the play, hadn't he?"

"My God you're right. What a fine, scholarly mind you have. Of course, he might have been into necrophilia."

"Oh no, that's... dead boring!" Howls of laughter.

"Sasha!" Peter had had enough of this, "For goodness sake stop blathering and open a bottle of something will you? I'm parched."

In the kitchen, Sasha quickly twisted the cap off an Australian red and gave it to Alice. "Take this sponge soaked in vinegar and, having placed it on a reed, run and put it to our father's parched lips."

"A reed?"

"Or you can use a glass if you prefer. Be absent. Leave us." Sash patted her on her way and turned to Fran, her eyes brilliant, excited, aroused. "Now, what was it you said you wanted?"

"I didn't."

"But you'd like something, wouldn't you? Sasha hipswayed closer. "What is it?" And closer. "Or do I have to guess?"

"You're crazy," laughed Fran, almost crying with relief. After the row with Peter at the motorway services, the rest of the drive here had not been great. She grinned at Sasha, sparring, enjoying this totally unexpected and more than a little sexually charged encounter.

"I could murder a cold beer."

Sasha pulls open the fridge, squats, hauls out a sixpack, slams the door.

"Tra-la!"

"Ah." Peter, framed in the doorway, glass in hand. "I see you girls are getting on all right. That's great. Ah... Sasha. I want to have a little talk with Mum... perhaps you wouldn't mind just entertaining Fran for a little while, er... we'll have some supper soon, but first... a little talk with Mum. Understand?"

"*Klar.*"

"What?"

"*Zum befehl, Papa!*"

"Alex... Sasha, sometimes I just wish you could..."

"Be normal, Father, I know. In this and all things I shall obey you, it will be a pleasure. I just love my new playmate." And she put her arm round Fran's waist, squeezing her so she giggled.

"Hm. Right." Bitterly, Peter looked Fran up and down, resenting her presence. Bloody little vixen, nearly had the applecart over, didn't she. Lead us not into... But now, seeing her with Sasha, bloody ridiculous, what was he thinking? There was a pause, one of those awkward ones, Alice would say, thought Sasha. Standing so close to Fran, she caught the way her dad was looking at her, wondered if she could possibly be reading the signs right... *surely not*! Abruptly, she let her go, went to the table and started pulling cans off the sixpack. Surely not... but Jesus, what if.

"Pete, why don't you let me explain things to Jane. It's a bit much just landing on you all and expecting her to just say like OK crash out or whatever..."

"Yes I know, Fran, but you're not actually part of the problem which I need to discuss, although God knows you could have been and I need to make sure first of all that Jane understands that, and then I have to tell her what the real problem is... I'll see you later. Perhaps you two could... go for a walk... or something." And he was gone.

Another silence started to lengthen. Sasha shook her head, cracked open a couple of lagers.

"I'm speechless. Take notes, it doesn't happen often. Here."

"Thanks. Cheers."

"Down the hatch. Of what problem might you have been a part?"

"Can I smoke in here?"

"Smoke? What other foul vices have you yet to reveal? And do I really want to find out about them? I suppose I do. I have one of those inquiring minds you read about. Come on, this way. I'll have one with you."

Peter returned from the kitchen, sipping his wine. He sat down, lips compressed. By now, Jane felt paralysed. She sat dumbly, staring into the empty grate. Where she had stood last night while Jack ran his hands all over her body. And now Peter was here. Her indignation and suspicion had mutated into fear. What was happening to them?

"Do you want some wine too, Mummy?"

"Yes. Yes please. Thanks, Darling." She quickly swallows a lot, coughs. "So, Peter..."

"They've gone in the garden," reports Alice helpfully. "I think they're smoking fags. Can I have some wine too?"

"No, Darling."

"Oh, Da-ad…"

"Oh, all right, just a taster."

"I had wine with dinner last night, didn't I Mummy? Jack let me have some. When are we going to have supper?"

"In a little while, Darling. Daddy's just going to tell me about his trip first. You can put the supper on, if you like. Have a look in the freezer."

"Can I read my book instead?"

"Yes, all right."

"Are you OK, Mummy?"

"Yes."

So Alice carefully climbs upstairs with her taster, *Jack let me have some-* and suddenly it's very quiet. Peter stares into his wine, takes a sip. This is my… bloody hell, Peter. It seems to Jane that she's never known such a silence. What's he going to say? And what did Jack let *you* have, Jane? *A feel of his cock, Peter…* she shudders, rehearses some lines. Peter, I've got something to tell you. Peter, Jack and I… Peter. I was standing here last night and Jack was feeling me all over. But I didn't… let him have me. But I might have. If… he hadn't said, *Sasha*. Yes, I definitely would have. And then what would we say to one another? When you arrived back unexpectedly with your little girlfriend and Jack and I would be here having slept together… Oh, and by the way, Peter, Sasha's come out. She's a lesbian…

"You've been right, and I've been wrong."

Startled from her thoughts, Jane looks at him open mouthed. Whatever she'd been expecting, it wasn't this. Peter sipped his wine, licked his lips, put his glass down in the hearth. Took his glasses off, rubbed his eyes.

"I'm talking about the, well, hardly a conversation, the… things you said on Sunday night. You remember. We were in the kitchen. You said you couldn't go on pretending. I said it seemed to me that you'd lost your faith, and you said it wasn't like that and I couldn't understand. Well, the good news is that I think I'm beginning to see now. You don't have to go on pretending any more."

He blinked at her: waiting for a reply, was he? Jane drank some more wine without taking her eyes off him. His words had meant nothing to her. She was gripped by the most awful feeling that after this conversation things would never be the same again. She thought of little Alice, innocent of all this grown ups' shit and almost sobbed aloud with compassion. Why did they have children if they were going to mess their lives up... but Peter was off again.

"It came to me quite suddenly, during yesterday, and this morning, and... I don't know just how- haven't had time to think it through- but I need to write it down. As a sermon. For this coming Sunday. Like no sermon I've ever preached before. Because this time I shall tell them the truth."

A silence began to expand, huge, threatening...

"The truth," he repeated, and bared his teeth alarmingly- or was that supposed to be a smile?

"What?" Jane's voice was a mere whisper. "Truth?"

"My whole career has been founded on a lie. I shall tell them that. The congregation. Bloody Alan and all the rest of the... I'll prick their cosy little bubbles."

"Peter..."

"Anyway. I felt I had to get away from them all. To be perfectly honest, I felt just a little bit as if was losing my mind. I didn't know where I was... couldn't see where I was going. Lost my... context. Does that make sense? No. Of course not. Well, when Sasha rang up something seemed to burst in me... I just had to get back to you, you and the girls... to reality. It's going to take a while to explain. But first, look. Let's get this girl Fran out of the way first. It's an extraordinary story, but quick to tell. It all began when she took some words from the gospels rather literally..."

"Ice cold. Fantastic. God, I've not had one of these for months."
"Why not?"
Fran doesn't reply. Too busy drinking. Aaaarp. "Pardon me." She puts the can down, takes her cigs and lighter from her jeans, then sits cross legged on the grass.
"You *were* thirsty."
"I've really missed the booze and fags. And, of course," she says, lighting up. Sash sits facing her, tilts her head inquisitively.
"And, of course?"
Fran takes another drag, flicks off the ash, watches Sasha through the drifting smoke with narrowed eyes, smiles slowly, her head swaying snakelike.
"Sex, of course," she hisses.

Sasha sighs, and, not without difficulty, for when you're sitting crosslegged in tight jeans removing your smokes from your pocket does present some difficulty, removed her smokes from her pocket.

"So, Fran," Sasha asks reasonably, fag in mouth, flicking the lighter, "have you fucked my daddy, then?" The little flame catches, the end of the fag flares bright. It's starting to get dark in the garden. Sash inhales, tosses her head so that the wings of her bob stir, exhales a twin jet through her flared nostrils. You've seen it in the movies a hundred times. Sash isn't beyond borrowing a little melodramatic gesture now and then. So as not to cry, because Sash doesn't...

"No." Fran is matter of fact about it. Not a trace of surprise that Sasha should ask, though.

"But you might've. Might've been a part of the problem which my parents are presumably chewing over even as we speak, right?"

"Right."

There. It was said. But the anger had seized him, by God it had, how he'd bundled her back into the car, driven off furiously, away from the damned motel, from the horrifying possibility... "I'm sorry, Sasha, I didn't mean any harm. You've no idea what it was like..." Fran finds she can't keep up the banter, doesn't want to. It begins to sink in. What she's done. The extent of her disillusionment. She sobs suddenly.

"Jesus, Fran, are you all right?"

Fran takes a long drag on her fag. Then sobs again.

"Got a hanky?"

"Tissue?"

"Thanks."

Fran blows her nose, manages a crumpled smile. "Have you ever noticed how hard it is to blow your nose when you're smoking?"

For some reason this seemed incredibly funny to them both.

"Perhaps it's time we had the *histoire de Fran*," said Sasha, moving in close so she could put an arm round her shoulders. Fran raised her head, found her face was very close to Sasha's, smiled, sniffed.

"Later," she said, and touched one wing of the bob. "I love your hair."

"Hey," said Sash, and smoothed the tangled flax from Fran's face, whispering in her ear, "What do you mean, later? Come on, Fran, what have you been up to? It must be fascinating. I want to be fascinated. Fascinate me. Go on, you know you want to."

"You'll think I'm quite mad."

"You haven't been playing with chainsaws again, have you?"

"You won't feel safe in your bed at night."

"I should hope not."

"Has anybody ever told you you're a dreadful flirt?"

"*Au contraire*. They say I do it rather well."

Fran laughs. "You do, actually." She stretched out her legs and lay back on one elbow, stubbing the fag into the grass. "You make me feel good," she said, smiling, and then: "Can we have another can?"

"We can. Here."

"Thanks."

"Now, *l'histoire*."

"It's quick to tell. It all began when I took some words from the gospels rather literally…"

2

"So." Eldan's voice was a reptilian hiss. "So what is it, this… great evil of which you speak?"

"The Vampire," said Derryn. "It has returned."

Alice got off her bed, went to the window. Starting to get dark now. The trees were still: beyond them clouds glowed a dull red where the sun was going down. Below the window, in the garden, Alice could just see Sasha and the beautiful lady sitting very close together. Who was she? Had Daddy rescued her from a Fate Worse Than Death at Bloody Woodwind? It was like in her book. Daddy was Derryn, saving Elise from a great Evil which has risen in the land. She switched on her bedside lamp, sat down to read, changed her mind, went out onto the landing, listened. Daddy's voice. What was he saying? She started to creep down the stairs, hesitated. It was wrong to listen to other people's conversations. But she felt so alone! She'd wanted Daddy to come with them on holiday, but now he was here, he just wanted to talk to Mummy. Nobody ever told her what was going on. If she asked Sasha, she'd just say a lot of stuff she didn't understand, and tickle her. Daddy was always a Bit Busy, and sent her to Mummy. Why had Jack gone away so suddenly? And without his cards. Cards of Power. Alice went back to her room, had a taste of her wine. Yuck. She got onto the bed, found her place.

"The Vampire! So. What has happened?" asked Eldan, stroking his long white beard.

"The Cartomancer is in danger," explained Derryn urgently. "Already the Vampire has tried to attack her once. You know the consequences for us all if she is turned to the Darkness…"

"Indeed, indeed. But what would you have me do, Derryn? I am old. It is for the young such as you to shoulder the burden of keeping the Middleworld free of those forces which would rule it for their own, ah… evil ends."

"Use your power to show me where the Undead One is. Then I shall go there and ensure that he never rises again."

"And how will you do that?"

"I will find a way. I must."

For a long time Eldan sat, watching Derryn, frowning, his thin lips pressed together. Then he seemed to make a decision. He stood up, smiled.

"Come."

He led Derryn through dark, low passages to the rear of the house.

"I do not remember this part of the house."

"Much has changed since you lived here. Yes, much has changed." Suddenly Eldan stopped, and with a whispered Word loosed the locking spell on a small wooden door. It creaked open, revealing a staircase winding down into the cellar. A dank and musty smell assailed Derryn's nostrils. Eldan took a torch from its bracket, and having lit it with another Word, handed it to Derryn, saying quietly, "Lead the way, boy."

The cellar room was square, earthen floored, and surprisingly large. By the dim light of the torch, Derryn could see that the ceiling was painted with signs of the zodiac, and other symbols he did not recognise. On each of the four walls an arch was painted, with, it seemed, incomprehensible dark forms jostling within. Was it a trick of the flickering torchlight, or were they actually moving? Derryn shuddered.

"Eldan- what is this place? Eldan?" Derryn realised with a shock that he was alone. The door- where was it? Frantically he ran from wall to wall, but he could not find it. "Eldan!" he cried again, but there was no answer. Then he heard it. The faintest rustling sound, as of leathern wings unfurling. He spun round, just in time to see a gigantic bat-like shape hurling itself towards him. The torch flew from his hand, and went out. In total darkness, Derryn crouched, his heart thumping, his mind racing. Then he heard the voice of Eldan again, but oh! how changed: it screeched, it howled, it dripped evil:

"Foolish boy! Did I not tell you never to return! It is necessary for you to die now, but before you do, I will show you what will befall the land now that I have arisen once more!"

"Eldan, no! It cannot be? You are... the Vampire?"

"He that was called Eldan is long dead. Weak he was, and easily bent to my will. I use his mortal form now and then still, when it is needful. Behold!"

Suddenly, one corner of the room was suffused in a silver and purple radiance, cold as a winter midnight. There stood Eldan- or so it seemed. Derryn gasped.

"You fiend! You evil, evil, fiend!"

"Now look, and see the future of the land! These things shall be!"

The arch before Derryn became translucent, revealing what must once have been a fair garden beyond, but all was spoiled, leafless and trampled down, and in the midst thereof the dark form of the Vampire: his eyes sparkled like wicked jewels, and his fangs gleamed, white, bright, enticing, and his arms stretched out to... no! It could not be! It was Elise! Horrified, Derryn watched as, drawn by an irresistible force, Elise moved, step by trembling step, closer to the hideous monster. Her flimsy silken nightdress gleamed in the evil half-light.

"No," he gasped, "No- you can't force her to do this. You cannot."

"Who are you, to say what I can and cannot do?"

"I am Derryn, and I am the Vampire Slayer!"

"You are... nothing!" screamed the vampire, and seized Elise so that her head fell back, her white throat helplessly offered ...then the scene froze, darkened, and at the same time the arch on Derryn's right grew bright as fire, and a terrible heat assailed him, with a loud buzzing of flies, and a frightful hissing noise. A giant snake reared up from a parched desert floor, its eyes blazing, its fangs bared. Its face, incredibly, seemed to resemble the face of Eldan... Within and beneath its massive coils men and women writhed half crushed, eyes bulging, mouths agape, soundlessly screaming for help. And he knew them: his family, friends...

"No! No! It cannot be..." Derryn sobbed helplessly as the hideous vision faded, but the anguish was not ended, for now the third arch glowed, and his tortured eyes beheld therein a darkling garden of eventide, in gentle rain, but he knew that the rain was blood: there were falling leaves as of autumn but all red with blood and a stream of blood flowed through the midst of the blighted garden with a trickling sound like blood spattering from a fearful wound. There sprawled a fallen angel, his wings and his robe all stained with blood, and in his hand was a cup of marvellous fine silver richly worked, out of which he drank copious draughts... of blood.

"Blood, blood, blood!" yelled Derryn. "What, you more than evil creature, wicked beyond words, will you never be satisfied? What will you do when you have drunk every drop of blood in the world?"

And that vision also faded in its turn, but the fourth arch did not lighten, nay, rather seemed to become more dark, if such a thing were possible. Within its depths, black shifted on black, and an icy chill struck Derryn, so that his spine seemed to creep and freeze at once.

"Can't you see?" The voice of the monster that had been Eldan came from behind him, cruel, mocking. Slowly, Derryn turned. The creature was coming closer, gliding over the floor towards him, it seemed.

"Go through the fourth arch, Derryn! Then you will see! Surely Derryn the Vampire Slayer is not afraid? Enter into the dark and learn! It's all about learning, remember?"

Derryn faced the arch, stepped forward: he could see nothing at first, but then, as his eyes adjusted to the dark, he saw a pale figure awkwardly shuffling towards him and trembled, for this was the worst torment of all... it was Elise, but horribly changed! All her grace of movement was gone: she limped, staggered. Her arms hung by her sides, her silken nightgown was ripped and stained with blood. The eyes she fixed on him were dull, lifeless. As she approached, she flicked her tangled, matted hair back over her shoulder so that he could see the red, raw marks on her throat where the evil fangs had pierced her flesh.

Speechless, Derryn tore his eyes away from her- where was the fiend who had done this?

The Eldan creature was standing in the middle of the cellar, a twisted smile on its loathsome face.

"There, Derryn- is she not beautiful?"

"You... you..."

"And look- she has a gift for you."

Beyond grief, beyond any feeling now, numbed by the horror, Derryn turned back to the living corpse that had been Elise. Slowly she lifted up one hand: it held a card. With a sudden flick of the wrist she turned it to him: it was Death!

Immediately Derryn felt the dreadful chill of the spell: his head reeled, and it seemed as if the life was draining out of him. With his last strength he twisted round, stumbled back into the cellar, perhaps to try some hopeless last gesture of defiance before he died. The loathsome face of the thing that had been Eldan was distorted with demoniac laughter: the terrible grating sound rang in his ears as he sank to his knees…

There was a colossal bang.

The laughter stopped at once, and through the swirling mists of his reeling awareness Derryn saw the Eldan-monster freeze, tremble, and then, with an ear-piercing screech, fall forward onto its face. Behind it stood Amanda, her arm extended in front of her, holding a pistol from whose barrel a whisp of smoke still curled.

3

"It's an extraordinary story."

"Yes. Well, that's why she's here. I'll take her back to her parents tomorrow."

"Are they expecting her tomorrow?"

"I don't think so. Unless Robert's been onto them."

"Well, let her stay. We'll take her home on Saturday. You've only just got here."

"I want to get her off my hands."

"Oh? Why?"

"Why? Well, she's…"

"What?"

Peter doesn't know quite what to say. His account of how he came to pick up Fran had been necessarily selective. Had to be. They'd be up all bloody night arguing otherwise. And there was the small matter of Jack…

"So what about Jack, then?"

Jane wonders on what level to answer the question. Better be a bit selective here. They'd be up all bloody night arguing otherwise.

"He had to go. Something came up."

"What?"

His cock, for one thing.

"He didn't say."

"Odd. He seemed so keen."

"Keen?"

"On having a holiday here."

"Yes."

Peter let his mind go back to- was it really only last night?- whisky and a sort of provisional sympathy from Robert.

"I must say," he said, "because I think a little more openness in our marriage is, er, necessary... that I had feared, I'm sorry if this sounds pompous... paranoid, idiotic, forgive me... I feared that his interest in you was... more than ordinary friendship."

Jane just looked at him. Still his move.

"Are you having an affair with him?"

"No." Jane is matter of fact about it. Not a trace of surprise that Peter should ask, though.

"But you might've. Right?"

"Right."

There. It was said. Neither of them could quite believe it.

"Are you having an affair with Fran?"

"No." Peter is matter of fact about it. Not a trace of surprise that Jane should ask, though.

"But you might've. Right?"

"Right."

Unbelievable. There was a very long silence during which the two of them made the necessary mental adjustments. Then Jane stood up and said, "Right."

"What?" Peter was aghast.

"I'll go and put the supper on."

"Good story. *Bonne histoire. Fabula bona. Gute Geschichte. Und so weiter.*"

"Do you think I'm really stupid?"

Sasha is suddenly all energy.

"Good God, no." She kisses Fran quickly on the lips, grabs her fags, pops one in Fran's mouth, one in her own, "I think you're absolutely super." Gives her a light, gives herself a light, lies back on the grass, and just as suddenly relaxes, staring into the infinite evening sky. "Super. What I don't get is why you had to throw yourself at Dad just because you'd decided Jesus wasn't coming. He's not much of a substitute, is he?"

Fran crawls across to Sasha, lies by her side, looking down into her face. She gets her looks from him all right, she thought, lucky girl, handsome bastard he must have been when he was young. Look at her dark hair, straight nose, high cheekbones, perfect eyes. Lovely.

"Have you got a lover?"

"Oh yes."

"Is it a girl?"

"Oh yes."

"What's her name?"

"Oh… Jess."

"She's a lucky girl."

Sasha swivels her head, refocuses her eyes on Fran's.

"Answer the question," she says.

Fran looks away, works her hair back behind her ears, sits up.

"I missed one bit of the story out. Last night, very late, must've been getting on for midnight, I was coming back from a walk. As I got near the house, I saw your Dad on the lawn. He was as pissed as a fart."

"What? My Dad?"

"Does that surprise you? He was well away. And upset. He obviously had a problem, so I tried to help, you know, do the good Samaritan bit. Gave him a cuddle- nothing really sexy, you know- just a friendly hug, really, OK?"

"OK."

"And then he got to talking about how his wife your Mum I mean obviously, Jane is it? had, er… lost her faith, right?"

"Don't ask me."

"Well he thought she had, and he was drunk and upset, so I started talking about Saint Paul, and how his teaching on sexual morality was conditioned by his belief in the imminent return of Jesus to the world for the last judgement."

"Hell of a chat-up line."

"And then I asked him to kiss me."

"Oh, that's better."

"Because I was lonely."

"Makes sense."

"Because, you see, I thought, it's been two thousand years now, and there's still no sign of him coming."

"Some men do take a long time. So I'm told."

"But he didn't kiss me. We just cuddled for a bit, and then it started to rain, so I went in."

"How Schubertian."

"That's simply amazing."

"No, it's *Die Schöne Müllerin.*"
"Do you know everything?"
"Not yet."
"Can I kiss you?"
"If you like."
"What would Jess think?"
"She'd think you were kissing me, what the hell do you think she'd think?"
"I'm not going to kiss you."
"Now who's a dreadful flirt?"
"The next morning, this morning that is, God it seems so long ago! this morning I'd decided to talk the whole thing through with him. His problem, my problem... he just seemed so much more real than the other people there, like that creepy Robert, ugh. But I didn't get a chance. He seemed really confused, his talk to the parishioners was all over the place, I mean, really wild. People were whispering, you know, What's the matter with the Vicar? That sort of thing. Then he just disappeared. I did a music session with some of his ghastly parishioners... Do you know a real paedo called Alan something?"
"Alan the Toad. Gets an erection every time he sees Alice."
"Yuck, right, well anyway I didn't see your Dad again until tea, but my God was he laying into that Alan."
"Really?"
"Shouting at him he was immature, ignorant, I don't know what else. Practically told him to fuck off and find a different church to go to. It was a great scene."
"Good for him. I'm impressed."
"Robert scooped your dad up and took him away. I think they had a row too. When he came out of Robert's study I tried to talk to him, but he just said he was leaving. That was the final straw- I don't know why. I just knew then that I couldn't stand it any more on my own. I had to get out. So I ran down the drive and hid in the bushes until I saw your dad's car coming. I stopped him and dived in. Drive, I said, get me out of here! Next thing I knew we were over the Severn Bridge and half way here."
Fran paused, found a can of lager, took a swig.
"And?"
"Yeah, there's more. I got really stupid, started crying, it was like I was, I don't know, hysterical or some shit. Your dad pulled off into a services, I got out and was like totally crazy, got some money off him,

got some fags, started prick teasing him about the bloody motel there, you know, how we could go in there for the night…"

"Well you obviously didn't, because you're here. Even I can work that out."

"I'm sorry, Sash, it was…"

"Load release faulting. Geological term. Come here."

Sasha gave Fran a big hug.

"You're incredible, Sash."

"It's raining."

"Very Schubertian."

"Let's go in," said Sash, and took Fran's hand.

But for some reason they didn't, not straight away. Stood together, really close, still holding hands, while the gentle rain fell softly on them both, righteous and unrighteous.

"Sash."

"Fran."

"Are we going to be friends?"

"Probably."

"I'd like to kiss you."

"But…?"

"I'm thinking of Jess."

"So am I."

"But I really want to… kiss…"

The back door flew open.

"Supper's ready!" said Jane.

"Oh, thank you, I'm starving," cried Fran, and dropping Sasha's hand ran up to Jane and kissed her on the mouth. Hard.

4

"Daddy, I'm sitting by you." Alice carefully comes from the staircase, bearing before her her glass of wine, like she's seen me doing, with the chalice, thinks Peter. She's not taking the piss, is she? Impossible. Too young.

"All right, Alice. Where's Mum?"

Sasha and Fran glance at one another, look away. Sash picks a chip from the dish in the middle of the table, bites off the end.

"I think she's still, er… in the kitchen," she chews.

"Oh. P'raps we ought to wait. Oh, yes, thank you, Fran, just a drop."

"It's nice having wine, isn't it Daddy?"
"So long as you don't have too much…"
"Like last night, eh Pete?"
"What happened last night, Fran?"
"Never you mind, little Sis," warned Sash.

Peter looked at them sharply. What had they been saying? And where is Jane?

"Here I am. Sorry." She comes in very quickly, sits.
"You look all hot, Mummy."
"Do I, Alice? Must be the heat of the grill. Fish fingers," she says, gesturing towards the steaming yellowish pile. Been grilling the… My glass appears to be empty."
"Oh, sorry…"
"Thank you, Peter."
"Daddy, are you going to say grace?"

Silence. Peter doesn't know what to do. Every mealtime, for years and years, their family has said grace. But now… he sees Fran looking at him, an ironic smile on her face. In the end, habit takes over.

"Lord, bless this food to our use and ourselves to thy service… Amen."
"Amen," says Alice, who looks around at the others in surprise: nobody else has spoken. "Jack said a funny grace, didn't he, Mummy."
"Yes. Have some fish fingers. Fran, do… please help yourself."

Fran smiled at her. "Thanks, Jane. I will." But she didn't move. Just kept smiling. Jane dropped her eyes to her empty plate. Awkwardly, she picked up her glass, took a mouthful, swallowed it. Put down the glass. It seemed to be impossible not to do things deliberately. Plates were being passed, someone wanted the ketchup, the salt: cutlery scraped loudly.

"Aren't you hungry, Mummy?" asked Alice.

Jane realised that her plate was still empty. She saw herself reach out mechanically, take a pile of chips and a couple of fish fingers. Like those robot arms you see, she thought; and then, what a stupid expression: fish fingers. Who thought of that? She shook salt, squirted ketchup, found herself chewing, swallowing. Just like everybody else. Situation normal.

"No one's saying much tonight," observed Alice. Not even Sasha. Odd.

"I expect it's because we're all very tired," explained Peter clearly.

"I'm not tired. I haven't done anything today. Except read my book. I've nearly finished it. It's very exciting. Amanda has just saved Derryn's life by shooting Eldan in the back." No one had an opinion on this, it seemed. "He was a vampire really, you see."

Or this.

"Yes," went on Peter, as if Alice hadn't spoken, "all very tired. I for one shall be getting to bed early tonight."

Jane then realised that of course Fran would have to have the spare room where Jack had been and that that meant of course that she'd have to share the double bed with Peter which would be the first time since... God how long had it been since they... She realised with a shock that she couldn't remember the last time they'd shared a bed...

"Because I shall have to make an early start in the morning. Right, Fran?"

Fran shrugged, smiled crookedly.

"Oh, Peter, for goodness' sake..."

"Daddy..."

"Got to get her back to her parents. They'll be worried about her."

"Peter, can't we just give them a ring and say she's all right?"

"Daddy, if you take the car tomorrow we'll be stuck here for another day with nothing to do... I thought we were going to have healthy walks in the hills. And I haven't seen you for ages and ages. You're always too busy doing something or other..."

"All right, Alice," Peter said, too loudly. Alice's lip started to tremble. "It's all right," he went on more gently. "Fran, would you like to stay here for the rest of the week? You could come back home with us on Saturday and it's not too far to Oxford from there."

They all looked at Fran. She had tipped a little salt onto the back of her hand. Now she raised it to her lips, put out her tongue, and worked it back and forth among the crystals until they dissolved, her eyes going from Alice to Sasha, to Peter, to Jane. Then she sat back in her chair, her arms falling by her sides.

"I don't know what's going to happen to me," she said.

"None of us knows that," said Sasha, pushing her plate away. It was the first thing she'd said for some time. She stood up. "Excuse, me, please. Going out for a breath of air."

The front door had opened and closed before anyone moved. Then Fran was on her feet, gathering the plates.

"Let me do the washing up," she said. "I've rather developed the ancillary habit over the last few months. Can I make some coffee for anyone?"

"Not for me... or you, Alice," said Peter. "No, sorry. We're off to bed. It's late, and if I'm not going to Oxford tomorrow I'll be taking you all for a long walk in the hills. Get some vigorous exercise. Right? You can practise on this little wooden hill here. Up you go." Peter shoved her playfully up the stairs, turned to Jane. Fran was in the kitchen: for a moment they were alone and looked at one another, knowing how much needed to be said, how impossible it was to say it. Now, at any rate: perhaps tomorrow.

"I take it," he said *sotto voce*, "that we're in the main bedroom?"

"S'pose," Jane nodded, bit her lip, couldn't, or wouldn't, meet his eye.

"Right. I'll see you in a little while, then," he muttered, and was gone.

Jane sat on at the table, thinking about sleeping with him. When was the last time? Around Christmas was it? Scratching at her bedroom door like a dog wanting to be let in. And she let him in, of course she did, because... oh, it had been such a long time, and she always hoped it would be different...

She didn't want it now, though! Not after all this. The sleeping arrangements could be different... He could go in Jack's room (I'll always think of it as Jack's room now) and Fran could come in with me...

Jane gave up the struggle. Let go the enormous effort she had been exerting throughout the meal to prevent herself from re-living that moment at the back door when Fran had kissed her. Hard, but so soft too, yielding. She compared Fran's kiss to Jack's: not the awkward, tight lipped fumbling last night, but the deep, yearning urgency of that first time in his workshop. What was happening to her? How could she feel like this? This is all because of what Sasha told me, she thought. I'm not. I've never. Women often kiss one another, it doesn't mean a thing. Mwah, mwah, affection only, or thanks for something... for cooking the dinner.

"I've done the washing up, Jane. Would you like some coffee?"

"If you're making some..."

"I'll have a cup with you. Just a quick one. Before bed."

Outside, it was raining. Sasha huddled under the little porch. Parents fighting, splitting? Probably. Why? Not funny. Why can't they bloody grow up? Because... she'd been over it all before. What a family. First Jack, now Fran. Bursting in on them, breaking up the fragile truce which seemed to be all Mum and Dad could manage by way of a *modus vivendi*. Fran. Have to admit it, she's cute. Have to admit to feeling more than a little guilty, here. Jess would be jealous. Not without reason.

It occurred to Sasha that she'd been incredibly lucky, not just to find Jess, but for their relationship to be unthreatened by the desire for anyone outside it- if you didn't count the ridiculous Jason, who stood about as much chance of getting into Jess's knickers as Neil did of getting into hers. Poor Neil. But now, she had to admit, she was tempted. An unpleasant sensation, lust mixed with guilt. This must be what it's like all the time for people who play around... how can they bear it? And yet she'd been keen enough for Mum to get off with Jack- even encouraged her. If it was all over with Dad, why not? But how did that leave him feeling?

And then...

And then she let herself think the thought she'd been repressing all through supper, the awful possibility that she was in competition with her Mum for Fran... She hated herself for thinking that, didn't want to dwell on it, it hurt... If Mum wanted to come out, well and good, but... Sash forced herself to see things in perspective. To recall all that she'd had with Jess, all the *love*... was she going to chuck all that away for the sake of a quick tumble with this pretty little stranger?

Of course not! She opened the door and went in quickly.

"Hi."

Ah. Another one of those *awkward* silences. Well, excuse *me*.

Sash goes upstairs.

5

"Goodnight, then, Fran. It's been so interesting talking to you. What an amazing story."

"I can hardly believe it myself. I think it's going to take me a while to get used to the real world again. It's so kind of you to let me stay. I do appreciate it..."

The coffee cups, upside down on the drainer, drain. A tap drips. The fridge hums. Their conversation has finally wound down, and Jane and Fran stand very close together by the sink. A real kitchen sink drama, this, thinks Jane, watching the dripping tap, and smiles. She looks up at Fran, who smiles back radiantly, so that Jane gets the full voltage right between the eyes, and gasps.

"What is it, Jane?"

"Nothing, sorry. Goodnight."

"Goodnight."

But neither of them moves. This would be the moment for a goodnight kiss, but Jane fears it would become so much more than that, and she's not ready... even if she's not deceiving herself... the moment passes, and she looks away. Fran opens and closes her hand in a little half wave of farewell, and is gone.

Jane leans back on the sink, sighs out all the breath in her body, rubs her face.

"Jane?"

My God, she's back.

"Jane, this is really stupid, but... I don't know where I'm going?"

None of us knows that, thought Jane, remembering what Sasha had said before. Then she realised what Fran meant, that she didn't know where she was supposed to sleep, and was seized by the very real possibility of saying, come on, we'll go in Jack's room, that is, the spare room, we don't want to disturb Peter I mean I don't sleep with him any more anyway... we could go in the spare room together... Her heart beat so hard she was sure Fran would hear it.

"I'm sorry. Of course. How silly!"

It was pitch black on the landing upstairs. No moon tonight. Jane went up and found the switch, then Fran switched off downstairs. A little conspiracy of going to bed behaviour.

"This way," whispered Jane, not wanting to wake anyone, but also because it felt good. "The bathroom's at the end. This is the spare room." Not *your* room: let's leave open the possibility of it being *our* room, shall we? Certainly not Jack's any more.

"Thanks, Jane," whispered Fran. And she paused on the threshold. "Goodnight."

This would be the time to kiss her. If. But no, Because what if.

"Goodnight, Fran." Not yet.

After Fran had shut her out (though why see it like that?) Jane crept to the girls' room. Door slightly ajar. Listen for the regular breathing. When they were little she'd listen for hours. Literally. When Sasha was Alice's age. She used to sit outside their room, just like this, the door ajar, listening, guarding, rejoicing in them. Her children. Now there's a pretty damn heterosexual thought, thought Jane, and found herself wandering downstairs again, away from the too too much of it all. Fourth one creaks? Yes. On the bottom step she waits: not a sound from any of them. She goes on into the room, switches the light back on. Why is she wandering around like this? Because she can't face him. Getting into bed with him. What if he tries to have sex with her- forces her? Rape within marriage, it happens. Like that time when... Horrid.

She goes through into the kitchen. This is ridiculous. Can't wander around all night. Get a drink- Dutch courage. Well, why the hell not. If Sasha hasn't drunk it all. There was some Scotch- ah, but that got spilled all over the place. Right mess that was. The spirit did wonders for the tabletop, though. Into the other room, the grotty little room we call the study. Not that it's seen much study lately. Dark. Dark, where's the light... ouch! Bloody coffee table or something, careful, break my fucking neck. Here's the pole of the standard lamp. Click. Let there be light. Ah. Brandy. Brilliant. Oh, not much left. Sasha! Might as well swig it anyway. Ooch! It burns. Good, though. Feel I'm taking charge of myself, by an odd paradox. 'Cos I'm really losing control, aren't I? Finish it. There. Now what? Those bottles still in the cupboard? There used to be all sorts. What's this? Oh, God, those foul liqueurs Tim brought back from Israel. And this? Port. Unopened! There's a stroke of luck. Pop! Now, one of these funny old glasses with the curly stems- antiques, Mummy said they were, always hid them away here in case the girls broke them, *shit*! Oh, what the hell, soft shoe shuffle it away under the sofa, get another one out, careful this time though, glug, glug. Good colour. Tawny, it says here. Ah. That's nice and sweet after the brandy. Look, Jane, you are a grown woman, you can do what the hell you like. You're yawny on holy holiday, for Christ's sake. The family? All in bed. Asleep. Yawny tawny. Yes, more. Goes down bloody quick. So. Now I've got a bit of time to myself. What's this. Samuel Beckett. Must be one of Sasha's. Where now? Who now? When now? Unquestioning. I, say I. Unbelieving. Questions, hypotheses, call them that. Keep going, going on, call that going, call that on. .. Uh?

What's on the telly. God! Where's the mute. Wake the dead, never mind them upstairs. Better. Better silent, like Charlie Chaplain and the Keystone Cops and... the rest. Flick through the channels. Flick... God! Look at that. Flick... flick... flick...

Little Alice woke to bright sunlight streaming through a gap in the curtains. She sat up and saw Sasha sprawled snoring on the other bed, and wondered not for the first time why her big sister so often went to bed without any clothes on at all. Breakfast, thought Alice, and went downstairs. Nobody about. Why do grownups sleep so much, she wondered. About to go into the kitchen, she noticed the study door was ajar.

Telly's on…

Mummy! Mummy?

Little Alice opened her mouth as wide as it would go and… but no. She'd got into trouble for screaming the place down yesterday morning. Very gently, she put her hands on Mummy's shoulders and started to shake her awake…

VI

1

Reluctantly, Jack's waking mind began to assemble itself out of the fragments of a dream: he'd fled, under the stars, he'd run away, hadn't he... the cards... awful things had happened with the star girl, with Jane... it was no dream it was real his cock in her hand his hand on his erection now. Now. Masturbation? Maybe. He was just beginning to explore this possibility when he realised that he was not alone.

Cathy was sitting on the end of his bed, watching him.

"*Bore da*, Jack."

"Good morning," he said, letting go and struggling upright, bending his knees under the blanket to try and hide the, must be obvious, er... "Don't you have any shirts of your own?"

"Hm, yes, it's one of Bryn's again. I just took the first thing I could find. What did you dream of?"

"What did I..."

"Say quickly before it goes."

Jack sat up, his dream flooding back into his awareness. Funny how you remember if someone asks you as soon as...

"The Star. I was working with the tarot... the Star card: a beautiful naked girl dancing in the night sky... it was like..."

"Go on, say it."

"Like when I did the reading for Jane. But in the dream she was doing it for me. Pointing to the Star."

"Your guiding star."

"I don't know. Why are you…?"

"Why am I here?" She slid along the bed till she was sitting right by him, and he became aware of her long naked legs. His erection throbbed. "I've been making sure that I didn't want to make love to you."

Jack thought about this.

"Where's Bryn?" he asked.

"In the workshop. It's his idea. He said I ought to come and check." She put her palms gently on his bare chest, covering the nipples, and leaned in to him till their foreheads touched: for a moment as he breathed her scent he had a clear image of a moment from their previous life together. Early morning. She was getting ready for school, stumbling around the bedroom, almost in tears, trying to find clothes which would make her feel she could cope with the day, while he lay in bed and watched her with something like amusement, something like pity… now he felt something like shame. She pushed herself away from him, stood up.

"I pass the test," she said, and laughed. Jack looked at her and realised that this was not the same Cathy. God, how she'd changed. Incredible. And she was with Bryn now, wholly his as he was hers: that was clear. Jack wasn't a part of her any more. He also realised his erection had subsided.

"So do I," he muttered, "I think."

"Here, this is for you." She took a folded piece of paper from her shirt pocket, chucked it down on the bed. "See you later."

The door clicked shut behind her. Jack swung his feet onto the floor, sat with elbows on knees. The dream came back to him again, but fading, quickly losing its fascination, its significance. Jane, pointing at a card. Jane? He looked between his legs at his limp cock. Which she had had in her hand. Which Sasha had gawped at in a drunken fury, had she? Did all that really happen? They were all pretty drunk. No, it happened. It was all wrong, farcical: what had he been thinking? Bryn was right. It was the same old story: too much baggage. And more to the point, too much hurry. Why hadn't he just left Jane to grow towards him in her own way? He couldn't wait. He'd just wanted to fuck her. Fuck her hard and then fuck off. Jane was never going to be a long term project. Was that the brutal truth? Suppose they had ended up in bed together, joyfully shagging the week away. What about the next week, and the next? Would she have left Peter, come to live with him in his little hovel by the studio? He tried to picture her getting out of his grubby bed in the morning, getting breakfast in the greasy chaos of his tiny kitchen... and did he want to deal with bloody cynical Sasha the teasing temptress, clever minx, and little Alice growing up too, did he want them on his hands for the rest of his life? Stepchildren, in effect, the responsibility of it all, you're not just taking on the woman alone, it's her whole life. Which includes all her guilt and shame and remorse and. And she is getting on a bit. Forty if she's a day. Damn sight older than me. Too old for me. But I did want her. So much.

Jack folded his arms tight, shook his head, hating himself. The cruelty.

The damage he'd done! What must she be thinking now? And what are they doing now anyway, still presumably stuck in the cottage, miles from anywhere, till Peter comes for them on Saturday. Peter. More guilt. Well, he doesn't know... unless she tells him. But why should she do that? Nothing to gain... just another nail in the coffin of their wretched pointless marriage. Should he go back? Just to see... to apologise? Imagine it... what could he possibly say? No. Better never to see any of them again.

But he had wanted her. So much. Should he...?

Go and check. Bryn's idea. Make sure that he didn't want to make love to her any more. Become free of her, as Cathy had made herself free of him... Could he go to the cottage, talk to her? Or creep in somehow tonight, sit on the end of her bed till she woke, see if... ridiculous fantasy. It's over. It was never really on.

And yet... would he pass the test?

Jack got off the bed, started looking for his clothes. Then he noticed the paper Cathy had dropped on the bed. Bryn's writing... The old bugger. A bloody shopping list.

2

Unbuttoning Bryn's old shirt and shrugging it off as she went through the back door, Cathy entered the little garden behind the cottage, stepping naked onto the grass. She faced east, and raised her arms, breathing in deeply, held the pose for a moment, then exhaled slowly, at the same time lowering her arms to her sides and closing her eyes. There she stood, opening herself to the four elements of the world, waiting for the eastern arch to arise in her imagination; and in due course it appeared to her, with beyond it, sweet birdsong and morning dew on scented flowers of springtime, and the stern piercing eyes of Raphael. "Hardd," he said, and she replied, "Raphael." Turning to the south, she acknowledged the silently blazing countenance of Michael. "*Ah, Michael*," she said, "*mae y neidr distaw yn awr*;" the serpent being dumb now: yes, there it lay, real, but no threat. And she turned easily from that high summer heat to the autumnal coolness of the west, and Gabriel's calm regard. Oh the peace, she thought, how lovely to stay by this gently flowing stream, with its serene guardian, old as the hills but ever vital, refreshing her, letting her be herself... "Dominus tecum," she heard him saying, "gratia plena," and wondered at his words, but then, "Ah," she said, "Were you not he that came to the maid Mary and blessed her beyond all measure?" What a dim and distant memory was called up there, she thought, she was no more than a maid herself when she was taught that salutation, and then, oh, what if? What if? A child? Bryn's child and hers? What if? Full of wonder now, and a little dread, she turned to the last arch, the unknown, the wintry north of earth and night. Oh, how dark it was, a landscape utterly empty and cold... nothing stirred, nothing. On her back she felt Michael's hot breath, urging her on, but did not want to be pushed into that gaping emptiness, and she staggered, throwing out her arms to either side, seeking balance: "Raphael! Gabriel!" she cried, "Hold me!" and at once she felt their arms about her, strong but very tender. "Stand fast," said the voice of Gabriel, "Feel the earth under your feet- feel how it founds you and grounds you and bears you on its broad back, ah, *Cariad*, you are rooted in the good earth and grow to the heaven of the angels..." Cathy came back into her body long enough to feel her toes dig into the grass, her feet firm once more, and then let her imagination take her again, more strongly than ever, as the domain of Uriel of earth lit up for her: lit up, yes, but it was lit with the light of a cold crescent moon; and it shone through silver clouds onto tall, still pine trees glittering with frost. "Uriel," she gasped, for she was in awe of this vision, "Where are you?" And what had appeared to her a dark mound of earth in the corner of her eye began to shift, with the faintest rustling as of branches of frosty leaves stirring, and the face of the fourth archangel appeared to her at last: for a long time he held her in his gaze, and she gazed back into his huge eyes, eyes jet black and shining silver, glossy blackness gleaming on deeper blackness until Cathy could see her own face reflected there, tiny, distorted, but recognised- a living part of the earth itself... At last Uriel spoke, one word only: "*Hardd!*"

At this, she let the vision fade, listened to the birdsong in the garden, felt the breeze ruffle her hair. The grass under her feet felt so good; and she clenched her toes in it for sheer delight. She spread her hands on her belly, dug the fingers in- what if? She lifted her hands to her breasts, cupped them, circled her palms on her nipples till they became erect, cried aloud for joy and flung her arms high. Only then did she open her eyes, and realised that she was not alone.

Bryn was sitting cross-legged on the grass, watching her.

"*Shw mae*, Cathy?"

She laughed with delight, and ran to him, pulled him to his feet.

"It was you, wasn't it?" she smiled, tearing his shirt off him, "Holding me up?"

"Just for moment…"

"Oh, I needed you just then." She was busy with his belt: when it was unclasped she seized it, pulled it out of the loops, and flung it across the lawn where it lay like a dead snake.

When he was as naked as she was, she lay on her back on the good earth and opened herself to him utterly, drew him down to her there on the earth under the sun in the wind and the rain too when that started a few minutes later. Neither of them even noticed.

3

Jack heaved the last bulging plastic bag into his car and slammed the hatchback. Bloody supermarkets. Something tells me you're here for a reason, Bryn had said last night. Very funny. Jack hadn't supposed it was to do the fucking shopping. Ah well. Now what? Take this stuff back, of course- but then? Jane?

He didn't know what to do. He folded his arms, leaned back on the side of the car, looked around the carpark grimly. Ordinary people came and went, getting on with their lives. While he… He almost saw himself going back into the store, asking to see the manager: got any jobs going? Better off stacking shelves in a supermarket in Brecon than trying to make a living as an artist in Oxfordshire. The rent he was paying on that place! What had he been thinking? Impossible to keep going. Give it up. Or try again here. Cheaper here, isn't it? Could find out. Why Oxfordshire anyway? Just because he grew up there. Got the contacts, a few friends. And his stuck-up bloody snooty sister and her precious husband. Mum and Dad…

Jack, desperate, even let his imagination tiptoe around the edge of the thought of throwing himself on their mercy. Swallow his pride. Yes yes yes, I'm sorry, you were right and I was wrong, I should have gone into business like you, Dad. I'm giving up all that arty smarty nonsense. Put in a word for me at The Firm, would you? In the meantime, any chance of a small loan…? No. Well you could always teach, his Mum had said that time, when they'd had the big row, teaching would be all right wouldn't it, Stewart? Jack could be a teacher? A *teacher*? Dad hadn't been able to put enough contempt into his refusal even to *entertain* the idea of his son being a, a…. A teacher, Monica, he had pronounced decisively, is a man among boys, and a boy among men. No, Father, you're wrong for once: a teacher is a poor little Welsh girl called Cathy Pritchard who cries her eyes out every Sunday night because she can't bear the thought of it all starting again in the morning…

He'd only seen them a couple of times since he dropped out of college. No. Can't go crawling back now, like walking into some kind of parable it'd be: forgive me, white-collared Father, for I have sinned by working with my hands. The parable of the practical son. If it hadn't been for Bryn… and being able to rent that place. It'd seemed cheap at the time. But the cost of tools, materials. Bit of advertising. Keeping the bloody car on the road. How much had he made this year? Not enough to break even. Try doing a bit of furniture too, like Bryn. But that takes time, the quality timber you need costs a fortune and anyway- new skills to learn, new tools to buy… the cost, the cost.

Right. I said I'd have a week off, so that's what I'll do. I am *not* going to worry about anything *now*. I shall just *be* in the present moment: go through the motions, wait to see what happens. What will be will be. Who said that? One of Bryn's, was it? He let his head fall back: the sky was overcast, changeable. He felt a spot of rain. Up there somewhere, his guiding star. He wondered if he could stand here all day, till it was dark, waiting for a star to shine, to show him the way… he remembered his dream again, and the astonishingly renewed Cathy sitting, watching over him. Enough of this. He shook himself and opened the car door, glanced up at the sky one more time. Right.

Right, then. He got in and drove off. Simple as that. That's it- just keep going. Watch it happen. Here we go. Not a bad little town this, he thought, rubbernecking as he nosed through the midmorning traffic: I could do worse. Find a place, not far from Bryn, stack shelves… The one-way system led him down a narrow street, winding, tall grey buildings looming on either side. Pub on the right: get pissed, forget it all. Cinema the other side: forget it all in a flickering fantasy. Too much of that. No more fantasy. Time to get real. He has to slow right down for the corner where the hiking shop is... Oh, Jesus!

Look at *her*! doing a kind of crazy clog dance in her big boots on the pavement in front of the huge mirroring windows, she sees him gawping at her, stops and guffaws self-consciously, pushes her hair out of her face, smiles the widest, happiest smile he's ever seen, gives him a funny little half wave, just opening and closing her hand. Then the shop door opens behind her and Jane comes out and he's round the corner and before he's had time to think about it he's run the car into the parking bay *which just happened to be free*- what the fuck is going on, you can never get parked here... Jack switches the engine off. *Was that Jane*? or am I seeing things...

Jack freezes, his fingers on the door handle. Go and check. Bryn's idea. Make sure that he didn't want to make love to her any more. Become free of her, as Cathy had made herself free of him... Would he pass the test? He thumbs his seat belt clip, shrugs it off.

Or, just don't be so bloody stupid. Drive off, quick, before... His eyes flick up to the rear view mirror. Nothing. His hand moves to the ignition key. *Turn it*! Go! No... he looks back at the mirror. Nothing- wait! *There*! Jane and the dancing girl- walking together. Towards him. His stomach churns: he's amazed at the force of his reaction, for a moment he thinks he's going to be sick... They are getting closer, the girl talking animatedly to Jane, who looks a bit grim, Jack thinks, his fingers feeling for the door handle again as he watches them...

Shit! There's Sasha and Alice coming round the corner behind them and *fuck*! Peter as well- what's he doing here... no way does he want to confront the whole bloody lot of them... Jack shrinks down in the seat, chin on chest, covers his face with his left hand as if massaging a fevered brow... this would be funny if it wasn't so fucked up, he thinks, as Jane and the girl go past, then Sasha and Alice...

Little Alice, who stops in her tracks, turns round with an expression of theatrical puzzlement and then loud enough for the whole bloody town to hear demands to know if that isn't Jack's car, and isn't that Jack in it?

Sasha flounces back to the car, flings wide the passenger door, and peers inside.

"It is indeed, little Sis," she says. "It is Jack. In a box." And she raps smartly twice on the roof. "Where have you sprung up from, then?"

Jack pulls the handle, leans on the door so that it flies open into the path of a passing cyclist, hears *fuckin' wanker* as he clambers out not without difficulty but at least he's holding on to his breakfast, somehow manages the long hike uphill round the back of his car and onto the pavement at last where Peter is standing looking as if he's got a big speech but has forgotten the first line... Jack thrusts out a hand, and Peter stares at it like he's never seen one before, takes it at last: saved by social convention!

"Peter," croaks Jack.

"Jack." Croaking back. Like a bloody college of crows. "Jane said that you had had...had had... that something came up."

"Yes. That's right." So that's what she told him. Useful to know that. He glanced at Sasha. She caught his eye, *Mum doesn't know*, slammed the car door shut and leaned back on it, taking out her fags.

"Mummy was ever so upset when you went," Alice informed Jack helpfully.

"Good old Ali," mumbled Sash, lighting up.

"Yes it was a great shame," Jack said quickly, "It really was. I felt pretty awful myself having to leave you all on your own. But it's obviously all worked out, Alice, because your daddy's here, eh? Did the, er... retreat finish early then, Peter?"

"No."

"Oh."

"Jack!"

"Hello, Jane."

"Hello again," said Fran. Sensation.

"Do you two... *know each other*?" Jane just could not...

"Oh yes," said Jack. Her eyes are stunning, he realises, a brilliant laughing cornflower blue. "We've known each other for, ooh, let me think, must be all of... two minutes!" Jane saw the expression on his face, hated him for it.

"I was doing a little dance in my lovely new clumpyboots." Fran demonstrated. "And *Jack*, is it? how do you do, by the way, Jack, I'm Fran, Jack was just going past in his car and I must've looked a bit funny because he only just made it round the corner." She smiled radiantly at Jack, the full voltage, right between the eyes. He gasped, gurgled rather, tried to make it sound like, well anything coherent... Then, thank God, Alice came to the rescue.

She had been trying a little clumpy dance of her own. "I've got clumpyboots too," she said, "but they're not new. We had to get Fran boots because she hadn't got any. So she could come with us for some Vigorous Exercise in the Hills. Are you coming with us for some vigorous exercise in the hills, Jack?"

Jack thrust his hands in his pockets, head down, toeing away an imaginary pebble. "I don't know, Alice." He did a little knees bend, shrugged a sort of gesture in the direction of exercise... "Could use some exercise, I guess." He glanced up: Fran was still grinning at him.

Jane looked miserably at her, at Jack, back at her. Hated him. And as for her...

"So where did you get to, then?" Peter wanted to know. The interview wasn't over yet, it seemed.

"An old friend- Bryn his name is- he's got a workshop near here. An urgent job, he needed a hand. Lifting some heavy furniture he'd made... into this van he'd hired. Delivery. Couldn't let him down. Old friend." He looked at Jane, who pulled one side of her mouth into a tight-lipped half smile. Bloody awful liar, her eyes said, and then she crouched at Alice's feet, muttering something about bootlaces. Sasha, he noticed, had turned her back on all this and was standing fag in mouth, elbows on top of the car, gazing across the street.

One of those awkward silences started to develop.

"Yes. He's good friend, is Bryn. So. Walking in the Beacons, eh?"

Peter seemed reluctant to admit this, despite what Alice had said, though the cags, rucksacks, boots and trousers tucked into big socks did rather suggest...

"We were going to fan her," he said doubtfully. This meant nothing to Jack.

"Sorry?"

"Oh God." Sasha, sliding herself round to face them again. "You mean *van hear*," she said to Peter, and added, aside to Jack, "Sounds a bit like *furniture van hire*, doesn't it, eh?"

"Oh, Fan Hir," said Jack, ignoring her. Been there before?"

"No."

"I've been up there a few times. It's a brilliant walk. You can see for miles from the top. All the way to the sea. Might not be so clear today, though..."

"If you know the way you could be our native guide," said Alice. "Except you're not really a native, are you."

"Er... no."

"Where're you from, Jack?" Fran wants to know.

"Oxford."

"Never! Me too!"

"Really?"

"Look, sorry, but I think we really ought to make a move…" Peter wished he'd taken her back to bloody Oxford like he'd intended. Then this… wouldn't have taken place.

"Yes, let's go." Alice, now securely laced, was impatient too. "Coming, Jack?"

"Well, I suppose that was the original plan." Go and check. Bryn's idea.

"Yes it was," admitted Peter grudgingly. "Before this other thing came up."

Jane, straightening up after bootlace duty, caught his eye. *Other thing, Peter? You mean… yes, you do, don't you. But it's over with him now. At least, I think it is. Think I hate him…* She watches Jack, trying to decide.

"I wouldn't mind coming with you, see Fan Hir again," he says, attempting to sound casual, not really succeeding. *Need to be sure, though, won't be happy till I've checked.* "That is, if you don't mind, Peter." *After all, I was trying to shag your wife last night and it'd be understandable if you were a bit pissed off with me…*

"No, of course not, why should I…" *perhaps because I've got a pretty good idea about you wanting to shag my wife, that's why. And she could have.* "All right Jane?"

"Of course." *Not. It was all a horrible mistake and I hate him and never wanted to see him again. Though now he's here, oh God, am I really finished with him? Find out.*

"Of course," she says again, trying for a smile this time. "It'll be… fine,"

So Peter awkwardly shrugs the great burden off his back, fumbles with toggles and zips awhile and eventually finds his Tourist's Guide to the Beacons and the cartographically challenged women have to kick their clumpily booted heels during the inevitable male ritual of demonstrating navigational competence, the girls just don't have the spatial awareness, do they, ha ha: are Peter and Jack even *bonding* here on some level? Take the A40, yes; go on through Sennybridge, got it; turn left at the pub in Trecastle, right; no I said left, ha ha ha; then it's about another five or six miles, you know, there's a lay-by. View of the hill on the right. Not sure? Follow me if you like, Peter, where's your car? Oh, I see, right. See you there, then. At last Peter resumes his burden, sets off down the street with Jane and Alice in tow.

"Bags I go in Jack's car," Sasha calls after them, chucking her fag end in the gutter. "No sense in us all squashing in the back of yours, is there, Dad?" And, she thinks, I want to have a word with you, Jack. "Fran had better come with me too. I'll need a chaperone."

Fran grins hugely at this, knowing what she knows… Sash gives her a wink, opens the door for her, shuts her in. Then she has Jack by the arm before he can get off the pavement and pushes her face up close to his.

"What sort of furniture was it, Jack? Stripped pine? A Welsh undresser? No, I know- Chippendales, *geddit*? Don't you dare breath a single fucking word to my father or mother about anything that happened on Monday night or I *will* have your balls…"

She lets him go, opens the back door, and gets in behind Fran.

4

"There's not much for lunch." Cathy, back in Bryn's shirt, squats in front of the fridge.

"There won't be till Jack gets back with the shopping." Bryn, still naked and dripping wet from the shower, is vigorously towelling his balls. "What's the matter, you hungry?"

"Starving."

"Not eating for two, are you?"

Cathy freezes, a lump of stale cheese halfway to her mouth. She stands up, turns to him. There is no way.

"There is no way," she says slowly, "you could have known what Gabriel said."

"Ave, gratia plena, Dominus tecum, wasn't it? Everybody knows what Gabriel said. Then he goes on to inform her about how she was benedicta in mulieribus and what is it concipies in utero, yes. Funny how the bible always comes to me in Latin these days, despite having had it bashed into me in Welsh when I was a boy." He chucked the towel away and walked over to her, embraced her gently, whispered into her ear. "Are you, then? Pregnant?"

"What would you say if I was?"

"Benedíctus fructus ventris tui."

"What's that mean?"

"It means shitty nappies all over the place for a couple of years."

They looked seriously into one another's eyes for a moment, then he relaxed, laughed, and so did she. She bit off half the cheese, pushed the rest of it between his lips, kissed them, still chewing.

"Mmph! What's this I'm choking on?"

"Lunch."

"Lunch? Sod this for lunch. Where the hell's Jack got to?"

"Perhaps he's gone to see his clergywife."

"Why would he do that?"

"To make sure. To go and check, remember?"

"Ah. Well, maybe that's what he's done. I'd better go and get some clothes on." Bryn picked up the towel, hesitated. "And you, Cathy? Did you go and check?"

"Yes." She smiled, but was troubled still, though she knew now it really was all over with Jack. "Back then, I thought I was in love with him. Now, I don't think there was ever anything there. Not compared to what we've got, Bryn. It was just fucking..." She shook her head.

"Fucking what?"

"Fucking nothing. Just fucking."

"Oh I see. Just fucking."

"It was good. Sometimes."

"Fucking is good."

"I have to admit that it was. With him, I mean. But it was just a comfort, or a consolation prize. Compensation for having such a shit life, you know?"

Bryn knew. This was a game they'd played over and over when she'd first come to him. It had helped her to get some purchase on who she was: working out with him who she had been. His role was to listen, his face mirroring her emotions, giving her time. But it was different now: there was no pain in the telling, it was just an anecdote. Even funny.

"Sex was just another thing to do. What shall we do tonight? Have a takeaway, watch TV, have a shag? We'd try and do all three at once sometimes, and I'd be so tired I'd fall asleep on the sofa and I'd wake up to find him still fumbling around trying to get my bra off. And then he'd get upset because all I wanted to do was go to bed and have a sleep..." She stood for a moment, eyes unfocussed, seeing again the horrid little bedsit, and him, pacing like a caged animal, frustrated, wanting something neither of them knew how to give...

"Cathy..."

"It's all right. I'm fine. Now that I've heard myself saying that, I'm fine. It's so different now, there's no comparison."

Bryn kissed her, and they searched one another's faces. For what? This was indeed so very different from anything either of them had known before. The words *Rwy'n dy garu* seemed to form on the edge of utterance, but *I love you* was not, they knew, quite what they were trying to say: it included that, but there was more, and they wanted it all. Wanted it to be complete. It would become clear in time. They could wait.

Bryn kissed her again, went upstairs. Cathy turned to the window, and looked out at the garden, now in bright sunshine again. If she had a baby... she hitched Bryn's shirt up, put her hands on her belly, as she had done before. Tried to imagine, what if, life stirring in me, in me. To be a mother. Gratia plena. And Bryn's... what? Wife? They'd never talked about that. Just been together. Lived in the moment. No thought for the future. But you couldn't go on like that with a child, could you? A child *is* the future... the mewling puking screaming future...

I must get one of those testing kits next time I'm in Brecon...

5

In the bedroom, Bryn sat at the table where his laptop was, clicked on the e-mails, and watched the usual invitations to penis enlargement pop into the window. He looked down, took it in his hand. No need for that, boyo. It was stirring again as he remembered kissing her in the kitchen just now, and what they'd done on the lawn earlier. Lucky boy, Bryn. Ding dong, went the laptop, you have male, mail. All junk? Oh, what's this. Not junk. Julian. *Cartomancer* still doing well, how's the sequel coming on? Bloody hell, the sequel. Bryn sighed. Glumly he opened a file called *Cart2* and read:

> The thunderstorm was over, but the evening was chill, and the western sky blood red as the sun sank behind threatening clouds: more bad weather was on the way. Derryn climbed down stiffly from his mare, and tied the reins to a passing tree. His riding boots crunched and splashed on the puddled gravel path that led up to the once familiar oak door. Had it really been a year? He knocked, and the sound echoed strangely inside the ancient house. After a while, he

heard footsteps approaching. The door creaked slowly open.

"Derryn!" Elisa stood open mouthed as Derryn brushed past her into the

He couldn't, he just couldn't bring himself to do any more. He didn't care what happened to bloody Derryn, he was sick and tired of Elisa or Elise it had been originally hadn't it? Does it matter? It had just been an exercise originally, a bit of a joke, see if he could hitch a ride on the vampire bandwagon. But somehow one chapter had led to another, and then Julian had seen it when they were trying to sort out the film rights for *Abraham* and insisted on giving it a whirl. And his agently instinct as he called it had been right: the little girls lapped it up, apparently. But he didn't want to write another, he'd go mad… mind you, the cash had been helpful. He couldn't complain. Most people trying to make a go of writing would be bloody grateful. Bryn stared dismally at the paragraph on the laptop. He couldn't, he just couldn't do any more. Hang on- *a passing tree*?

"You writing this afternoon, then?"

He hadn't noticed Cathy come in. She put her hands on his shoulders, kissed the top of his head where he was going bald.

"I don't know."

"More *Cartomancer*? The little girls I used to teach would have enjoyed that, the older ones, I mean. The titillation of approaching sexuality, all dark and dangerous."

"Hm. I might go down to the workshop and finish those bookshelves for Mrs Griffiths."

"They used to love reading about mysterious manly men and swooning maidens with firm nipples and opulent breasts. Before they'd got any themselves of course. Soon as they had, they stopped reading about them and started charging the boys a quid a feel in the shrubbery at lunchtime."

"Never in the world."

"Caught 'em at it." Cathy dropped Bryn's shirt on the bed and started fitting her own opulent breasts into a bra. He watched her broad shoulder blades moving under her lovely smooth skin as she reached behind her back to fasten it. God, he didn't want to have her again already, did he? He looked down. Penis enlargement, forsooth. "Bryn."

"Mm?"

She stepped into some panties, pulled them up, left her fingers lingering near her belly. She looked at him through the curtain of hair which had fallen over her face, and went to him where he sat smiling up at her.

"Bryn." She flicked her hair back over her shoulders, took his head gently in her hands and drew it towards herself, as it were towards her womb.

"I know," he said quietly, and tickled with his tongue her soft navel, so that she giggled. "I know. I understand." He ran his hands up her thighs, gave her buttocks a squeeze. Then he stood up, brushed a playful finger from her throat to the tip of her chin, and kissed her on the lips...

"I'm afraid this won't do," he said, breaking off, sighing, and picking up a pair of pants. "Mrs Griffiths wants her shelves."

"What about *Carry on Cartomancer*?" asked Cathy from inside a T-shirt.

"What about it?" Must have some trousers somewhere. Ah.

"The little pre-pubescents want their dose of Derryn and his big manly whatever." Pair of jeans? Ah. "You're not going to wear that shirt, are you?"

"Can't be bothered with bloody Derryn. Yes I am. It smells of you."

"Oh, Bryn."

"I'm going down to the workshop," he says, sitting down to slip some shoes onto his bare feet. "Mrs Griffiths..."

"...wants her shelves. I know"

He gets up, goes to the door but doesn't want to leave her yet. He lingers in the doorway, watching her as she stands in front of the mirror brushing her hair.

After a moment he says, "We'd better get one of those testing kits, eh?"

She turns, still brushing, laughing.

"We'll have to go fetch it ourselves."

"What do you mean?"

"I mean, it would be a bit tactless to add it to Jack's next shopping list."

VII

1

Then said young Country Wiseman, pointing with his finger over a very wide field, "Do you see yonder gap in the skyline, where it seems to dip down a bit?" And Pilgrim, peering through his spectacles said no at first but then actually yes I think I do after all. "That's Bwlch Giedd," said his young companion. "From there you can go either way, onto Fan Hir or Fan Brycheiniog. There are circular walks, but it's quite a long way. Maybe we could just have a look at the view from the top, and then come down the same way. Or indeed just stay down by the lake if people are tired when they get there. Llyn Fawr, big lake that means. It's very pretty."

Jack turned to Fran when he said very pretty, and repeated it softly, so the others couldn't hear, looking into her cornflower blue eyes, very pretty indeed.

Fran, who was not the sort of young woman who is given to blushing prettily and turning away covering her smile with her hand nevertheless covered her smile with her hand and turning away blushing prettily thrust the other through Jane's arm, squeezed up close and You all right, then, she whispered.

I'm fine, said Jane. What you thinking. Things you said last night. What. About when you were at Oxford. Before you. Made me think about when I was. With Peter. And look.

What?

Minibus.

White, longwheelbase, having disgorged a dozen or so red cagged apparent schoolchildren and their minders now fording splashily a transit of the stream below the carpark, a Ford Transit van, here. By Fan Hir, just fancy. And splashed on the side, Oxfordshire County Council. If found, please return to.
What about minibus?
Minibus from Oxford.
Oh. Co-incidence.
Mm.
Then said young Country Wiseman, "All set, then?" and Pilgrim, having made some small adjustments to the webbing whereby his weighty burden was secured upon his back, answered him with a main voice, Yea. Let us go forth. In the name of the Lord, Amen, for he found that he was indeed in remarkable good spirits now, such that Country Wiseman wondered greatly at him and he at himself also. Must be the fresh air. And he encouraged the females in their company in like wise also, they being weaker vessels unused to such manly marching that he might bring them abroad saying unto them, Escape for thy life; look not behind thee, neither stay thou in all the plain; escape to the mountain, lest thou be consumed.
"What are you talking about, Daddy?"
"Don't know, Alice! It just came into my head. It's in Pilgrim's Progress: John Bunyan, you should read it, I was glancing through it on Sunday afternoon while you were reading your, er, on the lawn.... But Bunyan's quoting... It's somewhere near the beginning and he's quoting..." Oh. Peter pauses. Now I know why it came into my head. Funny how the mind works. He turns, lest he be consumed, looks towards the mountain.
"Quoting what, Daddy?"
"It doesn't matter. I can't remember. Lot's... I mean, Let's... go!"
"Do you know what Daddy's on about, Sasha?" asked Alice as they started to pick their paths through the tussocky turf towards the stream, stone strewn bemerded by apparently German speaking sheep it seemed to Sasha, sheep who said *mehr...*
"Sasha?"
"You really expect me to explain our father to you?" Our Father. *Paternoster.* "Which art in Heaven."
"What?"
"Hello!"
"Sasha..."

"D'Bee thy name."
"'S not fair."
"Ewh. You said snot."
"Sasha!"
"What? Rhymes with snot."
"It *is, not* fair."
"Life isn't. Nobody ever said that it was."
"Every time I ask you a serious question, Sasha, you say something I don't understand, or you tickle me and throw me on the floor. I'll save you the trouble this time." And she plucked at her armpits apelike going ow ow ow before throwing herself into the long grass by the stream. After playing dead for a second or two she sat up and sadly watched Jack and their father splashing manly deep striding through get your boots wet through the stream while shrinking on the brink hand in hand on rocking clunky stepping stones teetering Fran and their mother trying to balance...
Sasha, still laughing at Alice's antics watched Alice watching and loved her. Realised how much she loved her. This was a new feeling, wasn't it? She strolled up to her, and then knelt down so their faces were close, put an arm round her.
"I think Daddy was saying some words from the Bible which are quoted, copied, that is, referred to, you know? in a book by John Bunyan called *Pilgrim's Progress*."
Sasha watches Alice's brows contract, the little frown lines come, her lips rounding, beginning to form who, what, why...
"I'm not sure, because I've only skimmed it- have to admit it didn't grip- but I think at the beginning the main character, Pilgrim, is comparing himself to Lot..."
"Lots of what?"
"No, that was his name, Lot. He's a character in the Bible who had to try to persuade his wife and... two daughters... ah. To go on a journey."
"Daddy's got a wife and two daughters."
"So he has."
A sudden shriek from Fran, who has apparently got water in her boot.
"Ow! It's really cold!"
Peter and Jack, some way on by now, turn back to see what all the... oh dear, the men look at one another knowingly, women eh? this is going to take all day at this rate... Pilgrim refrained himself as long as he could, that his wife and children should not perceive his impatience;

but he could not be silent long, because that it looked like being a bloody long hike and the morning was far spent and it was nearly lunchtime already.

"Come on, girls," calls Peter.

"I'm all wet. My boot went under."

"Aaah!"

"Oh no, Jane! You're up to your knees!"

"Come on…"

"Jane's gone in as well… Ow!! It's slippy!"

"Hop on, then, little Sis," says Sasha crouching, suddenly businesslike. "Let's go."

"Yay, piggy-back!"

So Sasha heaves little Alice aboard and strides straight through the midst of the waters of the flood thereof, splash splash enough of this pratting about splashy splash up the other bank and here we are.

"Off you get now, I'm puffed."

"Too many fags."

"You're right there, little Sis."

Now when all were safely arrived upon the other side there was great rejoicing and much laughter though some of it seemed a bit hysterical to Peter well that's not surprising he thought not really given the really rather odd party we are come to think of it. Really…

Jack, knowing the way, led the way, saying, This is the way, and in truth, this is the life: I love it here, out on the hills, great. And Fran hopped and skipped to catch him up while Peter, commiserating of his kindness with his wife's wetness, brought her along as quickly as may be behind. Last of all the two daughters, the long and the short of it.

"Why was he trying to persuade them to go on a journey?"

"Who?"

"Lot."

"Oh." Sasha glances at Alice, trudging along doggedly by her side, has a quick look at their parents' backs a dozen paces in front. "It's not a very… Not a very *easy* story to tell."

"Is that because I'm Too Young?"

"You guessed it."

"So it's about sex, is it."

"Well… it's got sex in it. But it's not very nice sex. If you see what I mean. Which you of course don't."

"Because I'm Too Young. Tell me anyway."

Dug myself a hole there, all right. Always doing that. Sasha walks a few more paces, checking her parents' backs again. Not easy. She's just decided she really loves this funny looking little bundle, and she really doesn't want to tell her a nasty story so corrosive of innocence... I mean, little Alice here has no idea that a father could offer his two daughters for the sexual entertainment of a lustful mob; neither does she know that the same father's same two daughters could get him drunk with wine and then make him have sexual intercourse with them so that they could have children. Sasha doesn't want to be the one to put these horrible ideas into her sister's funny little head.

"Oh, don't bother, then." Sulky again. Damn.

Sasha stops, takes Alice's arm gently, gets in close.

"Alice, love."

"What."

"Please try and understand. I'm not joking and I'm not going to tickle you and throw you on the floor. Please."

Alice's eyes flicker up to her sister's, look away, back; her head goes down, her lower lip starting to protrude. Like when she was a baby and- God it's no joke, she really is still Too Young... Sasha kneels down, kisses her cheek.

"Alice, there are horrible things in the world. So horrible that sensible grown ups just tend to keep quiet about them in front of children. So as not to frighten you."

"What, you mean like vampires."

"Well, I suppose a scary story about a blood sucking vampire is a sort of model of...well, it's a representation of... of something nasty. Do you see? It lets you try out your emotions without getting hurt, it's a sort of softened version- one that isn't too scary- of bad things that really do happen."

"Worse than vampires?"

"Yes. I mean, what's the worst a vampire can do to you? Bite your neck, huh? I mean, it's not very nice to think about, but..."

"He feeled her breasts too."

"Oh, right. Well, that's not too bad, is it? I'd rather have my breasts *feeled* than my neck *bited*." Though Jess did both, of course. Wonder if there's a signal up here?

"Girls! what are you doing?" Peter, yelling from half a mile away up the hill.

"Coming!" What I'm doing, Dad... "Come on Sis- race you!" What I'm doing is trying, Dad, to repair the, damage you've done... led me to do… to your younger, daughter, by referring to a piece of… of … three thousand year old… porn. Oh no it's not, I can hear you, saying, it's a parable about evil… evil and the wickedness of man and the inevitability of divine punishment, punishment God yeah, this hill's… pretty bloody punishing all right, have to walk the rest of the way. I know you could go on for… hours explaining but, the fact is… I don't want filthy Lot and his foul daughters anywhere near my little Sis. Look at her go. Running right up to you, Dad, leaping into your arms. You've no idea how much she trusts you, loves you. Don't go putting your horrible toxic bible stories into her poor little head. Phew.

"I'm puffed."

"Too many fags, Darling. You'd better watch it."

"You're right there, Mum."

But you'd better watch it too, keep on heading up the mountain. Look over your shoulder like that once too often, Mum, and you're sodium chloride.

2

"You could carry me all the way to the top, Daddy."

"No, I couldn't."

"You could."

"Not."

"Oh…"

"Down you get." Because I'm burdened enough already without… but in fact we carry our loved ones with us all the time, don't we? Worry about them. Shouldn't, but we do. Can't help it.

They set off again, no one speaks. After a minute, he looks at Jane, plodding, head down. So much to say. Can't really, with the girls here. But where to start?

Now as he went upon his way, Pilgrim pondered prayerfully upon these things, and especially upon that which caused the most distracting turmoil in his mind, namely whether it had not all been a great error, and should he not now confess as much unto his family and friends too, giving up that vocation to the priesthood which he had thought was good and true, but what is truth? And he thought how Our Lord and Saviour, when Pilate asked him, What is truth, answered him never a word.

Church on Sunday. Sermon, I'll write it. Tomorrow. Prick your bubbles, I will and Pilgrim waxed wroth in his mind and away with your steeplehouses they are condemned, he said, they will not stand up to the judgement that is coming. Being in that fellowship is no discipleship is not the way the truth what is…?

We are pilgrims on a road, That will bring us nearer God. Goad? Must've rhymed with road once. Some old hymns don't seem to rhyme any more. Like love and dove and pruv, prove. Don't seem to make any sense any more either. Singing hymns in the "church" is not the same thing as being a follower of Jesus. "Church." Always in inverted commas these days. How's that work, then? This is all a bit woolly, like that sheep there. Mare to you. Be patient, I will sort this out. This isn't funny. You're telling me it isn't.

Next? Have to face up to it. Can't put it off any longer. We make it all up. There, I've said it. Well, he glances at Jane, I've thought it. Religion is a human artefact, there is no such thing as supernatural revelation. No such thing as the supernatural. Can't believe I'm saying, thinking this. Oh boy, try that out on Graham. Peter, Peter, my dear fellow, where have you got these radical ideas from all of a sudden? Not like you, to be talking like this, is it? Do I detect the voice of one of our *christian atheist* brethren here? No life after death, no heavenly Jerusalem, no City Not Made With Hands? Come now, have a sherry- medium? Of course- and let's all calm down and drink like, I mean think like grown-ups for a bit, eh?

That's better, says Graham… Peter can imagine him sprawled all cheerful in one of the big leather armchairs in his study, stretching his legs out comfortably, with his golden pectoral cross reposing on the purple clad Golgotha of his big belly, a sherry in one hand, glasses dangling from the other, the eyes strangely pale, weak with age, but somehow still bright with what he at least is convinced is otherworldly wisdom come on Peter how does it help to think like this? You'll be putting "God" into inverted commas next, telling me you see him as a what was it an evolving historical concept, yes, a regulative, formative image of what a human being might become. I've read that book too. You can't *love* an evolving concept, Peter, can't be *loved by* a formative image. For goodness' sake, Peter. More sherry?

Mehr, sez a sheep. Oh, there's more all right. I see by this Book that I have in my hand, said Pilgrim, that Holy Scripture is just what it seems to be: a collection of writings very much *of their times*.... Saint Paul, for example, thought the world was going to end very soon- in his own life time, maybe, so that it wasn't worth planning for the future, normal family relationships suspended... all was provisional only, but more or *mehr* of that later, oh Jane, we *must talk*...The bible is a *part*- part only, mind, because the process is still going on, in literature, philosophy- even in science, for goodness sake- of that same slow evolution. Evolution of what we used to use the word "God" for, Graham. Try that out on Jane. The science bit especially.

She's still walking as if in a trance, eyes on the ground, face blank. Well, we've come a long way from *Shine, Jesus, shine* and shaking a tambourine, shouting hallelujah, Lordy Lordy... What else? I will have pity on the Alans of this world and be willing to minister to their needs- erring though they are. Even though they crucify you? Which they bloody will, snarls Robert's twisted face, suddenly appearing to Peter he can see him so clearly, blazingly angry, striding alongside him it seems, punching his arm to emphasise his points, They will, if you start spouting all this in the pulpit on Sunday morning. They don't want their bubbles pricked. Look what happened to Fran... Didn't I warn you? They don't want to go with you on your pilgrimage, Pilgrim, their idea of a prayer walk's a pleasant stroll by the sea not an interior struggle. How can it be, man- they haven't got interiors! Come on, Peter: Is this sermon really a very good idea? Why do you think they come to church on a Sunday? It's the fellowship, man, they don't want progress, Pilgrim...

Why not just take a sabbatical- Graham'd wear that- stress, yes poor chap, overworked, temporary loss of judgement, simply need some time to yourself...

Write a book.

Get thee behind me, Satan. And you, Robert and Graham and all... I will get this straight in my head and stand in the pulpit and... deliver. On Sunday. Stay in tomorrow and write it. Jane can take the girls off somewhere...

Jane is still mutely putting one foot in front of another, disconsolate. Is there any chance? That his new hope might include her too? What is she thinking?

She's trying to remember. When had they last made love? Love! Had they ever really made love? Had she ever recovered from that awful discovery? That he would only do it when he was mad with lust, drunk on accumulated testosterone? And how furious he'd been that time when he discovered she was on the pill. Children and the fruit of the womb, he'd ranted, crushing the little bubble pack in his fist, wagging it in her face, fruit of the...a gift and heritage from the Lord, they are: why do you think I'm doing this? *This* being what he did to her in bed. On those not infrequent occasions when he burned...

I thought you were doing it because you loved me... or at least found me desirable.

I do I do can't you see that's the problem? But how dare you force me, yes, force me to commit the sin of of of...

What sin, Peter? It is lawful for a man and a woman...

Of Onan. My seed wasted. For no reason other than to satisfy the burning burning.

So you only want to do this thing to me- I won't call it lovemaking- when you are driven to it by your hormones?

It is a sin to, to...

But at the same time there has to be a likelihood when you *do this thing to me* as I will call it that a child will be conceived. Am I right? Does that mean that children are just an accident of lust?

No no no you don't understand, you wouldn't would you, you're just a a a

Go on, say it: just a woman.

Jane plodded on uphill, just a woman.

So Sasha was conceived... She looked round at Sasha, chatting to Alice a few yards behind them

Sasha was conceived as soon as she came off the pill. Fertile she was, fecund, fruitful with fruits of the womb, yes, satisfied now? She looked at Peter's burdened back, the big rucksack bobbing a few paces in front of her. I have no love for him. I have never recovered from the horror of those first few weeks together. So I feel no guilt when I look at... She looked over her shoulder once more, at Alice. I feel no guilt.

But after another couple of paces tears sprang into her eyes and ran down her cheeks and she tasted them on her lips.

Salt.

3

They come to a shallow valley, where another stream runs quickly down over gleaming wet stones, sparkling in a sudden shaft of sunlight. The track turns to the right alongside it, leading them upstream, so that as they climb up they can look down at the busy water below on their left. A little way ahead, there is a miniature waterfall, only some dozen or so feet high, with alders growing out of the shiny black rock walls on either side, bending gracefully over the dark swirling plunge pool. A bearded youth in shorts and T-shirt, apparently untroubled by the size of his backpack and the couple of coils of climbing rope slung over his shoulders, bounds up the bank athletically, leading a sluggish straggle of red cagged complaining schoolchildren up from the grassy platform by the water below.

Alice stops to watch the water gliding smoothly over the lip of the little fall: its motion is hypnotic. Every now and then the spray flies up and catches the sun: momentary rainbows scintillate. She smiles at the beauty of it all, and she's still smiling happily when the last of the red cags comes up out of the valley. A boy, about her own age, his tanned face frowning with the effort of climbing. His eyes meet Alice's, and his face works as the reflex to reflect her smile struggles with the strenuous frown which he feels to be more appropriately manly. Confused, he halts, opens his mouth as if to speak. But he doesn't have the words, and, although she draws breath, neither does she. His expression collapses back into its default adolescent discontent, and he turns and jogs quickly away after the others.

Alice wonders what he's like really. What if he had been The One? She was sure that one day she'd meet Him, and it would all be lovely. The boys at school were all horrid. What if she'd spoken to him? Hi, I'm Alice. I'm Nathan. Hi. No, James. Or Stephen. And they might have gone up the hill together. He might have taken her hand. They might have had their picnic lunches together, admiring the view. And then…

Then she heard voices below. She went to the edge of the track, where the redcags had come up, and peered over the edge. Two grownups, with another big rucksack and a pile of climbing ropes.

"Hang on, Brian, don't go up yet. We'll catch 'em up in no time. Give us one of your fags, will you?"

"You old bugger, Geraint, I didn't think you did."

"I know I shouldn't."

Smoke drifts up towards Alice.

"Thanks."

"Every one's a little suicide, if the truth be known."

"It is… Hello, who's this?"

"Hello," said Alice.

"Hello. Not one of ours, are you?"

"No…" I could ask about that boy. "Are you going up Fan Hir?"

"Fan Hir?"

"Yes. Up there." Alice pointed.

"Is that Fan Hir?"

"Yes. Jack said it was."

"Oh no! I thought we'd been walking a long time. Our car's parked at Snowdon!"

"Snowdon? But that's…"

"I told you we should've turned back when it got dark last night, Brian…"

Puzzled, Alice stepped back from the edge and started to walk slowly up the hill, while crazed laughter rang out in the little gorge behind her. Snowdon was in North Wales. She knew that because she'd got an A in her Physical Geography of the British Isles test last term, beating Emma Brayne by a whole seven percent…

There's another waterfall a little further up, then another, and another, and still another as you climb up alongside the little valley, each one with its guardian Alder or Mountain Ash trees leaning over its pool. Jack and Fran, having outpaced the others and the school party too, sit side by side on a flat rock, looking up at one of these. Jack had taken Fran's hand to help her down from the track, and somehow hasn't got round to letting go yet. The noise of the fall speaks for them, for they've run out of words.

Fran, roars the watery rushing voice, all on your own in the world with nothing to call your own, how you yearn for someone to give your life meaning…

Jack, Jack, splatters and splashes the echo back off the wet rock wall, flaxen hair and cornflower eyes: tremble with hope: she's lovely, and she's told you she carries absolutely no baggage at all…

Tricky, trickles the stream, tricky to say what to say since you've both been such bloody fools once already by the sounds of it you with your unsubstantial Jesus and you with your, well, you've sort of said about Cathy in a sort of roundabout way but haven't told her about Jane yet have you? Shouldn't, not if I were you, Jack… not yet. Better not at all…

Wet, wet. Wait, wait, don't bugger everything up by rushing it, you twat… the splat, splattery trickly rushing stream of life goes on for ever, there's time… patience…

Jack looks from the fast flowing glossy pouring out of the fall dropping heavily to the thundery white water below to his own hand and hers in it: looks into her face and she into his. Her eyes say, this is fun! And Jack has the wisdom at last to smile back, yes it is! And leave it at that. He stands and pulls her up and leads her laughing back up the bank…

The roar of the fall's voice fades behind them and the quiet immensity of the hillside is suddenly over them like a benediction, so that they walk quietly for a while, heads bowed. I would have kissed her back there, he thinks, that would have been the moment to do it, that's what I would have done, he thinks, before. Before what?

He was going to kiss me, she thinks, back there, I know it, and I would have kissed him, but I'm glad we didn't kiss then because that kiss is still there in the future for us now. Perhaps.

"Where are the others?"

Jack lets her hand go at last, jogs a few yards back down the track.

"There they are. Hello!" he waves, and Fran hears Alice's excited squeal.

"Look, Mummy, there's Jack!"

Now when all were safely arrived in that place there was great rejoicing and much laughter though some of it seemed a bit hysterical to Peter well that's not surprising he thought not really given the really rather odd party we are come to think of it. And as he stood there pondering these things in his heart Pilgrim was ware of how his children were complaining mightily of their hunger and wasn't it well past lunchtime? We thought we might have lunch at the lake, he said, and asked Mr. Country Wiseman how far off that might be, and being informed by that worthy that it was in truth no more than a few minutes' walk away, he at the last did let be wrung from him his hard consent, whereupon

Jack, knowing the way, led the way, setting off at a great pace, saying, This is the way, in truth, by my life. And Fran hopped and skipped by his side, and Alice ran circles round the two of them like a puppy and Peter, as befitted his dignity, strode on purposefully behind, bearing yet upon his back the burdensome sack *sine qua*, for therein he bore the lunch, *non*.

Sasha stepped in front of Jane, stopping her: put her hands on her shoulders.

"You all right, Mum?"

"I'm fine."

"Mum?"
"I'm… fine."
Sasha nuzzled her Mum's cheek. Wet. Kissed her. Tasted salt.
"Mum-mee. Tell me what it is."
"Oh God, Sasha, I wouldn't know where to start."
"It's Jack, isn't it?"
"No, no."
"He seems to have attached himself to Fran. Not without encouragement."
"Jack can attach himself to who or what the hell he likes. I don't care any more. I told you. He was a mistake." She sniffed, shrugged away from Sasha's embrace, set out after the others. "Come on," she said too loudly, pulling out a hanky and wiping her face. "Funny how the wind makes your eyes water."
Sasha almost has to run to keep up with her.
"I know you've been crying."
"So?"
"Is it Dad?"
"I don't know what you mean."
"Yes you do. We talked about him becoming your ex, don't you remember? When we went to the village? It was only yesterday…"
"Sasha, please…"
"Because as I said at the time he's my Dad as well as your… your…"
"Look." Jane stopped. They were going to catch the others up at this rate. "Please don't get cross with me, I just couldn't bear it. Listen. I said to you I thought you were old enough to understand. And I do. About Jack, yes, but forget him now. And about the other things that I said to you, what I told your father, remember them? That I felt I was *living* a *lie*? That I can't support him as a priest any more because it's become obvious to me that the church is all…"
Jane, almost crying again, flapped her hand in front in front of her face as if to clear it of a troublesome fly.
"Bollocks, Mummy," Sasha reminded her gently, seriously, "I remember that seemed to be the *mot juste* at the time."
Jane looked bleakly at her lovely, tall, handsome daughter, seeing Peter in her so clearly, the bastard. She turned her head slowly, and her mouth set in a tight, grim smile as she watched little Alice capering about.

"But there's more. I can't say what. It seems to me, Al… Sasha, that there are some things a mother just doesn't discuss with her children."

Jesus, thinks Sasha. Now what. And I thought I was the expert excavator or excavatrix it should be I suppose of bloody great holes for myself…

"Right, so… "

"Perhaps when you have children of your own, you'll…"

"Unlikely."

"Oh, yes. Foolish of me. Sorry." Jane took Sasha's hand, kissed it.

"That's all right. I'm sorry if… I mean I'm sorry if I can't help."

After a moment, Jane kissed Sasha again, took her arm. They walked on together in silence, both wondering, from their own very different perspectives, what it meant to have a secret so big.

They were so preoccupied by this, that they found themselves, without realising they had walked so far, by the shore of the lake.

"There's supposed to be a wartime bomber sunk at the bottom," said Jack, chewing an apple as he stood looking out over the water.

"Really? Must've been a bit of a shock for the Lady of the Lake and her cattle when that fell in on her head." Peter was packing, lunch done with now, got to get on.

"You're thinking of Llyn Fach, Peter. Over there."

"Lady of the Lake?" asked Sasha. "Like in Tennyson?"

"Nah. It's a Welsh folk myth. There are legends about all these places."

"Where's Alice got to?" Jane wanted to know.

Sasha points her fag along the shore, where some red cags were skimming stones.

"She seems to have found a friend."

Fran got up and went to stand by Jack. Me too, she thought. Me too, I hope.

Peter, peering along the lakeside, finally spotted Alice.

"Alice! Come on, we're going!"

"That's my Dad calling."

The boy glanced at her, hurled another stone.

"One, two, three, four, five… uh."

"You're very good at that."

"I did a tenner once."

"A what?"

"Ten. Bounces."

"Alice! Come on, will you?"

"Oh. I've got to go."

"OK." He picked up another flat stone, chucked it hard... "Six. Oh. Sir's coming."

"Darren, come on, we're off."

"Yes, Sir."

Tall, slim, bearded, smiling man in shorts and T-shirt, great big backpack, coils of climbing rope.

"Hello, there, little girl. I think your dad's calling you." Laughing now at pantomime of Peter gesticulating wildly.

"Yes." Alice could barely speak. It was... incredible. The tall teacher turned away, and the boy trudged after him. Alice took the plunge. "Derryn..."

He stopped, turned round slowly, frowning his frown.

"It's Darren."

"What?"

"Not *Derrin*." He couldn't stretch his lips contemptuously enough. He shook his head slowly as he stomped away.

4

So up they went upon the steep and rugged pathway up towards Bwlch Giedd, Jack showing the way in front with Fran, he himself poor pilgrim soul struggling to keep up, the others way behind, below. Now when they had gone some way Pilgrim bethought himself and said in his heart, I don't need this Pilgrim crap any more. What am I hiding from?

So Peter stopped and stood there, hands on hips, breathing hard, for it was yes pretty bloody steep and rugged. He took out his handkerchief and mopped his brow and looked back the way he had come.

Back over the landscape he had travelled, back over the journey of his life. Life was a pilgrimage, he thought: and then, hang on, who says? It's only an idea, a story. If it isn't helpful- or, worse- if the imagery starts to leak into your real life, it's time to give it up.

We trudge on sorrowing through this vale of tears, but if we're strong in faith we'll reach the heavenly Jerusalem in the end. So the story goes. So we put up with all this nonsense because we know it'll be All

Right in the end. Except it won't. We know that now. This is all that there is.

What is there?

There is what I see now. Let's start from there.

Looking back down the way he'd come he saw little Alice following after him up the steep like stairs path and remembered again on the stairs in his house how she'd said to him, with tears in her eyes, Daddy, and he had shouted down at her looking up at him, saying, And you can shut up as well, don't you think I've got enough to deal with, with her I don't know who she thinks she is… Sasha was loping along just behind Alice, and Jane next, what a row they'd had.

And he remembered trying to pray on the prayer walk, praying for forgiveness, in the woods he had prayed, saying our Father, which art, he himself a father though not in heaven, sitting there wretched in the windy wood among the shifting patterns of sunlight on the undergrowth, the heady stench of wild garlic. Up here it was all different. Wide open. He had to forgive himself… a moment of panic. Identity. He wasn't sure who he was for a moment. We rely on our environment for our identity. He wondered what Alice and Sasha were saying as they came up to where he stood panting. Would they forgive? He stepped aside to let them go past him, looked at Alice, she didn't look at him, silent and intent now she was, frowning. Lovely little girl though, with her long fair hair done up in a little pony tail, sweet little tilty uppy nose and her big eyes oh how she reminded him sometimes of Jane.

"Where've Jack and Fran got to?" Sasha, also breathing heavily, he notices, can't see them. Neither can he, come to think of it. Out of sight, up there somewhere.

Now Jane caught up, stopped, blew her cheeks out. "Phoo. Steep. Feeling my age."

"I'm really sorry about Sunday night," Peter blurts the words out, all in a rush, "It's been impossible for me to say before but I want to try…"

"Sasha, just run on and catch up with Alice, would you? I'm afraid for her on her own on this steep path," says Jane.

"Yes, Mummee. I'll try." Jane watches her go, then turns to Peter.

"Peter, listen. I've been very very unhappy for years now. This you know. Sunday night was only the tip of the iceberg. It's no good being *really sorry*. It's too late for being sorry. If we're going to stay together, and for the sake of the children if nothing else I think we might have to, then we've got to come to terms with one another. We need to talk seriously, at home, not try and patch things up here, perched half way up a bloody mountain like a couple of..."

"I've changed."

"So you say, but..." She waves her hand helplessly, out of words again: after all these years of loveless marriage, what hope is there? What change could ever make her desire him sexually again? Or even want to live with him? If it weren't for the children... she looks up the path where the children are, and then starts plodding up once more, away from him. After a moment, he follows her slowly, and sadly, wearily, and so sadly. Sadly.

They'll crucify him. Up he goes. Via dolorosa. Up. Golgotha. He preached salvation to others, himself he cannot save. Up. Higher. What pains he had to bear. And still does. In us. Our suffering. God, incarnate, suffers. Suffers as he tries to become himself in us. As we try to become his image, what a human being might become...

"Come on, Peter!" He can see the top at last. Fran is jumping and waving, her hair flying; Jack is frankly admiring her; Jane and Alice are sitting huddled together having a little heart to heart, it seems; and Sasha is struggling to light a fag in the stiff breeze.

Setting his spectacles firmly on his face he more or less legged it the rest of the way up the path and out of the gully up to the very top and on a sudden lo! Could we but stand where Moses stood, and view the landscape o'er! Clear as could be after all that cloud earlier. He was not sure, for his geography had ever been but hazy but was that not the sea in the distance shimmering and he had an idea that... was it not in fact Swansea and Gower over there?

"Sasha, isn't that..." A swirl of acrid smoke whipped past him on the breeze.

"...Swansea, Yeah. The Promised Land."

5

"So we got our walk in the hills after all, Jane."

Jack had somehow contrived to drift into the cottage along with everybody else. Peter was busy, unpacking his rucksack, and Alice seemed to have lost something under the table. Fran, he saw, was whispering with Sasha in a corner.

"Yes, we did, didn't we, Jack. Thank you for driving the girls, by the way. Now if you'll excuse me I must go and get the supper on." And that was that. She ducked into the kitchen, and there was immediately a loud clatter of falling pots and pans, and lots of swearing too. Fran ran to see.

Peter padded towards the kitchen also, thought better of it, sat down, grunted, got up again. What's this on the seat? Alice's book. He chucked it irritably on the table, sat down again. He looked up at Jack as if to speak, but thought better of that too, and polished his spectacles instead. Awkward. Can't just tell him to sod off after... but he is going, isn't he?

Alice came to the rescue again.

"Oh, there it is. It's been on the table all this time. I've nearly finished it."

"Of course! *Cartomancer!*" Jack picked it up, smiling at the silly vampirish artwork on the cover, turned it over to read the blurb. "I knew I'd heard that title before somewhere. It's one of Bryn's."

"Bryn?"

"See? On the cover. Bryn Vaughan-Price."

"So?"

"He's the guy I went to see yesterday. He wrote it."

Alice's eyes were saucered, her jaw dropped.

"You *know* the author of *Cartomancer*?"

"Sure. I've known him for years. He only lives a few miles away."

"Go on, little Sis, say it: Oh, My, *Gaaa...d...* He's a remarkably versatile furniture removal man isn't he, Jack?" Sash adds quietly, slinking up very close to him, thumbs in waistband. "What else does he do in his spare time? Pine strippergrams?" She is smiling, but there's a warning here too. Jack looks her straight in the eye.

"The furniture's just a hobby these days really. A useful hobby. *Really* useful." Raising his eyebrows on that *really*... I won't talk if you don't...

Alice is showing her book to Peter.

"Isn't that brilliant, Daddy, that Jack actually knows...?"

But he has been looking busily brow furrowed at another paperback he's just taken from the mantelpiece. Well, if that isn't the most amazing...

"Amazing coincidence. Look!"

"*Abraham and his seed.* Yeah. That's his as well. They're going to make that one into a film hopefully."

"*Hopefully* indeed." But Sasha finds she can't be bothered to correct Jack, she's too pissed off with Dad just brushing Alice's enthusiasm aside poor little thing it's just not on. So she says, "Hey, Ali, here's a thing. You know that holiday essay you've got to write? Well, don't you think it'd really be a bit special if it had an actual interview with the author in it?"

"Wow. Yeah!"

"What do you think, Jack? Would he be up for it?"

"I'll ask. I'll pop back in the morning and let you know. Were you planning anything particular for tomorrow Peter?"

"Well as a matter of fact, Jack," oh dear, going to get further indebted to him here but never mind, "I was hoping to be able to do some writing tomorrow and so if by any chance Mr er, Vaughan-Price did happen to be available..."

"I could take Alice off your hands for a bit. Sure, why not?"

"Oh, Jack! That'd be wonderful. Wait till Emma Brayne sees my essay..."

"Take Alice off our hands?" Jane is in the doorway, wineglass in hand. "What's all this?"

"Mummy, Jack actually knows the author of my book! He only lives a few miles away! He's going to see if I could actually meet him tomorrow and interview him and get lots of ideas for my essay..."

"And while she's doing that," says Peter, "I can get lots of ideas for *my* essay. My sermon, that is. That'd be OK wouldn't it, Jane?"

"Well..." Jane looks at Jack with no enthusiasm. Fran appears behind her and tops up her glass, winks at Jack and vanishes again. Jane takes a couple of large swallows, leans on the doorpost. Christ, thinks Jack, she's downing it like orange squash. "I'd better go too, then. Hadn't I, Ali... Can't have you all on your own with all these *strange men*..."

"Oh, thank you, Mummy."

Jane shoulders herself off the doorpost and stretches out her free hand to Alice, strokes her hair, still in its tight little outdoors ponytail. Her expression is unreadable as she kneels down and kisses her daughter on both cheeks, then squats back on her haunches, looking up at her smiling little face, looking for... what? She doesn't seem to be sure...

The moment lengthens uncomfortably.

"I'd better go." Jack's had enough of this. He's been and checked, and he's passed the test. No way does he want to... and besides, he can't stop thinking about... He calls through to the kitchen, "Bye, Fran," and she pops into view again, smiley pretty Fran.

"Are you off?"

"Yes. I'll see you in the morning, then."

"That'd be nice."

Don't say anything stupid. Don't push it. He waves the little hand open, hand shut wave he's seen her do, and she copies it back to him. "Bye," he says, and is gone.

6

"Where the fuckin' hell have *you* been?" Bryn wants to know.

"I've been up Fan Hir," says Jack, dumping carrier bags on the table.

"Fan Hir? *Fan Hir*? They haven't opened a bloody supermarket up there, have they?"

"I didn't see one. I'm afraid the butter's melted."

"We've been fuckin' starvin' to death here, boyo! It's past my dinnertime. I was just about to send *her* out with a shotgun to get us a fuckin' *rabbit*. Did you remember the booze? Ah, thank Christ for that. You're not completely useless, then."

Bryn cracks open the Sŵn y Môr, pours himself a large one. Cathy, smiling serene in the big chair by the fireplace, watches Jack as he unpacks the bags.

"What's her name, Jack?" she asks quietly.

Jack smiles, weighing a carton of milk in his hand.

"Alice," he says, after a moment, and goes to put the milk in the fridge.

"Have you shagged her yet, then?" Bryn wants to know.

"She's ten years old."

"Is she, by God. Well? Have you shagged her yet, then?"

"She's a great fan of yours, Bryn."

"Answer the question."

"*Cartomancer*. She absolutely loves it."

"P'raps I should shag her myself."

"And she wants to meet you."

"There! I'm in, see?"

Jack empties a bag of apples into the fruit bowl, sits down, nods at the whisky.

"Mind if I have some of that?"

Bryn slides a glass across the table.

"Actually, I said I'd ask if it would be all right..." Jack pours whisky, "to bring her here in the morning, Bryn."

"Did you, now. And how did you come to meet this little vampire fan... ah, I get it now. She was sitting reading her book on the top of *Ffan* Hir... and you're going to bring this *fan here*... Oh, very good, Jack, very good shaggy dog story, I didn't think you had it in you."

"And her mother, too."

"What?"

"He can't just bring the little thing out here all on her own, can he?" says Cathy. "I'm going to get some food. I'm starving."

"Me too. Thanks. But hang on, Jack. I'm just beginning to get a glimmer of what might be going on in that devious little mind of yours. Is this *mother* by any chance...?"

"I was just checking, Bryn. You know."

"What?"

"Checking, you know. To see if it was over..."

"Oh no, here we go again. So it is the same one, it's the bloody wanking woman again. But that means... Oh Jesus Christ on crutches, Jack! That means this is the daughter you thought was wanking you off before... and she's fuckin' *ten*..."

Cathy squealed.

"That was her older sister, Bryn..."

Cathy squealed again.

"You bringing her too? Is she a fan as well?"

"No, she's not a fan. But I might bring *Fran*." Jack got up and went over to Cathy, who was still giggling over the cooker. "That's the name I should have given you in the first place, Cathy. Fran. She's just come into my life today, from nowhere. Like magic. I'd like to bring Fran here."

"Fran? Have you...? Oh God, you ask him, Cathy, I just don't have the..."

VIII

1

...Amanda, her arm extended in front of her, holding a pistol from whose barrel a whisp of smoke still curled.

"Amanda!" gasped Derryn.

Then he felt the ground shake under his feet, and with a terrifying rumble a section of the ceiling collapsed: he heard Amanda scream as light flooded into the awful vault, and he saw her falling. He tried to reach her, but could not move. Then, as debris showered around him, he saw a hideous change come over the prostrate body of the creature that had been Eldan. As Derryn watched with appalled fascination, it seemed to melt, sinking into the earthen floor. A foul-smelling fog arose, and when it had drifted away, there was nothing left. Or not quite nothing. Something was gleaming on the ground where the body had been, reflecting the bright daylight which was now streaming in through the cracked ruin of the ceiling. He staggered towards it, picked it up: it was a silver bullet. Then he heard a faint moan near at hand. He slipped the bullet into his pocket, and ignoring his pain, forced himself to move towards the sound.

"Amanda?"

"Oh... Derryn..."

Her voice was very faint, and when he saw the bright red blood trickling down her alabaster skin he feared the worst: but she was only hurt by a fragment of falling plaster. Summoning his last remaining strength, he gathered her up in his arms, and bore her up the spiral staircase which seemed to shift and slide under his feet as more of the house collapsed: but at last they were out, and he did not put her down until he had carried her right out of that cursed place. At last he set her down by the little stream that flowed past the end of the orchard, and wetting his kerchief, tenderly bathed her head, gently washing away the caked blood and dust.

Her huge eyes searched his face as he worked, and when he had finished she put her hand behind his head, thrusting her fingers into the thick abundant curls of his hair, and drew him close. For a moment he hesitated, and then suddenly his lips were melting into hers, and her heart pounded with delight: she had never known such a passionate kiss. At last he broke off, breathing heavily.

"Amanda," he said, "Oh, Amanda!"

"Derryn," she whispered, "Don't leave me again. I need… Oh, I need…"

He embraced her with his strong arms, held her body tight against his, and she gasped as she felt his urgency growing.

"Oh Derryn, Derryn…"

She felt his urgency growing. Urgency. Where's the…

Urgent. a. Pressing, calling for immediate action or attention. Hence urgency, n, f. Latin *urgere* press, drive.

Felt his urgency pressing. Gasped.

The moon had risen and the first stars were out already before they rose from the grassy bank of the stream and walked hand in hand to the place where Derryn had left his faithful mare. He helped Amanda up into the saddle, and led the great horse up the steep track, away from the ruined house which had seen such evil days.

As he walked holding the reins, by chance he thrust his free hand into his pocket and his fingers closed on something round and hard. He drew it out: the silver bullet. For a moment he was minded to throw the gleaming sphere into the bushes and be rid of such an ill-omened thing: but then he thought, no. This present evil is no more, but who can tell what the future holds? He looked over his shoulder at Amanda, swaying half asleep in the saddle, her face beautiful in the bright moonlight, then back at the bullet glinting in the palm of his hand. His lips tightened in a humourless smile, and he put it back into his pocket. You never know with vampires.

The end.

Alice switched off her bedside lamp, fell back into her pillows. Ahh... swaying half asleep... her face beautiful in the moonlight. Oh Derryn, Derryn... She sees herself lying by the water's edge, watching the ripples among the reeds; one of his strong arms is crooked round her neck, with the other he softly bathes her averted face. Her hurt healed, she turns to him, sees his frown of concern fade to reflect her own timid smile... she puts her hand behind his head, drawing him close and.

Alice wonders what it would have been like to lie by the lake with him, with his red cag over them to keep off the wind, snug and cosy. To turn her face to his, to get closer, closer, until their lips... touched.

And then she tried to imagine how he might have embraced her with his strong stone chucking arms, held her body tight against his, and how she might have felt his... urgency. Growing?

And then... she is asleep.

2

Peter looks up frowning from *Abraham*. It's Jane. Jane coming out of the study, where she's been watching TV with the others. Through the open door behind her, the shrieks of a studio audience, a braying of brassy music. Someone slams the door shut from inside, and in the sudden hush they regard one another, he sitting with the book on his knee, she standing, swaying slightly, he thinks. Drunk, she is, but I'm not saying anything. Bit worrying, though. If she starts... regularly, I mean. Then what?

"I'm a bit drunk," she says, "So our *talk*, you know, our *talk* when we suddenly magically find the all right things to say and all shall be well and all manner of thing shall be well, will, you know, our *talk*, will, have to be... post, poned." She sets an empty glass down on the table with a click. "I am going to bed. And I these days like to sleep... alone. As you may have noticed. It's your turn for the sofa tonight. If you can get those two off it. Have to peel them apart, first, mind. Very physical they are, these young... friends. In fact, I think Sasha wouldn't mind... and neither would I for that matter. Oh, but of course, you don't *know*. Do you?" She took a couple of unsteady but bloody aggressive steps towards him.

"Don't know what?"

She watches him, catlike, waiting, ready to jump in with claws out as soon as he loses patience and repeats...

"What don't I..."

"It's a secret," she yowls at once, gotcha, banging the table and pushing off it right up to him, one hand clutching the back of his chair. "A secret. And I tell you, I'm bloody good at secrets- *Peter Thomas.*"

She spat his name in his face.

Appalled, he could only watch as she reeled away to the bottom of the staircase. There she twisted round against the wall, halted, staring, as if at bay. But he wasn't about to start chasing her: he didn't even dare move.

Jane slowly deflated, wondering where all that had come from suddenly. She grasped the banister rail, glared at Peter across the room, cringing in his chair by the fireplace, his silly book open on his lap. Didn't he care any more at all? If she had secrets? If she provoked him enough she could get him to beat it out of her... could she? Would he? At least if he beat her up she'd be able to feel there was something between them... She felt her expression softening; she was tired now, and anyway, there was nothing to say. She turned away from him, God she must be so drunk, and she went up step by careful step upstairs, up, stairs, clinging on to the rail. As she so often did, she went to listen outside Alice's room: the door was ajar, but she didn't dare go in in case she fell drunkenly over a chair or something and woke her up with a fright that wouldn't do poor Alice. So instead she leaned on the doorpost and stood, her head against the blessedly cool woodwork, her face turned so that she could just see into the bedroom where her little daughter lay, all quiet, dark, and secret.

For a long time after she'd gone, Peter sat as if petrified. Well, I would be, wouldn't I, be petrified I mean, *tu es Petrus,* after all, and *super hanc petram...* and the rest. Funny: no matter how bad things get, one part of the mind still keeps coming up with silly jokes and puns and trains of thought that are quite irrelevant, unhelpful... but on the other hand, perhaps it's a sort of defence mechanism. Keep on smiling through. Nothing much to smile at there, though. More than a bit worrying. She says she wants to stay with me for the sake of the children, but if she turns into an alcoholic it's not going to help them much, is it?

He removed his specs, inspected them, found some possibly flecks of her spittle perhaps on them. Unpleasant, more than that, frightening to have her right in my face like that. Throwing my name at me like a... well I don't know. Perhaps I should be grateful it wasn't that wineglass.

Peter, having wiped upon his handkerchief embroidered with an ornate P his glasses settled them back in their customary position and, have first marked his place, placed his book *Abraham and his seed* by Bryn Vaughan-Price upon the table, picked up the glass his wife had left there and carried it through into the compact kitchen at the rear of the premises. Having rinsed it under the tap, he placed it upon the drainer and leaned upon the sink with both hands. His life was, he felt, very difficult at the moment and this was certainly a situation which, in the past, would have drawn forth from him much prayerful sighing and beseeching of that Benevolence which Holy Scripture teacheth us is ever at hand to aid us in our hours of darkness and distress. Indeed his head was bowed over the sink with its plastic washing up bowl containing two teaspoons and a souvenir of St. David's coffee mug indeed sunk almost below the level of his shoulders but this was with weight of woe rather than being that inclination customarily understood as being preparatory to prayer.

This won't do, he thought, I will lift up mine eyes unto the hills, and looked up. His reflection in the window glass, for it was now dark outside, looked longsufferingly back at him so that he was moved to pity it. Those eyes had lifted up unto the hills today, all right, well a good part of the Brecon Beacons at any rate, and whence came their help? The hills were empty, the sky above them empty, my heart empty. My God my God why hast thou forsaken me? Asking the wrong question. That's the point. Work on that tomorrow, when they're out. Too late for writing now, too tired. Still a bit shaken by Jane's outburst. Read some more of that book. Really rather good, in parts. Curate's book.

Bloody Tim the incurable curate. None of this would ever have happened if. Not Very Well, indeed. *I'm* not very bloody well and *I* keep going because *somebody's* bloody got to, haven't they, *eh*? See if any wine left. Half a bottle! That's a surprise. That's where she was off to in town this morning while we were in the hiking shop, just pick up a couple of things quickly, meet you back here in a minute... Pour myself a glass, take it through, funny how I thought Alice was imitating me with the chalice last night so proud of her grown up glass of wine she was I don't think she really likes it very much.

After sipping with satisfaction from the glass in his hand several mouthfuls of the blushful hippo cream as he thought the poet had it (not being much of an expert on literature other than Holy Writ) and having immediately returned to the kitchen where he had left the bottle to replenish his glass, (for he found he had inadvertently almost finished it at once,) and having indeed sipped from it once more, for it was, he decided, a fine wine (which must have cost his wife, and, through the circumstance of their having a joint account, him, a lot of money,) Peter finally felt a sufficiency of equanimity had returned to his mind such that he might be able to resume his comfortable seat and once more take up that work of Mr Bryn Vaughan-Price, which, for some reason not immediately clear to him, and though written in a style of which he did not entirely approve (though who was he to judge? being not much of an expert, as explained *vide supra*) was nevertheless currently giving him considerable satisfaction.

3

I can only guess what was going through Pontius Pilate's mind that morning when he condescended to come forth in the name of Rome and meet the representatives of the temple. He'd had to come out to them, mark you, because if they'd entered the praetorium they'd have become *unclean*. Unclean, I ask you. Compared to a Roman Governor who'd just been bathed in three different temperatures of water and strigiled to within an inch of his life? No, *unclean* here meant tainted. Tainted by the foreign, the different. That must have seemed to Pilate to be their big problem, these *Jews*. They just couldn't accept that the rest of the world mattered at all. He'd been told that it was because they believed their God had chosen *them*. Not anyone else. Bloody strange way he had of showing it.

You can imagine the one who seemed to be their leader talking, very fast, very urgent. Arms flailing- big on gesticulation, these Levantines. Someone had upset them, and that was intolerable, it seemed. Why? Ah- it's a *religious* matter. They wanted him punished. *God* wanted him punished. How did they know what *God* wanted? Silly question. Anyway, Pilate couldn't make out more than the general sense. He turned to his interpreter. "Sextus?"

"They are holding a man prisoner because he claims to be the King of the Jews, which they say he is not. They say he deserves to die because apparently saying you are King of the Jews when you are not is an offence to their religious beliefs punishable by death. They further say that it is an offence to Rome because saying you are the King of the Jews when you are not is…"

"Yes yes yes I think I get the picture." So he wants to get rid of Herod, does he? thinks Pilate. Huh. Him and half Judea. Ah well, we'd better have a look at him. "Tell them to bring him in round the back."

Pilate and the attentive Sextus march away, Sextus mincingly skipping into step with his Governor, back to the inner part of the palace. It is early, but already getting hot.

"Immortal gods. What a place."

"Sir?"

"Bloody people with their bloody religion."

"Sir."

"Ought to be more grateful."

"Sir."

In the audience chamber, Pilate sat down. It was going to be one of those days. His wife…

"My wife."

"Sir?"

"Had a dream. About this one they're bringing in. Shook her up something rotten. Where's he got to, anyway? Optio!"

An NCO snapped to attention. "Sir?"

"Where've they got to with him? We haven't got all day."

"Go see, Sir?"

"Go see."

Shook her up something rotten. As if he hasn't got enough trouble, what with her drinking and… He got up and went to the doorway. The Optio's nailed sandals clacked away, *sinister dexter sinister dexter* across the…

"What was their word for this…"

"*Gabbatha,* Governor."

…stone pavement. Bloody awful language. Like they're sicking it up all the time. Pilate heard the Optio in the office bellowing where's this bloody Yid, then, the Guv's waiting, well get him over there now then, immortal gods, what a shower. Shook her up, she'd said. Have nothing to do with him, she'd said. Leave the bastard alone, let the local cops deal with it, it's nothing to do with Rome anyway if they want to kill one another let'em. Drink. He goes back inside.

"Drink!" Slaves scurry in the background. He picks up a scroll off the table, glances at it, throws it down. A tray is offered. He grabs a goblet, sniffs it, scowls, drinks it anyway. "More." The goblet is full again. Again he drinks. There is a clattering and a shuffling and the doorway darkens as prisoner and escort enter.

He doesn't look like much. Not a king, anyway. Pilate sits down again, gathering his robe and what he can manage of their ghastly lingo about him. "King of the Jews, you are?" he manages, glancing at Sextus, who puts the question more idiomatically, perhaps sarcastically too? Certainly at greater length. The Yid listens, shrugs, smiles, and answers, surprisingly, in fluent Latin.

"Am I the King of the Jews? Is that what they told you I said I was?"

"They didn't tell me you could speak Latin. Well, that should make it a bit easier. Yes, they told me you said you were the King of the Jews. Also that you thought you were the Son of a God or something. I didn't really understand. That's why you're here. So that I can decide what to do with you. So let's have some answers, all right?"

"All right. I spoke of a kingdom, and I could be understood as its king. But it is not a political kingdom. It is a kingdom of the spirit: a way of seeing the world. The priests accused me of blasphemy because it was the only way they could articulate their frustration and incomprehension. They're good people really."

"They want you dead."

"It's not their fault. The message I bring came as quite a shock to them."

"And that message is…?

"Ah. I don't know how familiar you are with our religion…"

"Do I look like a Jew?"

The Yid's grin became an easy laugh. "No, you certainly don't. I'm sorry, Governor, but it's difficult to explain in any detail without giving you a certain amount of background, and something tells me that you don't want a theological symposium just now."

"Theological symp… do you speak Greek as well?"

"Yes. Let me put it to you very simply. My message is that human beings- all human beings- ought to be nice to one another. We should all be brothers and sisters together, living as citizens of the heavenly kingdom, if you like the image. We should love one another. That's the message. There. Now you have it."

Love. Tell that to my wife. Pilate raised his cup to his lips, found it empty. "More," he shouted, and a slave came hurrying up with a jug. The Yid watched him calmly as he poured, bowed, retreated.

"Should I love my slaves, then?" Pilate caught sight of the Optio stifling a snigger. "Should I love the Optio?" The snigger became a short bark of laughter, quickly suppressed.

"Why not?"

"Because he's an ugly ignorant pig of a non-com who needs his arse kicking, that's why not."

"He's a man like you and me, like your interpreter, your soldiers, your slave there. As men, we have more in common than the things that differentiate us. The differences are all to do with the value we give people. But we give it- we ourselves- and we can change it. If we want to."

"Yes, well, that's as may be. But right now the difference between you and me is that I'm the one in charge. And if I say you go to the cross, that's where you go."

"Agreed, but you only have that power because of the valuation society has given you- call it power, authority, whatever- and that valuation isn't inherent in you. It's given, isn't it? And it can be taken away. The Emperor will not be pleased if there is a riot in Jerusalem, will he?"

"What's that got to do with it?"

"Come on, Pontius, that's what the priests are threatening you with, isn't it? Kill him for us, or we'll have a mob of bloodthirsty zealots roaming the streets before you can say Hail Caesar. Couple of squaddies get knifed, you have to react, and by sundown the place is like a battlefield. Not good government. Believe me, I understand your dilemma."

Pontius? He had called him... but it had been done so easily, so naturally, and his Latin was mesmerising: how had he...

"How did you learn to speak such good Latin? You scarcely have a local accent."

"Words are important. And in any case, if you love someone, you'll try your best to talk their language, right?"

"You love the Romans?"

"Of course."

"No wonder your priests want you dead. You're a traitor."

"I love the Romans as people. I didn't say that I loved their imperialism."

"Nothing wrong with the *pax romana*: it keeps the peace." Obviously- Roman peace. And any bastard who doesn't like it gets the chop. "You should like that- peace."

"I do. But if you'd been able to live peaceably with your neighbours in the first place, it wouldn't have been necessary to conquer the world in self defence, would it?"

"Conquer the world in... that's a good one." Pilate was laughing now: was he a bit drunk? Or was it just that, somehow, it wasn't possible to feel anything but elated in the presence of this, this... no. It can't be that. "I still don't see why they... you know, your fellow countrymen, priests, religious experts, want you dead."

"We've already agreed that you are not a Jew, Pontius. Without that background it must be hard indeed to understand the rage they feel when I speak to them of love: let me try to explain a little more. They hope for so much from God, you see. They've invested so much of their aspiration and ambition as a people in their apprehension of him. They don't want to hear all that devalued."

"Devalued?" *Evilescuntur*? Can one say that?

"The poor and those defined as sinners come first. They must be raised, lifted into God's family where they belong. They too are to be loved, not rejected, ignored, avoided..."

"You said, sinners. What are they?"

"Anyone who disobeys God is a sinner. You can pick some of them out easily, because they will be poor, or diseased."

"Poverty and disease are caused by disobeying God?"

"Apparently God would not allow a righteous man to suffer so."

"Remarkable. And the rest of the sinners?"

"Prostitutes, tax-collectors and others who work for you. And of course the rest of the human race. The heathen. The people that know not God. You, in fact, Pontius."

"So why aren't all those people diseased or poor, or otherwise showing the symptoms of God's displeasure?"

"Because it's all bollocks. God doesn't punish. God loves everyone. We need to show that through our actions. We need to *be* the love of God acting in the world."

"So if God loves everyone, why is there poverty, disease...?"

"We need to be the love of God working to create that perfect world where such things are no more. Take away this crippling nonsense of sin, these absurd religious laws, simply *be* the loving God to one another..."

"Ah. Got it. That's the blasphemy, right? They hear you saying that, but report it as you saying you think you *are God* full stop. It all makes sense. And of course, from what you've said, there isn't much left for the professional religious to do, is there?"

"There would be a lot of redundancies at the temple, if…"

"If you got your way. Right. So you can see their point of view. You go round telling your own people they're getting their religion wrong, of course they're upset. They think you've claimed to be God, of course you're a blasphemer. And being a volatile bunch, they want you permanently silenced. But where do you get these ideas? How do you know all this? You seem to have practically invented your own religion."

"It's not new. We have books- the books of the prophets- full of these ideas. They've read them, but won't apply them to their own situation. They're either too comfortable for change, or want the wrong sort of change- the sort you're afraid of, Pontius, fierce beards slipping the knife in during the night while you dream of Empire. How is your wife, by the way?"

"My…?" How did he know? *Could* he know?

"It must be very worrying for her, having to live in a place like this. I expect she'd prefer it if you were posted somewhere a little more stable. Alexandria? One of the Greek provinces? Or even back to Rome. Is that what she'd like? What would *you* like, Pontius?"

Pilate was about to tell him when

The door of the study flies open to girlish giggles. Annoying. Annoyed, Peter looks up. Sasha and Fran, arms round one another. Something seems to be very funny.

"We're off to bed now, Dad."

This, apparently, is hilarious.

"Sasha, stop it…!"

"I want to give her a goodnight kiss, but she's being frightfully coy."

"Sasha! All right, you *dreadful* flirt, just one."

So Peter finds himself watching as… well, really.

"Girls…"

"Papa?"

More hysteria. Fran breaks away, runs upstairs: Shhh! goes Sasha hissing after her, Be quiet, Fran, you'll wake up Alice… and Mum. She guffaws again, turns to her Dad, grinning.

"Actually, I don't think there's much chance of Mum waking up. I mean, until the morning! Ho ho. I don't think she's drunk herself to death. At least, not yet."

Sasha sashays across the room towards him, face ecstatic, arms outstretched, fingers flexing, hips a-wiggle, bare feet flicking the floor, dancing to some wild music only she can hear... she stops abruptly as if it's been switched off: holds the pose, slowly lets it go, arms down, feet flat, goes suddenly hipshot and tilts her head at him. Her brows contract, her lips pout.

"Poor Daddy."

Peter shrinks in his chair, his book face down on his crotch, its inverted V a protection and a camouflage too... He takes in the long bare legs, the fashionably ragged blue jean shorts, the lean bare belly and too skimpy black blouse hardly done up, the white bra showing, pushing up the breasts, the fine moulding of the throat, the strong expressive features in their nest of glossy black hair, the gleaming eyes transfixing him. His daughter.

"I'm sorry things are so hard for you just now."

"Sasha, I..."

"I mean about Mummy. We talked a bit, yesterday, you know, and..."

"Sasha, please."

"What?"

"I don't want to discuss..."

She kneels by his chair, her right elbow on the arm so that her hand falls by his neck, and she can caress his cheek, affectionately, fingers curled backhand, raking her knuckles through the sharp dark evening stubble above the shaved line of the beard, while her left hand finds his knee, inches up his thigh, squeezes his flesh. Filially.

"Daddy. Why not?"

"Because... I've got *so* many things to worry about..."

"What things? Mummy? The church?"

"Lots of things." The smell of her. Lovely...

He finds that he is looking down into the black chasm between her breasts. Like two young roes that are twins. More beautiful than wine, and the sweet smell of thy ointments above all aromatical spices. Falling into that soft abyss, he tears his eyes away, but knows that she knows...

"Lots?"

"Leave it, will, you, Alexandra?" He twists himself in his chair, shrugging her hands away from his body... Anger, anger. He must find...

At once there is a distance between them, hostility: and father and daughter are estranged, distanced, but man and woman are still close, sexual... He is looking fixedly away but her eyes are on his face, avid, waiting for the moment when he will look back, as he must, and yes, now he does and their eyes meet widening in a challenge that suddenly terrifies them both... He is not her Daddy now, he is just a man like any other, aroused but frightened, hating himself, biting his lip with self loathing but wanting, wanting...

So this is how it happens, she thinks... What would it be like? It would start just like this... Her world tips upside down. Never, never, had she imagined... but there, do you see, little Alice? Do you see now, trudging along beside me on the mountain path while I try to explain wickedness which I myself had not apprehended... Such thoughts as this have been thought before, lots of times... Perhaps that's what such hideous stories as bloody Lot and his horrible daughters are for, to let us know that we are not alone in our misery... Others have splashed despairing through these foul swamps, it's not just us...

Shaken, Sasha levers herself to her feet and plunges away from him. She puts her hands flat on the table, recovers herself. This is... unnecessary. Don't work it up into a bloody great earth-shattering tragedy. Hey, it's no big deal. See the funny side. This is, after all, the same table upon which I had Jack, flat on his back, with his big cock and balls all a-dangle... Which we were eating our dinner off earlier. The table, not the... She laughs, bright and cheerful, see this gloom away, swings and roundabouts to him.

"Sorry, Daddy. I think I must be a bit drunk too."

And very quickly, she runs to him and kisses the top of his head where it's just getting a bit bald on top and then skips to the stairs calling night night daddy see you in the morning and with a tip tap top she's gone

After some minutes had elapsed since the departure of his daughter, during which he had been sitting in a condition of more or less complete stupefaction, the Reverend Peter Thomas, feeling shaken, though not, he added to himself, recalling with amusement a popular cinematic entertainment which he had enjoyed some years previously, stirred, bestirred himself sufficiently to leave his chair and, taking up the glass into which he had previously poured a measure of that so refreshing wine, made his way to the kitchen at the rear of the premises where, he felt sure, he would find something left in the bottle. In this he was not disappointed, and after steadfastly consuming the same, all of it, he rinsed his glass and repaired to the downstairs bathroom for the purpose of micturition. This accomplished, and having brushed his teeth and splashed with water his face, he returned to the chair where he had left his book of Abraham, for it must be said that he found it inexplicably cheering, and made his way through to the study which, as his wife had made clear to him during their conversation earlier in the evening, was to be his place of repose for the night. But for all his determination to face with equanimity the slings and arrows of outrageous fortune as he had heard his elder daughter remark that she for her part intended to do all her life long on more than one occasion his heart was heavy as he went. Upon entering the small chamber which he called the study, though in truth there had been precious little study done there for as long as he could recall, his nostrils were at once assailed by the strong reminiscence of girlish perfume and tobacco smoke lingering in the air, and the sight of a litter of light alloy cylinders and glass tumblers together with a saucer onto which a great many filter tips had been pressed in extinguishing them upon the low table by the couch which was to be his bed did little to elevate his mood. His realisation that he had neither pyjamas nor bedclothes lowered his spirits still further. A book, not his, one of his daughter's by the look of it, lay on the carpet. he picked it up, flicked it open, read:

Where now? Who now? When now? Unquestioning. I, say I. Unbelieving. Questions, hypotheses, call them that. Keep going, going on, call that going, call that on.

Peter smiled, chucked it down. All right, I choose to call this going, going on. I will not despair. I will find out where, who, when… Unbelieving, questions, yes I will, I will, yes. And he threw himself down on the sofa just as he was without one plea and read from the book that he had in his hand, Bryn's, not hers…

"How is your wife, by the way?"
"My…?" How did he know? *Could* he know?
"It must be very worrying for her, having to live in a place like this. I expect she'd prefer it if you were posted somewhere a little more

stable. Alexandria? One of the Greek provinces? Or even back to Rome. Is that what she'd like? What would *you* like, Pontius?"

Pilate was about to tell him when…

Alexandria

Alexandra

Sasha

Peter fell asleep.

4

It's good to get it off your chest but God I came a bit close there, nearly told him All but let him wonder on if he does wonder he doesn't look like he gives a shit, sitting there with his bloody book all night while I make the supper serve the supper wash the supper things up afterwards like a good little Martha how he thinks a wife should be when he thinks about me at all it'll be his Last Supper all right one of these nights I'll just say right that's it I'm off. With Alice. Take her of course, Alexasha's big enough to look after herself these days she's off anyway to uni soon it'll just be me and Ali against the rest of the world. Ah, she's so excited isn't she, fancy this bloke being the author of Cartowhatsit Jack didn't say he was a writer what did he say he was at first a sort of artist or woodworker, all that new age crap with magic runes and his bloody silly tarot cards there's nothing in it still it's weird I must admit the number of co-incidences but there that's just the way things are you do what you do because it's what you do there's no point in pretending it's all part of some Great Plan or fate or destiny things happen because other things have happened before them it's obvious really

God the bloody room's going round I drank so much I shouldn't what if Alice was ill in the night or something and I was too pissed to look after her he'd be no bloody use faffing about he looked a bit suspicious when I went to get the extra booze this morning but then he's been looking a bit suspicious ever since Jack started dropping in to the vicarage for a coffee as well he might be what a fool I was Jack, Jack, should've taken him upstairs to my own bedroom at home while the others were out no one would know or no I know I should have gone out to his workshop again do it there oh he did feel good when I kissed him he was so hard under his jeans

And when I crept into his room in the dark and there he was in the moonlight by the window and I got on the bed and reached out to him his legs so strong and my fingers going up, up, up into the secret places nearly bursting ready to come he was and then he said her name. How could he have stood there thinking it was her all that time just standing there enjoying it he was he wasn't going to say Get out you little tart how dare you was he no by God he wasn't the bastard men they're only after one thing and they don't care who they get it off and what a story that would've been to tell bloody Bryn if it had been her instead of me, you can imagine him laughing with a beer in his fist Well, the mother's a bit hung up but the daughter, oh, wait till I tell you

So he ran away he must've thought the damage was irrep, rep, bloody hell my stomach irreparable and he was right there what on earth could we have said to one another over the breakfast things just imagine Ah there you are, good morning Jack, my goodness what a laughable misunderstanding last night you'll never guess what Sasha I went to Jack's room after you'd gone to bed and I was giving him a bloody good handjob he was loving it but guess what just when he was about to come he said Oh Sasha, Sasha, yes, he thought it was *you*. And see Sasha choking over her toast, crumbs spraying everywhere oh *Jack* you silly didn't you realise I'm only interested in girls? And little Alice looking up all puzzled from her cornflakes asking Mummy what's a handjob? to general hilarity what a night well I never so we're going to Fan Hir today then are we?

Still thank God he did go and thank God Sasha came out so I knew there really was nothing going on but he must've thought there was how come what did she say? She'd had a go at him earlier on after I'd gone up to bed, yes, having a good row could've done the trick for him, Mummy's friend and Mummy's friend's daughter have had a nasty row and turned their backs, but the Man and the Woman in them are still toe to toe eye to eye and all that emotion's got to go somewhere having a row could've brought them closer as it were pa, para, pardon *me!* paradoxically. He must've thought she was up for it somehow at least he thought she might come to him. At least he hadn't gone to her. What am I, making excuses for him now? Well he couldn't could he, not with Alice in the room. Or had he already arranged for her to come to him was that what he was doing standing by the window waiting for her but I just got in first spoiled it for them no Sasha wouldn't would she she's not interested in boys or did she actually want to find out all that talk about Welsh boys well what if she did want to go to him out of curiosity she might you couldn't go your whole life without knowing what it's like with a man, could you. Or what it's like with a woman if you're…

What's all this commotion outside stomping banging and giggling for God's sake shut up you'll wake Alice what's that? Sasha's voice what's she saying Be quiet, Fran, you'll wake up Alice… and Mum. Oh great. Stage whisper loud enough to wake the dead, thanks Sasha well thanks a lot for the bulletin from the home front nice to know Fran's going to bed at what is it have a look one o'clock in the morning and all's well, well, well. Lonely. On your own in bed. Ought to be used to it by now. There's the bog flushing that's her coming out of the loo and that's her door that was Jack's door opening is it yes the latch is a bit stiff, yes and shutting? No. Left it open? Why's that not expecting a visitor is she who might that be well let's see there's a choice of three four if we include Alice but for heaven's sake no let's be sensible is it Sasha if it is it's goodbye Jess or is it is it possible you can have lots of lovers like in Islam they have four wives is it four just imagine being number one and seeing the new models brought out every few years I suppose it would make some things easier I mean if Peter wanted to with her he could've just added her to the roster couldn't he instead of all this guilty excuse making I wonder if he really did it with her what if that's why her door's open tonight he did and she's expecting more

Mind you she was pretty keen on Jack today but then she'd have to be wouldn't she with me there but she was being ever so friendly and last night God I would've if only I hadn't been afraid is that true would I? If she's not expecting Sasha or Peter or for heaven's sake Alice yes well that's just silly then it's got to be me. If it's going to be. That lovely shiny poster I liked so much in Robert's study in bloody Wind whatever it was called Ward was it psychiatric ward more like funny it was though wasn't it with him banging on to Peter about the Christian fellowship so boring boring and what was his wife called Sheila Sarah Sara that was it got into trouble for calling her Sarah silly bloody fat or corpulent cow with her logging on and logging off and faffing about with the endless coffee and I was bored half silly so I started gawping round the room like you do and there he was all of a sudden on the wall, such a lovely picture wonder if I could get a copy somewhere clinging on to a cliff it looked like he was, bronzed and fit as they say well fit he was all right with his lovely strong limbs gleaming golden in the sun

And that was where he met her then he must've made quite an impression on her for her to just drop everything and follow him like the disciples leaving their nets in the boats and there we go again the bible everything comes back to the bible it's in me so deep I'm always remembering some story or other I don't suppose it ever leaves you once you've had it hammered into you yes they hammer, thrust it into you so deep sexual it is really, all those men pushing it in as hard as they can they love it no wonder some of them won't have women priests its not the same for them is it without a great big erection out there somewhere ready to poke and shove and stir up the fire of faith like totem poles and standing stones and even steeples really they say they point to heaven but we know better don't we girls they're just fucking great cocks with a weather cock on the top very often too just to make it clear in case you missed the obvious symbolism so here's a clever little pun as well to as it were thrust it home, ladies. Got the point?

She must've got the point all right for her just to drop everything and jump into his car like that if that's the truth what a tale of cock and balls he told me I don't believe it mind you what she said was amazing if it's true just selling everything she had and spending her time singing songs to Jesus and waiting for him to wrap it all up and carry her off to heaven she must have been a bit soft in the head if she thought that was going to happen but that's religion for you. So now she's decided it was all a mistake, well well well there've been plenty of those made this week. What a week this has turned out to be. Some bloody holiday. God what is it, Wednesday? Thursday morning really. Oh, look at the time. Horrible when your mind seems to just pass through some threshold or other and you know you're not going to get to sleep. Lie still, lie still, time will pass you just have to wait and the future will happen the way it was always going to, it will, and soon comes the dawn, morn. Try counting sheep. That thing of Sash's when we were up on the hill. Made me laugh in spite of everything. Why can you never finish counting sheep? Because you fall asleep before you've finished, said Alice. Nope, said Sasha, it's because there's always one *mehr*. Need another pee now.

Quietly with the latch. Not a sound. Can't see a bloody thing. Go back and put the bedside light on, just enough to see down the corridor if I leave the door open a crack. Ouch what's that my shoes. Where's the. Here. Switch. That's better. God I do feel weird. How much did I drink? Find my way carefully, don't want to go flying crash bang wallop imagine it the other doors fly open and out pop Sasha and Alice and Fran all gawping at me rolling around on the floor moaning trying to find out which way is up. How they'd laugh. Not funny really, being this drunk. What if Alice. This is a bit of a *déjà vu* experience, come to think of it, except it's not is it, it's an action replay as they say on TV. There's his door now, open a crack, no, hers now, and she's in there. Asleep? Listen. Nothing. What if I? Just had a peek. Stupid. Really need to go, anyway.

Bright! And such a loud click. Why do they have to have pull switches in bathrooms? So you don't electrocute yourself with your wet hands on the dodgy toggle. Stupid idea. What do they think towels are for? Shut the door. Quietly! And slip the bolt across for uninterrupted peeing. Gather up this nightie. Don't know why I'm wearing such a long one in this weather. Tie it round my ankles if he comes scratching at the door with his monthly erection sticking out of his pyjamas. Ahh. God, I'm doing gallons. How much did I have? Those cans of lager didn't help. Trust Sasha to stock up on those when I was getting the wine. There's not much bog roll left, get some more tomorrow. Give myself a wipe. Men don't. Can't be bothered. Do it standing up, give it a shake after, goes everywhere. Dribbles on the floor. Horrible, having to wipe up his piss for him. Hate that. Funny how it's the same hole for pissing and coming. Penis. Pee nice. Hardly ever touched Peter's. Didn't want me too. Afraid he might enjoy it. Jack's though. Nice. His kiss in the workshop, deep. Tongued him, I did. How much longer am I going to sit here wiping my. Funny how I don't have a word for it like cock. Don't think about it. Fanny. Sounds funny. Cunt. Sounds crude. Labia major, clit, me bits. Nice feeling it. Mm, that's nice. I could keep going till I. Not here. In bed. Help me to get off. Get off, ha ha. Off to sleep. Flush? Make a noise. Leave it. What the hell. Leave the light on? Such a loud click. Leave it. What the.

Enough light from the bog to see into. Her room. What if I? Just a peek? When she kissed me. Last night. Deep. I feel so ready now after. Just creep in, see if. So dark where the bed is. Mind I don't fall over anything. Where is it, here. Ah just enough light to see her hair, so fair like flax it is and so fine… kneel down, careful now… kiss her hair, yes, mm it smells so good, kiss her bare shoulder kiss

"Mm…?"

"Fran…"

She stirs in her sleep she's not awake yet stroke her lovely hair smooth it is like silk down the side of her face her chin there and her little collar bone so fine under the soft warm skin kiss her lips

"Huh?"

"Shh…"

Kiss her lips again, Shh, no sound, God her little breasts she's naked under the quilt of course she is she hasn't got a nightie or anything here's her nipple

"Mm…"

"Shh…"

Heavenly this is I never dreamed I never realised never thought it could be so

"No…"

"Shh…"

"No, no this is lovely, mm you are turning me on I'd love to but we can't it's so unfair remember you said we were only playing and that's all right but this is too much I think you're lovely really I do but you'd better go before… before it gets too… you know it would be wrong… please don't be hurt I'm only thinking of Jess…"

Out quick not a word before she has time to have a good look and shut the door clatter of the latch but what the hell get back into bed before anyone sees door shut light out get this bloody nightie off so hot so hot get on the bed before my heart gives out oh its thumping, thumping hell what have I done what have I done what if I had got in with her hell so soft she is so slim and her little breast in my hand how delicate, how gently I'd have caressed it and kissed her mouth deep, deep, my tongue on hers while I'm stroking her slowly down, down, over her flat firm belly until ah there I'd touch her soft bush and linger on her little clit and slide my hand between and slip a finger in and find she's all wet like me I am so wet I am too the lovely juice mm I'd keep stroking till she moaned and see her face if only I could see her face as she started to come imagine imagine her blissful blue eyes rolling up and her lips apart, breathing faster, faster and pushing up again and again up on my hand faster and faster her arms around my neck now and ah, ah, her voice catching as she gasps and comes and comes yes my love yes yes yes

Oh I'm done I'm absolutely done my heart my God it's thumping thumping listen God it'll burst with a bang, wake them all up and they'll come in to see and find me here flat on my back stone dead with my hand on my fanny and they'll know I died for love love mm, Fran, Fran, Fran…

Ah there you are, good morning Fran, coffee? My goodness what a laughable misunderstanding last night! Pass the marmalade please Peter you'll never guess what Sasha I went to Fran's room after you'd gone to bed and I was giving her a bloody good snog she was loving it but guess what I was within an inch of her clit when she goes no no no this is lovely but we mustn't, must we, it's not fair on Jess! Yes! She thought it was *you*. And Sasha choking over her toast, crumbs spraying everywhere oh *Fran* you silly didn't you realise if it'd been me you'd've been coming so hard the moment I touched you you'd never've got a word out? And little Alice looking up all puzzled from her cornflakes asking Mummy what's a clit? to general hilarity what a night well I never so we're going to see the Great Author today then are we?

But what when she tells she's bound to she'll say something to Sasha in the morning or perhaps not you can always hope and hey what's done is done let's not dwell on the past we all make mistakes and that but oh in the clear light of day what will she say? She'll at least look at her a bit funny and Sasha'll say what's the matter with you today then and she'll say she's bound to isn't she should I get to Sasha first and explain everything then, guess what, I'm coming out too, love, you've shown me the way I'm gay, no lesbian it is with girls isn't it? Am I? Never even thought about it before well that's not quite true, wondered about it obviously but I didn't know I'd really want to I surprised myself but it's not surprising really the experience I've had of men well Peter anyway.

Peter in his prime, pumping away, inout inout it never occurred to him did it that it could be gentle, that softness and silkiness and ever such delicate caresses were part of it? Sinful that would be oh hell must I think of it our wedding night when I thought it was all going to be so lovely I was so happy I cried when we got to the hotel room but when we got back up there after dinner and it was Time to Do It for the First Time and he was so crazed with lust the bloody maniac I thought he'd gone mad it was like being attacked and he didn't even manage to get it in that time before he was spurting all over the place oh God I don't want to remember.

Horrible couple of days that was all right, driving round to see the sights such as they were during the day smiling and smiling and pretending to enjoy myself and then back to the grotty hotel room at night where he'd pray long and hard ha ha long and hard before he got into bed but he didn't want to try again it would've been a sin to so soon after like he enjoyed it or something yawning now I'm so tired what's the time Christ I'll never get to sleep and when he did finally work out how to shove it in that was about all he did do wasn't it inout inout in and then he'd say aargh and pull it out and roll over off me and go to sleep that's his lust sorted for another few days and he hated it if I seemed to be enjoying it that wasn't in the script no no I had to lie still and take it I don't think I ever came properly until until I until I went

That was the time yes when trumpets fanfared fulfilment and jazzy joyful clarinets trickley tickley oh how high and oh how low the swooping trombone brassy flashy big bell blaring ching ching ching went the funny little cowbells crash sizzle sizzle cymbals thump daddy mummy daddy mummy drum drum drum can't hear a bloody word you're saying drum drum sorry what I said I can't hear a bloody... let's go outside. Into the pouring rain across the road ow shriek it's pissing down oh splash splash mind that fuckin' car for Christ's sake *parp* yes, and up yours too you careless bastard here's a good pub let's have a couple take that mac off you're soaking no take it off no I can't I'm naked underneath oh nobody here minds that come on that's better here I'll hang it up for you. Now then, what would you like to drink? I'll have a Bloody Mary like that sheep's having. Do you see, the one at the bar, talking to my husband. You Bloody can't have a Mary, they've run out, there's no *mehr*. Bloody *Mary* Christmas to you all, says Santa, red trousers puddled round his ankles as he picks up the sheep's hindquarters in his hands and without so much as a by your leave begins to bugger away, his white woolly beard wagging in time to his inout inout the sheep doesn't seem to mind, or even to notice, certainly doesn't let the rogering he's receiving interrupt the interesting theological conversation he's having with Peter, who is very relaxed in full Eucharistic garb for the season of Christmas, elbow on the bar, chalice in one hand from which he sups in between pronouncements leaving his lips bright red, rolled copy of the Church Times in the other, with which he whacks the sheep on the head to emphasise his points, in the name of the Fatherwhack, and of the Sonwhack, and of the Hold it right there, she shouts, that poor sheep stop it stop it but nobody seems to be taking any notice of her however loud she shouts, so that she leaps up and down, arms flailing, tits aswing, stop it stop it and then Sasha turns to her from behind the bar where she's polishing glasses, fag in bright red lipsticked mouth, cheeks rouged, in full barmaid fetish rig, skimpy white blouse barely containing her sturdily bodiced underwired and upthrust embonpoint, bursting buttons popping off like shrapnel, Cool it Mummee, it's all right, he loves it, don't you, Angus? And *Mehr, Mehr* goes the sheep, so that sodomitical Santa redoubles his efforts while Peter puts his chalice down the more violently to belabour the ovine arse enthusiast using both hands, and when even this proves insufficient punishment throws the inadequate journal away and produces from within his robes a hardback copy of Crockford's Clerical Directory and sets to work with renewed vigour on the poor sheep's head, now bloody but still unbowed He loves it, Mummee, shouts Sasha, he's taking it for all of us, aren't you, Angus, Angus Daily qui tollis peccata mundi, Tuesday, wedding night. Thirsty? Good. Friday night's always a bit busy in here, whole of Saturday's the same, harrowing experience, hell's bells ching ching ching, thump that sheep, daddy mummy daddy mummy drum drum drum can't hear a bloody word you're saying drum drum sorry what I said I can't hear a bloody single symbol and by the way have you realised you're stark naked as the as the day you were raped I never says Peter processing across the bar to remonstrate with her but coming over all hurt and petulant or if I did, he whines and whinges, polishing his glasses with a pair of skimpy pink panties, you asked for it flaunting your wicked woman's body stark naked kneeling by the bed I prayed, God knows I prayed to be saved from nightly fantasies and all unchastity though not yet, Lord, not just yet, because I'm enjoying it all far too much at the moment oh is it Sunday yet? Yes: another womanish weakling's past it's time to *mount* the pulpit steps once more and *thrust* my phallocentric *faith* right *into*, *your*, open-mouthed *ears* ha ha if you can have open mouthed *et cetera* you know I always like to start my sermons with a joke! Help your child-like women's minds to engage with the serious male matter in hand. In hand! See? Here's my *male matter* in my hand now! Ha ha all right I'll put it away now missus only joking only joking. Here we go then, no seriously now, in the name of the Father, and of the Son, and of the other one, Spirit that's it thank you Tim make mine a large one! Sorry sorry sorry. Well, what a relief it must have been, belovèd, to be standing there gawping at Him in your sandals and your dressing gown with your tea towel on your head and be told, "It's all right. Really. Sins? Forget it. Oh, if you insist: they're forgiven. Yes they are. Because I say so. Now stop pissing about and get on with your lives. Oh, and don't forget to be *nice* to one another. Religion? You don't need all that crap. It's cut. That turd is nipped. Finished. The kingdom is here, the tabernacle of God is with men, whatever. All that snipping at little boys' winkles and sacrificing of sheep and oxen and doves and pigeons and trying to give the Romans the chop and no nice pork chops either is all over and done with. It's served its purpose. That's it. Game over. Insert coin. No, actually give it to Judas over there, Sir, he's the treasurer, looks after the pieces of silver for us. Lovely lad, trust him with me life. Ay thang yew. Sorry, no more questions, I'm late for a cripple in Capernaum. Healing? Yes he is- heeling over to the left something dreadful when he walks ha ha ha b-boom don't worry I'll sort him out love and peace guys love and peace joking Jesus they call me Saulpaul wasn't having any of that. Yesyesyes he'd been wrong to persecute them, they'd been right all along, fulfilment of the law and the prophets, but they couldn't just leave it all behind. God did choose them to be a holy people, right? So show some bloody gratitude. Down on your knees, Sir- yes, you too, Madam. Now. That's better. Nonono, least of the apostles. But do what I say! Get your hands off me, Roman citizen I am, wait till I tell the Procurator. Thank God for the Romans. Now, you stupid Galatians, Corinthians, Thessalonians, and and and the rest of them, you can just fill in the name when you send it off, can't you? Thanks. Where was I? Oh. Concerning the matters you wrote to me about. Sex, sex, sex. Can't you think about anything else? Why can't you all be like me, chaste and pure? The day is almost come when the Lord Jesus Christ the Alpha and Omega the beginning and the end will return in great glory with more than twelve legions of angels, the heavens will be rolled up like a parchment, stars dropping from the sky like rain, the trumpet will sound and we will all be changed in a moment in the twinkling of an eye and the whole world will be driven trembling before the judgement throne, and you want to know if it's all right to have a shag? No no no don't put that, most unseemly, put instead something about living after the will of the spirit not the will of the flesh you know the kind of thing by now. Put how, yes- put how those that are married already, yes yes I know I did just leave a space you can do it later I'll lose my thread, those that are married already can stay married, but there's not much point marrying if you're not married already because damn it I've forgotten what I was going to say. Oh just say they can marry if they must, weak vessels full of lust that they are it won't make any difference anyway in the long run. Not that there is a long run anymore. It could all be over before that ink's dry, you realise that, don't you boy. You married? Good. Stay that way. You're engaged? For God's sake, you young men. I'm sure she is, yes, very lovely. Has she indeed. She- now, boy, that's more information than I need. Oh all right then if you must. Better to marry than to burn with lust. Hey, that's good- put that in. Better to marry than to burn. God I'm tired, tired of all this. Come, Lord Jesus. End it all. So tired. How far have you got? Well get on with it for goodness' sake, what's the matter with you, still dreaming about that girl of yours, are you? Handwriting? It doesn't matter about the bloody handwriting you're not exactly writing for posterity are you? Nobody's going to be reading this stuff in two thousand years' time. All be over then. All over. Wish it was over now. What a life. Sometimes I wish I'd never heard of Damascus. Things used to be so different in the old days. Those peaceful Sabbath days. Oh, Sabbath rest by Galilee, we used to sing, oh calm of sheep flecked hills above, rising and falling like waves of deepest emerald, they were, so lovely sloping down to the water. So cool by the lake it is, I can see it now- in my mind's eye, boy, in my mind's eye- almost silent save for the lapping of the ripples on the shingle shore, but now I hear just the faintest melody, growing louder now in my imagination, a shepherd is it, with his pipe, sitting on a rock overlooking the waterside, handsome lad he is, not like you you bloody scruff, just listen to him he's what they call cool, real cool he is, a cool cat we used to say in those days, oh yes I used to know all the lingo, me and my mates we used to go every year, the town used to buzz and oh sure the up tempo numbers used to have all our feet tapping but for me it was the gentler sounds always that I used to love, I remember one time when the mood was so cool, so glacially cool that gentlest of jazz, with softest shuffle of brushes and beat of bass, and I see her now sitting listening, rapt, her elbow on the table her hand under her chin, so cute she looks but melancholy too, as if she's been hurt so bad sometime, and she's still hurting, hurting, she takes a drink, and then I think, I'll take a bet, that when this set, is over she, will talk to me, and so in the sudden loud applause and whoops and bravos, encore, more, I get up and start to pick my way through the smoky air between the crowded tables but no matter how many I step round with excuse me and whoops and sorry was that your foot do you mind if I just come through… she's always just as far away, and I seem to've lost my trousers somewhere along the way, and people are pointing and laughing and shouting hey, but still I go on and on until at last I'm nearly there, she runs a hand through her long heavy hair, Would that it were shaken out over my breast, I say, and she turns and smiles and replies, There is enough evil in the crying of

"*Bryn, Bryn, Bryn...*"

"Mm."

Enough evil in the crying of wind in the reeds by the edge of this desolate lake of the lady of sorrows the

"*Bryn, Bryn, Bryn...*"

"Huh?"

"Bryn, there's someone outside."

"Mm."

"Bryn."

"What?"

"There's someone outside. I heard a car."

"Fucksake what time is it? Jesus. I was out like a light. Someone outside, you say?"

"Better get some clothes on. Oh God, they're knocking. Who can it be?"

Bryn rolled over and landed his feet on the floor, heaved himself up and padded naked to the window, pulled aside the flimsy curtain, fumbled with the latch and flung it wide to a burst of birdsong, and suddenly the joy of last night's long magical working took him up, and for a moment he saw again the flowery glade, the waterfall tumbling laughing into the crystal pool, felt himself breathing in gratefully the scented air of that fairy world... then voices coming up from somewhere below brought him back and he felt exhausted, sagging on the windowsill, no longer as young as he was. Still, he thought, it looked like another fine day. Except there was a strange car in the yard. Not Jack's.

"Cathy?"

But she was going out of the door, still pulling her jeans up. He heard her bare feet pattering down the stairs, renewed knocking. Then her unlocking, and the creak of the front door. He crept to the top of the stairs, stood listening. Jack's unmistakable bray, and other voices, quieter. Then some laughter. And... was that a child's voice?

Bloody hell! He's brought them! The wanking woman and her vampire loving kid! Fuck!

IX

1

Ow that sun's bright now I've got some shades in the glove compartment somewhere where are they here we are that's better it's odd having Jack driving our car but the five of us wouldn't have fitted into his very well with all the junk he's got in it and anyway I bet I'm over the limit still pissed look how he handles it he's so relaxed and easy with it compared to Peter see his thigh move as he changes gear oh no don't even think it oh can't you shut up you girls jabbering away in the back all the time you don't have to shout do you what's so bloody hilarious for God's sake but I shouldn't complain I'd never have been able to face them again if Sasha hadn't come to me I just wanted to die I felt like that who was it Damocles with his sword hanging over his head so bloody miserable waiting for the blow to fall she's a lovely girl I'm so proud really I am oh no here we go it's Are we nearly there yet Are we nearly there yet they always start that sooner or later Fran's enjoying herself by the sound of it well that's something I suppose what's Sasha saying now oh it's questions for Alice to ask the Great Author good idea we don't want to just sit there gawping at him like he's exhibit A well I hope he's got some coffee on for us black and strong would suit me right now try and wake up a bit my God that was a sharp turn and where the hell are we going now this is a bit bloody narrow down here and bumpy too ooh my guts I hope he doesn't scratch the paintwork or Peter'll be off again on one like when we'd only had it a week and I backed it into the gatepost hello we're here are we it wasn't so far after all thanks Jack everybody out it's a bit run down isn't it for the Great Author to live in wait a minute it's. It's like. Oh My God it can't be…

"Hello, Cath!"
"Jack! Good morning. And…"
"This is Alice."
"Hello, Cath."
"Hello, Alice. Nice to meet you. I gather you're a really keen reader, then. Oh, you've bought *Cartomancer* with you! Well, you'd better come in. And you've brought Mum too, have you?"
"Jane here is yes Alice's Mum of course and, er…"
"Hello, Jane."
"Mm."
"This is big Sis, Sasha…"
"Hello Sasha."
"Enchantée."
"Behave, Sasha. And this is Fran. A friend…"
"Hi, Cath."
"…whom I just met yesterday, in fact. In fact she's…"
But Cathy saves him from making a complete arse of himself.
"Hello Fran, you're very welcome. Please come on in, all of you, make yourselves at home. Jack, you know where the tea and coffee is, would you mind? Sorry about the just got out of bed look, by the way, but that's because I've just got out of bed. Bit of a late night I'm afraid. Would you excuse me for a moment? I'll go up now and tell Bryn you're here."
"Is he busy writing?"
"I'm not sure, Alice. He'll come down in just a moment."
"If he is, tell him I'm really sorry to interrupt him."
"I will, Alice. What a nice polite girl you are. See you in a minute, I won't be long."
Cathy skipped away and ran up the stairs. Bryn was coming out of the bathroom, brushing what was left of his hair and grumbling to himself. She put her hands on his shoulders, quieted him, engaged his eyes, smiled.
"Gabriel," she whispered, and…

And it was as if he had stepped out of a tangled thicket into a sun dappled glade, sweet with the scent of wild flowers, where birds sang and a laughing spring spilt its fresh life eternally into a brilliant pool of clear water…

"Hardd," he replied, and then, "Soror mea."

"Frater meus," she whispered, and kissed him and…

…and sent him on his way downstairs laughing for joy. Quickly she went into the bathroom and stripped and stood under the shower rejoicing because she could see that what had happened in the magical hours of last night was still real and present in them this morning… oh the enchantment, *hud*… the fullness of being… as she washed herself she could hardly believe she was truly under the old shower with its battered chrome rose for she saw beyond it and through it the fairy falls that had showered their healing water on her in that blissful valley where they had walked together…

Bryn was still laughing and full of the joy of her when he flip flopped into the kitchen, so that Alice loved him at first sight and leaped to her feet with her eyes wide and would have run excitedly up to him, but for her excellent vicarage manners.

"This must be Alice," Bryn said, grinning, and…

And splashing barelegged through the brilliant pool under the sunlit willow branches loud with birdsong a beautiful happy little child, a girl, her bright eyes sparkling in glad greeting, her white dress like gossamer floating around her as she held out her hands to him…

…and thinking what a pretty little thing she was. Stooping slightly, he held his hand out to her. "How do you do, Miss?"

"I'm very well indeed, thank you Sir," she replied as she shook it solemnly in her best polite prep school pupil manner, so that Bryn laughed again, and…

And as he took her hands and felt her bounding energy surge into him, he gasped in wonder, for he knew her face, knew it so well, how could he ever have forgotten that long flowing fair hair framing those quick, intelligent features, those eyes crinkling in laughter now…

…and bent his head in close to her, saying, "I'm a bit nervous, actually, Alice."

"Why's that, Sir?"

"Why, actually meeting one of my readers… it's a bit scary!"
"Is it? I feel a bit nervous meeting you, Sir."
"Well, that makes two of us, then."

…and the birdsong faded and the pool darkened and sunlit glade became shadowy, the complex patterns of the willow branches shifting over his head became the simplicity of his homely kitchen and the child was this child, this little girl he knelt by, whose pretty little face and charming manners had won his heart at once: and he tried his best to make her feel at home so that this visit would be a success for her. He said:
"I'm sure we're going to be friends, Alice. You must call me Bryn, for a start, like everybody else does, all right?"
"Yes, Sir, I mean, Bryn."
"Good. I'm looking forward to having a long chat with you. Is that *Cartomancer* you've got there?"
"Yes, Sir, Bryn. I've got some questions…"
"Questions? Ooh, I love questions. Fascinating things. But first: coffee. Is it on, Jack?"
"Yes, Bryn, just coming."
"Excellent. I need something to wake me up. What do you like, Alice? Juice?"
"I like wine."
"Do you now. Me too. But we can't go getting drunk before we've had our conversation, can we? Work first," said Bryn very seriously, patting her on the shoulder. He glanced up from her, realising with something of a shock that he'd ignored all these others, so strongly had he been moved by the little girl. Where were his manners? But he felt compelled to look back at Alice again- he *knew* her! Surely that was impossible. For a moment he felt the kitchen fading again, saw with his inner eye the luminous faery landscape of last night…

"You all right, Mum?" whispered Sash, bending to Jane quickly.
"No, I feel terrible."

Bryn forced himself back into the present. There was a smiley little blue-eyed blonde fussing round Jack and the coffee things, the older sister, he presumed, and a tall striking looking girl with intensely black bobbed hair who was stooping solicitously over some weird female slumped on a chair at the far end of the long table, her eyes hidden behind dark glasses. Jack's woman I suppose she is, he thought. Christ, looks a right bloody misery.

"But Alice," he went on, rubbing his hands together, "You haven't introduced me to all these people who've come with you. Quite a houseful we've got."

"This is my Mum," said Alice proudly. Mum, not Mummy. Grown up now. Real Author.

"Hello," said Bryn, smiling, nodding, getting nothing but a slight inclination of the head back, wondering why the shades, dark enough in here isn't it? Has she got weak eyes? Too much bloody wanking perhaps.

"Mummy's feeling a bit under the weather this morning, I'm afraid! But she'll be fine. This is Sasha, my big sister. She was helping me think of some good questions in the car."

"Yeah, we'll make you scratch your head, Bryn," sez Sash, striding over. "Hi. *Bore da* and all that." That's a surprise, thought Bryn. I'd have guessed the blonde one was the sister. Firm handshake, manly almost. Wonder if she's…

"And this is Fran." Jack butting in here, proprietorial, wanting to be the one to introduce Fran for some reason. "Here's your coffee, everyone. " He sets a tray on the table, passes round mugs and cups and a glass for Alice, not wine. "Hey Fran. Let's take ours outside. Show you round. There's a lovely walk down to the lake."

"Sure, why not."

Bryn still couldn't take his eyes off Alice. He sat her in one of the big chairs by the fireplace, took the other himself, got out his smoking kit, started talking to her about her school, what her favourite subjects were, what her friends were like, while Alice sipped her orange squash and answered him with a kind of awe, wondering at the clouds of fragrant smoke… she'd never seen anyone smoke a pipe before! He was concentrating on her, enjoying her cute little mannerisms and the turns of phrase she'd picked up… while at the edge of his awareness he felt the dark eyed presence of the mother still sitting at the table, knew that he ought to try and include her in the conversation. He almost threw her a question, but just then Sasha dragged a chair across to him and started telling him about her father's enthusiasm for *Abraham and his seed.*

"Likes it, does he? Oh, good. I must admit I'm pleased with that one. Bit old for you, I'm afraid, Alice. It's going to be filmed, all being well. Next year, so I'm told."

"Was Abraham an Arable Farmer, then?" Alice wanted to know. Arable was a good word. She'd used it in her Geography essay on Land Use in England and Wales.

"No, I don't think so. He was a herdsman. Sheep, you know."

"So what did he need the seed for?"

"Oh, good question. Ah… it wasn't that kind of seed. It's a metaphor. Have you learned about metaphors yet?" The innocence of her. *Semini eius*… not suitable.

"Yes. A simile's got like in it and a metaphor hasn't."

"Oh, very good. Very concise. Well, what is meant by seed here is all the generations that are going to be descended from Abraham. Like the seeds of a plant."

"But that's a simile. You said like."

"So it is. So I did. Damn. I knew I had reason to be nervous this morning."

"*Sicut locutus est ad patres nostros,*" sez Sash conversationally, "*Abraham et semini eius in saecula.*"

"Oh, you know Latin do you? That's good."

"Language is my thing. I'm going to Swansea next term to read English. Wouldn't mind trying my Welsh out on you later, *os gwelwch yn dda.*"

"*Wrth gwrs.*"

"I'm going to give up Latin next year."

"Oh, don't do that, Alice. That would be a bad move."

"Really?"

"I'm sure of it. If you think my advice is worth anything, learn Latin. You'll never regret it. Now, we're supposed to be talking about *Cartomancer*. Enjoyed it, did you? Good. Who's your favourite character?"

Jane had recognised him at once. Ten years had fallen away, the rotten tapestry of ten years had simply fallen away, dropping with a dull thump which she had felt in the pit of her stomach, leaving her numbed, sick. In her head she was howling with rage at the injustice, screaming inside with anger at the sheer improbability of it, it was so unfair, why had the blind unravelling of one damn thing after another brought her back here after all this time… Thank God he didn't seem to remember her. Of course, she'd had long hair then, was wearing completely different clothes. It'd been ten years, a decade… Keep the shades on, keep quiet. As she put her coffee cup to her lips, trying to stop her hand shaking, she stared at him over the rim, through the dark disguising lenses. Trying not to see Alice's face in his…

Quietly, hoping he wouldn't notice her and speak, she eased herself out of her chair, went to the window that looked out onto the little garden at the back. She remembered it all so well now. How was she going to survive this? What if they were invited to stay for lunch? Make an excuse and go. She couldn't sit at the table with him without him realising, surely. Half listening to their talk with the blood pounding in her ears, she suddenly became aware of someone at her elbow. Christ, it's his woman. Cathy, was it?

"Hello, Jane. Sorry to be antisocial, I just had to get freshened up. We were so late last night." Jane couldn't think of anything to say, just stared at her through the concealing lenses, swallowed hard. His woman. She's beautiful. Of course she is.

"Are you all right, Jane?"

"Sorry…" Jane kept her voice low, in case the sound of it reminded him… "Perhaps I could get a bit of fresh air. While they're talking. Sasha will…" What? I don't know what I'm saying…

"No problem. Here, I'll let you out the back door. Don't get lost!" Too late, Cathy, oh far far too late…

After Jane had gone out, Cathy went back to the window and looked out at the sunlit garden: after only a moment it faded before her and she found herself led again into the enchantment of last night: sitting with Bryn in the centre of the circle they'd hallowed, holding him close and gazing unblinking into his eyes while the magic worked, shuddering deliciously as the energy pulsed and flickered all over and through their bodies; the intensity growing until she truly felt she was not in her body any longer, but was walking free in flowery fields, breathing the scent of broom and meadowsweet, hearing the sweet voice of the Flower Maiden Blodeuwedd herself by her side, telling her stories of owls flitting by night in the old oak forests, of emeralds and blood and the tarot card of death; and that we must always be responsible for our actions… then Cathy remembered the wonder of that moment when she and Bryn came back into their bodies simultaneously and found themselves telling one another their true names for the first time; and after that the sheer joy when…

A shadow passed in front of her, reasserting the everyday view of the garden. Head down, her mouth a tight line, Jane was moving slowly past the window.

Troubled now, though unsure why, Cathy took a cloth from the sink, feeling its cold everydayness claiming her, and started to wipe the glass where it seemed clouded. Lines from a hymn she had not sung for years came to her:
A man that looks on glass
On it may stay his eye,
Or if he pleaseth through it pass
And then the heavens espy.

2

The sheer hell of that week in the cottage with his bloody parents. Both dead now, thank God. Good riddance to the pair of them, interfering busybodies that they were. Never left her alone for a minute, always found something wrong didn't they, they always managed to make it clear somehow without actually *saying* anything, that she didn't really measure up to their high standards, that she wasn't really quite good enough for their impeccably perfect Peter. She'd thought it would make things better when Alexandra came along- she'd given them a lovely grandchild, hadn't she? But no! That only made it worse, there was so much more for her to get wrong then, wasn't there, oh yes and every year when we went for our compulsory annual so called holiday the hints fell thick and fast from how to dress her I see she's wearing those jeans again, don't you like the little frock we got her (no I don't it makes her look like a fucking freak) to what to feed her oh you're giving her tinned sausages and beans, are you? (yes she's hungry now and can't wait while I sod around chopping veg and if you're so worried about her nutrition why don't you bloody feed her yourself) to whether she should be allowed to watch the television I was reading in the paper how children's intelligence is adversely affected by long hours in front of the screen (were you really well no one's stopping *you* from playing a stimulating game with her, *I've* been out with her all day so *I* haven't had time to read the bloody paper and *I'm* bloody knackered) to what time she ought to go to bed when Peter was her age he'd have been tucked up long since (yeah and look how well *he* turned out, you tucked him right up, didn't you he's well tucked up now look at him) it was a living hell and it had all come to a head that week, her annual penance of a holiday week in the cottage she'd hoped to avoid it that year she'd had a terrible time getting ready for the move to Saint

Jude's and of course she'd had to do it all on her own hadn't she because Peter was *too busy* so there'd been endless arrangements with removal firms and finding a new school for Sasha, who hadn't wanted to leave all her friends poor little thing and Peter couldn't even make time to come to see the headmaster when I took her to visit for a day before the end of term oh she'd cried and cried and. And there was the Parish Leaving Do and saying goodbye to everyone and then on top of it all just when it was all sorted and I was looking forward to a rest his bloody mother ringing up oh you must need a rest so do come down to Wales with us as usual, I'd been hoping to use the move as an excuse to avoid it, so oh we'd love to I said but Peter's too busy this summer with the move I was saying but he heard me and took the phone and miraculously happened to have a free week after all, well just fancy that.

And having to share a bedroom with him. One thing about living in Victorian vicarages, plenty of rooms. But only three in the cottage, of course. The parents snoring away in the middle one, Alexandra in her own pink boudoir with the silly cartoon wallpaper and the mobiles- oh yes, they knew how to decorate a little girl's room better than I did too- and him and me in the one by the bog. Jack's room, Fran's room, ours then. Twin beds, but that didn't stop him trying to wriggle his way in murmuring Jane Jane oh Jane. I'm too tired, I said, go to sleep. You always say that, he says, come on Jane come on no Peter no and all this in frantic whispers in case the parents heard through the wall he wouldn't stop and I was fighting him off but he got mad and he was stronger than me and he had my nightie up round my waist and he was all over me and then I said still whispering but furious through my teeth I hissed it in his ear you bastard Peter this is rape, you understand that, don't you this is rape you bastard bastard it's rape

That was the magic word all right. He pushed himself off me, hurting me so I gasped aloud and flung himself on the other bed. Silence. Nothing. Then the misery hit me and I started to sob and had to stuff a handful of the pillow in my mouth to stifle it in case the bloody parents heard the bloody bloody parents oh I just wanted to howl but I didn't want the humiliation of them knowing how bad it was, I could just see them exchanging looks and sighing and looking sympathetically at Peter and saying it's the child I feel sorry for the stupid stupid ignorant stupid

And when I woke up in the bleak and featureless grey light of another hopeless morning and turned my head and saw him snoring there I knew the rest of my life was going to be just more of the same, a loveless marriage his bloody horrible parents poor little Alexandra in the middle of it all learning that life was hell and hopeless and I didn't want that for her I thought of Mum and how she'd gone to pieces after Daddy died and knew if I didn't get away from this I'd end up like her and so I got dressed quickly but he woke before I could get out of the room so I told him Peter I'm going home I've got to get out I need some time on my own and he sat up in bed looking bewildered but then last night must've come back to him because I saw his face change and I knew he understood without me having to explain he said nothing. I had my hand on the latch and was about to go when he spoke But… and I looked back and nearly felt sorry for him, no I did feel sorry for him, he looked so miserable and lost I might almost have relented and stayed if he hadn't come out with, What will I tell my parents? Tell them what you fucking like you fucking shit I shouted and clattered the latch and slammed the door and ran down to Alexandra's room but she was still asleep for all the banging about and I didn't want to have to explain to her and anyway his parents were so bloody good at children weren't they, she'd be all bloody right with them so I turned and practically fell down the stairs I couldn't get out fast enough I grabbed my coat and my handbag and snatched at the front door I hurt my hand on the lock I was in such a hurry and slammed the bastard thing behind me as hard as I could and ran, God yes I ran all the way to the village, thinking at any moment to hear the car behind me with him chasing me to get me back but no, I was clear I was away.

    The place was empty it was still early no one much about and then I heard this bus coming and looked and it said Brecon on the front and that'll do I thought and flagged it down and got on I saw there was no one on it it was so early I said Brecon please and the driver said return? No fucking way, I said, and he nearly pissed himself and said go on sit down it's a free ride for you for giving me the first good laugh of the day, looking me right in the eye and checking me out it was obvious he didn't try to hide it and I thought Oh God a man a real man he is with a sense of humour they do exist then and I had to laugh too at his cheeky smile I smiled back in spite of all. So I sat on the seat at the front and off we went and he turned and said I can't say I blame you, Miss, it's right hole, he said Miss that was nice and then after a while So what's the bastard's name? He'd got the picture all right I thought and something just gave way inside I didn't care anymore what the hell so I just laughed and laughed it was the relief or something I said Peter and he goes Peter! Ew Pay-tah oh very posh what's he then and I said he's a vicar and my God that was nearly game over he laughed so much he nearly had us off the road

When we got there I said thanks for the ride and he says hang on I'll give you me phone number and I laughed again he made me feel so good I said thanks but no thanks and got off but he shouted after me OK Miss but you keep off those vicars- you think you can have one and that's it but before you know it you'll be cravin' another and another after that and in no time at all you'll be...

Jane found she'd walked nearly all the way to the lake. The noisy diesel smelling crowded jabbering townscape of ten years ago faded from her senses and she apprehended the reality of the dusty path ahead, glowing in the bright sunshine: just about, its harsh brilliance attenuated by her dark glasses, bearable. Except that, now she looked more closely, she made out, silhouetted against the sparkling water ahead, two figures, very close together.

She made her way right up to them. As she approached, they drew apart, so that when she halted the three of them stood, she realised, with the queasy sensation that she was seeing the world from a very strange perspective today, at the points of an equilateral triangle.

"Very strong," she said, knowing that this was a crazy thing to say, but the whole day was crazy. "In engineering. Bridge construction, for example. Sorry."

Jack and Fran exchanged glances, uneasy for different reasons.

"But," Jane ploughed on anyway, "bridge building- not a bad thing. Better than burning them, eh?"

Fran took a step towards her.

"Jane..."

"You two must think I'm absolutely awful. Let's be honest for once, shall we?" Jane took off the shades at last, looked at them both, her eyes narrowing, not just because of the strong sunlight. "You both know what I'm talking about."

Jack sensed some appalling catastrophe approaching. He looked at Fran, but she was calm. "Jane," she said, "It's all right, really."

"No, it's not." Jane was calm too, perfectly matter-of-fact. "I'm getting tired of hiding. I'm tired of secrets. I want to stand in my own truth. Accept the truth of how things are. No matter how difficult that might be. I've been very emotional, recently, as they say. I've not been too sure who I am. I've been behaving very strangely. For weeks now, to be quite honest. Which I do so badly want to be. Honest. You know this, Jack, don't you?" she said, turning to him, her mouth twisted into a half smile in which Jack read something like a plea for understanding, something like acknowledgement that it was over between them, that she wouldn't spoil it for him now. Jack didn't dare speak: too much hung on this. Jane paused, then turned to Fran.

"I've only known Jack for a little while, Fran. God knows what he must think of me. He's got to know me during a very difficult time. And you, Fran, I've only known for a couple of days. You know how much affection I have for you already." Again the quirky little smile.

"Yes, Jane, I think I do."

And again a short pause. Both women were thinking of last night, they knew they were. And they knew they weren't going to discuss it.

"Please forgive me, both of you, if I've caused you any pain. I just want to get things right from now on. With Peter, from whom I feel… alienated? Sorry, I'm sounding ridiculous."

"No, Jane…"

"And with the girls. It's so difficult for both of them- Sasha seems so confident but I know a lot of her apparent sparkle is just her way of trying to keep going, going on…

"Jane, it's all right."

"Easy to say, Fran. All right indeed. Wait till you're my age. Wait till you've… Oh I wish I hadn't said that, it sounded cruel. I know you only want to help. Do you see how easily I'm… oh, just buggering everything up nowadays?"

"I understand what you're saying..."

Jack couldn't bear it any longer. She said she wanted to accept the truth, but what was it?

"What are you going to do, Jane?" he blurted. "You want to get things right with Peter, you say. What does that mean?"

"I have to try to accept the truth of how things are, Jack. Even if I can't see what that truth is. I have to accept that it is as it is, whatever that may be, and go along with it."

There was a silence between them, which extended gradually beyond any awkwardness until it passed a threshold and became a communion. At last, without a word, Jack took Fran's hand and started to lead her back to the house. Jane remained for a few more moments, sensing the peace of the lake, the calm of the sheep flecked hills above, rising and falling like waves of deepest emerald, so lovely, sloping down to the water. So cool by the lake it was for her, and almost silent save for the lapping of the ripples on the shingle shore, but somewhere in her memory there arose just the faintest echo of a melody, a solo clarinet, perhaps, so cool, with softest shuffle of brushes and gentle beat of bass... Alice, she thought, my Alice. The truth starts with you.

She turned from the lake, shoved the shades in her pocket and strode back to the house.

3

Peter was sitting with his arms folded on the table, his lips compressed, reading slowly and with increasing despair through the page and a half he had written so far. Finished, he looked up, his eyes wrinkling at the bright rectangle of the window. It seem to mock him with its sunshine. A fine day. For some. He wondered how the visit to Bryn Vaughan-Price was going. He glanced at *Abraham* lying on the table, within reach. Read some more? Remarkably good. Not yet. Must get on. He looked down, re-read the last sentence he had written, groaned, pushed his glasses up, tried to massage some truer vision into his bleary eyes.

What a morning. He had crawled off the sofa in the study, stiff and miserable, still in yesterday's clothes, got to his feet and stood there swaying for a full five minutes, afraid to face the others, because the horror of last night had suddenly come flooding back. At last the need for the toilet overcame everything else, and he blundered out and through to the back. He had been some time in there, frankly hiding, and when he returned, Sasha was at the table with the breakfast things, and Alice was jumping up and down at the window.

"Morning, Sasha," he said briskly. She looked at him sideways past the black wing of her hair, opened her mouth for a moment as if to speak, but shoved a piece of toast in instead, bit it off and chewed slowly, all the time keeping her eye fixed on him. Playing her bloody mind games, was she? Well surely neither of us can stand that for much longer, he thought. Not after last night... a bout of despair hit him. He leaned with both hands on the back of a chair. Alice was still jumping. Jack-a-Jack-a-Jack, she seemed to be saying, over and over.

"What are you doing, Alice," he asked, irritated.

"I'm trying to make Jack come," she said, and resumed her Jack-a-Jack-a...

"I should stop it if I were you, little Sis. What if you succeeded and the shock made him drive off the road with fatal consequences? Could you live with that?"

"Alex... Sasha- will you stop this."

"Stop what?"

"I can't wait for Jack to come, so as I can meet Bryn Vaughan-Price, author of *Cartomancer*, my favourite book. Isn't it amazing that Jack knows him, Daddy?"

"Remarkable."

It had been tense, difficult. He'd made some strong coffee, sat miserably drinking it, wishing he'd got a paper to read, anything. Most of all wishing Jack bloody well would come and take them all away. Fran appeared, strangely muted for once, just mumbled morning, then sat at the table so uncharacteristically silently that after a moment Sasha looked up sharply at her and said, What? Fran looked back quizzically, shook her head. Nothing, she said, but kept on looking, as if waiting for something. Sasha shrugged, poured her a coffee. Drink this in remembrance that Mr. Bean died for you, she said consolingly, and be thankful. Peter frowned at this, it might be a joke to you Alexandra but it's bloody sacrilege to me but he caught her looking at him sideways, just as before: again she held his eye for a second, and then inclined her head in a kind of bow of mock courteous acknowledgement before sweeping her gaze deliberately round the room till it locked on Fran, hitting her with the full voltage so that her coffee cup rattled in its saucer as she put it down.

"Sasha," she said, glancing at Peter, but he had gone stalking over to the window by Alice, muttering it's all right Alice, I'm sure he'll be here very soon and so on, "Sasha, can I... have a word?"

"A word? Let me see. How about, deoxyribonucleic. As in acid."

"In the kitchen. *Please*."

Peter turned round from the window to find the two of them gone. What the? He looked at his watch. Nearly nine. Then he realised Jane still wasn't up. Should he go? Too difficult. What if she starts... Send Alice. Why not.

"Alice, just nip up and tell Mummy will you? She ought to be down by now."

"Yes, Daddy."

No sooner had she gone than there was a shriek of laughter from the kitchen, quickly stifled: Sasha. Being wild again. Wish she'd bloody well grow up. Thinks she's so ruddy smart with her mind games but it's just hurtful. Plain hurtful.

"Daddy?" Alice down again. But what on earth...?

Alice's little face is tilted up to his, her eyes brimming, lip starting to tremble.

"What is it?" He crouched down to her aghast: for God's sake don't tell me she was so pissed last night she puked and choked on it... Alice seemed unable to speak. He was gathering himself to go up and see when Sasha and Fran burst back in giggling, froze at once. Alice's distress was obvious. She sobbed.

"What is it, little Sis? Ali?" Sasha had knelt quickly, had her in her arms.

"Mummy... on her bed... won't wake up... no clothes on..."

Sasha bounded up the stairs. Peter and Fran wildly gawped at each other, open mouthed, appalled. Alice burst into loud tears. And then there was a knock a knock at the door, and Jack waltzed in with a cheery Hello hello hello...

4

Peter heaved himself up from the table, went into the kitchen and stood there while the kettle boiled, trying to empty his mind, and failing as he always did. Thoughts raced, independently of him, it seemed. He spooned fairtrade decaff into a mug with a *faux naïve* drawing of Ely Cathedral on it. Faith: simple faith... he used to have faith that all would be well and all manner of things would be well. That God held the world in the palm of his hand like a hazelnut. That the sufferings of this present time were nothing compared to the glory that shall be revealed in us. That... the kettle was boiling. He poured water into the mug, flinching lest the steam steam his spectacles. Keep going, going on. Read that somewhere. Recently? Forgotten now. He fetched milk, poured, replaced it in the fridge. Situation normal. He carried his coffee carefully through to the other room, and placed it by the armchair which he had found he preferred for reading, took *Abraham* from the table, and settled down.

...Is that what she'd like? What would *you* like, Pontius?"

Pilate was about to tell him when he realised that this wasn't what was supposed to happen. What would he like indeed. Out of all this, for sure. He glanced at Sextus, who seemed to be concerned about the state of his nails; looked back at the prisoner who was still standing calmly smiling, head tilted interrogatively. Nails, indeed.

"Never mind all that. Right now I'd like to know what to do with you."

"You'll do what you do. Just like all the rest of us."

"I don't understand."

"You can't do anything other than what you're going to do. Think about it."

Don't you tell me what to think… but Pilate couldn't help it. He wasn't going to give up without a fight, though. "I have a choice. I can condemn you or set you free."

"That's how it looks. But all the conditions are in place already. We just have to wait and the future will happen the way it was always going to."

"Are you talking about fate now? The will of the gods?" Heard of that, all right.

"That's a rather poetic way of expressing it, Pontius. Fate, the will of the gods or God, these are things we invent, and they change with us. We are the real agents of fate, every tiny word and action, insignificant though they are, all working together to produce an endless stream of what we can understand as reality. It works through us and beyond us. We make it and are made by it: you, your wife, Sextus here, me, your slaves and your soldiers. Even those enthusiasts waiting outside for your decision, though they'd be the last ones to see it. Stand in your own reality, Pontius, remember to value human beings, to love them, as I said, and that's about it. You can't do more. Oh, do stand at ease, sergeant-major, you're making me tired."

"Sir, thank you Sir," barked the NCO, his harness jangling as he gratefully obeyed. Then his jaw dropped as he realised what had happened and he gasped his apologies to Pilate, his mind spinning, blushing furiously as he tremblingly resumed the position of attention, sweat pouring down his face. It is said that some ten years later he was one of the first to carry the new Way to the island of Britannia, working his passage on a tin trading ship out of Tyre, or it might have been Sidon, opinions vary.

Pilate ignored him, though normally a flogging and reduction to the ranks would have been the price for such a breach of protocol. He was studying the calm face of Jesus, trying to read it, but the text was in no alphabet he recognised. Look at him, he thought, smiling still despite the danger... he must know he's had it... The governor noticed that a faint trickle of blood had run down the side of his prisoner's face, from his hairline to his beard. They must've roughed him up a bit before they brought him in. That was unnecessary, surely.

"Who... Why... ?" if only he could understand. "What are you trying to achieve?

"I want people to see the truth."

"Truth! What is truth?"

"The truth, Pontius, is that the world is as it is, and hidden from us utterly. I can't put it any more clearly, really I can't. Oh I've told parables, indeed I've tried to live out the truth- to set an example, if you like, but it's so hard to grasp. Does a fish know it's wet? Does it really understand water? It lives in it, but takes it so much for granted that from its fishy perspective it hardly exists as a concept. Well, that's a bit silly isn't it, I mean fish don't have concepts, don't philosophise! Or at least none of the ones my Galilean friends catch ever do! They taste good, though..."

Pilate leaned forward slightly. The prisoner was running his tongue over his lips, frowning for once... then he sniffed. His eyes were averted, downcast. Perhaps he was recalling quiet days by the Galilean lake, chatting with his fisherman friends, thought Pilate, while the smell of fresh caught fish cooking on an open fire hung in the still air... the distant sound of a shepherd's pipe... he saw himself sitting with them on the shingle, sharing their bread and wine and...

Jesus lifted his head slowly, deliberately, and brought his eyes up to meet Pilate's. The smile came back, but from such a long way away now, it seemed, and it carried such a weight of woe... When he spoke his tone was lower, valedictory: and Pilate realised with astonishment that he was being told, very gently, that the interview was over now...

"But look at us, Pontius. Do we know what *our* world actually is? Any more than a fish knows what water is? We try to make sense of it with our language, don't we, naming the things we see and giving them value or condemning them: we invent laws, religions, our sense of who we are. But in the end, all that we can be sure of is that things are how they are- whether we understand them or not... Come on, Guv, let's get it over with."

5

The faintest hint of a melody, a solo clarinet, so cool, with softest shuffle of brushes and gentle beat of bass had drawn her as she wandered aimlessly through the crowds of, she realized, jazz fans, what was she getting into now? Some kind of full-blown festival going on here... she found herself following the fans into a darkened hall, not wanting to be alone any more, buying a ticket without thinking about it, smiling as she remembered her old music teacher muttering in an unguarded moment, Jazz, jazz... mere musical masturbation... What the hell, nothing wrong with a handjob now and then if you're married to someone like Peter... you can't rape yourself, can you. Can you? She stood uncertainly, taking in the spotlit stage, a scatter of tables, filling up quickly, a bar, doing a brisk trade though it was barely lunchtime: again, what the hell. She bought a large gin and sat at a table near the stage, exhausted, sat on listening, rapt, her elbow on the table, her hand under her chin, the slowly beating passage of time the same for her as the shuffling beat of the music, each melancholy four four ratcheting her further away from her past... from her hurt, still hurting, hurting, but...she takes a drink, and then in the sudden loud applause and whoops and bravos, encore, more, she sees him standing by her table, a beer in his fist, glancing at her, smiling uncertainly, and she runs a hand through her long heavy hair, smiles back, says hi.

And later, how much later? Later, when another band trooped on and trumpets blared and clarinets were squealing, trombones flashing brassy in the hot spots and drums thumped loud he said sorry what I said I can't hear a bloody... let's go outside. I'm into the cooler jazz myself, he said, that was too up tempo for me just a lot of thrashing around but it was cool enough outside all right pissing down it was a cloudburst into the pouring rain we splashed across the road together and mind that fuckin' car for Christ's sake he yelled and we got honked at up yours too you careless bastard he shouted back I had to laugh there's a good pub just here let's have another he said and I said I didn't mind if I did so in we went and take that mac off you're soaking he said so I did and he hung it up and got us drinks and we sat there chatting while time passed and passed and the past just wasn't there any more just him and me and I loved it I did I did

And later still, how much later? Much later, we'd run out of things to say for a moment and I sat there looking at him as he stuffed his pipe and lit it God it was so long ago you could smoke in pubs then I watched how he did it, how he shook the match out and dropped it in the tin ashtray it was so quiet that moment you could hear it fall a little tick it made and he grinned at me through the drifting smoke his eyes screwed up but so gentle he wasn't fast God no he wasn't coming on heavy like that no way we could've chatted on and parted ships in the night strangers on the shore but looking at him as he turned his head and looked out of the window watching the crowds going past the sun was out now and in that light he shone somehow he was luminous larger than life and something clicked in me like that little tick the falling match made you'd scarcely notice it but it changed everything I decided I wanted to make love to him

Shall we go, then, I said, standing up and he got up too but his face had fallen and I saw what he was thinking, God no Bryn, I said I'm not a. One of those. Please, I've left everything behind, given it all up, lost everything, please, will you help me get it back? A long time he stood there looking at me, wondering and so was I wondering who I was so out of context you lose your sense of self and then he tapped his pipe out in the tray ching ching ching like the funny little cowbells in the jazz band and he looked up smiling and said, well, well, well. Come on then, Jane.

And so he brought me here.

Jane looked up at the house, remembering that evening, the meal he'd cooked for her, the talk they'd had, how they'd gradually, gracefully, laughingly danced slowly through the hours of that strange day towards the late evening and the act which they both knew was inevitable now, inevitable and wanted so much, though there was absolutely no hurry. She had thought, with irony, there was no avoiding it, of that dreadful wedding night in the hotel with Peter when they both knew they were going to Do It but with Bryn it was so different, so utterly unlike, it was how she'd wanted it to be then. He was so gentle, self deprecating, his embarrassment at his own body neutralising her modesty as as they undressed one another tenderly and

Right there on that big sofa. And, later, in his bed upstairs. And, in the morning, when they woke up, in his bed. And, after they'd had some food, a drink, some talk, on that long table in the kitchen where they were now, she guessed, about to have lunch. She pulled her shades from her pocket, went to put them on, hesitated. Why bother? She thought for a moment, then she did put them on and went into the house.

"Mummy! We wondered where you'd got to. You're just in time for lunch. We had a lovely talk and Bryn showed me his workshop."

Bryn was at one end of the table, with Alice on his right, Sasha next to her, and Cathy on his left. Fran was next to Cathy, Jack next to her. The empty chair was at the opposite end to Bryn's, so that when she sat down she'd be facing him. So be it. For what we are about to receive… she sat down.

"Wine?" asked Sasha, proffering a bottle.

"Mm." Jane drank most of it down, while the chatter arose, re-starting conversations which her apparently rather dramatic entrance had interrupted. Well, she could do dramatic when it was called for, all right. She leaned forward on her elbows, looking steadily at Bryn, and peeled the disguising glasses off her face.

The movement attracted his attention. He held her gaze, still chewing, then his jaw froze. For a long moment they were the only two not moving amidst all the lunchtime passing and spreading and drinking and commenting… He dropped his eyes to Alice, finished chewing what was in his mouth, swallowed, licked his lips, looked back at Jane, and knew. She stood up.

"Bryn," she said, and inclined her head towards the door. "Would you mind if…?"

Slowly, he got up too.

"Sure," he said, glancing at Alice again, and then at the others. "Would you excuse us for a moment?"

"What is it, Mummy?" Alice broke the surprised silence.

"A secret." Jane smiled at her. "Won't be a second."

They walked a little way into the yard, stopped. After a moment Jane said:

"I won't say anything if you don't."

"It is you then. Fuckin' hell. It must be ten years."

"Yes."

"You had long hair."

"Yes."

"I saw you in her, straight away. I swear I saw you…"

"I saw you. In her."

Bryn ran his hand over his face, turned to her, his eyes narrowed, troubled.

"How old is Alice?"

"Ten."

"Alice and… Sasha. Look very different."

"Yes."

"And you think…?"

"Almost certainly, yes."

"Ahh… Why didn't you tell me?"

"You forget. You dropped me off in Brecon and that was that. I didn't give you a number, address, anything. That wasn't part of what we wanted then."

"I want to do something for her now."

"Don't even hint. She loves Peter. My husband. He's her Daddy."

"I can write to her. She'd like that."

"I don't mind."

"I can do better. I know- wait and see. I know what I can do for her. We'd better go back in now, they'll be wondering… Jane, this is… Perhaps…?"

"Cathy looks like a wonderful person. Are you happy?"

"I can't tell you how happy I am. But…"

"Don't worry. Everything's fine. Let's go in."

"Mummy! What's the secret?"

"It isn't a secret any more," said Bryn, reaching out and smoothing her hair. God his heart would burst! He looked at Cathy, and touched her cheek, needing in the face of this blinding shock to remind himself of the reality they shared, not just the world of enchantment which he had made with her but also their everyday in this house which included this simple wooden table which he had made with his own bare hands and which they were eating their lunch off and on which, who knows… Alice might well have been conceived. He smiled at his secret daughter, but his eyes brimmed with tears.

"Like I said to you earlier on, Alice, my publisher has been bullying me to finish the second volume of *Cartomancer*. And I told you I wasn't sure if I would, being too busy with other things. Well, your Mum was asking me just now what I'd decided, and… I've decided I *will* write it…"

"Oh, Bryn, thank you!" Alice bounced in her chair, clapping her hands.

"And… you know how at the front of a book there's sometimes a dedication, you know, someone's name who the book's especially written for?"

"Yes?"

"In the front of *Cartomancer Two* or whatever title I eventually decide to give it you will find the words, *To Alice Thomas, with love.*"

"Oh, Bryn, Bryn…" And little Alice forgot all her vicarage good manners and jumped into his lap and hugged him and hugged him and he smiled weakly over her shoulder down the table at Jane and they could all see the tears of joy streaming down his face…

"It's the least I can do," he sobbed and laughed at the same time and he buried his face in her hair and kissed her and kissed her again…

X

1

"Are we nearly there yet? Are we nearly there yet? Are we…"
"We are in the Promised Land, Little Sis."
"I can see the sea!"
"If you look the other way you will see the entrance to *Prifysgol Abertawe* with Abandon Home All Ye Who Enter Here written in letters of Welsh gold over the gates…"
"Is that where you're going to Uni?"
"It is."
"You'll be able to go on the beach every day."
"Yep. Surf's up for Sasha."

Listen to her. She can't wait to leave home. Abandon the sinking ship of us. Can't blame her. What am I going to do, then? *What am I going to do*? Shit, look at my knuckles on the steering wheel, white as… must relax, relax, for goodness' sake. For His *sake*, remember looking that up, funny word. But do what? See if Graham would let me have a sabbatical. Give him a ring tomorrow. Explain about leaving the retreat. Bet Robert's been at him by now, though. Tell him stress, overwork, that's better. Just six months perhaps. Think a bit, write a bit, come back refreshed, hit the ground running, get the parish back on its feet, go for something different after that, promotion, if I play my cards right I could still have a chance, be wearing purple myself by the time I'm fifty, then who knows? Get out into the world, get some respect, pull the strings myself instead of rotting in the Cotswolds while everybody else moves up and on in the big cities. London, why not? St Paul's Cathedral...

"Right here, Peter."

"I know, I know."

Get some bloody power for once. Red light, stop. Frustrating, sitting in a queue. Been doing that for too long. I want to be at the front for a change. Be the boss. Who doesn't want to be top dog? Got the collar already, ha ha. Just need to be let off the leash. But have I got it in me? Ambition? Up against the best? Me? Maybe not...

"It's green."

"What?"

"Go."

"Oh."

Green like bloody Jack. Had he really been after Jane? Imagine if I'd come back to the cottage to find them in bed together. Or if I'd got it together with Fran... could've gone her way, started talking to Jesus again... But her way doesn't lead to the top in the Church of England, oh no, we're a bit suspicious of the gifts of the spirit, aren't we, Paul? Oh, or I could just give up. Get myself into a nice psychiatric hospital, wander round the grounds all day talking to Jesus nobody would even notice much. Oh, that's Peter, they'd say, he talks to Jesus. And she's given it up now anyway. For Jack. A pretty poor substitute for Jesus. Still. Go for charisma again, like the old days, eh? Be the biggest fish, but in a smaller pond. Still have the power, have them swooning like Jane used to back in Oxford. In the old days. She was turned on to me then all right, juicy Jane. How many nubile Frans are there out there waiting for charismatic me to just... I could start over, knowing what I know now, yes, get back on that bandwagon. That's the path Alan would like me to take, and he's not the only one. Get a music group in to do the pop songs, sorry worship songs, boot Mervyn out, drop all the Byrd in four parts and the serious exegesis and the ritual and *just*-where would the charismatics be without the word *just*? Just say O Jesus we just want to thank you for just dying for our sins and just help us poor sinners to just pretend that the last two thousand years hasn't happened and... Be like Fran was. Dance for the Lord. Stick up a gospel tent on the village green. Take a megaphone to the Market Square on a Saturday morning. Do a bungee jump for Jesus off the church tower. As it were the highest pinnacle of the temple. It could get me on TV, a stunt like that. Bring in the young people, that would. If you're on TV you're real. It wouldn't bring Sasha in of course, not that sort of young person, not the ones who've learned to think, their heads so full of ideas that they can't see the truth which is…

"Right here."

"I know I know I've been here before." …that Jesus died…

"Careful!"

"It's all right." …for their sins. Oh shit, that was close.

"You didn't indicate."

"Look, do you want to drive?"

"Are we nearly there yet?"

Fucksake she can bloody drive on the way back and what on earth's that noise?

"Jessee…"

Sasha's phone. What was I…? Oh yes, two down one to go, episcopal purple power or public pinnacle plunge. Pair of perplexing possibilities. Tempting. Two down, one to go, turn stones into bread now… Challenge: turn *stones into bread* into alliterative pee peeing? Ha ha, got it- *pierre en pain*: a miracle! A miracle I can remember any French at all after all this time when did we last go to France? Years ago. Driving on the wrong side of the. Hm. Tight bend, that. Must be more careful. Concentrate. What's this now. T junction. Which way is it? Look at her, arms folded frowning she's not going to say anything now even if I drive us off a bloody cliff I think it's left…

"…there yet? Are we…"

"Yes, that's Alice you can hear enthusing in the background…"

"Are we nearly there yet? Are we…"

"Yes we are, Alice darling, do calm down. Very nearly there."

"…nearly…"

"Ali do put a sock in it, I can't hear Jess."

"It's just round the next bend I think. Slow down, Peter."

"I am. I am slowing down."

"It seems we're going slowly round the bend now, my love. So no change there, then."

"Hooray! We're nearly there, Sasha! Sasha! We're nearly there!"

"Excuse me a moment, beloved, my sibling has some matter of grave import to impart."

"I said we're nearly there!"

"Nearly where?"

"There!"

"Oh, *there*. I see. It seems we're nearly there, Jess. I don't know. Can't remember. Pen something. Place of outstanding natural beauty. The seaside. But I see no sea. Just a lot of trees and hedges and interesting bilingual roadsigns and amusingly rustic drystone walling and, wait... Ah. "

"Yes, this is it- turn right here."

"I hate these bumpy... Whoops!"

"No, that foul noise was not Alice for once, it was in fact a cattle grid. Commentary continues. The scene before me is almost mediaeval in its colourful banality. How's that? All the coloured motor cars lined up upon the sward and indeed some familiar faces among the milling throng of gaily clad grockles. Grockles, yes. Well, this looks like journey's end all right. What? Oh, I get it, Journey's End yes, very good, no, no casualties yet. Yes, I'll try not to go over the top, ha ha..."

"Look, Daddy- there's Bryn! That's him over there with the lady she's Cathy and oh look there's Jack and Fran too I can't wait for you to meet Bryn Daddy he's really nice, isn't he Mummy?"

"Yes."

"I'm looking forward to meeting him. I must say I really enjoyed his book. Very moving actually. Just what I needed. Who's the girl with him then? Is that Cathy?"

"Yes."

"She's beautiful, isn't she, Mummy."

"Of course she is..."

"Look, they're waving. Hello...!"

"Those present include Bryn Vaughan-Price the famous author... no well neither had I but I gather he is; his rather tasty girlfriend Cathy..."

"There's a space, there."

"I think I can back in here, actually."

"Outstanding natural beauty. Long legs, blonde... biggish, I suppose you'd say they are, nice... yeah, cute enough given how *old* she is. Real *Erdmutter* potential..."

"Don't get out yet, Alice, wait till Daddy's parked properly..."

"And of course the famous *Jack*... Don't be silly, Jess..."

"Right! That's it. Out we get!"

"Don't forget the picnic things."

"And then of course there's Jack's friend Fran. Actually she's sort of everybody's friend as you may have heard in previous bulletins but she's with Jack at the moment. Yes, she was but they couldn't be prised apart yesterday afternoon and so last night she stayed with Jack at

Bryn's. Well, exactly. *Rem acu tetigisti*. No, Plautus. Anyway, that's the question we're *all* asking ourselves. Except Alice, of course. I mean, apart from being *too young* she's wholly absorbed by the personality of the Great Author and has no time for the trivial flirtations of *hoi polloi*..."

"Sasha, I want to lock the car."

"My father has informed me that he wants to lock the car. A simple enough ambition, and easily fulfilled: he only has to thumb the tit and lights flash and various things go *clunk*. I've seen him do it many times before: I don't know why he's making such a fuss about it today."

"Sasha!"

"Oh, I understand now. It's another example of fatherspeak. Fatherspeak? Haven't you? It's a sort of game we have in our family. Father makes a statement, such as *I want to lock the car* but that isn't really what he wants to communicate. There's a subtext, you see, which actually carries his true meaning and we all have to guess what it is or else there's big trouble. In this case I have cleverly deduced that the statement *I want to lock the car* actually means get the fuck out. It's easy once you get the hang of it."

"Sasha, for goodness' sake..."

"Oh I'd better go, he's starting to show the symptoms again... hey it's been lovely talking to you darling, see you tomorrow, hey? Yes tell your yummy Mummy she's a sweetie for driving you over to be with little old me in the madhouse. God I can't wait to see you. I will. All night long, you just wait. Mm. Love you, babee, love you. Bye."

"Who were you talking to, er Sasha?"

"Jess."

"*Jess*? Oh. Er..."

"Daddy! Come and meet Bryn!"

Clunk!

So this is it. The cold box with the picnic and the rucksack with the towels and the suncream and oh shit I've left my shades in the car no can't go back can't put it off any longer this is it this is it oh look at Alice holding her Daddy's hand already she *looks* like his daughter... Peter's bound to see it! He'll guess! There he goes loping up to them his hand out to Bryn ready for the firm manly... so this is what it's like when the two fathers of your children meet for the first time...

So this is him. Jesus. Intense looking bastard. Bryn took a deep breath, let go of Alice, and held out his hand to the man whose wife he'd made pregnant with Alice ten years ago who took it and shook it all unknowing...

So this is him. Peter took Bryn's hand, half listening to Alice's enthusiastic introductions, half wondering why he looked somehow so familiar ... I guess when you've just been reading a book like that you get the feeling the you know the author somehow...

"Hello, Bryn. I've heard all about you."
Have you, by Christ.
"Nothing too bad, I hope."
"I've been telling Daddy all about yesterday."
Daddy. Right.
"I'm so glad you could join us today."
Right, Vicar.
"Well, Peter, this is Cathy."
"Hello, Peter."

Cathy knew, of course: they could have no secrets. In the hour or so while Jack was driving the others home last night Bryn had taken her in his arms and told her that Jane was the strange lonely lovely woman he had met in Brecon all those years ago, and yes, she remembered his story about her; but now there was more- Alice was their child: and at that she had felt her heart leap, she was amazed at the rush of fulfilment the news produced in her, for she found Bryn's astonishment and joy flooding her, becoming hers also. Oh yes, from somewhere far away in the distance she heard a voice, faint but shrill, raised in jealous protest, of course she did, but she accepted that it had to be there, let it be, knew that it too was part of the truth. As Bryn held her, she had wanted to make love to him at once, but as she started to kiss him she realised that part of that wanting was selfish, only wanting to claim him more strongly for herself, to distance him from Jane, and so instead she just held him, waiting, waiting for the new knowledge to work more fully in them both. And in any case, Jack had come back soon after, with, to no surprise, Fran... Now Cathy looked at Jane and loved her as she stood there awkwardly, burdened with a big box and a rucksack, her mouth drawn into a lopsided ironic half smile she thought she understood and well, yes, partly pitied. Partly admired.

"Jane, let me take that. Here. Goodness- it is heavy! have you brought the kitchen sink?"
"Very nearly. Thanks."
"You're looking better today."
"Thanks."
Cathy wondered if she guessed that Bryn had told her. No matter. The truth is as it is, and we all have our own little versions of it. No one can see it all.

"Up there, on the hill." Bryn was pointing enthusiastically. "An excellent place for our picnic, Alice. If we go straight to the beach to have it, we'll get sandy sandwiches. Not very nice at all, you wouldn't enjoy that. And there's a view. Now, who's got my bag? Oh, well done, Jack. Come on, then, this way."

2

Peter was slightly bemused. For some reason meeting Bryn had seemed a bit of an anticlimax to him. And now everybody was somehow assuming that Bryn was in charge of the expedition and seemed to know everybody else better than he did so that he felt a bit out of it, let himself fall behind as they passed out of the dusty carpark and up towards the winding track which apparently led to the top of the hill. Cefn Bryn, it's called, Bryn was loudly explaining to Alice, yes, I'm so famous they've named a hill after me... And holding hands with her. Well, why not? Funny how she's taken to him so quickly. Holding hands also, he saw, were Jack and Fran. Bloody fast worker, that Jack. Jane was talking to the beautiful Cathy, he saw. Bryn's... wife? No. Living together. The usual these days. What ever happened to marriage? His marriage. What had happened? How did it all go so wrong? He knew, he knew now exactly what had gone wrong. And why. Was it too late to repair all that damage? Jane, Jane, I love you... say it over and over, like a mantra, make it work, God, God... They'd even fallen out over the driving, though, they're always arguing, what hope was there? It had been convenient, of course, that lucky Jack had taken the besotted Fran back to Bryn's with him last night. Lucky? Probably. Freed up the spare room at any rate. Couldn't face another night on the bloody sofa. When did Jane and I last even share a bed, never mind... can't remember. He plodded on up the hill. God. God. That was the...

His nostrils twitched. A whisp of acrid smoke. Sasha had stopped for him, waiting for him. That's... nice of her. After the bad time they'd had the other night... and she'd been in such a funny mood this morning... and that conversation on the phone... she'd been talking to *Jess* like that, had she?

"Come on, Dad. The Devil takes the hindmost. Or so I'm told."

Peter stopped, searching his daughter's face. He loved her, he knew that, God how he loved her. But how to say...?

"Penny for them," she said.

"What?"

"Your thoughts."

"I was thinking... just thinking... I love you."

Sasha gasped, laughed, flung her arms round him.

"Dadeeee... I love you too! But what's brought on this uncommonly frank expression of paternal affection?"

"This what?"

She laughed at him, took another drag, kissed his cheek.

"Phoo! You'll have to stop this smoking."

"It shall to the barber's with your beard."

They started walking again, side by side. After a moment he reached out, twined his fingers in hers. She squeezed his hand, let him keep holding hers. Was it only the day before yesterday they'd last been climbing up a hill together? So many hills to climb, it seemed to Peter. Such steep hills, steep learning curves.

"Things have been difficult lately, Sasha."

"With Mum?"

"Yes, and..."

"And?"

"No, I can't really... You see I'm actually desperate to explain, but it's so hard to find the words. Simple enough words."

"Hm."

"Oh, don't get me wrong, I'm not trying to patronise you, Love; God knows you've probably got a bigger vocabulary than I have. It's more a sort of technical issue. There's so much theological background involved, you see. So much spadework before you can even see what the problem is, never mind understand the solution. I wish I could explain to you."

"You can try if you like, but I'm afraid theology's not really my chalice of wine, Daddy."

Peter stopped, turned. All around them was rough tussocky grass, patches of heather further up, bracken. Already from this far up, there was a view of the bay, the coast of Devon hazy beyond the glimmering sea of the channel.

"Could we but stand," he said, sighing, taking it all in, "where Moses stood, And view the landscape o'er..."

"Not Jordan's stream, nor death's cold flood," replied Sasha, who wasn't to be outquoted even in third rate Victorian religious verse, "Should fright us from the shore." She hadn't been in Mervyn's choir for nothing. "Curious rhyme isn't it? Do you think he meant oar shore or ower shower? Maybe he just had a funny accent." Her voice tailed away as she realised he wasn't listening. She dropped her fag, stood on it. Mustn't set the bloody hill on fire. Named after him indeed.

"But that's the problem, you see!"

"Sorry Daddy, what is the problem?"

"We *can't* stand where Moses stood! We're modern people, not Bronze Age herdsmen: we just don't see the world in the same way. We can't. And it's no use pretending that we can. Do you see what I mean?"

"That's obvious, isn't it?"

"It's amazing how it *wasn't* obvious for so long... it's *becoming* obvious to me... Your mother said something, on Sunday night. When we... had that awful row. I think the truth of what she said hit me hard. I was ready to hear it, I'd sort of got there, but I lost my temper because I couldn't see where..." Peter broke off, walked on briskly.

"What did she say?" asked Sasha, having to almost run to keep up.

"Something like... She said something like how it was obvious to her that our lives start without us being able to do anything about how or why they start, and that after we've been born we gradually become aware of things going on around us: our lives happen, in other words, and then... then we simply cease to be aware of them. That is to say, we die. She said that that was all there was to it. I told her I found that profoundly depressing. You see Sasha, my difficulty was, is, that I think she's right..."

"So what's the problem?"

"The problem is," said Peter, stopping abruptly and in his querulous tone of voice giving Sasha the uneasy feeling that he was on the brink of hysteria, "I don't quite see where that leaves God..."

She watched him against the brilliant backdrop of the bay while he took off his glasses and polished them vigorously on his handkerchief with an embroidered P in one corner and quickly wiped his eyes and put his glasses back on and glared at her through them.

"Do you, Sasha?"

Well no, Sasha wanted to say, I'd always wondered where he was supposed to fit in, but no... not this time. She just took his arm and squeezed it tight. She *did* love him...

"Daddy..." And leaned her head against his shoulder.

"I used to believe," Peter said, "that God made us to share his being and love us but that the Devil made us sin so that he had to become man himself to pay the price of our sin so we could all go to heaven together to behold Him and enjoy him for ever... to gaze and gaze on Jesus..."

Now, to her astonishment, she saw that the tears were flowing freely, and he broke loose from her and staggered aside from the path, taking his glasses off again, wiping his tears away.

"Sorry, those words... always make me want to cry. So moving. Why is that do you suppose?"

The two of them stood there, a few feet apart; but it might as well have been a mile. After a moment Sasha pursed her lips and looked away.

"I don't know, Daddy. Strong poetry..."

"Anyway, it came to me just the other day, almost a casual thought, ridiculously simple... the thought that we make it all up. Do you hear, Sasha?" He took a couple of strides towards her so that she turned to him, and was shocked by the intensity in his face.

"I've been living with this all week, Sasha. That's been the problem for me, ever since your mother put it into words for me on Sunday night. I saw, with a shocking clarity, which was not to be denied, quite suddenly, that we've made it all up ourselves. Our ideas about God, the great narrative of creation, fall and redemption. It isn't a pre-existing reality set apart from us out there somewhere way beyond our understanding which we can dimly apprehend through a glass darkly by faith and prayer and reading the scriptures and all the rest of it. It's a cultural artefact like any other: we've made it up. All of it."

Peter threw his arms out, let them fall to his sides with a smack. Then he sighed, and sat down, shaking his head.

"I'm in the wilderness. Lost." He tilted his head up, squinting at her in the strong sunlight. "I'm sorry, Sasha. Not much of a Dad, am I?"

Oh shit, thought Sasha, and glanced up the path. She could see Bryn, Alice, Mum and Cathy a good way ahead, almost out of sight amongst the tall bracken, passing over the broad shoulder of the hill. Fran and Jack were some way behind them, walking hand in hand. She turned back to her not much of a Dad, sat down by him, hugged him, almost cradled him. A skylark was pouring its crazy music out of the blazing blue above their heads. She looked up: but there was nothing to be seen in the blinding glare, nothing at all.

"Daddy... It's all right..."

"In Bryn's book... the crucifixion... last night in bed I was reading it... I was on my own of course, in bed, I mean, your Mummy was in the spare room because well, oh dear oh dear..."

"Quite."

"I cried. His description of the crucifixion. It was so moving. He made it real. Oh!" And his shoulders heaved and heaved.

"It's all right. If we can't cry when we see a good man killed by ignorance and prejudice, what are tears for?"

"Cried, not because his description isn't true... but because it's truer than ..."

"Sorry, Daddy, you've lost me..."

"Bryn's book... truer than... the Church..."

"You must tell him. He'll be dead chuffed..."

"His Jesus... truer than... and he died for my stupid stupid stupid..."

"Daddy..."

"You see... sorry, my handkerchief, I must..."

"Here you are."

"Thanks. Thank you so much my dear, dear. Oh dear. You see, I know what sin is, now. I'll tell you what it is. It's this. It's denying what is obviously true. What we used to call the sin against the Holy Spirit which couldn't be forgiven... how can you be forgiven if you're consciously denying the obvious truth? Jesus came to bear witness to the truth. For us to insist that there really is a supernatural world with lots of intelligible consequences for human life when there obviously isn't anything of the sort is therefore sinful in a funny sort of way...yes, funny..."

"Daddy, are you laughing now or still crying? I'm a bit confused."

"*You're* confused... ! Try this. I think nowadays it's actually a sin to believe in God! Yes! Do you see the logic of it? It's the new idolatry! It's come back, the old commandment, Thou shalt make no graven image nor worship it. You weren't to invent a God to believe in, not then, and not now either! Not now that we *know* that that's what we've been doing all along! We didn't know before, do you see, Sasha, we *didn't know*! Me and all the holy boys as your Mum calls them, back in the old days at Oxford, we were so innocent we didn't realise that what we were doing was making up a God and then pretending *he'd made us*! It was the other way round all the time! And the scriptures! We thought it was God talking to us when oh if we'd only seen it was so bloody obvious we were just reading whatever we wanted to into these old, old, past their inspire-by date writings! That's what all the…

"Sorry, Daddy, 'scuse me laughing, that's very good, past their inspire-by date, oh you *are* a lovely funny Daddy…"

"That's what all the blasted sermons we had to write actually were. When we were training for the priesthood. We were inventing relevance where there was none, helping one another to make believe that these ancient texts, these *provisional* texts, documents entirely of their time, were in fact timeless and eternally true…true! Truth. Ha. What is. Bloody Saint Paul, for example… Just imagine taking that stuff literally. Like Fran did, though I think she's changed her point of view recently, ha, ha… And oh your poor mother. Your dear mother. I was horrible to her, back then, you've no idea…"

"Daddy…"

"Women. We young lads were afraid of women, see, that's one thing you need to understand, thanks to Saint bloody Paul, absolutely terrified of them and what they could make us want…"

"Daddy, for goodness sake…"

"No, listen, you need to know. You are a woman. Women were reality. Sex… Sex was, is, reality."

"Daddy, stop it."

"Every one of us knew, though we couldn't admit it to ourselves, that what we wanted more than *anything* else in the world was to have a really good *shag* we wanted it much *much* more than we wanted Jesus or the beatific vision or anything else but *that's* why we couldn't allow ourselves to have it you see because if we did we'd know the *truth* we'd get a bit of bloody *perspective* and the whole damned house of cards would come tumbling down…"

Sasha suddenly found she'd had enough of this. She stood up, swallowed hard, looked up the hill again. The others were out of sight, must be at the top by now. P'raps someone would come back to see… Lower down, just coming up from the carpark, another couple of grockle families, their children shouting cheerful insults to one another.

What to do with Daddy? She looked at him, now curled up in a nest of heather, his knees drawn up to his chin. Practically foetal, she thought, well, that figures. He wanted to be born again once. Now perhaps he will be. But he does pick his moments. Sasha blew her cheeks out, scratched her head. Then she shrugged and lit another fag.

After a few moments a couple of football-shirted children dashed past squealing, their fat or corpulent sunglassed mother gaspingly plodding on by a few moments later complaining about them kids, the heat, the roughness of the path, the lack of toilet facilities. The thickset father, in holiday uniform of trainers, baggy shorts, and a white England T shirt that left his tattooed arms bare, his shaven head a shining brown egg in the sunshine, stopped and stared slack jawed at Peter.

"He aw right, is he?"

"Knackered," said Sash. "It's pretty steep."

"Steep? This hill ain't steep!"

"I didn't mean the hill. His learning curve. Bloody near vertical."

3

"What you thinking about now, Fran?"

"Just now? You really want to know?"

"Mm."

"Well, I was thinking about..." She looked back, saw Peter and Sasha some way below. The others had gone on ahead, were nearly at the top. "I was thinking," she said in a stage whisper, stepping closer to him as they walked and putting her arm round his waist so that their thighs brushed together, "If you really really want to know my secret thoughts, I was secretly thinking about last night. At Bryn's place. When it was bedtime, you know? And Cathy showed us *our* bedroom with the emphasis on the *our*, remember? She just seemed to assume... and so did I... But you didn't sleep with me, did you, you said good night Fran very sweetly and went off somewhere else..."

"The sofa downstairs. Yes."

"Why?"

"We've only known one another since the day before yesterday."

"Two whole days. Yes, it must have been about this time two days ago that you drove round the corner and I was like...." She stopped, did a few steps of her clumpy boots dance. "Remember?" She grinned at him, holding the hair out of her face: there was quite a breeze up here, near the top. They walked on for a few more paces. "So, Jack," she asked him sweetly, "What is the standard period of time which has to elapse before cock may decently be inserted into cunt?"

Jack stopped, turned, pulled her close. He wanted this strange beautiful girl desperately- and the force of his desire hit him now so hard he found he couldn't speak: his reaction to her was so visceral, overwhelming... he knew he'd never seen anyone, ever, so lovely as Fran looked now against the shining backdrop of the sea out there in the channel, her head lowered, but her bright cornflower eyes gleaming up at him from the wildly waving nest of her windswept hair. She bit her lower lip and lifted one hand to his cheek, ran its back down the stubble, and went, "Hm?"

"Oh, fuck..." He let her go, turned away shaking his head, started walking again.

"Fuck, yes- that's what I wanted!" She was laughing now: she took his hand and swung it as she skipped along beside him. Wryly, he glanced at her sidelong- she was funny all right and fuck, oh fuck how much he wanted to fuck too. Who wouldn't? But he could feel, countering his desire for her body, an equally urgent desire that it should not be with her like it had been with other girls: fun at the time but casual, meaningless, the flirting leading to the snogging leading to the shagging and then the inevitable drifting apart, the resentment, the emptiness, the dreadful feeling of loss. And then, oh then... the whole dismal cycle starting all over again at some party or other or in a pub... He couldn't face that. He wanted this to last.

"I've made some mistakes in the past," he said. "I've tended to be a bit fast."

She laughed, and improvised all singsong happy:

"He made some mistakes in the past,
He tended to be a bit fast:
But now he's met me,
It's easy to see
He has found his true love at last."

"What's that?"

"Limerick. We are both poets and we did not know. It's..."

"What?"

"Nothing. I just said *know it's* to rhyme with *poets*. Sort of."

Jack wasn't sure what to make of this. Sounded like one of Sasha's incomprehensible rants. They walked on, further up, reached the place where the track swung off to the top. It was steeper here.

"I don't want to make another mistake," said Jack, pausing to look back at the view of the bay. "Cathy…" He couldn't think how to say…

"Was a mistake. Like Jesus."

It took Jack a moment to digest this. Then he said:

"Jane…"

"*What*? You've fucked *Jane*?" Fran was open mouthed, wide eyed.

"Shh!" Jack glanced up the track, but they were out of sight. "No. No. I sort of flirted with her… I was depressed, mixed up. It was another mistake, see? And I don't want to make a mistake with you! Don't want all that…" Jack took both her hands in his. "But Fran… you hardly know me… I can't expect you to drop everything and come to live with me…"

"I already have."

"What?"

"Dropped everything. As for living with you… Don't you believe in love at first sight? I do. Now I've met you."

"But Fran, I'm thirty four, for Christ's sake…"

"I prefer older men…"

"I've got nothing to offer you. … you don't really want *me* do you? Look at me, for God's sake! You don't know me. Who am I?"

"You are my Jack."

"Your…"

"And as for offering stuff and that what the hell do you think *I've* got to offer? How do you think I feel about *my* life? Hey? I chucked everything away because I thought I heard the voice of Jesus telling me to. How crazy is that?" She broke away from him, flung her arms wide, stood staring at him, not laughing now.

"It was unbelievably courageous."

Fran's face contracted: it was as if she was going to cry. Then she slowly smiled again, and so did he, and after a moment they walked on in silence, a little distance apart. Then she took his arm and said:

"Jack, I don't understand the way things happen in the world. How was it that lovely lovely you just happened to be driving round the corner in bloody Brecon of all places at the exact moment I came out of the shop and did my silly dance on the pavement? Because if you hadn't, or if I'd stayed in there a moment longer, we'd never have met." She looked into his face every few paces as they climbed higher, but he said nothing. His eyes were on the ground. At last she leaned in to him, said, "It's meant, Jack… it's meant." And then, halting him, standing in front of him, "Jack? Won't you even kiss me?"

4

Alice ran ahead and leapt up onto the little rocky outcrop right at the very top of the hill.

"Wow! Look!"

She gazed on the beautiful bend of bay and sinuous swerve of shore, the glint of sun on blue green sea and there in the distance the faint hazy shadows of another coast.

"Three Cliffs Bay," said Bryn, climbing up behind her and pointing, "and over there Oxwich. Rhossili Down's that way, over there's Llanmadoc Hill, and back over there are the Brecon Beacons, where we've come from today."

"And what's that over the sea? Another country?"

"If you're Welsh like me, yes! It's England! That's the coast of Devon."

"It's lovely up here." Alice sat down, inspected the rock between her feet. "Look, it's all crumbly."

"The frost breaks it up in winter. Freeze thaw action it's called. Haven't you learned about that in Geography?"

"No. We learn about Land Use. And why there are car parks in Milton Keynes." She picked out a tiny piece, held it up to Bryn. "Look how it sparkles!"

"Quartz conglomerate," he said. "Very old rock indeed. Even older than me. That sparkle is from the tiny crystals embedded in the sandstone."

"How old is it, then?"

"I don't know exactly. Three hundred million years? Something like that."

Alice frowned at the little fragment, trying to understand what it meant to be holding three hundred million years in the palm of her hand. The she looked up.

"Where are the others?"

"Oh, they'll catch up in a minute. You led us up here at such a pace, didn't you, Alice?"

"I'll go back and see." And pocketing the stone she sprang to her feet and scampered away. Bryn grinned at Jane, at Cathy, at the seascape. He felt madly happy.

"Well, I need a sit down after that climb," he said, and found a place. He started fumbling with his pipe, managed to get it lit despite the wind, under the cover of his jacket. When he looked up again, he found that Jane had come to sit by him. She slipped her arm through his.

"Bryn," she said.

"What?"

"Nothing. Just let me sit for a moment…" She looked up to where Cathy was standing, hands in pockets, the wind playing with her hair. She looked lovely, so lovely against the distant seascape and the sky, she thought, lovely. His woman. "Cathy," she called, and when she looked round said, "You don't mind if I…" Cathy smiled, came over and kissed her.

"Of course not." Meaning, I understand. "I'll go see where Alice has got to."

"Tell that Jack to get a bloody move on. He's got my bag with the lunch in it." He turned his face down to Jane's, spoke her name softly.

"Don't say anything, Bryn. I just want to sit with you for a moment." And she leaned her head on his shoulder. Alice's father. She closed her eyes, felt the blessing of the sun on them, the wind gently ruffling her hair, and then she was back again in the moment when he dropped her off in Brecon so long ago- goodbye, thank you, lean over for a last kiss, get out quickly, close the door, walk away into the crowd, not looking back to wave, no, just going, going on… that was what they'd wanted… she had thought she'd never see him again and now here he was… what a journey back she'd had, bus to Abergavenny, train to Newport was it, yes, then to Reading, then to Oxford, then… When she finally got home- home!- call that home? it was late and of course the new vicarage was still unfamiliar, strange, half the things were still packed, she couldn't find anything. In the end she managed to make herself a cup of tea, no milk, of course, and sat there with it in the huge bare kitchen and cried and when she was tired of that went upstairs and cried there and then fell on a bed and cried again until she'd cried herself to sleep.

And in the morning she'd sat staring at the ghastly wallpaper in the bedroom and wondered what it would be like to divorce him. Then she thought of little Alexandra, and decided not to divorce him. But she couldn't go on like this. She would wait until Alexandra was grown up, and then divorce him. Ten years, maybe? She'd be old, the best part of her life would be gone. Ten years. She'd stick it out somehow, for little Alex. And for now, she'd work. So as not to have to think about it any more. Sort out the house this week, and from then on work on the cooking and the cleaning and the washing and the entertaining and taking Alexandra to school and helping her with her homework... And perhaps he'd be pleased with that arrangement, and would leave her alone at night.

So. When he finally came home with Alex at the end of the week she was waiting for them in the kitchen, which was clean and tidy and well stocked and smelled of freshly baked bread and newly made coffee. And little Alex ran up to her and asked her if the doctor had made her better, and Yes, Darling, she said, kissing her- so that was the story, was it?- much better. And look- I've made the new house all nice for us. Go and have a look around. You know which is your room, don't you? I've put up all your pictures and arranged your books and things... So off she went, leaving them to face one another.

"Coffee?"

"Oh- yes, please. This is... really, well- you've worked so hard!"

"So you told them I was ill, did you?"

"Yes."

"I see. Here's your coffee."

"Thanks."

"There's milk in the fridge. I've done shopping for a week. Everything's unpacked. I've cleaned the place from top to bottom. Your post is on your desk in the study, with a list of phone messages you might want to deal with fairly soon."

"Thank you so much, Jane... I've been so worried."

"What about?"

"Jane..."

"How you'd cope without me? It's all right, I'm not leaving you. Yet. Now, I'll get your dirty washing unpacked and put it in the machine. Then I'm going to make supper. After we've had that I'll bath Sasha and read her her story. You'd better take that coffee in the study and deal with those phone calls."

"Jane..."

"Just go now. Get on with it. That's what we've both got to do from now on, for Alexandra's sake if nothing else, just... get on with it!"

And that would have been that, with him settling into the new parish and me doing all the vicar's wifely things and sorting Sasha out ready for the start of term at her new school: it would have been all right I suppose, we'd have managed, it would have been so simple, if I hadn't realised after a week that my period was late.

Couldn't remember the last time I let Peter do it to me. Well before my last one, to be sure. Oh, great. Now what?

By the way, Peter, I forgot to mention on the way back from the cottage I stopped overnight with a really nice man who shagged my fucking eyes out it was brilliant, just what I needed, the only thing is I'm going to have his child now, OK?

Peter, we've got to be very grown up about this. Peter, it's hard to explain but after I left you in the cottage I was in an emotional turmoil and when I was in Brecon waiting for the bus I got talking to a really lovely man who helped me, really gave me such a lot of my confidence back. I know you'll find this difficult to understand but I stayed with him overnight and one thing led to another and…

Peter, love, there's something I need to ask you. You know how the Virgin Mary conceived our Lord by the Holy Spirit? So that he was born without an earthly father? Yes, Jane, that's what happened, all right, parthenogenesis it's called, why, what is it? Well, Peter, do you think it could happen again? I mean, seriously, supposing a woman found she was pregnant, but hadn't, you know… done it recently…

No way.

Just let him think it's his.

So there I was hanging about on the landing in my nightie like a bloody tart on a street corner waiting for him to come out of the bathroom in his pyjamas so when he did I could switch on the snuffles and say goodnight then Peter in a really sad little voice so as he'd say what's the matter and I could say oh nothing really, it's just, oh nothing and he could say tell me and I could just take the lapel of his pyjama jacket in my fingers and say oh and step a fraction closer to him have to be careful here because if he thinks for a minute I'm after it he'll back off bloody sinful that'd be: tell me he says tell me what's the matter

Lonely, I say, so quiet he doesn't hear at first and bends his head closer I'm lonely I whisper into his ear very close now this is it one false move and I'm fucked or not fucked rather in this case but no it's going to be all right because I'm looking down to see and his pyjama trousers don't hide much in fact it's starting to poke out already as if to say hello hello what's all this then don't get much of this anymore damn right you don't but tonight's your lucky night my son and he goes Jane, all gooey and Jane, it's been so long and not that long I want to say, only about four inches last time I saw it but this isn't funny oh no there's nothing funny about the lusts of the flesh is there Peter

So he took my hand and led me into his bedroom and shut the door lest poor innocent Alex be awoken by our screams as we hit orgasm simultaneously ha ha that'll be the day and he put out the main light so there's just the bedside light to see by he likes to see he does so all right let him then just for once I thought and stripped my nightie off over my head and chucked it on a chair and I don't know when he'd last seen me standing starkers but he just sat on the edge of the bed gawping and I suddenly thought oh Christ I'd never have done that before I had Bryn I hope he doesn't guess I've just been on a crash course in advanced erotic practices I haven't put him off have I I must look pretty bloody sinful like Eve with a whole bag of Cox's Orange Pippins except for my navel of course so I thought let's get to the point of no return before he starts remembering St Paul and fearing for his eternal soul

I started to unbutton his pyjama jacket but he couldn't wait for that he ripped it off himself and then there was a real moment of mirth when he stood up and tried to drop his trousers but he hadn't bothered to undo the silly string things you tie to keep them up so his cock got caught in them and I looked away and went round the other side of the bed to climb in so he wouldn't see I was pissing myself laughing but I managed to get a suitably solemn face on for him as he started pawing at my tits as befits a Christian wife who is bravely risking hell fire and damnation that a child may be brought into the world though why the hell anyone would have wanted to do that in the days when people actually believed all that shit God or Saint Paul only knows oh well actually I guess that was his point really, Paul, that is, no copulation equals no population which is fine because it'll all be over anytime now and we'll all be lining up to be issued with a harp or a pair of asbestos pants depending on how we've

Ouch! He'd been getting himself nicely worked up while I'd been lying there thinking about this that and the other and I nearly missed the big moment but here we go here we go uh uh uh bloody hell he's coming he's coming already is he? Is he? Yes. Oof, God he's heavy. Roll off, there's a dear. Listen to him panting, not a secret smoker is he? Anyone'd think he'd just run the thousand metres. Well, that didn't waste much of my evening. I could still go downstairs and catch the end of Newsnight.

Sorry, Jane, darling... He was off on his usual litany of post coital apologies. Finished a bit quick Love, sorry... it's been such a long time. Yeah, like Bryn said he hadn't had a woman for months and he managed to make it last all night and most of the following morning too, ah well anyway, don't worry Peter, I said, don't worry.

And I nearly added, that'll do nicely.

5

The light! So very bright. Shut them again. Dark now, but flashing colours cut across, crazy patterns. Open. Bright! And see, very close, clutching skeletal roots of heather. Shut. Chaotic spangles dancing on the darkness. Open. The sandy earth in which the roots dig. Dry, grainy. Blackish yellowish brown the earth, some grains almost white, most of it black, peaty, crumbly, warm to the touch as fingers, my Petey fingers, pry a little into its peaty secrets. Tiny pieces of rock. My head is lifting. Why is that? Because. Now there's more. A greyish outcrop there, with yellow patches, lichens? Here and there stiff stalks of grass, whipping in the wind. And more. Beyond, burning bushes, trees all shades of green leaves rippling burning bright in sunlight; somewhere beyond their flickering swaying tops, the shining sea. Above, the blue bowl of the sky, and the crazed endless trilling outpouring of the skylark.

I do not know what any of this means, Peter thought. I have named some of what I can see, I have made it: I mean I have made it intelligible to me. I can describe it to others I can tell them stories about it but I do not know what it really is. Or who I am to be naming, describing, inventing ways of speaking of all this. If I ceased it would not cease but my bones would sink into the soft soil among the roots already skeletal always here being what they are though what that is is not known truly

And what's here? Here are the finely muscled backs of the long smooth suntanned legs of a tall tall girl. Up they go, her long long legs, into the short blue denim of her skimpy skirt which flares out over her pert crupper. There's a hell of a word for it. But I can name things how I like. She's got a pink top on which leaves her neck bare, so you can see the faintest gold line of the fine chain she wears there, and her shoulders are bare too: over the left one she's slung her little brown leather bag with no doubt her phone, her fags, her purse, perhaps a towel for after she's swum in the sea. Oh, and a book, knowing her. And I do know her of course, and I love her. I named her name too, like I name everything, but she changed the name I chose. Well, so be it.

Ah, the telltale whisp of smoke round her raven black bobbed hair, she must give it up, really. I know what she looks like from the front too, this pose is habitual, characteristic: I know just how she'll have her left arm folded across tightly under her breasts, her right elbow on her left hand, the smouldering fag held out in her palm-up right hand as she looks out defiantly at the world with those challenging expressive eyes narrowing over the high cheekbones as the ideas come and go in her mind, her full lips now and then osculating the filter tip and staying pursed as she exhales the twin jets of acrid smoke from the elegant nostrils of her fine straight nose…

My daughter.

Peter stood up awkwardly, coughed. Sasha spun round. Now what?

"Daddy? Are you all right?"

He looked around, blinking.

"Yes. Was I asleep long?"

Sasha looked him up and down, frowned, still unsure of him. Then she relaxed and said with an uncertain smile, "Only about *that* long," indicating with finger and thumb of her left hand the length of an unsmoked kingsize added to the stub in her right, which she then dropped and stepped on. "Are you sure you're OK to go on up, then? They'll be wondering where we've got to."

"Sure I'm sure. *Lay* on, Macduff."

"Oh, very good, Daddy. Full marks for Eng Lit. There's hope for you yet."

"You think so? Well, we'll see. Come on. Race you to the top!"

"Oh, Daddee… it's too hot for racing…"

"Too many fags…"

"Daddee…!"

6

"Here they are at last. Come and have some lunch, Peter."

"Hello everyone. Sorry… I lingered rather…"

"We saw you from the top, Sasha. When me and Cathy went to find Jack and Fran."

"Cathy and I."

"I, sorry. They were *kissing*."

"Oh my word. Whatever next. What are you eating?"

"A peanut butter sandwich. Do you want one?"

"No, I eat the air, promise crammed."

"What?"

"Pass one over."

"Here you are. It was very romantic. Like in my book when Derryn and Amanda finally get to kiss on the desolate moorland. Bryn's been telling me lots of stories about this place. There are ancient burial mounds and all sorts..."

Sasha was watching her Daddy dubiously as he sat himself gingerly down on a rocky seat near Bryn. Sat himself. Seated himself. Sat himself down. Not the same meaning. Tricky. To do with intransitives? Must be. Using the verb to sit transitively. I seat him down, no. I sit him down, yes. I sit him on the chair. Yes, if he can't do it himself, or has to be forced... I was sat on a hill..."

"...don't you think? Sasha?"

"Mm. Got a drink?"

"There's orange squash in here."

"It's not second hand, is it?"

"I made it myself."

"That's what I'm afraid of. It looks like a urine sample."

"What?"

"Give us a swig anyway."

"Give *me* a swig."

"Me, sorry."

"Give me a swig *please*... Ow no, gerroff stop tickling me ow ow ow...!"

"And it's going to be filmed, I gather."

"Apparently, Peter, apparently it is. It's out of my hands now, though. Julian says they've got someone working on a treatment, whatever that is. I'm too verbose for the big screen, it seems. All right, Cathy my love, I'm too verbose full stop, I know." And he put his arm round her and kissed her lovely giggling face. Peter watched the two of them sadly, oddly reminded of Robert and his dreadful big arsed Sarah or Sara. It was the ease of it, that was all- they couldn't be more different otherwise. The ease with which they spoke, touched, understood one another. Sadly, he looked at Jane sitting nearby, saw that she was watching them too. Her gaze shifted to him, caught his eye, held it. He wanted to cry out- are you thinking what I'm thinking? Look what we've lost! Or what we've never had... where's the ease between us...? He opened his mouth to speak, but Jane got in first.

"They're making the book into a screen play, then?"

Bryn released Cathy.

"They're making it more likely to sell in America," he said, producing a hip flask. "I'll believe it when I see it. Anyone fancy a swig?"

"No thanks. I'm driving..."

"Huh. He's trying to," Jane snorted. "I'll have some. I've got to sit next to him on the way back." Peter watched as she upended the flask, shuddered. "Meh. What on earth is it?"

"*Sŵn y Môr.*"

"I'm none the wiser."

"Sound of the sea."

"That explains the sudden ringing in my ears." She handed the flask back, looked at Peter, smiled faintly, so that he felt a flicker of hope, very faint, oh if only... He pushed on.

"I hope they don't lose the truth of it, Bryn. That was the part I liked best- when Jesus talks to Pilate about truth. That's the whole point, isn't it? To know the truth."

"Which is that the truth cannot be known. Yes. That'll keep the box offices busy. I expect they'll have to bugger it up quite a lot. It's not exactly *Star Wars*, is it?"

"But Bryn... there is a difficulty. Which I really wanted to put to you."

"Go on, then."

"I'm not sure that anyone living in Judea in that period would have been able to think that far outside the box. I mean, isn't your Jesus's attitude to truth anachronistic?"

"Oh, Peter..." Jane stood up, her mouth pulled into that ironic half smile again, and walked across to where Jack and Fran were chatting together a little way off.

"Mind if I join you? It's getting a bit philosophical over there."

"Sit down quick," said Fran. "You can chaperone me. It's getting a bit sexual over here."

I'd have done better with the philosophy, thought Jane, as she made herself comfortable in the springy heather, and felt that ironic grimace getting tighter still. Is there anyone here apart from my children I haven't slept with or wanted to sleep with? Cathy. Oh, don't go there, for heaven's sake... She lay back on one elbow, stretched out her legs.

"Sexual? Oh, yes, I remember sexual..."

The three of them grinned ruefully at one another; each one knowing what they knew of the other two, of what fumbling attempts they'd made in their own ways to find something in other people and in themselves... but what?

"What is it, though? Sexuality. It's crazy," said Jane. "Sex is so important to us, but what *is* it? What's it *for*? Making babies? Try telling that to Sasha. But why don't we understand sex better, if it's so important? Peter and I..." She bit her lip, paused. Was she really going to give Jack the answer to the question he'd asked her on Monday night, when he'd been doing the bloody awful tarot reading? What, he had wanted to know, had the sex been like?

"Peter and I didn't know what sex was, really. We were virgins, of course, when we were married. More than that. Hadn't even had our clothes off. I can't believe I'm telling you this."

"I'm a virgin." Jack hadn't realised this. Oh... "Sorry, Jack. That was my big secret. There. Well, it's out now. Perhaps you were right. We do need to know one another a bit better..."

"So this Harry you told me about..."

"My first proper going-out boyfriend. Met him at church, you see. Where we'd both been told the bible made it clear that sex was an awful dangerous force which could destroy our souls, but that if we were married it was all right to have it if we really thought we had to. You can read all about it in Corinthians something or other I'm trying to forget where."

No one spoke for a while. Fran took out her pack of cigs, got one lit in her cupped hand, looked seriously at Jane as she lay there, playing with a pebble she'd found in the heather. Jack was still trying to take in what she'd said... so what she'd said coming up the hill, all that cock and cunt I want to fuck now stuff and why didn't he sleep with her last night was all just... what? From further up the hill they caught Bryn's voice or Peter's now and then, as the wind shifted, or a squeal of laughter from one of the girls. Jack's eyes were remote, searching the horizon. At last Jane said:

"Sex... we have to invent it ourselves. I think that's what I want to say. Come up with your own ideas, don't try to make somebody else's work..." She glanced at Fran, added, "Least of all Saint Paul's."

Fran made a face, shrugged as if to say, yeah, that's over now.

"What's Saint Paul got to do with it?" Jack wanted to know.

"Nothing." Jane was very clear about this. "Like I say, you have to work it out for yourselves. It's a shared project, just between the two of you. A project which you have to work hard at, if it's going to succeed." She smiled at Jack ruefully. "Sometimes, however, it *is* best just to bin the project, Jack." She crawled over to him and kissed him, ruffled his hair, and they both remembered how much they'd wanted one another just a few days ago. Well, that project came to nothing. Thank goodness. Then she went to Fran and kissed her as well, and thought yes, that could have been another story too. If … She took her hand, squeezed it. "I'll see you later."

It's all about *incompetence*, really, thought Jane, as she picked her way across the tussocky broken ground towards Peter and Bryn. Sexual incompetence, like religious incompetence, people fumbling about with ideas they think are so wonderful and they are, but they just don't have the imagination to use them properly… And just generally not being very good at being human beings…

"Well, Bryn?" she said. "Is your Jesus's attitude to truth anachronistic or not? What's the answer?"

"Oh Jane, goodness me, we sorted all that out a long time ago, moved on to other matters, we have, Peter and me. In fact we've been having one hell of a chin-wag, haven't we?"

"Bryn was just telling me about the time he saw a dragon sitting on *Pen-y-fan*."

"You saw *what*?"

"It's true. On a certain level."

"We've been hammering that word truth, haven't we Bryn?"

"We have."

Jane felt an urgent need to say, well Peter, if it's truth you want, try this: the man you've been chatting to about truth is in truth Alice's father… she shut her eyes and took a great lungful of air, throwing out her arms wide as if to embrace the two men at once, stretching, up on her tiptoes for a moment, thrusting her breasts out at them: then she slowly exhaled, put her heels back on the ground, bent her elbows till her hands rested on the top of her head. She opened her eyes, looked from one to the other, knew that somehow she would keep the secret for all their sakes, and that somehow… she dropped her arms, held out a hand to Peter.

"Come on," she said.

He looked at her hand, and at her face actually smiling at him. He didn't understand. Jane glanced at Bryn's twinkling eyes: he understood all right, and she drew strength from him now as she had before- strength to go on, to make this work… She reached down and took Peter's hand in hers, pulled him to his feet. She kept hold of him, they were standing very close. She put her other hand on his shoulder, kneaded the muscle; she felt her lips drawn back from her teeth still clenched from the effort of pulling him up: her brows lowered, narrowing her eyes as she looked into his, swimming behind his glasses.

"We've got to get on now," she said, quietly, nodding, "Yes, get on with it. That's what we've both got to do, do you see, just… get on with it!" She looked round him to where the girls were still chatting. "Ali! Sasha! Time to go to the beach!"

"Yay!"

"Jane…"

"It's going to be all right, Peter."

"Where's my blasted bag? Oh here it is. Have we got everything, Cath? *Rydyn ni'n mynd at y traeth.*"

"Traeth? Were you telling Cathy we've been talking about the truth?"

"Truth? Na, that's *gwir, gwirionedd… Traeth* is the beach!"

"Where are Jack and Fran?"

"I left them over there just now."

"I can see them," says Alice, who is up on the highest point of the rocks. "They must be tired after all the walking. They're having a little lie-down together in the heather."

7

Well I never.
They're together.
In the heather.
Aren't I clever.

Clever enough to make up silly little… ditties? But there's more to it than stringing together rhyming trochaic di-meters, if that's the word which I think it is but bloody well ought to know. Look it up when we get back. Still, shows some fluency in the mother tongue… got the A levels now… A-stars actually, my dear… But I won't be satisfied till I can improvise poems in Latin, French and German too, and Greek and Welsh once I get stuck in next year…vocabulary, it's all about vocabulary. Read, read. Memorise. And *don't forget to look at the endings*, well thank you for that, Mr Ablative Absalom, you certainly hard wired that one into me. I'll wait here a minute, let them get on ahead, just have one more look at it before I go down. The Promised Land. Old Bryn's a laugh, and Alice just loves him- look at them hand in hand again like he's her Daddy not just her favourite author... Mum and Dad walking together, actually having a pleasant chat for once, well that's something God I hope they patch it up I wouldn't like to start at uni with them splitting up in the background and poor Ali all in the middle of it on her own. Perhaps if they can avoid driving anywhere together, what was he on this morning? There go Jack and Fran well who'd have thought it? She's dead cute all right, hell of a giggle I had with her and as for him, well... wonder if I should tell her I had him on the table with all his bits out Christ no let's just hope it all gets forgotten and to think I was afraid *he'd* tell well well I suppose in the frantic hurly burly of daily life *chez* Thomas a daughter inspecting her mother's boyfriend's privates is just a mere detail soon forgotten, swept away in the tsunami of one damn thing after another ... let's hope so, anyway.

Mustn't stay up here too long. Ah, look at it. Swansea itself over there to the west, bit of a hole compared to Oxford if the truth be known but Oxford hasn't got a beach and the Gower twenty minutes away on my faithful mountain bike which that reminds me I really must buy next week I wish I could have a car but the cost... the campus is OK, get a decent enough little room in a peeling and patched sixties tower block with a bed and a desk and a bookshelf, somewhere to take a shower and a crap, functional if communal well, who gives a. Me, I can live with it. See how hard those Welsh boys really are. Will I? Jesus, there's a thought. I ought to get on the pill in case. What if I was off my face one night and some bloody Geraint or Wyn went and stuck it in. What would Jess say? Is she going to get on the pill? Why have we never talked about that? Living in never never land we are, Jess and me... Got to talk, tomorrow. Not on the phone, in bed. Where it's real. Or is it?

Oh, the beautiful bend of bay and swerve of shore. *Finnegans Wake* without an apostrophe yes God what a fantastic explosion of language. I must try again. So hard though Joyce. His vocabulary. Damn, yes that reminds me. Joyce knew Italian too. Have to learn that as well, then. Oh there's so much, I'll never never... What is it with Daddy? What if he has a breakdown? Is he having one already? Is that what it is? Mummy isn't going to leave him for Jack now because Jack's with Fran or at least he is today who knows what if she gets off with someone else she was so pissed off with him before that would finish him I think if she found someone else and left him where would that leave Ali and me

And now Sasha did. Cry. It came out of nowhere really, it seemed to her. Suddenly it's time, apparently. So she sat on that ancient high stone seat looking out at the too too much of it all, the sheer bloody beauty of it, and let it happen at last, the huh huh huh shoulders shaking oh fucking shit I can't help it I don't care I'm just going to cry now and I'm too small too stupid there's so much to do and oh Jess, Jess... next term you'll be in Parks Road with your deoxyribonucleic acid with its alternating pentose sugar and phosphate groups arranged in a double helix and the hydrogen bonded AGCT bases always paired in the same way A with T and G with C see I can remember it all just like you told me oh Jess and the laugh we had looking at the photos of Crick and Watson on the computer and you said you fancied Crick and I said no Watson's more my type: oh, oh I'm not used to crying funny how it sort of takes you over and runs itself after a while so you can even have a laugh while you're doing it well that's handy still I'd better get some practice in because I'm going to miss you so so much Jess

What if she meets someone else? She's so bloody lovely there's bound to be someone to make a pass and what if she? Like I nearly did with Fran. I could have, I think she'd have let me. But she was good when Mum tried... Oh God, I can hardly believe that happened, but it's a funny old world, and Fran thought it was me and she said what would Jess say... I would have, if it hadn't been for you, Jess, when we were on the sofa watching the telly and started getting a bit giggly and silly and I kissed her and she kissed me back and we were having a bit of a romp but it was only playing, wasn't it? We both knew it, but what if she'd gone serious on me could I have resisted it? Would I have wanted to?

That's funny the crying's stopped and I didn't even notice. It goes on and off sort of independently, lets you get on with any other business as it were all very convenient really. Oh, Jess, it's because of you and your gorgeous family that I'm going to be here next term, miles away from you. Paradox! Because I didn't just fall in love with you last summer it was the place, the crazy campsite the tent the weather, the sun and the rain and the wind and surfing the waves just over the dunes at Rhossili and climbing the three hundred million year old limestone cliffs and that magical day when we took the canoes at high tide and paddled around Three Cliffs the sea was like a mill pond but oh it was lit up and sanctified and sealed and delivered and blessed by you and what we did in that lovely little tent at night my lovely warm scented sweetheart…

Got a tissue here somewhere. Right. Eyes wiped, face briskly rubbed. Thank God no mascara to give the whole pathetic game away. Time to follow on down before they call out the coastguard. Just light another one of these first, umph, bloody windy still, have to pack it in, I will they're all saying it except Bryn the Human Chimney of course. Right. Off we go.

Have a little run at it catch them up with a Gerard Manley Hop, skip and a jumpkins Oh, half hurls earth for me off, under, my, feet Hurrahing in Harvest good one that with silk sack clouds and wilful wavier mealdrift Anthony Burgess reckoned he knew the whole of Hopkins off by heart but I don't know he was boasting or saying what he wished was true or perhaps he did some people memorise the phone book but that's autistic not artistic though some will say it's the same oh God I'm puffed. One more drag at this, there. Stamp it out, stop it. Now. Off we go again it's not far really the interior monologue continues it doesn't have to I could stop

stiff stalks of grass *agrostis tenuis* whipping in the wind and burning bushes trees every shade of green leaves rippling burning bright in sunlight beyond their flickering swaying tops the shining sea and the blue bowl of the sky and the endless trilling outpouring of the skylark *alauda arvensis*

There they are just going through the carpark Dad's turning round looking wave here I am it's OK I'm coming catch them up while they're waiting to cross over mind the cattle grid it's pretty busy on the roads today and every day I suppose in the summer with all the grockles and the Birmingham Navy on manoeuvres but here's a gap in the traffic so over we go don't dawdle they won't stop for you not till they're well down the M four and need a piss come on Sasha join the happy throng well that makes a pleasant change quite cheerful we all are for once what's going on Dad's saying look at these houses lucky people living here and didn't this one use to be a post office yes it did Peter because don't you remember we used to buy ice creams there and once we came and it was shut and you were pissed off and so we said it was the pissed office don't you remember? Hello Sasha, caught us up then. We were just saying how nice to live in one of these houses. Wonder what they do for a living? Retired *Sais* they'll be, made their pile in England and come here to die, says Bryn. No they couldn't have come here to die, says Jack, we'd have seen the removal van. What? Long and tedious passage while this is explained to Alice so Sasha moves on ahead and finds herself leading the way past a tumbledown farm and into the sudden shade of a narrow pathway of cracked concrete with tall hedges on either side loud with insects that say buzz and thorny branches leaning some of them heavy with elderberries or blackberries and mind the dog poo God some people have no idea really and here's a right bunch of beach barbequed beauties coming up from the bay they're done already better step aside while big bummed incongruously sports clad Mum in her shades and paunchy thick thighed Dad in his on back to front baseball cap sweat past with the bags, Good afternoon, sez polite Sash and Arr, pants Dad a bloody pirate is he oh well to arr is human so they say and then along comes the red faced red shirted short haired short arsed grunting boy with *Rooney* on his back dribbling his football oh joy let's see it's inevitable Ow Mum… oh rapture yes, straight into the poo. Sort that one out, Fatso.

Love thy neighbour. Who is my neighbour? A man was going up from Torbay to Penmaen when his son's football went into the poo. A tall, intelligent, well-read, strikingly beautiful lesbian undergraduate-to-be at the nearby university saw, but sniggered and passed on. A pair of lovers, he a handsome, green eyed, curly haired and virile youth though no longer that young if the truth be known, she a slender smiley blue eyed flaxen haired maiden who knew he was no longer young but claimed that she preferred older men anyway, had eyes only for one another, though presence of mind enough nevertheless to step daintily around the cause of the disaster. Then came a priest, though not in priestly garb, and seeing the plight of the boy, that his football and expensive trainers alike were woefully bemerded, did have pity on him and indeed his parents in like wise, for they were at their wits' end and minded even to curse their son for his carelessness and to swear in their wrath so that the young boy's lower lip protruded frightfully, and his brows were knit together like one sore aggrieved at a dodgy refereeing decision. And the priest said unto his goodwife who was with him upon his journey, wife, open thou the burdensome pack which I have on my back, though since we had lunch I admit yes it is not quite so much of a burden, and see if by furcking around therein thou canst not find a packet of tissues, and give thereof unto these good people, for indeed their state is most parlous. And she did his hest and handed the said tissues unto the parents of the boy, saying, go on, take the whole packet, it's quite all right. And so as the stricken family grunted their heartfelt thanks, and set to work on the cleansing of their son, the priest and his goodwife wended their way onwards once more unto the *traeth* or beach, not without a quiet chuckle at the amusing scene they they had just left behind them. Now, my children, which of the three do *you* think was a good neighbour unto the frightful grockles?

"Oh dear," says Bryn, striding past briskly with Alice and Cathy in tow, "mind your feet, here. It's like I say, you're always in the shit, it's only the depth that varies...."

Sasha was leaning on the gate which led onto the sandy heath above the shore, a maze of winding paths through scented gorse, dark prickles and yellow flowers. She was waiting because she was unsure of the way. Unsure about next term... Stupid. It's only natural to be anxious about leaving home. But that's the whole fucking point, leave home get as far away as... But away from Jess too. What if... Tears, near, maybe? No. An obvious opportunity for a fag break, this, but again, no. Let's see if we can break the habit. I don't have to. When Jack and Fran strolled up hand in hand five minutes later, she was just grinding the stub out beneath her toe. Fags, she was discovering, like tears, seem to have an independent life of their own...

"Well I never," sez Sash, "still together. How long's it been now? Two days?"

"Two days and four hours and about twenty minutes," laughs happy Fran. "We were just working it out."

"Made in heaven."

"I hope so, said Jack. "I really do."

8

After the prickles and yellow flowers, a steep and stony pathway winds down to a final slither of warmsoft sand, and onto the beach itself: a little semicircular arena, the white horses of the incoming tide its gently beating radius, embraced by curving cliff walls like two grey arms of steeply tilted strata, each with massive tors for fists jutting out into the waves, huge, impassive, dwarfing the dozens of tiny humans who pick their way over the jumble of rocks at their bases or stroll across the sand or paddle in the sea or just lie basking in the sun.

Bryn didn't swim because the water kept getting in his pipe and making it go out so he minded the bags and the clothes while the others went in, leaning back on the near vertical limestone of a three hundred million year old sea bed. Through half closed eyes he watched the tiny figures almost silhouetted against the vast brilliance of the channel as they danced and ran and waded and plunged and splashed, and he soon lost track of who was who as the shallows became crowded with other people too, mums and dads and children alike bewitched by the magical influence of the flowing skirts of our great green mother the sea, he thought, we're drawn back to her, aren't we. Ah, some god is in this place...

The children. Alice. Which one's she? Can't tell at this distance. And Cathy? Oh, Cathy, wait till we get home tonight with that kit I got this morning funny that with Jack and Fran on board, Why are we going this way, Bryn? Just got to pick something up first, Boyo, patience is a virtue, and then having him drive around the block while I nipped in and got it. Shoved it in the glove compartment PDQ but not before our Jack had spotted Boots on the bag and so mind your own business I said it's just my weekly viagra prescription help me keep up the good work, eh Cathy? Ah, Cathy, ah, Hardd, soror mea, oh we'll know tonight: you've only got to pee on it... two blue lines! She could nip up into the bushes here and do it. No, wait till we're alone. Just her and me and... perhaps...

Alone. Hm. Actually of course there's Jack now and apparently Fran too, well, quite a little commune we're turning into, if he goes for the offer. Suit me if he did. Suit me very nicely actually. And of course if she's still with him when Cath... if Cath does have a baby she could help with that too... Yes, if he'll take on the furniture and the bits and pieces of odd jobs and leaves me free to get on with the writing. For Alice. Have to be quick, get her a printout, don't wait for publication, or she'll have grown out of vampires by the time Julian's finished with the bloody thing. Hundred and twenty thou, good enough length. What's that? Four thousand words a day for a month? Hard work, though. And that's without any interruptions. Good old Jack. Yes. I knew he'd come back for a reason. Hell, he could even do up the old barn for me and they could live in there if they wanted to. Wouldn't cost a lot in materials and if he did the work himself for his keep, why they could be in there by the winter. If they're still together. Our Jack... But there's something about him when he's with her. Different. Maybe this time it'll work for him. I hope so. I really do.

Ah, look at the sea. See it at night, in the moonlight. See a ship nearing shore, white sails gleaming or, no, sails as black as night itself. And on the beach waiting, men, cloaked, hooded, horses ready. Who's on the ship? Why such a secret moonlight landing on this deserted beach? On the clifftop secret watchers, Derryn and Amanda spying on the men below... he passes her the telescope, do you recognise them? No... Something arising again, out of the dim and distant past... something known once, half forgotten, but coming back, it's a woman...

It's Jane. Down the length of the table yesterday when I knew her God it shook me it still does *we had a child* it's been a life changer all right, well, I had a feeling, didn't I? Didn't I say to Jack I thought something was on the way? ... Alice, little Alice, my God she's my daughter my own lovely daughter. Loved her as soon as I saw her she came to me out of the enchanted land... Growing up all this time she's been in Oxford somewhere is it? And I never knew, all I had left was the memory of a wonderful day and a night and the next morning and then it was over- I thought: though for days afterwards I wandered around in a daze, didn't I, thinking Jane, Jane... I would have let her stay. If she had wanted to. How different it would all have been then. No Cathy. Unimaginable now. But no, off she went back with never a backward glance off to her life with Peter. Because of Sasha. To make it work somehow. What did she think when she found she was pregnant? Imagine that. Well, he thinks Alice is his. So be it, why should I mess his life up now? Funny talking to him. So serious he was about *Abraham*... And all the time while he was banging on I was seeing Jane there and Alice and oh such a big secret. The truth, eh Peter? You want to know what that is? Well it's hidden from you, guarded by me and by Jane. And Cath. Alice is our little bit of the truth.

Guarded. The guardians. The guardians of... the secret that is coming back into the world out of the mists of the past on that sinister black-sailed ship, that's who they are, Amanda, said Derryn quietly, collapsing the brass tube and stowing it away in his leathern bag. *The Secret of the Cartomancer*. That'll do, that's a good title. Amanda stirred, and would have fled, but Derryn put his arm around her and roughly forced her to keep still. Don't stand up, he said, they might see you on the skyline. Oh Derryn, she gasped, breathing hard, I'm frightened. You are? Of course I am, you fool, it's part of the genre. I tremble, my bosom heaves with emotion, and soon the guardians will capture me and imprison me in their dark tower full of secrets and do unwriteable things to me at night and you'll have to come and slay them with the silver bullet in your pocket left over from last time and rescue me and press your passionate lips to my yielding…

"Oh it was great, Bryn, we had a lovely swim, didn't we, Cathy?"
"We did, Alice. Bryn? Bryn! You've been asleep, Bryn."
"I have not. I was just closing my eyes for a moment."
"Jane, have you got a towel for Alice? Thanks. Here you are, love."
"Thanks, Cathy. Bryn, you'll have to turn your back now in case you see my opulent breasts and firm nipples."
"*What* did you say?"
"It was in Bryn's book, Mummy. When Elise was in bed, and the vampire…"
"Bryn, you corrupter of youth, drink off this cup of hemlock at once."
"Right, sandcastle competition, and then we can all have tea. Oh no, someone's sat on the cake!"

9

And after tea, as high water slighted the sandcastles and the shadows of the western tor began to creep up the wall of the eastern cliff, and Jack and Fran kissed and Peter and Jane dozed and Sasha perched on a rock watching the waves and smoking her last ever fag, Bryn and Cathy sat with Alice a little way off from the others, one on either side, holding her hands.

Alice's eyes were closed, and after a little while, Bryn said:
"Imagine a cave in the cliff. Can you see it? It isn't very big, the entrance is quite narrow, and low, but if you just bend down a little you can walk in easily off the beach. Can you see it, Alice? Can you imagine what it would be like to walk into a cave like that?"
"I think so, yes."
"Do you want to go in?"
"Yes…"
"Go on, then. Cathy and I will come with you…. there. The floor of the cave is wet sand at first, you can feel it with your toes, can't you?"
"Yes. It's bit cold. It smells of the sea."

"Yes, it does, doesn't it. The sea comes right in here at high tide, so we mustn't stay long. Look at the seaweed on the walls. Put your hand out, feel it."

Bryn felt Alice's hand twitch slightly as she imagined the texture of the cave wall.

"It's rough too. Barnacles."

"Yes. Careful- they can be sharp…"

"Are you there, Cathy?"

"I'm here, love."

"I'm glad you're here too. It's a bit scary."

"It's all right, though," said Bryn. "We can go out again at any time- you've only got to say. But there's someone here you might like to meet."

"In the cave?"

"Yes. We need to go a little further in. Are you OK with that, Alice?"

"Mm. I think so. It's dark."

"Yes, but if we go a little bit further you can see a patch of light. There's a hole in the roof of the cave that goes all the way up to the cliff top, like a big chimney, and the sun shines straight down it."

"Oh yes…"

"There's a little step up here, careful… up you go off the sand onto a rocky ledge… all right with that?"

"Yes. I'm holding your hands tight in case I fall."

"You won't fall. It's a broad ledge and the rock's been made quite smooth by the sea."

"Oh yes. Can I keep going towards the light?"

"You can… now, just ahead, lit up by the light from above, there's a lovely rock pool."

"So there is… can I have a look?"

"You can sit down on the edge and bathe your feet in it: the water's lovely and warm."

"There aren't any crabs, are there? To nibble my toes? That wouldn't be very nice."

"There's nothing in here to harm you. The lady of the cave wouldn't allow that."

"The lady? Is that the person we're going to meet?"

"Yes."

"All right, then, I'll sit down. Oh, yes the water's lovely and warm. I feel safe, and oh- I feel something else too… as if this is a place where,

I don't know what to say. It's like this is a place where special things happen. Look how colourful the rock is where the sun's coming down, and see, it's shining on the water. I can make ripples with my feet. Look, it's sparkling."

Bryn glanced at Cathy. She raised her eyebrows as if to say, wow, she's a natural.

"Alice?"

"Yes, Bryn?"

"I think in a moment the lady's going to come to see you. She'll walk out of the shadows at the back of the cave. Do you see where I mean?"

"Yes..."

"Now I'm not going to say anything else for a while, so that you can talk to the lady when she comes. Listen very carefully to what she says to you. And of course be very polite to her, as I know you always are."

"I will be, Bryn. Oh- I should stand up."

Bryn and Cathy felt Alice stir slightly as she imagined herself getting up out of the pool, ready to greet the lady. Bryn looked across at Cathy again. Her head was inclined, listening, waiting. For a moment there was complete stillness. Then they heard Alice's sharp intake of breath.

"Alice Thomas, so please you," she said. Bryn and Cathy felt her hands tightening on theirs.

"My friends, Bryn and Cathy, brought me here….oh… I didn't think… wait… yes… in my pocket, I've got…" Alice let go of Bryn's hand, reached into the pocket of her shorts, and brought out the fragment of sparkling rock she had picked up on the hill. She held it out in front of her.

"It's all I've got… sorry…" She opened her fingers, and the tiny stone fell into the sand in front of her. At once she was groping for Bryn's hand again, seized it firmly. He could feel how she was trembling.

"Oh. That's really very kind of you… Oh thank you… I don't deserve it, I only gave you a little piece of rock… was it? Was it *so* precious? …How come…? …Oh, I see… Anything? I understand, yes. Very serious indeed… Oh but I don't need time to think about it… there's only one thing I want… Please, please… I want my Mummy and Daddy to love one another and stop arguing all the time…"

Bryn could hardly bear it. Cathy was open mouthed with pity and awe, her head slowly moving from side to side as she tried to take in what was happening…

"Oh thank you, yes, oh thank you so much… You're very beautiful… and so kind… Can I really? I will… I will when I get home I'll come again… Oh but can I come on my own? …I'll try to be brave…"

There was another long silence, then:

"Thank you, dear Lady… Yes, because the tide's coming in… Goodbye… Yes I'll mind my head… Goodbye…"

Suddenly Alice's eyes flicked open, and she saw where the lowering sun was striking the top of the opposite cliff so that it blazed brilliant gold.

"Oh look!" she cried, "There! On the cliff top!"

"What can you see?"

"Oh Bryn… a huge lovely creature, look at its great scaly wings, its head all fiery…"

"*Y Ddraig*!"

"Don't look into its eyes, Alice! Look just past it, over its shoulder… No, don't speak… just listen to what it has to tell you!"

The little girl started to sob, and her trembling hands gripped Cathy's and Bryn's so hard it hurt them, and they saw tears start from her wide eyes as she gasped and shuddered and gazed and gazed on the beauty of it…

"Oh, thank you, thank you, thank you…"

They held her gently, waiting, while she gradually came back to them.

"It told me… my name… oh Bryn, Cathy, it told me my name is…"

"Shh! No! Don't say it! That is your secret name and you must never ever tell it to anyone unless they are so so special to you. No, not someone like me or Cathy… someone you will meet in the future… you'll know. Oh Alice, you are very blessed!"

And joy and love and pity overwhelmed them and they all three found themselves crying and laughing at once…

XI

1

"Do you love me?"
"Yes."
Tired now. And salty from the sea. Hair feels all… yuck. Have a shower later.
"Do you love me?"
"Yes."
Soon be bed time. Wonder if… tonight?
"Do you love me?"
"You know that I love you…"
Cold in here, though. Borrow a jumper. Must get some clothes. But no money. No nothing. Because I loved you, did what you told me…
"So why are you behaving like this?"
"This isn't easy for me, you know."
Make a cuppa. Get warmed up. Kettle. Water? Enough. On. Mug? Here. Dragon on it. *Croeso I Cymru.* Welsh, I suppose.
"What are you trying to say?"
"I'm not sure. I think…"
Teabag. Milk? In fridge, yes.
"Do you…?"
"You know I love you. But…"
Nearly over. Getting dark now. Lights? Not yet.
"Tell me what's on your mind."
"You know what's on my mind."

Creaking overhead. Footsteps. Bryn pacing. Thinking what to write. For Alice?

"I think of things to say, imagine them being said in your voice…"

"… love me?"

"You know everything."

Boiling. Pour. Teaspoon? Here.

"Where have you been?"

"You know where I've been."

"Yes, I do. But you have to tell me."

"Been getting on with my life."

Stirring. Teabag in bin. Milk in mug. Take it over there. Comfy chair. Curl up. Look out of the window. Reflection. Look at me looking at me looking out. Who am I? The girl with the dragon mug.

Getting dark now. Lights? Not yet. Creak.

"When the golden evening brightened in the west, and you danced for me…"

"In the sea, yes, and…"

"Soon, soon, to faithful…"

"You said it would be soon."

"Cometh rest. And on a rainy morning in town too, you danced."

"I did. Clumpily bumpily on the pavement in my new boots."

"And I came to you."

"He came to me."

"Where is he now?"

Still out. Walking. Wanted to have a think. On his own. By the lake? Perhaps. Thinking about me? Probably. Sip tea. Back soon. Then we'll see…

"I am coming back soon."

"When?"

"Soon."

"Nonsense."

"You will see me coming in the clouds."

"Yeah."

Creak. Creak. Still pacing. Wondering what to write. Story for Alice. Something happened to her. On the beach. What? With Cathy. And Bryn. Those two! And then! Soon as we got back here. Upstairs for a minute, creak, then yells and laughing and back they came practically falling over themselves, they could barely speak. A thin blue line, he was saying, over and over, a little blue line, that's it! I didn't know what he was on about, till Cathy said. I could be pregnant too, if Jack had come to me last night. What would it be like? To make love with him? To have his child?

"Do you love him?"

"You know I do."

You have to actually *make* love... What did he say? When we were on the beach, talking about sex. Again! Enough talking...

Sex should be something you invent with a particular person, he said, didn't he, something you design with the someone you've got to know and love...

"Do you know him?"

"You know how much I know him."

It's like the difference between pornography and erotic art, he said. In pornography you don't know the people, they're just nameless bodies posing, copulating...

"He said that?"

In an erotic artwork you know their story, how they came to be together, what they mean to one another. Their lovemaking has some relevance to reality, to you. The erotic situation calls for some imaginative input from you, the observer, the reader...

"He said that? Jack did? Bit brainy for him..."

And being in a love relationship yourself is like making an erotic artwork or any artwork: you have to invent, to discover, explore, try out ideas which don't always work but have the faith in yourself and in your partner to keep on trying even when it seems it would be better to bin the whole project and start again somewhere else...

"Try telling that to Jane."

"She knows."

Jack the craftsman, using his artist's eye and his sense of what works... He's been gone a long time. Going for a walk, he said. Think about... things.

"You're making this up."

"Sure. Just like I'm making you up. And I shall stop doing that very soon. Talking to you's just a habit I've got into. It doesn't mean anything any more."

"You loved me once."

"Sure."

"When you walked down the aisle and gave yourself to me."

"Down the aisle, yes. Like a wedding."

"Mystical union that is betwixt me and my Church..."

"The leprous bride, the loathly lady..."

"My love transforms you."

"Bryn says love isn't a thing that exists independently of relationships. It has to be made, he says, invented, tailor-made, custom built. Like the love of God. You have to make it. He was on about that when we were driving back. Funny how he talks. Like he knows."

"As one that hath authority, and not as the er…"

"Scribes and Pharisees, yes. My love for Jack isn't the same thing as Cathy's for Bryn or Jane's for Peter or Sasha's for Jess. All these loves are different…"

"My love sustains you."

"My love for Harry…"

"You loved Harry once."

"We went out together. He said he loved me. I was unfaithful to him."

"You chose me instead."

"I didn't make love to him because we needed to keep ourselves pure and then when we got to heaven it would be so worth it… I remember saying that. What a laugh."

"You chose well. Now, about Jack…"

"I left Harry for you. Now I'm leaving you for Jack."

"Whom you hardly know. And in any case, you love me still. You said you did. Still."

"Like Bryn said he loved his Jesus. The one in his book. The one he'd made up."

"But I am real."

"No."

"I say real things to you. Things that matter."

"It's me. I'm letting my mind speak to itself."

"Strange."

"Not really. Just using my imagination."

Get my life back. When did I last touch a piano? Or sing anything other than silly love songs to Jesus? Schubert. Oh. With Peter on the lawn, in the rain. With Sasha. *Die Schöne Müllerin… Die liebe Farbe*. I loved singing that.

"Why that song?"

"The loved colour is green." Green. Well. Jack o' the..

Green.

"Do you love him?"

"Fran Green." Meh. Keep my own surname. No. It's theirs. Horrible reminder. Should ring them, Jack said. Don't want to. They don't fit in with all this. They didn't understand then, and they won't now. If I marry him…

"It's now Friday evening. You met him on Wednesday morning. That means you've known him for three days. And you're thinking of marrying him?"

"A lot can happen in three days. You should know that, Lord."

"Love at first sight…"

"Yeah."

Should ring them.

"You should. Ring them. See, there is the telephone on the window ledge."

"Not a word I'd have thought you'd know."

"*Telos, phonē*… common words in Greek…"

Mess of papers by the phone, some scribbled with numbers, messages. Saul! Saul! What's this? A4 sheet, palimpsest of scribbles and coffee cup rings over printed words… something Bryn tried out, discarded?

Fran tilted the paper to catch the faint light from the window, read:

Saul! Saul! Why do you persecute me?
Who are you, Lord?
You know who I am.
I do. I see now. I see what's going on.
Answer the question.
Because… it must not be so.
But it is so. And there's nothing you can do about it.
Oh but there is. I will not see it,
But you can see it. Have seen it.
And can just as easily unsee it. Chosen people, chosen by God…
Meaning?
Meaning what it has always meant. This new way… blasphemy.
Don't be ridiculous. You're too intelligent not to realise…
Get thee behind me, Satan!
You know I'm not Satan. Unless you want me to be…
No.
Who am I then?
I know who you are. But I cannot, will not…
What?
See.
So be it. Be blind, then, Saulpaul.

I shall.

There's more on the back.

"Sir?"
Saul had stopped in the middle of the road. The men shambled to a halt. Now what, thought Samuel, what's up with the weird little bugger this time?
"Sir?"
"What is it?"
"You want us to stop here, Sir? Rest break? Fall the men out?"
"What?"
Samuel took his helmet off, blew his cheeks out. Bloody hot again.
"Do you want us to stop?"
"Stop?"

-he won't move, so they take him by the hand and pull him on his way.
-he doesn't want to face Damascus and some hard decisions.
-what if he can't accept that it's just internal dialogue.
-it must be supernatural- has to be!
-then the scales fall from his eyes- but what does that mean?

"Something of Bryn's."
"An old sketch for his book, maybe."
"He writes well about me."
"You think so?"
Fran put the paper down, looked around the darkling room. Was this what she wanted? To leave Him for Jack? Must check.
"I love you."
"Mm."
"Lord, come quickly."
"Mm, mm."
"Lord, speak: for thy servant is listening."
Fran waited, listening, heard nothing but another creak from upstairs as Bryn paced around, thinking, thinking. Then out of nothing, it seemed to her that the world remade itself around her: on the darkened stage of her perception the scenery was shifting... ready for the next scene. The scene with her and Jack... she visualised him, and smiled. I love you, she thought, and then said it aloud:
"I love you, Jack."

She sighed, and picked up the phone. Jack had said she should ring. Give your parents a ring, he'd said, because if this bloody Robert or whatever his name is has told them you just fucked off with some deranged priest they'll be out of their minds with worry. There. How mature is that? She pouted, felt very young. Their daughter. It hurt her to remember that that was who she was. Even remembering the number was painful. How could a phone number carry so much grief? Frowning, she prodded the buttons, listened to the ringing tone, visualising the phone at home- *home*- sitting on the hall table under the stairs. Home... her heart sank. She saw the piano, a volume of Schubert open on it...then she heard her mother's suspicious, querulous recital of the number she'd just dialled. Why couldn't she just say hello like everybody else in the universe...

"...Hi Mum. It's me. Fran! Yeah... well, everyone calls me Fran now, OK? Anyway, surprise, hey? Yes, I'm with some friends... I'm not sure exactly- somewhere in the middle of Wales. There are mountains. And sheep. You don't need to worry Mum... How did you hear that? Robert? I wish he hadn't... Because I knew you'd worry of course... No, actually I'm not going back there any more... No, I'm not coming home either... it's not that I don't want to see you. No. I told you, friends. I honestly don't know. We drove here the other day. It isn't near a town. I told you, it's in the country. I don't know. What? Oh.... Hello, Dad..."

2

The talisman *had* worked! Just not in the way he'd expected. *Hod*!

The sun was setting over the hills, the lake was tranquil. Jack sat on the bank where he'd been fishing with Bryn, and marvelled. On Sunday he'd wanted Jane so much... but now: he felt a sudden shame like a punch in the stomach. The harm he might have caused! If she'd gone to bed with him, like he'd wanted, and Peter had come back and found them at it... Or even if he hadn't, what would have happened once the holiday was over and they were back in their everyday world? The keeping up of a deception or the horror of confrontation, the recriminations, the tears... But Peter had come back- with Fran: and he'd met her... because he'd gone shopping and stood in the carpark, delaying, *being kept back* until just the right moment to see Fran doing her little dance on the pavement...

The talisman. Magic. What other explanation was there? It was the most amazing coincidence- and she'd come out of the shop at *just that moment*. He watched the flight of a couple of birds, swift and low over the softly rippling lake. Beautiful. Amazing that things work out the way they do. Those birds... those *particular* birds, flying *just that way now*... what are the chances? But it has to happen somehow. What did Bryn say? Jack couldn't remember. Something about causation. No, it's gone. He felt another kind of shame, a sense of there being ideas which would always elude him. Too stupid. Never much good at school. not like Sasha. She made him feel stupid all right, every time she opened her mouth she lost him. The way she'd smirked at the talisman, knowing how to read the runes, and sneered at the the tarot cards. And that wasn't all: he remembered a drunken fumbling late at night and shame hit him again.

But Fran though. She talks to me so easily, makes me feel good! He traced the course of their being together, from the Romeo and Juliet moment as she called it: Romeo and... has she read all that Shakespeare stuff? What if she's just as clever as Sasha and after we've been together for a few weeks she finds out I'm thick and gets fed up with me... Jack has a moment of doubt, pulls up his knees, hugs them tight.

Try again, think it through. After that moment of love at first sight let's call it, driving her out to Fan Hir, Sasha sulking in the back... gradually finding himself with her all the time as they walked, then driving her back to the Thomas's place, fixing up the trip to Bryn's next day. Waving goodnight. Funny little wave she has. Then calling for them in the morning- strange bloody mood they'd been in, and no wonder after what she'd whispered to him about *goings on in the night*... well. But walking with her all around here, that'd been great though he'd been scared in case Jane made a scene... Last night, though, where to sleep? Cathy had assumed, so had Fran, it seems... don't want to screw it up, mustn't rush it, give it time. But after today, kissing her for the first time, on the hill, on the beach... What about tonight?

It is difficult, thinks Jack, when you're out of your usual world of everyday, to see things clearly. How does anyone ever know if a person they've met, are attracted to, is going to be a life partner rather than a casual shag? Isn't it a matter of faith in the end? Trusting your instincts? What have we got to go on? He remembers her standing before him on the hill earlier on in the bright sunshine, her hair wild in the wind, her eyes glittering: it's meant, she'd said, it's meant…

He realises that he's been thinking of her ever since as a life partner. That's it. He wants to marry her. The realisation is so astonishing that it drives him to his feet. How can this be? How can he be so sure? He doesn't know. But perhaps he's understood what faith is…

3

Fran put down the receiver and fell back in the chair, exhausted. She had tried to explain. It was hopeless, though, as she'd known it would be. At least they'd heard from her, had heard she was safe: the dutiful daughter has reassured her parents, even if they didn't like what they heard. Did they seriously think she could go back and live with them? Not now. Not after meeting Jack. Jack! He could make sense of her life, he would! He could show her how to find some meaning in the real world, away from the crazy make-believe of Windwood, Robert's castle in the sky: could show her how to live without giving in to the self-destructive impulse which had driven her away from everything she'd hoped for in the days before she'd got in with Harry and all that crowd… self-destructive? Yes, it was, a little suicide, turning her back on what she'd valued- not the possessions, not the status, but life itself…

She'd been in thrall to death. A lifeless fantasy that had sucked the living blood out of her till she became a pale shadow of herself… A pretend Jesus whom she'd imagined so vividly that he'd become a reality in her mind, preying on her as she prayed to him, growing huge and powerful as he fed on her energy and creativity, like a… like a vampire.

She gasped aloud as this thought came to her. Blasphemy… But no, idolatry was her sin here; she'd invented her own Jesus and worshipped him. Instead of the real one, the one who had brought the old vengeful sky-father down to earth with a bump, ripped away the veil of the temple as he died two thousand years ago but still saying love, love… salvation is learning to love, to live in love with one another… and you don't do that by hiding away in a retreat house.

What now, then? Life with Jack… Fran tried to see into the future: where would they live? How would they live? It's all very well giving everything away when you're going to sponge off the likes of Robert.

Would Jack think she was sponging off him? Not now, perhaps, but in three or four years? Children. Must have… because I want to give something back. Give life, not see it sucked away…. Life, love…

Bryn and Cathy came down and switched on the light.
"Oh… Hello, I must have nodded off."
"It's been a long day, Fran." Bryn was busy with the kettle, tea. "Fancy a cuppa?"
"Mm. Thanks." Yawning, stretching. "Then I must go and have a shower. My hair…"
"Sea water," said Cathy. "You've got lovely hair. In fact you're a lovely girl all together. Isn't she, Bryn."
"Pulchritudinous," called Bryn, "very. Sugar?"
"No thanks."
"Sweet enough already, she is. Lucky Jack."
"Bryn! Don't tease."
"Still out, is he?"
"Yes. Wanted to have a think, he said."
"About time."
"Bryn!"
"Soar-y. Hey, what a day, though." He kissed Cathy, and they smiled. Yes, it had been a very special day, though not all of the specialness could be shared with Fran. He took her a cup of tea instead.
"Thanks. I rang my parents." Bryn and Cathy waited, but that was it. Then she suddenly went on, "You've written a lot about Jesus, haven't you?"
The change of subject raised Bryn's eyebrows, but he guessed at the connection she was making.
"Yes."
"And vampires."
This time Bryn didn't get it.
"Vampires? Well, only the book Alice was reading."
"Religion can actually be quite dangerous, don't you think?"
Bryn frowned, looked over at Cathy. She said:
"Why do you ask, Fran?"
"Because it nearly killed me. But now I think I'm being offered a new life."
"Are you talking about Jack?"
"Yes. I'm almost sure…"
"There's always a risk in loving. If you commit yourself utterly."

"It's a matter of faith, in the end," said Bryn.

"Yes. Yes it is, isn't it? I'll take my tea upstairs if you don't mind. Have that shower."

4

As Jack opened the gate and stepped into the yard a vivid memory came to him, stopped him. He had woken up that morning out of a profound dream: and he felt again the sensation of weaving through moonlit woodland, in and out around the black boles of ancient oak and ash, slipping on drifts of dry leaves, ducking under low looming branches, crashing through curtains of hanging foliage, leaping mossy fallen trunks, but she was always ahead of him, a slender pale figure, twisting and turning, half seen, half sensed, never any closer... One particular image came back to him now, very strongly- a gap in the leafy canopy revealing a night sky where one bright star stood brilliant, shimmering, summoning. He had heard her voice, singing, somewhere close: and there! dancing in an open glade so near, her white skin gleaming and making the night bright... then, slowly realising that he was awake, that he lay under a blanket on the sagging old sofa, with cold morning light filtering through the curtained windows, he had seen her, like a strange vision from his dream, sitting cross-legged on one of the kitchen chairs, a few feet away, watching him.

"Good morning, Jack."

"Good morning." He had shrugged off the blanket, swung his bare feet onto the stone floor, and sat there in his boxers yawning and trying to massage some life into his face. "Been there long?"

"A little while. You don't snore…"

"Don't I?"

"…much."

"Oh." Still half asleep, he had seen again a girl running, always ahead of him, a slender pale figure, twisting and turning, half seen, half sensed, never any closer…

"What are we going to do, Jack?"

"Today?"

"And the next day and the one after that… that's what I've been wondering, sitting here watching you sleep."

Now, remembering all this, he realised that he knew the answer. He walked quickly up the path to the house and pushed open the door.

"Hello boyo. We're just havin' a brew."

Jack stood for a moment blinking in the light. Their big news came back to him. Quite astonishing. He grinned, and clapped his hands on their shoulders.

"Mum and Dad," he said, laughing.

Bryn's eyes twinkled.

"A little blue line, Jack," said Cathy. "Incredible what it means."

"I'm really pleased for you. For both of you."

"Thanks." Bryn sipped his tea. "Think about what I said before, by the way. The building project, and the furniture work, right? I'd like you to take that on for me. And of course, if you find that... well... things work out for you, you know; she's welcome too."

"Thanks." Jack looked around. "Where is she now?"

"Gone up for a shower. It's not easy for you, Jack. It's not easy for her. But, if it helps the two of you to be here, you'd be doing me a favour. Especially as I've got another book to write ASAP. I've just been making some notes. I must get started properly in the morning."

"This is the one for Alice."

"That's the one."

"You really liked her."

"Oh yes. Oh yes." Bryn and Cathy smiled at one another, and moved towards the stairs, but Jack said:

"Bryn? How does it all happen?"

Bryn looked at him with something like pity, something like love. He understood. Poor Jack. Shaking his head, he went slowly across to the table and sat down, taking out his smoking kit. Cathy sighed.

"Oh, he's getting his pipe out," she said, going to the sofa and stretching out."It's going to be a long answer. I might as well make myself comfortable."

"Sorry, Cathy, it's late- perhaps tomorrow..."

"To start with," said Bryn, ignoring this and stuffing in tobacco, "Tell me why you're skulking around here."

"Skulking?"

"Instead of milking the Cotswolds wealthy of their disposable income like a good little artist should."

"Because..." Jack picked up the kettle, found it had some hot water left, started to make himself coffee. "I don't know, that's the point. That's what I'm asking."

"But you do know," Bryn insisted, lighting up. "Work it backwards. You're here because I was the any port in a storm you fled to when you made it too hot for yourself with Jane. You got to know Jane because you were showing some work which you wouldn't have created if you hadn't learned the ideas and the skills from me. You came to me in the first place because you couldn't stand it at the bloody college and decided to get as far away as you could hitch which turned out to be in the middle of nowhere and were standing there in the rain like a bloody half-drowned scarecrow when I happened to come along in a good mood and gave you a lift. Suppose I'd had a bad day and decided to drive on and leave you for someone else to pick up. What then?"

"I wouldn't be here now."

"And neither would I," said Cathy. "Think about that."

"I'd never have met Cathy. Right." Bryn blew out a lot of smoke. "And I'd never have met Jane again. I mean…" he coughed, flapped his hand in front of his face, "…never have met Jane. Or Alice. See? And you'd never have met…" Bryn waved his pipe towards the staircase. "Her upstairs. It's obvious, really." He grinned, clenching the pipestem once again in his strong teeth. He sat back and puffed away happily while Jack stood leaning back against the sink, dubiously rubbing his stubble.

"That isn't quite what I meant, Bryn. It's the coincidences!"

"No such thing."

"No, listen, Bryn. It's incredible. Wednesday morning. She was just coming out of a shop with Jane… *exactly* at the moment I was slowing down for the corner and saw her there on the pavement. Fran and I were talking about that yesterday. She said it was *meant*."

"By whom?"

"And Alice and Peter were reading your books. How do you account for that?"

"I'm a very popular author. No seriously, Jack… can't you see it's the same thing? Coincidences are just what happens. It sounds as if you're looking for some kind of supernatural explanation. Fate, or destiny or the will of God or the gods or some such nonsense."

"Magic?"

"What about it?"

"Well, spells," said Jack, to no response. He felt he ought to say something else. "You know, making things happen that are going to happen anyway, but somehow making them happen more deliberately and positively. You said that once, or something like it. I remember."

"Everything you do, whether it's casting spells or pathworking or reading the paper or going fishing or taking a piss will affect what happens next. It's obvious. Magic's a way of getting yourself on the right side of things, engaging your imagination, so that you feel part of the pattern. You see? You're emotionally connected to what's going on. Feel you're a part of it, not just the helpless toy of fate, in fact, since you mention fate. Fate is a misunderstanding, like that infantile nonsense of karma. Of course your actions lead to other actions. There's no need to get all bloody mystical about it."

"I tried to use runes to get Jane to…"

"So you said, I think. It doesn't work like that."

"I knew that really. I think if I'm honest I was trying to impress her."

"But in fact it was just that kind of supernaturalist mysticism she was on the run from. Had enough of it from the church, by the sound of it. As for using tarot cards… it takes months to get anywhere with that imagery. It isn't an after dinner game. Still less a seduction technique."

Jack turned away, and stared bleakly out of the window towards the garden, but there was little to see beyond his own perplexed reflection. Nearly dark, another day gone... He picked up his coffee, sipped at it, turned back to Bryn.

"But it got me Fran, didn't it?"

"Did it?"

Jack realised that he still didn't know. Three days…

"Three days," said Cathy. Jack glanced at her sharply. She smiled back gently. He looked at Bryn, who had got up and was knocking his pipe out in the fireplace.

"I've got a lot to learn, still, haven't I?"

"Ah, learning, Jack, yes. It's still all about learning. And now Cathy and I really must go to bed. And in the morning I've got to get on with *The Secret of the Cartomancer* or whatever I'm going to call it. You think about what I said, about the work, you know? Be a good project for you, all right? Good night, Jack." He reached out a hand towards Cathy and she took it so that he could pretend to pull her with a great effort from the depths of the old sofa. "Come on, you two," he said, and they went upstairs laughing.

5

Jack finished his coffee, rinsed the mug. Then he went and sat down at one end of the long table, arms folded, staring at the grain of the wood. Nice piece of oak, lovely. And a well made piece of furniture, work of a real craftsman. But had he got it in him to do the same? Yes, he thought, or if not, I'll bloody learn. It's all about learning. Then Fran came down again, wearing a vast Wales rugby shirt that came down almost to her knees.

"Been on the scrounge?" he asked.

"Enter the dragon," she said, "Grr!"

"Do dragons go Grr?"

"I don't know," she replied, pushing up the too long sleeves and sitting down at the other end of the table, arms folded just like his, facing him seriously down the polished surface. "But if we're going to stay here together, it might be as well to find out."

For a moment they said nothing, searched one another's faces, wondering. Jack said:

"You look different."

Her face worked as she recalled what she had been thinking while he was out. Different, yes, perhaps; but in the end she just smiled and said:

"Washed my hair?"

It was still damp, brushed back, so that her features stood out, her eyes seeming larger, yearning: her neck thin and delicate in the rough collar of the big rugby shirt. She looked young, vulnerable, thought Jack, but so beautiful, and she could be mine.

"Fran. I've been thinking. While I was out."

Her guts turned over. What if he was going to end it? Her mouth fell open, and she had to make an effort to close it, felt her lips meet unevenly, swallowed hard. Her heart was pounding and she thought she was going to cry.

Jack saw her distress, wanted to hurry on, say it, save them both, but he found himself literally at a loss for words... too many clashing emotions, drives, memories, wants... finally he gasped her name- it was all he could manage.

"Fran..."

"Jack?"

"Fran..."

This was absurd.

"Jack?"

And this was... too, too ridiculous! Out of tension, nerves, out of somewhere came bubbling up at last the huge relief of giggles and splutters and sheer out loud belly laughter. They sat there, one at each end of Bryn's great oaken table, helpless, rocking with mirth.

"Shh...! They've gone to bed..."

"I know… must be quiet…"

But this too was for some reason extremely funny…

At last they subsided, biting their knuckles, wiping their eyes, looking down the length of the table at one another with complete understanding at last…

"Oh," Jack gasped, recovering enough to speak, "Like we had an… orgasm."

"Was it?" asked Fran, pursing her lips primly, though her eyes were glittering. "I really wouldn't know."

"Ah. Of course. How silly of me…"

"But I *do* hope I'm going to find out."

For a couple of heartbeats they are silent, waiting. Then Jack says:

"Like I said, I've been thinking. I've decided I will take Bryn up on his offer of working for him here. It would be really good. But only if…."

"If? What?"

"If you'll stay here with me. If you'll… I mean, if you really want to…"

Fran stood up. She crossed her arms, grabbing the hem of the big shirt, and pulled it off over her head. Then she chucked it onto the table, tossing the hair away from her face. She hadn't been wearing anything underneath it. With shining eyes and parted lips she looked at him, breathing hard.

"I take it that's a yes, then," said Jack.

Gracefully, like the dancer that she was, Fran extended one arm towards him, turned the palm upwards, rippled the fingers in invitation. Marvelling, he got up and walked the length of the table to her, let her take his hand in hers, and lead him upstairs.

XII

1

"Glass of wine, Julia?"

"Better have a coffee. Driving. Well, thank goodness you're back, anyway." Julia pulled a chair out and sat at the kitchen table. "Jess's been impossible this week. And there's no phone at your cottage and mobiles don't work there, apparently. So they weren't able to speak whenever they felt like it, which young people *have* to do these days, you understand, it's some sort of inalienable right."

Jane, arms folded, leaned her bum against the sink, waiting for the kettle to boil, tilted her head and wondered about this tall, strangely confident woman, who had always intimidated her slightly in the past. She'd visited the vicarage often enough because of the girls, but always gave Jane the impression she was an anthropologist exploring some primitive jungle village. Now, Julia's quick eyes were running over the front page of the *Church Times*, her expression one of tolerant bemusement. She sighed, shoved it away, and leaned back, flinging her right arm over the back of her chair, crossing her long bare legs, tracing the grain of the tabletop with the fingers of her, she noticed again, ringless left hand. At ease with herself, thought Jane, and with the world she lives in. Like me, she thought, now. Perhaps…

"Medullary rays," Julia said, looking up. "Make lovely shapes, don't they? So. What kind of a week did *you* have, Jane?"

Jane smiled, avoiding the sharp interrogative glance. She let her eyes rest on the polished surface of the table by Julia's hand. Medullary rays, for heaven's sake.

"It was... not quite what I'd expected it to be."

"Oh?"

"No. Not at all what I'd expected. In fact..."

The kettle was boiling. Jane got busy with the fairtrade and the milk.

"Well, do tell..."

Jane was wondering just how much she could tell when Peter came in, preoccupied.

"Ah. Coffee."

"Evening, Vicar."

"Julia- sorry, didn't see you there. I was miles away. Brought Jess over have you?"

"Yes, Gavin's been out with the bothers all day, so I'm on taxi duty."

"Hard luck. How are you, anyway?"

"Fine, thanks. And you? Still peddling opium to the masses?"

"Hah." Good old Julia, always having a go. "Not exactly. More a kind of analysis of the drug, this time."

"Peter's been writing ever since we got back this afternoon, haven't you. The big sermon."

"They'll crucify me."

"Oh, Peter." Jane was putting the milk back in the fridge. She shut the door, and embraced him, hugged him tight. "Peter, it's very brave of you... don't worry." She released him, smiled into the tired but hopeful eyes behind the spectacles. "Now, here's your coffee. Get back in there and finish it."

"Right, I will," said Peter, "One way or another." He glanced out of the window at the garden, getting dark now with evening shadows, noticed the sunbed still out there in the middle of the lawn. "Where's Alice?"

"Upstairs in her room. She's been writing too. You see, Julia, Ali's holiday work for English was to write a review of a book she's enjoyed over the summer. And my goodness..."

"Just a minute," laughed Julia. "Just a minute. Never mind the holiday work. I need footnotes. Why do you expect the congregation to get the hammers and nails out for you? What on earth are you going to tell them?"

Peter left the window, took his glasses off, found he was encumbered with coffee, put it down, rubbed his face, realising how tired he was. Running on empty. Not much longer now, though. What a week.

"It's not easy to explain in a few words. Or indeed in quite a lot of words. It took me a couple of hours just now to even get the outline of it down... in fact, sorry about this, I really must get back now or I'll lose my thread if you see what I mean." He looked at Jane, felt full of hope. He put his glasses back on, picked up his mug of coffee, sipped it. "Thanks for bringing Jess over, by the way, Julia. I'm so glad those two are... you know, so *happy* together. I'm really pleased." He nodded vigorously, and was gone.

Jane put a mug down by Julia, who was still looking after Peter, her lips parted as if to speak. They heard the study door shut firmly. Still open mouthed, Julia turned to Jane as she took down a bottle of wine and rummaged in a drawer for the opener.

"So..." Julia wasn't sure what she wanted to say. Better to say nothing perhaps. Suppose she'd misunderstood that last bit, and Peter and Jane didn't know in fact and blew their little Christian tops off. Better say nothing. She didn't fancy having to drive a screaming kicking Jess back home again tonight...

"Sasha told me they were lovers on Tuesday, Julia," said Jane, heaving at the cork. Out it came with a pop. "I hadn't realised, believe it or not- call me naïve if you like! It's pretty obvious really, isn't it! And it only came up because of a silly stupid mess I got myself into with this man Jack, he's an artist friend of ours who took us down to the cottage while Peter was away: it's funny really, though it wasn't at the time." She sloshed a lot of wine in to a glass, took it to the table and sat down, sketching a toast to Julia. "Cheers."

So they do know... But, *what*?

"You got into a *mess* with a *man*, Jane...?"

Jane swallowed wine, giggling, and edged closer to Julia, beginning to realise how much she was enjoying this, it was like being a schoolgirl again. Scandal! Delicious!

"*Scandal*! Wait till I tell you. You see I'd lost my head over this chap a bit I have to admit it God I was actually, you know..." She nodded, meaningfully, you know...

Julia didn't know, couldn't imagine, but nodded back anyway.

"And I got into a right strop with Sasha because I thought she was letting him get into *her* knickers when the only knickers I wanted him getting into were *mine*!"

Julia was shaking her head, blinking... was this really *Jane* talking?

"So I accused her of trying to take Jack away from me, and she, oh Julia it was so sweet, do you know what she said?"

Julia dumbly headshook no.

"She said, Oh Mummy, I wouldn't do that. I only want for you and Jack to be happy like I am with Jess... and then I realised, and it all came out. She came out, I mean. About Jess. Peter and I think it's rather wonderful, don't you?"

"But I thought... aren't Christians against..."

"Lesbian relationships? Who knows? Who cares?" She flicked at the *Church Times*, took a swig of wine. "I quite fancied Peter's little girlfriend myself."

"*Jane!*"

"He met her at this retreat he was supposed to be at. He was meant to stay there all week while I played with my toy boy, but he found he couldn't stand it any more after the first day, and arrived at the cottage on Tuesday evening with her in tow."

"Peter's been having an *affair*?"

"No no. She hitched a ride with him because she couldn't stand it there any more either, so I gather. Luckily the toy boy had fled by then. Anyway, the next day we were getting her some stuff in Brecon because she'd got nothing though that's another story and lo and behold, there he is again as large as life and the two of them fell in love on the spot like Romeo and Bloody Juliet."

"Who? The toy boy and...?"

"Fran, and Jack, yes."

"Jane, this is extraordinary..."

"A week ago, you see, I had a terrible row with Peter. I told him I couldn't go on pretending. All this ... nonsense."

"What nonsense?"

"That there is a real supernatural world. That religious practice is anything other than the exercise of the imagination. That consciousness is anything other than, well. What would you say, Julia? It's your field, isn't it? An effect of the organism's interaction with its environment? Cheers."

"I'm sorry, I really don't get it. You've lost your faith?"

Jane snorted, spilling wine. "Don't *you* start!" she laughed, putting her glass down and going to fetch a paper towel. "That's what Peter said a week ago." She wiped up the spill, said, "Faith isn't something you can just give up, like membership of a club- though plenty of people think it is." She binned the paper towel, and plenty of people's thinking with it, picked up the bottle. "Come in the other room. You don't have to go back just yet, do you?"

So Julia followed Jane out of the kitchen and into the hallway. From upstairs, romantic music swelled: Mahler? she wasn't sure. Jess and Sasha getting reacquainted. Or coming to terms with their forthcoming *Abschied.* Jane led the way into the sitting room, swinging the bottle by its neck.

"It's a creative process." She sat, curling her legs under her, on the big sofa. "Faith, that is. A positive attitude. Oh no, Julia, I haven't lost my faith- I've realised what it is. Choosing to be a part of what's going on. Making it work. No matter how difficult or weird it seems."

"Weird. You said it." Julia sank into the cushions at the other end of the sofa, looking at Jane with new eyes. She realised how little she understood her. "This is all a bit sudden, this..."

"Yes. But you know how things just build up over the years and then something- or someone- comes along and... well it's like birds getting ready to migrate. They sit around for ages in a great squawking flock and then when the conditions are just right, off they go all at once. You know the kind of thing."

"The system reaches a critical value and..."

"That's it, Professor. Everything flips over at once. One of your postgrads ought to write a thesis about us."

"So Peter's leaving the church? This sermon is actually a resignation speech?"

"No no. Not at all. He doesn't want to go. But they might make him."

"Sorry, I don't get it. What's he going to say?"

"He's going to burst their bubbles. Tell them what they all know but don't admit."

"Which is?"

"The truth."

2

In the soft light of scented candles, Sasha and Jessica sipped Calvados and listened as *Das Lied von der Erde* faded into its blue distance of gentle scintillating celestas, hazy cloudy strings, and the plangent poignant pluck of the lonely lover's lute as she laments her loss, her lover wandering in the mountains, seeking rest for her lonely heart...

Silence. Jess put her glass down, stretched out luxuriously on Sasha's bed.

"That's lovely."

Sasha, crouched in the armchair, watched her sadly.

"*Ich geh'. Ich wandre in die Berge.*"

Jess turned her head on the pillow.

"I know. You're going to go and wander in the hills and on the cliffs and along the beaches in Wales while I walk up and down Parks Road in Oxford with my lute, twanging it plaintively because I miss you so much."

"*Warum… warum es müsste sein…*"

"You know why. Come here."

Sasha slowly unwound herself from the chair, stood up tall, took a deep breath.

"I haven't had a smoke for over twenty four hours."

"You're doing really well, Darling. Come here."

Sasha drained the little glass of spirits in her hand, put it down by the bottle, refilled it.

"More for you?"

"Later. Come here, Sash."

"Third time is the charm." Sasha sat on the bed, stroked Jess's hair, her cheek, leaned forward and kissed her lips. "I shall miss you so much."

"We've got weeks yet," said Jess. "Don't be sad. And we'll be home for Christmas, won't we?"

"I was sitting on a three hundred million year old hilltop yesterday, looking at the gleaming blue sea, thinking about you."

"That's nice."

"I cried."

"Oh, Sash…"

Sasha stood up and went to the window, opening it wide. It was almost dark. The silver moon, a stricken ship driven before the storm, ploughed through wave after wave of ragged cloud above the treetops. Then Jess was behind her, her body pressing against hers, her arms around her waist, her lips on her neck.

"*O sieh!*" Sasha couldn't take her eyes off the moon. "*Wie eine Silberbarke schwebt der Mond am blauen Himmelssee herauf…*"

"Yes… a silver ship to carry us both on the gleaming blue sea up to heaven, Sash, my heavenly love, my…"

Sasha twisted around in Jess's arms, saw her sweet face in the moonlight, the eyes half closed, dreamy, candles glowing behind… "*O schönheit!*" Such beauty! She ran her fingers through Jess's shining hair, kissed her deep, deep. Jess broke off sighing, pulling Sasha's shirt out of her jeans, and off over her head; she held it to her face, breathing in the scent, as Sasha shrugged out of her bra, dropped it. Jess picked up the little glass of Calvados, took one sip, and poured the rest onto Sasha's breasts, a libation to love, quickly stooping to take it on her tongue as it gathered in exquisite droplets at her nipples…

3

Jane shut the front door, and stood there for a moment, hearing the tyres scrunching on the gravel as Julia turned her car in the driveway. The house was quiet now. She walked down the hall to the bathroom, locked herself in, leaned her head against the cool woodwork, remembering how she'd done the same thing a week ago nearly it was though God it seems longer, that afternoon when bloody Alan had called and she'd brought Alice in here for some suncream.

She ran some water into the basin, looked at herself in the cracked mirror. Jack. Only a week ago. What an idiot I've been, she thought, still, got away with it somehow. She turned her head this way and that as she splashed her face, thought about growing her hair longer, like it was when… she thought about Alice, and how much of Bryn there was in her looks… Must lay off the booze, though. No need to guzzle it like I did tonight but Julia's a bit, formidable? Needed something. Interesting what she had to say about the way things happen, though. Causality? Determinism. Something like that. She's got a brain all right. Pity I'd got most of a bottle in me by that time so couldn't really… Maybe have her and Gavin round for dinner. Grow it out a bit, get highlights? Not too old.

Jane pulled the plug, watched the sluggish spiralling away of the dirty water. Gone. Now then. Try again. Have faith.

As she came out of the bathroom, she heard the study door opening.
"Peter?"
"Hello. That's that, then."
"Finished?"
"Have a look if you like. It's on the desk."
"I'd like to. Want a drink before bed?"

"No thanks, I'll just get straight up."

"All right."

"Actually, Jane..?"

"Mm?"

"There's something I wanted to say. Just come in here a minute."

Now what. She followed him into the study, saw at once the notepad on the desk, the lines of neat handwriting. Funny how he always wrote his sermons by hand...

"It's about something that happened yesterday. It keeps coming back to me. On the way back from the beach, do you remember? Alice?"

"What, the way she held our hands, you mean? It was odd. Wouldn't let go till we got to the car, would she?"

"That's right. She'd been with Bryn and Cathy playing some game for a long time as I remember, but then, just as we'd got packed up and were about to set off, she suddenly got hold of me and led me to you, she said something like, Come on, Daddy, we need Mummy. And we had to set off as a threesome. Quite awkward it was in places on that narrow path."

"She's funny, isn't she?"

"Yes. But... the really strange thing is, after we'd been walking a little way, I started to feel her hold on me in a very odd way... I hate the way these New-Agers talk about 'energy', but that's the only way I can describe it: she seemed to be transmitting energy or something from me to you and from you to me. I felt as if she was, mediating between us... does that make sense? Sort of holding us together... And it was only then, as we walked up the path together, that I really began to feel I was OK again... Yes, it was like a kind of healing... as if... Oh, Jane this is very difficult."

Jane waited. She'd felt something too, but needed to hear it from him first.

"Jane, this sounds ridiculous, but it's as if she was forgiving me for all the hurt I've caused you and showing me that we could be together... I won't say together again, because I think in a sense we've never really been together thanks to my stupidity and blindness over the years. I've no idea how this healing could be. I'm only telling you what I felt. Little Alice, somehow, I felt, has healed us, made us whole. Has been the healing love of Jesus to us, if you like... well, that's how I would have put it theologically, though I'm not sure how helpful an image that is... Jane? Does any of this make sense to you?"

Jane went to Peter and put her arms round him gently, leaned her head on his shoulder.

"I felt it too. Alice has been the thread running right through this week, Peter. I don't know how. Don't understand. But yes, her love for us was literally holding us together yesterday. And we needed it. What a week it's been." She turned her head, kissed his cheek. Then she walked over to the desk, picked up the manuscript. "I'll read this now, if that's all right."

"What? Oh. Yes, of course. Well, I'll be getting up to bed, then. Goodnight, Jane."

"Goodnight, Love."

He froze half way out of the door. *Love?* Did she say..? He looked back, but she was already reading. He sighed, and went out.

4

Twenty minutes later, Jane put the manuscript down, turned off the light, and went upstairs. Alice's door was open a crack, and Jane could see her bedside light was still on, though Alice was in bed and fast asleep. She had produced a manuscript too, she saw, as she went to switch off the light. A bold title in capital letters read, *CARTOMANCER A REVEIW*, and in smaller letters above it were the words *To Bryn Vaughan-Price, with love*. Carefully, so the click wouldn't wake her, Jane switched off the light. As she passed Sasha's room, she heard a stifled cry, a gasp, a high pitched moaning... well. She reached Peter's door, knocked, opened it a crack, peeped in.

He was sitting up in bed in his pyjamas, eyes closed. He breathed out, opened his eyes, turned his head, said, "Jane!" He held a hand out to her, and she took it, sat on the bed. "I was just re-living that walk with Alice and you," he said. "In my mind's eye. Trying to remember every detail. It's astonishing how vividly things come back to you sometimes, isn't it. Important things. I felt that sense of connection again, very strongly. I suppose it's a kind of prayer. Yes, that was a real prayer walk, that was, not like... Ah well."

Jane squeezed his hand. "I read your sermon."

"Oh, good."

"I loved it. Thank you."

"Hm?"

"Thank you for making everything so clear. Dear Peter. It's been so difficult. I'm sorry about last week and losing my temper and bloody Jack and all the rest of the nonsense…"

"It's all right. All shall be well."

Jane got up and shut the door. Then she turned back to Peter and started to take her clothes off.

"This is just between you and me, Peter," she said. "And no one else. Least of all bloody Saint Paul…"

5

Mervyn looked with love on Lucy as she led the choir into the chancel. His improvising fingers found the *Tristan* chord, their secret signal, and her eyes met his, narrowing with understanding, while her lips pouted into a kiss which modulated into a modest smile as she looked away at her hymn book. She is as sensual in a cassock and cotter as she is in bed, thought Mervyn, sighing, as he dropped his right hand onto the lower manual and wove the tune of the the first hymn seamlessly through the shifting sequence of Wagner's harmony, pressed a combination piston with his thumb and eased the swellbox open with his right foot so that like the sun rising over the sea the organ's voice grew brilliant, flooding the resonant space of the church with a vision of glory…

Mervyn became aware of a nervous presence hesitating at his side. Peter, one hand on the edge of the console, leaning in to him.

"Just bring it to a close, will you, Mervyn? Doing it a bit differently this morning."

"Meh…" So as Peter moved away towards the nave Mervyn moved away from the blazing dominant seventh he was holding to the submediant… *coitus interruptus*… he thought, catching Lucy's eye as she glanced quizzically across: he shrugged- the ways of the clergy are not our ways- and after a second's pause during which he shoved in stops played a soft plagal cadence, ironically flattening the third in the subdominant chord as his comment on this latest example of how priests just don't get ritual.

Mervyn sat back, arms folded, peering through the roodscreen to where Peter was standing by the lectern placed at the entrance to the chancel, ready for the gospel reading later in the service. He had not put on the coloured Eucharistic vestment: he wore the plain white alb only over his cassock. The congregation of some thirty or forty people, not many of them young, were scattered around the tall mediaeval nave: they had stood up at the entrance of the choir, and now looked towards him blankly, hymn books in uncertain hands. There was a long silence. Now what?

"I'm doing things a bit differently this morning," said Peter, his amplified voice echoing strangely. "I'm preaching the sermon first. Would you please be seated." And he made his way to the tall pulpit, climbed the steps slowly... for the last time?

He put his sermon on the reading desk, noticing that his hand was shaking. Fumblingly, he switched on the reading light, and looked out at the upturned faces below. There was Jane, in her usual place in the back pew on the left, just in front of the west aisle, and next to her as usual, Alice. But what made him almost cry out was that Sasha and Jess were there too... it was over a year since Sasha had vowed never to set foot in the place again: and now... he nearly called out to her, he was so grateful. Dear Sasha... and Jess too. Well.

He realised that he needed to get started. He gripped the wrought ironwork at the edge of the desk, and began to speak.

"Some of you will be aware that the Parish Retreat didn't go quite as planned. For those of you who don't know what happened- although I'm sure word has got around- I felt it necessary to leave on the second day."

His voice was playing up. Alan, he saw, lurking by his habitual pillar, was frowning around at some of the others who'd been there. Peter cleared his throat. Right. Well just you listen to this.

"A lot of things which had been troubling me for years suddenly became very clear. Overwhelmingly clear. I felt I had to get away and do a lot of thinking- beat a retreat myself, in fact. And all week since then I've been trying to put into words what I feel. I'm preaching the sermon now instead of in the usual place in the service because... everything we do after this will be in the light of... what I say."

Get on with it. Stop putting it off. His hand was hurting. He looked at it, and noticed, appalled, that his white-knuckled grip had actually distorted the ironwork. He let go, massaging the painful hand with the other, looked at his notes.

"I take as my text the Gospel according to Saint John, chapter eighteen, part of verses thirty seven and thirty eight: For this was I born, and for this came I into the world; that I should give testimony to the truth. Every one that is of the truth, heareth my voice. Pilate saith to him: What is truth?"

He looked down the nave again. Faces, faces. He nearly said, Are you sitting comfortably? He took a deep breath, and read:

"Once upon a time, about three thousand years ago in fact, a small group of nomadic people were wandering around the middle east. Like everybody else in the world at that time, they believed that powerful invisible beings called gods demanded their attention, and influenced their lives for good or ill. But these particular people, who were of course the Jews, had a revolutionary idea. Their god, they decided, was not just one god among many. He was actually the most powerful one of all, the one who had made the whole world and everything in it. And what is more, he had singled them out for special attention, chosen them out of all the other people in the world, made a special deal with them. These were the terms of the deal. If they would acknowledge him alone and do exactly what he told them to, then he would give them a wonderful land to live in- no more wandering around- and would make them the greatest nation upon earth. It was as simple as that. Obey, and be blessed.

"They got their land eventually- though only after much fighting, because some other people less favoured by their god were living in it at the time- but they were not blessed. On the contrary, not only were they still subject to death and disease and famine and war like every other nation, but they were politically weak too: and although they liked to recall a time of prosperity under their great kings David and his son Solomon, as time went on they were increasingly oppressed by the more powerful surrounding nations. In the end they were enslaved, taken into exile, and by the waters of Babylon, far from their promised land, they sat down and wept.

"What had gone wrong? They remembered their god's promise to them: he would not have gone back on his part of the bargain; that was inconceivable. So they must have failed in theirs. They had promised to obey him, but were clearly not doing so. It was the only explanation.

"Attempting to understand their situation, they began to compose a national epic, collecting together stories about their god: how, long ago, his word had caused the world to be made and made perfect in every way, and how by disobedience the first human beings had spoiled its perfection and become alienated from the very source of their life. They wrote about the fathers of their nation, Abraham and Moses, and the deals which they had made with their god: and they produced a vast body of laws governing every aspect of their lives which would, they were sure, enable them to obey their god and return to a state of blessedness- if only they could keep them exactly.

"Round about the time they were putting these stories and books of law together, some of them found their way back to the promised land, and to the capital city, Jerusalem. But the temple had been destroyed, and the land overrun by foreign armies, so that the process of reconstruction was long and painful, and their observance of the law necessarily more and more stringent: their only hope lay in obeying God: any failure to do this was not only a religious but a political crime. The nation could not survive unless the law of the god was kept absolutely.

"But all the time, alongside the making of laws and the edifying telling of histories, there was another stream of thought: a critical commentary if you like, the tradition of prophecy. Isaiah, for example, who saw God as being ready to act to save his people through his suffering servant, and Jesus too was in this tradition of criticism: indeed some say that Jesus was Isaiah's suffering servant, a special person sent by God to save them from their sinful disobedience- an anointed one, a messiah.

"Jesus' message was simple enough: the kingdom you have always hoped God would establish is here already, but you can't see it because you're not letting your religion develop: in fact now the traditions you've established are actually getting in the way. New skins for new wine! God isn't out there somewhere, endlessly condemning us for being who we are. God is in our simple love for other human beings, Jews and Gentiles alike: in our sheer joy at the gift of life. Let us be glad therefore, and when tragedies do occur, as they will, deal with them together!

"But the new wine of the kingdom was too heady a vintage for those who loved their religion more than they loved their fellow humans. How long did the message of Jesus survive his death? A generation? Less. Already by the time our New Testament was being written the old ways were creeping back. To those who called themselves Christians- those who were supposed to believe that Jesus was God incarnate, that God had come down to earth- God was back again in his unreachable heaven, and mankind was once more crawling under the same old burden of guilt, endlessly condemned to fail in their efforts to obey the divine imperatives. This world of the senses was unreal: and the Christian's hatred of himself and his world was reinforced by influences from Greek philosophy which saw human beings as imperfect creatures in an imperfect world: only God was perfect. For now we see but as in a glass darkly, but then face to face. No, Paul. The glass is all that there is. That's *it*. Nobody saw that that perfection was just an idea like any other, or in what sense assigning ultimate value to a philosophical concept instead of your fellow human beings could have had anything to do with the message of Jesus.

"But the critical voice of prophecy wouldn't go away: always down the centuries it sought to nag and prod the inert complacency of the powerful religious authorities. It took on new forms: instead of attacking religious practice directly as in the time of Isaiah, it created new ways of seeing the world which gradually relativised religion, made the blinding certainties of faith look provisional, anecdotal, and, eventually and most tellingly, artificial. From Galileo to Newton to Darwin to Einstein the voices of prophecy went on, until at last, let's say a hundred years ago at the latest, it became obvious: religion is a human invention, through and through. There are no absolute, eternal truths: there is no supernatural, there is no perfect world above. There is only language. And our language cannot point beyond itself. This life is all that there is: and what has always been obvious- that is, that we become aware of the world, use language to express our feelings about it, and then cease to be aware of it- is indeed all of what human existence is."

Peter looked up. No one moved.

"That's it," he said, and repeated, "That is indeed all of what human existence is."

Alan, he saw, was stifling a yawn. Peter adjusted his spectacles, plunged on.

"*We* invent the stories which tell us about God. God does not reveal himself in the scriptures- they are a record of the evolution of the concept of God in the imaginations of the writers. In Genesis we read that God made man in his own image. But it's actually the other way round. We make God and always have done. His decline has been in proportion to our growth into autonomy.

"In ethics..." They're not listening, try a joke, "That's not that county next to Thuthex, it's the study of morality..." Not a flicker, apart from a snort from the direction of the organ console. "In ethics too, we've invented the rules ourselves. Take Paul again: his teaching on sexual morality, which is causing so much trouble in the church today, is his own invention, and it's terribly dated: it was written to give Christians guidance at a time when they literally thought the world was likely to end at any moment and they'd all be summoned by a trumpet blast to the judgement throne. I don't think any of us seriously imagine that's very likely now, do we?"

Not a flicker. Dangerously, desperate to get some reaction, Peter started improvising:

"Ironically, you see, and this would make me laugh if it wasn't so pathetic, Paul's constraints on sexual behaviour, if taken at face value today, actually have the opposite effect to that intended- make sex within marriage seem like the meaningless copulation of two random strangers! See why? Because the husband and wife's sexuality is so hedged about with awful warnings it isn't part of the growing relationship... It was almost imposed from without. It wasn't about what we felt, I mean what they feel for one another as people, not about love at all. It was like... a necessary discharge." Like going to the toilet together, he thought, but didn't, thank goodness, actually say. What was going wrong? He felt light headed, crazy, forced himself to concentrate, got back to his notes.

"And Jesus? What of him? He is not an invisible friend we can talk to in prayer: he has no real supernatural existence: but that doesn't mean that by the exercise of our imaginations the thought of him can't sometimes become almost unbearably moving! To gaze and gaze on..."

No, he couldn't. It was, is, too too. Peter took his glasses off, ran his hand over his face, replaced them, read on:

"And he's not coming back to catch us up with him into the clouds, either. He is a symbol of what we could be, if only we could rejoice in our lives, live by love instead of fear and guilt. Saint Matthew tells us that when Jesus died, the veil of the temple was rent in twain from the top to the bottom: suddenly there was no longer any difference between the sacred and the profane. Although the expression *the death of God* is nineteenth century- I think, I think it was Nietzsche but I didn't have time to look it up last night- we could say that the old God, the old punishing projection of male power and anger died at that moment too, on the cross if you like. My God, my God, why hast thou forsaken me? No answer, because he's dead. Gone from Jesus's religious consciousness, gone from ours: fully incarnated, fully identified with suffering humanity at last. I'm inventing that idea, do you see? Just like every other idea about God which you've ever heard, it's made up. Does that mean it can't be true?

"So, what is truth? Not something out there beyond us that exists in a Platonic world of ideal, ultimate, superhuman reality. I don't see what that could mean. The only reality we can apprehend is the reality of our language. I don't see what we could possibly mean if we say that there is a superhuman reality beyond our human language. What could such a reality be like? We cannot get outside our language: it is to us as water is to a fish. We cannot imagine anything beyond the system of signs with which we think and feel and express ourselves to one another. Can we? You just try and conceive of anything at all without using words or some sort of mental image."

Peter waited a moment, glanced up to see if anyone was obviously trying to conceive of something without using words or some sort of mental image. He got the impression that they probably were not. Well, he had wondered about including that bit.

"I quote Saint John again," he went on. "He has his Jesus saying, For this was I born, and for this came I into the world; that I should give testimony to the truth. Every one that is of the truth, heareth my voice.

"What is that voice saying to us, here in this church? I'll tell you what it's saying to me. It's saying that all of this... the building, the music, the ritual action of the mass, the reading of the scripture and the saying of prayers is a drama: a dramatic and imaginative statement about value: about the high value we assign to human life, to love, to beauty, to endurance and selfless giving. It's a play of metaphors which celebrates the religious imagination and develops it. These great images that have come down to us from the past, even though we now know they are poetic metaphors- indeed we may even use them with irony or a gentle humour- are still sharp tools with which to work on our shared project of growing together in the world, indeed of discovering the world. It's an artwork, you see. Everything- *everything* you see done here is a product of the imagination. God is a product of our imagination. Fragmented as the bread is fragmented on the altar, but coherent as an abstract artwork is coherent."

Peter nodded towards Jack's *Corona Spinea* hanging in the Lady Chapel. He'll learn, he thought, and wondered how he was getting on with Fran.

"You see, we may not understand very clearly what the truth can be, but that's because there isn't any great once and for all Truth any more for us to understand: there is only the ongoing project, which we all share, of experiencing the world together and using all forms of language- verbal, visual, musical- to articulate our response to it in loving communication with our fellow human beings.

"What is truth, then? Truth is a young man and a young woman who are only just starting out on their life with one another, sitting on a beach together, tired after swimming in the sea, their lips meeting in a tentative kiss. It is a beautiful girl smoking a cigarette on a hillside, watching over her poor father as he lies writhing in the heather, lost in an interior wilderness. It is an old man standing under a stormy sky in the Brecon Beacons, rooted to the spot with awe and wonder because he can see a dragon crouched on the top of *Pen-y-Fan*. It is me, holding one of my little daughter's hands while my wife holds the other, and the three of us walking home, together again at last."

Peter licked his dry lips, picked up his notes, looked out at the congregation.

"There," he said. "Amen."

There was a slight stirring, an easing of buttocks on pews. It was over. He swallowed hard, turned, and made his way carefully down the pulpit steps. Don't want to slip and go arse over tip now- that would spoil the effect, he thought, trying not to laugh, must be a release of tension or something: he suddenly felt quite ludicrously light-hearted.

"Mervyn," he called.

Mervyn was leaning back against the wall behind the organ bench, his eyes shut. He pulled himself together; and it was as if he was coming back from some very distant place in his mind. He focussed on Peter with some respect.

"Yes, Vicar?" he said quietly.

"We'll have the first hymn now, please."

Afterwards, in the priest's vestry, Eric the server helped Peter take off the heavy embroidered cope, while *Joie et Clarté des Corps Glorieux* rang around the building.

"Thank you, Eric."

"No trouble, Vicar," said Eric, carefully stowing the vestment in its wide drawer. Peter watched him for a moment, but he didn't seem to have anything else to say. Ah well, time to face the music. There was plenty of that, thanks to Mervyn, he thought. *Joie* indeed. But he didn't feel very joyful. Anxious, even slightly afraid, he stepped out of the vestry, and made his way along the aisle towards the south door.

"Terribly loud, isn't it?" shouted Mrs Travers, nodding towards the organ.

"No, Messiaen, I believe," said Peter.

"What?"

"Vicar," busy Glenda wanted to know, "Have you fixed a date for the garden party yet? We need to get it into the Parish Magazine, and the last day for material to be handed in is this coming Tuesday..."

Peter stared at her.

"No," he said after a moment... "I'm sorry, would you excuse me?" He turned away.

"I got a dolly." He looked down. Little Katie held the plastic gynomorph out for his inspection.

"Very nice," he said, peering, adding automatically, "What's her name?"

"She's Dolly."

"Ah." Katie's Mum, he saw, was hovering nearby. He smiled weakly at her.

"You love your Dolly, don't you, Katie." she said, with a wink at Peter. "Come on, Katie and Dolly, Daddy will be wanting his lunch."

Peter, frowning, watched them go, then passed on down the aisle, to where Jane was still sitting, apparently inspecting the roof. Alice was on her knees beside her, hands folded on the back of the pew in front, staring fixedly towards the altar. Sasha had her arm round Jess: Jess's head rested on her shoulder. Their eyes were closed as they listened to the organ. The rest of the pews were empty already: the four were the only ones still in their places. Peter walked quickly to the door. A small knot of people were in the porch waiting for him. Ah, this is it.

"Hello, Vicar," said Mrs Mountjoy. "I couldn't really talk in there. I don't know why that young man has to play so loudly."

"I think it's an image expressive of the joy and brilliance of the risen body," explained Peter. Mrs Mountjoy blinked at him.

"What I wanted to ask, Vicar, which I'm not sure about because you failed for some reason to read the notices today, is if the midweek communions will be taking place as usual now you're back and poor Tim still so unwell?"

"I suppose so, Mrs. Mountjoy. I suppose so..."

"Well, I should have thought, Vicar..."

"Yes, do that, Mrs Mountjoy. Do that."

"Ah, Morning Vicar."

"Morning. Visiting, are you?"

"Yes indeed. We're from Kent. We're staying with my sister, Glenda. She said the music here was very good."

"Oh, it is."

"We didn't recognise the mass setting."

"Neither did I. Something Mervyn found on the internet, I gather."

"Mervyn?"

"Our organist."

"I see. A very fine player. Even if the hymns were, well, a little on the fast side. Difficult to catch one's breath, you know."

"The choir manage to. And so do I."

"Ah, really. Yes, but..."

"Good morning, Major." Peter was beginning to feel light-headed again... "And how are you today?"

"Can't complain, Vicar, can't complain."

"What," asked Peter, almost desperately, "did you think of my sermon?"

"Your sermon? Oh, very fine, Vicar, very fine, as always."

"God," Peter insisted, "is a human invention. There is no supernatural world. This life is all that there is."

"Absolutely, Vicar, absolutely. Very fine. But I must be going, I'm lunching at the golf club at one. Have to leave all the, ah, *theology* to you professionals, eh? Speaking of which, is poor Tim still unwell?"

"Apparently, yes."

"Poor chap. Still, curate, cure thyself, eh? What? Ha! See you next week."

In disbelief, Peter watched the Major walk his cane down the path. A hand, touched, his elbow. Evelyn, softly spoken, a churchwarden.

"Peter, a word."

"Yes, Evelyn?"

"I wonder if at the next P.C.C. we could raise the matter of the sidesmen's rota again. David should have been here this morning but wasn't. And last week if you remember..."

"Evelyn, God is dead."

"I'm sorry?"

"And you killed him. You and thousands like you..."

"Peter, what are you talking about?"

"Did you actually *hear* my sermon?"

"Yes."

"And?"

"I'm sorry, I don't understand. What do you want me to say?"

"Why, anything but to the point..."

"Well it was very interesting..."

"*Interesting?*"

"Vicar."

"Ah, Good morning Alan." Perhaps *this* is it.

"I'm sorry to interrupt your conversation, Evelyn, but I must protest. I thought you were going to have a word with Mervyn, Vicar. I have had to listen to a number of complaints…"

"From whom?"

"From… people here."

"Name two."

"It's time we had this out once and for all."

"I thought we'd had it out once and for all. And I told you that if you didn't like the music here, there are plenty of other churches in the area to go to…"

"That girl. That girl you went away with. Fran. We were making some progress. You should bring her here. With her guitar."

"Oh I don't think she'd want to do that, Alan. You see, she came to understand that her songs to Jesus were complete fantasy. She knows now that she was making it all up."

"She was. She told me."

"She did?"

"Yes. They were all her own original compositions."

"Not the songs, man, the whole thing. The reality of the supernatural. The second coming of Jesus. The whole salvation story… she understood that that is exactly what it is- a story. Nothing else."

"Exactly. Wonderful girl. So why can't she at least come and, you know, do a what d'you call it- a *workshop*- with Mervyn and the choir?"

Peter couldn't take it in. He turned abruptly and went back into the church. It was almost empty now, except for the little group still sitting at the back. The music was over, and Mervyn was locking up the organ console. He edged into the pew in front of Jane and the girls, rested his bum on the back of the next one, and got his feet up so he was sitting facing them.

Sasha gave him a thumbs up. "Well done, Dad. If a bit over simplified."

"I've never heard a vicar tell it like it is before," said Jess. "Thanks."

"What did they say?" asked Jane, her voice strained, and he realised how anxious she was. He smiled, shaking his head slowly.

"Nothing," he said.

"*What?*"

"They asked me about the parish magazine, about the midweek communions, about the sidesmen's rota, bloody Alan was banging on about the music… after all that, after all we've been through, it made absolutely no impression at all."

"I wouldn't say that, Peter," Mervyn was there, hand in hand with Lucy. "I thought it was a brilliant sermon, and very honest."

"It certainly was," said Lucy. "Thank you."

"You're not… shocked?"

"Shocked? Why should we be?"

"You didn't think that a plain statement from the pulpit that there is no supernatural revelation of truth, that we make it all up ourselves, isn't a bit… well…"

Mervyn exchanged glances with Lucy, shrugged.

"We were at Cambridge, of course," she said. "Hi Sasha, don't see you here very often."

"I felt I had to be present on this historic occasion. And to rescue Dad from the mob if they turned nasty and decided to burn him at the stake in the churchyard. This is Jess, by the way."

"Hi."

"Meet Merv the maestro and the lovely Lucy."

"Hi."

Jane still couldn't believe it. While Sasha and Jess chatted to Mervyn and Lucy, she bit her lip and watched Peter, still sitting there slowly shaking his head from side to side.

"What's the problem, Daddy?" asked Alice.

"They just took no notice," he said faintly. "No notice at all…"

"Come on, Topsy, *die müden Menchen geh'n heimwärts…*"

"Stop it, Merv."

"*Um in Schlaf,*" murmured Sasha, kissing Jess on the cheek, "*vergess'nes Glück und Jugend neu zu lernen.*"

"You know your Mahler," said Mervyn.

"And you know your Wagner," replied Jess. "We spotted your cheeky *Tristan* quote when you saw Lucy come in."

Lucy gasped theatrically, put a hand to her throat.

"Alas, my love, our secret is out. We must flee the country. Actually we'll be back in time for evensong."

"If you're not still in sleep forgotten happiness and youth re-learning," grinned Sasha. "Better set the alarm."

Lucy squealed. "*Sasha!* Come on, Merv. *En avant!*"

"Oh! Lucy… not in church, *please…*" And they were gone.

Peter had been trying to explain to Alice why the sermon had been so important to him, and why he was so astonished at the reaction, or no reaction…

"Perhaps they didn't understand it," said Alice. "*I* didn't understand it *all*, but I expect that's because I'm *too young*. But I did like the bit at the end about dragons. On the beach, I saw…" She stopped suddenly, put her hand to her mouth, remembering Bryn's advice: no, not even Daddy. She asked instead, "Was that actually Bryn you were talking about?"

"The man who saw the dragon?"

"Yes."

"Yes."

"And then were you talking about how you and Mummy and me walked up…"

"Mummy and I."

"Mummy and I thank you Sasha walked up from the beach together?"

"Yes."

"That was lovely. Really lovely. Didn't you think so, Daddy? Mummy?"

"Yes, Darling, we really did," said Jane. "Didn't we, love?"

"We did." Peter could barely speak.

He put his feet on the floor and awkwardly knelt on the pew and Alice stood up so he could sort of put his arms round her and Jane leaned over and somehow managed to more or less embrace them both… Sasha put her hand out and squeezed Alice's shoulder affectionately, turned her head and said to Jess, who was still snuggling in the crook of her arm, "Love, eh?" and gave her a kiss. And then another.

10/10/10